DEATH IN BLITZ CITY

East Yorkshire-born David Young began his East German-set crime series on a creative writing MA at London's City University when *Stasi Child* – his debut – won the course prize. The novel went on to win the 2016 CWA Historical Dagger, and both it and the 2017 follow-up, *Stasi Wolf*, were longlisted for the Theakston Old Peculier Crime Novel of the Year. His novels have been sold in eleven territories around the world. Before becoming a full-time author, David was a senior journalist with the BBC's international radio and TV newsrooms for more than twenty-five years. He divides his time – and his writing – between Twickenham in the UK and the Cyclades islands in Greece.

Also by David Young

Stasi Child
Stasi Wolf
Stasi State [previously A Darker State]
Stasi 77
Stasi Winter
The Stasi Game

DAVID YOUNG
DEATH IN BLITZ CITY

ZAFFRE

First published in the UK in 2022 by
ZAFFRE
An imprint of Bonnier Books UK
4th Floor, Victoria House, Bloomsbury Square, London, WC1B 4DA
Owned by Bonnier Books
Sveavägen 56, Stockholm, Sweden

A CIP catalogue record for this book is
available from the British Library.

ISBN: 978-1-83877-434-9

Also available as an ebook

1 3 5 7 9 10 8 6 4 2

Typeset by IDSUK (Data Connection) Ltd
Printed and bound in Great Britain by Clays Ltd, Elcograf S.p.A.

Zaffre is an imprint of Bonnier Books UK
www.bonnierbooks.co.uk

In memory of my late mother, Barbara May Young (née Gibson), 1926–2002, who served with the Women's Royal Naval Service and later taught at Hallgate Infants School in Cottingham.

'. . . The town that suffered most was Kingston-upon-Hull . . . Morning after morning the BBC reported that raiders had been over a "north-east town" and so there was none of the glory for Hull which known suffering might produce . . . Hull often suffered for what might be said to be no rhyme or reason except that it was an easy target. But it was night after night. Hull had no peace.'

HERBERT MORRISON, Home Secretary of the wartime coalition government, from *Herbert Morrison: An Autobiography* by Lord Morrison of Lambeth (Odhams Press, 1960)

1

Stumps of houses still managed to stand upright, somehow, towering over the rubble. But it was as though some giant beast had devoured most of their softer parts: the roofs, windows, even much of the brick walls. The thicker structure of the chimney stacks was all that was preventing everything from collapsing to the ground. If the aim of the Luftwaffe bombers had been to destroy civilian homes, they'd done it well. If they'd been aiming for the nearby St Andrew's fish dock, then they'd missed. But that would be of little comfort to those who had lost their homes or loved ones.

Detective Chief Inspector Ambrose Swift picked his way delicately through the rubble. He didn't want to trip, and have to be helped up by his deputy, Sergeant Jim 'Little' Weighton. Or worse still, to fall on his false arm and damage its harness, which, as it was, made his right shoulder ache at the end of every day. But as they walked closer to the centre of the devastation, Swift found himself concentrating more on the smell than on the debris underfoot. He used his good left hand to take out his handkerchief, whipped it open, and then held the white cotton fabric against his nose and mouth. There was a cocktail of aromas – none of them pleasant: the whiff of raw sewage, and perhaps, the start of something worse. The stench of decaying flesh.

But the dominant smell was that of damp plaster – and Swift had no doubt that it would have been present in many of the homes even before this latest bombing raid. Terraced housing stock, like this off Hessle Road, was considered little better than slum dwelling. Even before the Nazi bombers helped the demolition squads, Swift was aware of the rehousing projects, with communities from Hull's fishing industry transplanted into newly built corporation homes, mainly to the north of the city.

'Why are we even here, sir?' asked Weighton. 'It's a job for the uniforms, ARPs and firemen, isn't it?'

'I'm not entirely sure,' Swift replied. 'But in the call to HQ, one of the doctors at the scene said CID needed to look at one of the bodies. Something not quite right, apparently.'

Weighton gave a grunt. With his oversized body – the one that had probably given rise to his sarcastic nickname – he looked like a disgruntled ogre told he'd eaten quite enough humans for one day. Although Swift was never entirely sure that was where his sergeant's 'little' moniker *had* come from. A more prosaic explanation was it had been borrowed from one of Hull's satellite villages – Little Weighton, nestling in the foothills of the Yorkshire Wolds.

'I don't know why you need that over your face, sir. Before the war it smelled much worse here. The stink of fish from the docks. You didn't need a bloody BBC weather forecast then, I can tell you. The rotting fish smell was always worse when it was about to rain.'

With Swift only having transferred to Hull from London two years earlier, Weighton's local knowledge was something he usually valued. He was a useful man to have around. Not least because of his size and strength. After picking out his sergeant as a potential number two, Swift had soon perused the man's personal file, curious as to why someone so fit and powerful hadn't signed up to fight. There was nothing obvious, unlike Swift's own Great War injury. The answer was a faulty heart valve; Weighton had tried to volunteer but had been rejected. What the file had also told Swift was that his deputy was from traveller stock on one side of his family, and a bare-knuckle boxer in his spare time, to boot. Why a semi-legal form of fighting was tolerated in the Hull police force, Swift wasn't entirely sure.

A middle-aged male in a dirty white surgical coat had spotted the pair and was advancing on them through the rubble. Dressed in suits and fedora hats, they no doubt stuck out like sore thumbs among the shirt-sleeved workers trying to clear the rubble. The doctor had obviously realised these were the detectives he was expecting.

'Dr Stephenson?' asked Swift.

The man nodded.

'I'm Detective Chief Inspector Ambrose Swift, and this is Detective Sergeant James Weighton.' The doctor gave Weighton a smaller nod. 'We were told there's something amiss with one of the bodies.'

'That's right, Chief Inspector. Follow me, please, gentlemen.'

A makeshift tent had been set up to the side of where the workmen were digging through the rubble.

'Are there still folks missing?' asked Weighton.

'We don't think so,' said the doctor. 'They just want to make doubly sure.'

'How many dead?' asked Swift.

'From last night's bombing raid?'

'Of course.'

'Well, it was a big one here. Possibly the largest high-explosive bomb dropped on Hull so far. That's why there's such a mess.'

Swift stopped himself sighing. Why couldn't people just answer the question that had been asked?

'How *many*?'

'Sorry. Altogether ten dead, another dozen seriously injured. That's across all last night's bomb sites. Here, the Avenues, Sutton and over by Alexandra Dock. The worst was here. The shelter took a near-direct hit. But in addition to those killed by the bombs, there's this other one.'

The doctor pulled back the flap of the tent. Various bodies – both large and pitifully small – were lined up neatly in a row, covered in sheets. In the early-summer heat, they were indeed already starting to smell.

'Shouldn't these all have been moved to the mortuary by now?' asked Swift.

'Normally, yes. But these aren't normal times, Chief Inspector, as you can imagine.'

He led the two detectives to the end of the tent, where he pulled another flap aside.

'The last in the line, so to speak. Now I hope neither of you is squeamish.'

Swift couldn't imagine Weighton was, given he was prone to smashing his fists into others' faces and bodies in the name of sport – or fun. And he certainly hadn't seen any evidence of it in the time they'd been working as partners. As for Swift himself ... well, he'd seen enough dismembered bodies in north-eastern France to fill a lifetime's nightmares – including his own severed arm, which he still regularly dreamed he could use as he once had. The rounds of golf in his head, threading a drive through an avenue of Surrey pines down the centre of a lush fairway. They were things he could never do again. But he was still dexterous enough with one good hand, and one good arm, to drive a car, ride a horse.

The doctor drew the cover sheet down to just below the victim's chin. She was young – early twenties, Swift guessed – and with pretty, small facial features. A snub nose, symmetrical face, and one which gave no inkling to the trauma her body had suffered. That only became clear when the doctor pulled the sheet further down her unclothed body.

'Jesus!' exclaimed Weighton.

Even Swift felt a sudden rush of bile into his gullet. He looked away briefly, and swallowed.

'Is that what I think it is?' he asked, looking back at the gaping wound in the young woman's chest.

The doctor nodded. 'Her heart has been literally ripped out. At first we thought it was a blast wound from the bomb, but it clearly isn't. It's too neat.'

Neat wasn't the adjective Swift would have chosen, but even from his non-expert experience of blast wounds in the Great War, he could tell the conclusion was correct.

Weighton had leaned forwards, almost as though he wanted a better view. Swift couldn't imagine why. He was struggling to prevent the bile rising in his throat.

'While ... she was ... still alive?' asked his sergeant. The question came out in a series of gasps, as though he couldn't quite believe what his brain was conjuring up.

Swift, too, was imagining what that would have involved. The breaking, or sawing, of the breastbone at the very least. Surely even at that stage there would have been too much loss of blood. It wasn't even possible, was it?

The doctor's answer, after he'd left a slight pause as though he was seriously considering the question, came almost as a relief.

'The pathologist will tell you for certain, but for my pennyworth it was done post-mortem.'

'A trophy of the killing?' postulated Swift.

'Who knows?' shrugged the doctor. 'Possibly. But it wasn't the cause of death.'

He pointed instead to the woman's neck. Now Swift could see the light bruising encircling it. He'd missed it at first glance. Normally, he prided himself on his advertence.

'Strangled?'

'Yes. Some form of ligature, I'd say.'

Swift found himself subconsciously rubbing his own neck with his good arm. He was tempted to remove the covering further down the body to check whether there was any external evidence of sexual assault. Perhaps his glance was enough, because the doctor answered the question without being asked.

'There's no obvious sign she's been interfered with sexually, if that was what you were thinking, but it's something I'm sure the pathologist will check.'

Swift gave a thoughtful nod.

'Do you know her identity?' he asked.

Before the doctor could answer, Weighton intervened.

'I do!' he cried. Swift turned to his number two, surprised to see his eyes glistening.

'She's Sweet Sarah.'

'Sarah Sweet, surely?' said Swift.

'No, sir. Sweet Sarah. Sarah Houghton. She used to work at Smales – the fish processors at the docks. There's not much actual processing happening there with the war on. Sarah had to find other work, if you know what I mean.'

The doctor intervened. 'You're saying she was a prostitute?'

Swift glared at the man.

'The poor woman is a murder victim, whose life's been cruelly taken away, and we'll all treat her with the same respect as any murder victim, please.'

Then he turned back to Weighton.

'How do you know all this, Sergeant?'

'Well, to earn a few bob she used to work at George's Café Prestige down Hedon Road. When I was in uniform, we raided it, sir. But really, she's just a young girl fallen on hard times. She would have had her dreams, like anyone else.'

Swift took one last look at the violation that had been performed on the woman's body. The removal of her heart had to have some significance, surely?

'I don't suppose anyone's found the missing body part?' he asked the doctor.

The man, looking slightly chastened after Swift's mini-lecture a few moments earlier, shook his head.

'Not as far as I know.'

Swift turned back to Weighton. 'Get a uniform team down here, Weighton. I want an inch-by-inch search near where the body was found.'

'That's going to be difficult, sir, when they're still clearing the rubble.'

'Just sort it out, please. Then you and I need to pay this Hedon Road café a visit.'

Swift took the sheet and covered the body again, pausing at the woman's face. He leaned down slightly and said his next words to her, even though she was long past hearing.

'I don't know what kind of madman or madmen have done this to you, Miss Houghton. But we're going to find them and make sure they pay for their crimes. You can be sure of that.'

Then he covered her face, gave a curt nod to the doctor, and turned on his heels.

2

George Camilleri's Café Prestige seemed to have missed out where the 'prestige' part was concerned, thought Swift. It was little more than a working man's 'caff', as they'd say down south, with fixtures and furniture that had all seen better days, catering to the workers at the nearby Alexandra Dock. Those docks that had been repaired after the zenith of the Nazi bombing campaign the previous summer were still busy, supplying goods to the Soviet Union and receiving Russian timber in return. One recent change had been the arrival of American GIs, all of them black – almost without exception – but with white officers overseeing them. The common soldiers seemed to have been accepted well by the local population, but Swift and others knew there were racial tensions between the officers and men.

A hush descended as soon as the two detectives walked in, and Swift noticed a few shady characters – and provocatively dressed women – swiftly exit by what was, presumably, a back door. But Weighton was known here, if only for raiding the place. Swift would let him do the talking.

His deputy walked up to the counter and took off his hat. He nodded at the man standing behind it, wearing a greasy apron.

'George.'

'Sergeant Weighton. I hope you're not here to cause trouble again.'

The man had a Mediterranean complexion and an accent to match. Possibly Italian, although Swift wasn't sure. If he was, why hadn't he been interned? Perhaps he just had an Italian-sounding name. Swift made a mental note to check that out.

'You know how it works, George. You don't cause us trouble, we won't cause you trouble. Step out of line and we'll come down on you hard. But this time, all Chief Inspector Swift here and I want is a word.'

'I'm listening,' said the man.

'In private, if you wouldn't mind, Mr Camilleri,' said Swift.

A look passed between the owner and a busty woman who Swift assumed was his wife. Then he opened the counter flap and beckoned them towards a room at the rear of the establishment.

'Sit down, George,' said Weighton. He waited until the man had parked himself on a rickety-looking chair. 'We've got some bad news, I'm afraid.'

'What?'

'Sweet Sarah. Her body was found in the rubble of the public shelter in Scarborough Street, off Hessle Road, early this morning.'

'Good grief. Poor lass.' The man seemed genuinely affected, with a catch in his voice. He passed his hand over his face and through his hair. There were tears in his eyes. 'First I've heard about it – well, that she were caught up in it. I knew about the bombing – couldn't miss that. It were a direct hit, weren't it?'

Weighton nodded.

'Mind you,' the man continued, 'I don't know what she were doing on that side of town. We live over that way, but she's from East Hull.'

Swift drew up a chair and pulled it close to Camilleri, who was glancing nervously at the detective's prosthetic arm, as though he feared the policeman was about to lash out at him with it.

'Was she working here last night, George? Could she have gone over to Hessle Road way with a client?'

'I'm not sure what you're driving at, Chief Inspector.'

Weighton slammed his fist down on the table.

'Don't play the innocent, George. You've been up twice in front of Hull Magistrates for running a disorderly house. Don't forget, I was involved in one of those raids. I know what goes on here.'

Camilleri shrank back in his chair.

'The arrangements the girls make if they meet men here are nothing to do with me.'

Swift gave a long sigh. 'Look, Mr Camilleri. Perhaps you've got the wrong impression. We're not here about what the girls get up to, or what they don't, or what your involvement in it is – or isn't. That doesn't concern us ... at the moment.' He let the rider to his statement hang in the air and sink in with the café owner. 'We're simply trying to find out what we can about Sarah Houghton. Her last known movements. The normal things you ask in a murder inquiry.'

'Murder? What do you mean, murder? I thought you said she were found in the Scarborough Street shelter after the bombing.'

'She was,' said Swift. 'But that's not how she died, and probably not where she died either. Where were you last night, Mr Camilleri?'

'Me? Why are you asking me that?'

'Why shouldn't we?' asked Weighton.

'Well, I was here. Until about ten o'clock. Then me and the wife got the trolley bus back to our place. Here, I can get Elsie. She'll back me up on that.' He got to his feet, and shouted through the doorway into the café itself. 'Elsie! Come here a sec.'

The busty woman with curled jet-black hair bustled into the room, panting slightly, wiping her hands on her apron.

'It's busy out there, George. Why are you round the back here, skiving and nattering?'

'It's these gentlemen. They're detectives.'

Swift saw the look of recognition on Elsie Camilleri's face when she saw one of the police officers was Weighton.

'Ooh. Is that a promotion then, Jim? Your mam'll be dead proud.'

Swift watched Weighton blush slightly.

'No. Not exactly. Still a sergeant. This is my boss, Chief Inspector Ambrose Swift. Sir, this lady is Elsie Camilleri, George's wife – and the person who keeps everything running smoothly round here.'

'Delighted to meet you, Mrs Camilleri,' said Swift, rising to his feet and doffing his hat.

'Wish I could say the same,' replied the woman. 'When the police come here, they bring nothing but trouble – a bit like the bloody Nazi bombers.'

Swift offered her his chair. Mrs Camilleri was about to refuse when her husband intervened.

'You'll want a seat, Elsie, when you hear what they've got to say.'

Swift cleared his throat and raised his eyebrows at Weighton. His sergeant drew in a long breath.

'It's not good news, I'm afraid, Elsie. Sweet Sarah's been found dead.'

'Oh my God. Where? How?'

Weighton gave her the same information they'd just imparted to her husband.

'But why would anyone want to murder a girl like that? She was a real sweetie, kind and gentle.' Like her husband, she had tears in her eyes. 'I don't want you getting any ideas in your head about her, Jim. She were only doing it for a bit of pocket money on the side, as it were. To help her family, keep the wolf from the door. Times are hard.'

'We're not here to judge, Mrs Camilleri,' said Swift.

'Who the heck are you, anyroad?'

As Weighton had already introduced him, Swift interpreted the question as a put-down. Elise Camilleri had already been eyeing him suspiciously, as though she didn't take kindly to having posh southern interlopers in the café.

'I've already told you, Elsie,' explained Weighton. 'He's my boss, Chief Inspector Swift.'

'We simply want to know Sarah's movements,' said Swift. 'Whether you saw her with anyone, whether she'd seemed troubled recently, whether she looked in any way different.'

'Well, that's a lot of questions and things to think about. Nothing springs to mind straightaway, although . . .'

'Although what?' prompted Swift.

'I'm not sure it's my place to be saying anything, really, not if the lass has been murdered.'

Weighton snorted. 'Oh, come on, Elsie. That's precisely why you do need to tell us what you know.'

'Well, if anything, she'd seemed a lot happier recently.'

'And that was unusual?' asked Swift.

'Well, I'm not saying she were a miserable bitch – she wasn't. She were a lovely lass. Gentle soul, who didn't really realise her own beauty. Came from a poor family. Anyway, that's beside the point. The point is, we reckoned she'd found a fella.'

'We?' asked Weighton.

'Well, the girls.'

Swift leaned forwards, at the same time wafting away the cigarette smoke that Elsie seemed determined to blow into his face. 'And do you know who he was?'

'No. Bit of a mystery. But she'd started going to dances in Cottingham. Mebbe she met him there, like.'

'Cottingham?' echoed Swift. 'I thought you said she lived in East Hull. That's a bit of a hike.'

'Whereabouts in Cottingham?' asked Weighton.

'That I dern't nerr.' It had taken Swift a while to get used to the Hull version of *don't know* and similar such phrases. In any case, when dealing with authority figures, many of the locals attempted to use their version of BBC English they'd heard on the wireless. Under stress, however, especially in police interviews, they tended to lapse back into the local dialect. Elsie Camilleri didn't appear particularly stressed – but it made Swift wonder if she was hiding something from them. 'You'd have to ask one of the girls,' she continued. 'Jessica's the one she used to go there with.'

'And where would we find this Jessica?' asked Swift.

'She's usually in later if you pop back round six. Altherr what wi' all the bombing last night, mebbe people will be staying in tonight and keeping out o' t' way. But she dun't like policemen.'

'Who the fuck does?' piped up George Camilleri.

Swift glared at him.

'All I'm saying,' continued Mrs Camilleri, 'is if you want to get anything useful out of her, I'd bring one of those women officers along. What do yer call 'em? The hawk-silly-is or summat?'

'Auxiliaries,' said Swift. 'Women's Police Auxiliaries.'

'Aye, that's it. Bring one of them lasses along with you. Or if you can't do that, you just come alern, Jim. At least you're from Hull. Leave Mr Snooty Chops back at Alfred Gelder Street.'

'Come off it, Elsie,' said Weighton. 'There's no need to be rude.'

'I'm just trying to help you, Jim, as a friend of the family, so to speak. Bring a lass along and you might actually get somewhere.'

'Sorry about that, sir,' said Weighton, as they made their way back to Swift's Morris. 'What Elsie Camilleri said. She's never been one to mind her tongue.'

Swift shrugged. 'She's got a point. Perhaps a female officer would be useful. Are there any bright ones you can recommend?'

'Well, there's Kathleen. Works in the records department. She's always helpful and a bit of a brainbox. Wasted there, in my opinion. She's from a farming family up in the Yorkshire Dales, but won a scholarship to a posh school in Harrogate.'

'Sounds promising.'

'Not only that – she was very interested when she heard about my move to CID. I remember her saying that's the sort of thing she'd like to do one day.'

'All right. No harm in giving her a chance, I suppose. Will you have a word with her?'

'I'm happy to, sir. But wouldn't it be better coming from you? I think she'd appreciate it more, and be more willing to put in the extra hours.'

'Quite right, Weighton. I'll do it. What are the Camilleris, anyway? Sounds like an Italian name, but the husband obviously hasn't been interned.'

'He's actually Maltese, sir. So, one of us – or at least part of the British Empire.'

'Aha, that explains it. And very brave they are, too, Weighton. Without Malta, we'd be in danger of losing North Africa completely.'

As they climbed into the car, Swift glanced over at his deputy. Despite his less than salubrious 'hobby' of fighting with his bare fists, Weighton was someone Swift had been glad to have at his side in the year they'd been working together – since their first encounter during the height of Hull's own Blitz.

Those two nights of bombing in early May 1941 had been almost apocalyptic – as though what had just happened at

Scarborough Street had been repeated in every corner of the city: the sky above Hull blazed a fierce orange, visible from as far afield as the top of York Minster, some forty miles distant.

The demarcations between CID and uniform had been forgotten, with Swift called out to assist with a communal shelter which had been hit just off Hedon Road.

Even getting there had been a struggle in a city transformed into a giant fireball. The word was that Hammonds and Thornton Varley – the main department stores – were ablaze. All around he'd heard the rattle of incendiary bombs raining down on the city, and the drone of warplanes above. Several roads were already blocked by rubble, requiring detours, and eventually Swift had abandoned the Morris, setting off at a run down Hedon Road, ducking and diving into doorways as the bombs fell and the ground shook beneath his feet. He remembered it as though it was yesterday – as though the Blitz he'd left behind in London had followed him up to Hull.

When he'd turned the corner into Wyke Street, he'd been faced with a scene of utter devastation. Men were already frantically pulling away collapsed masonry.

'Who's in charge here?' he'd asked.

'Sergeant Weighton there,' replied one youth.

Swift looked up to the top of the pile of rubble, where a giant of a man was silhouetted against the burning orange skyline, desperately throwing bricks and wooden beams to each side, making light of their weight, while bellowing orders to the others. His first encounter with Weighton, the officer who would soon become his sergeant.

'I'm going in!' Weighton suddenly shouted.

'Don't be daft, Jim!' another policeman yelled. 'It'll collapse on you.'

'There's bains in there. I've got to get them out.'

Swift rolled his sleeves up, joining the rescue efforts, issuing orders even though the other officers at the scene had little idea who he was.

He awkwardly climbed up to the top of the rubble pile, careful not to fall on his false arm, and shouted down to where Weighton had disappeared, asking if he needed help.

'I'm all right, thank you, Chief Inspector. Just freeing the bains.'

Swift could hear muffled screams and groans.

'How many, Sergeant?'

'Three, I think, sir.'

Then Swift heard the shout of one of the children.

'What about our mam? We're not leaving her!'

The operation had been incredibly dangerous. Swift had climbed down inside to help, conscious that at any moment everything could collapse around them, burying them alive – both rescuers and victims. All the nightmare images of the Great War, the hell and mayhem at the front, had assailed Swift – but somehow Weighton had the sort of presence that made you believe everything would turn out all right.

First one wriggling, cursing child had been pulled free, reluctantly led to the surface by Swift, and then handed to the other rescuers above ground.

Weighton had insisted Swift keep out of the way – that he could cope – and, in truth, with his prosthetic the chief inspector had realised he would be little use yanking away collapsed masonry and beams.

Weighton had been true to his word.

First, one by one, the other children.

Then finally, looking half-dead, her face creased in agony but crusted in dirt and dust, their mother – Mrs Nancy Greaves – carried over Weighton's enormous shoulders as though she was merely the lightest of feather-stuffed eiderdowns.

'You're going to be all right now,' Weighton had whispered to her. 'You're going to be all right now.'

Looking at the woman's ashen, pain-etched face, Swift hadn't been so sure.

But Mrs Greaves and all her children did survive, and two weeks later, as Swift searched through applications from uniformed police officers who wanted to transfer to CID, that night at Wyke Street was fresh in his mind. When he saw the name of Sergeant James Weighton among the list of applicants, he didn't hesitate.

Jim 'Little' Weighton was exactly who he needed as his right-hand man.

They'd both hoped those two nights of sustained attacks by the Nazi bombers would be the end of it. It was a forlorn hope, of course, but – until last night at Scarborough Street – the ferocity and regularity of the bombing raids had at least abated.

They stopped at the nearest police box to check in with control. Swift could imagine a time not too far in the future when the police box would be redundant. Already, patrol cars had begun to be fitted with radios, and no doubt CID wouldn't be far behind. But for now, the ubiquitous boxes – blue here, as in the rest of the country, unlike Hull's anachronistic cream public telephone boxes – were a way for the police to quickly phone in information, and find it out. What Swift wanted to know was when and where the post-mortem on Sarah Houghton was being carried out.

A victim who'd been found in the wreckage of Scarborough Street – but one who, very obviously, hadn't been killed as a result of the Luftwaffe's bombs.

3

The mortuary hadn't been as busy this year as the previous one – Swift knew that. The peak of the city's own Blitz had come on that night Swift met Weighton during the rescue in Wyke Street, and the following night. An intense two-day bombardment which had killed four hundred people. But tens of thousands more had been made homeless, and each night up to a third of the city's population trekked out to the countryside to sleep in the fields and avoid the bombs. Everywhere, buildings were missing, or left as rubble.

The city would be scarred for ever.

Hull Royal Infirmary, site of the mortuary, hadn't survived unscathed. One of its buildings had been destroyed, although the mortuary was undamaged.

Professor Herbert Jackson gave off the air of a crusty Oxford don, with half-moon reading glasses permanently sliding down his nose, and a tweed suit and waistcoat showing under his unbuttoned white surgical coat. Swift hadn't warmed to him on his previous visits, but was determined this time to try to keep his dislike in check.

'I suppose you two want to see the prostitute,' Jackson growled.

Swift counted to ten in his head before he answered.

'If you mean the young woman, Sarah Houghton, then yes. But our information is that she wasn't a full-time prostitute, and whether she was or not is beside the point.'

'If you say so. *I* would have thought it's very much to the point, given they tend to be the victims of crime more regularly than the rest of the populace. But then I'm not a detective, I'm a Home Office pathologist.'

Swift sniffed, then wished he hadn't. He'd been trying to hold his breath. The smell of mortuaries, disinfectant and death always took his mind back to somewhere he didn't want to go – the Great War. When death was commonplace, and seemingly every life expendable.

'So, what can you tell us?'

'That you don't already know? I gather you talked to Dr Stephenson at the scene. He probably filled you in on the salient details.'

The man's manner was so exasperating, Swift found himself on the point of losing his temper. But rubbing a pathologist up the wrong way was never a very sensible tactic for a homicide detective. Thankfully, Weighton came to his rescue.

'Don't be such a misery guts, Herbert.'

'*Professor* Jackson to you, Weighton.'

'Well, if that's how you want to play it, it's *Detective Sergeant* Weighton to you. And *Detective Chief Inspector* Swift. Now are we going to play word games all day, or are you going to tell us what we want to know?'

'You already know everything,' said the professor.

Swift sighed. 'Confirm it for us then, please, *Professor*. How did Miss Houghton die? When do you think she died? Was her death *in situ* or had the body been moved? And have you found out anything else that might assist our inquiries?'

The man looked slightly taken aback that the two detectives had tired of his verbal jousting before he'd even really warmed up.

'Well, she was strangled, with a ligature, and died of asphyxiation.'

'There's no doubt about that, then?' asked Swift. 'The asphyxia couldn't have been caused by being suffocated under the rubble.'

He knew this wasn't the case, of course; he just wanted to try to draw some further information from Jackson, despite his recalcitrance.

This time it was Jackson's turn to sigh. He indicated to his assistant to wheel in Sarah's body.

Once he'd locked the wheels of the mortuary trolley and uncovered it, he leaned over and beckoned Swift and Weighton forwards.

'That,' he said, hovering his finger over a thin line of bruising round the dead woman's neck, 'is the result of ligature strangulation, and that is what caused her death. So, no – no doubt.'

'Any signs of resistance?' asked Swift.

Again, Jackson pointed with his finger to a series of crescent-shaped lesions.

'Yes, but very limited. It suggests she was caught by surprise and by the time she realised what was happening, it was either almost too late, or she wasn't strong enough to do much about it.'

Weighton frowned. 'Do you think this happened where she was found?'

'I doubt it very much.'

Jackson again signalled to the young male assistant, and together the two men rolled the woman's body over. Swift immediately saw the abrasions.

'The body was dragged along the ground?'

'I would say so, yes. A concrete floor – something like that. They are grazes rather than jagged cuts. And they happened post-mortem. The other clue, of course, is that, according to Dr Stephenson at the scene, rescuers found her body lying in a prone position.'

'On her front?' asked Weighton.

'That is what prone means, Detective Sergeant, yes. But lividity was found in her back.'

Swift cocked his head. 'So immediately after death, she'd been supine?'

'Exactly. And I'd put the time of death at least three hours or so before the Luftwaffe dropped their blessed bomb on that shelter. So, in summary – she was strangled by a narrow ligature, possibly rubber- or plastic-covered wire, hence the limited bruising. Perhaps surprised from behind, which would explain why there aren't more signs of a struggle. And all this happened away from the bomb site – I would surmise – and she was moved there after the bombing, with the murderer possibly hoping the cause of death would go unnoticed in the general mayhem that always follows such tragic events.'

Weighton frowned. 'Any signs of a sexual motive?'

'There were indications of recent sexual activity, yes. But then given her profession, part-time or not, that's unsurprising.'

Swift rubbed his left hand across his forehead. 'You're not convinced this was a sexual attack, then.'

'I can't say with any certainty. What I can tell you is, there is no evidence of actual genital injury. But aren't you failing to ask me about one of her most *obvious* injuries? Something the killer surely knew would not go unnoticed?'

'The mutilation of her chest and removal of the heart?' said Swift.

'Yes. Though I would hardly describe it as *mutilation*. More like surgery. Almost as though your killer had some knowledge of what he – or she, indeed – was doing. The sternum, for example, has been sawn through quite skilfully.'

'But Dr Stephenson talked of the heart being *ripped* from her body.'

'Hyperbole, Chief Inspector. Hyperbole. It's not easy to access the heart, never mind remove it. It's not in a particularly accessible part of the body, and is well protected. So your killer possibly has had some medical training in the past. If not as an actual surgeon, then maybe as a general physician, or a vet.'

'A butcher?' mused Swift.

'Perhaps, but I doubt it.'

'Or a pathologist,' ventured Weighton.

Swift looked at his colleague in surprise. His deputy appeared slightly embarrassed – as though he'd involuntarily spoken aloud what he was thinking.

Professor Jackson, however, took the remark in his stride, giving a wry laugh.

'Yes indeed, Sergeant. *Or a pathologist.* However, given there are so few of us for the amount of work that needs doing these days, I'd put the odds on that as rather high.'

Swift rubbed his chin with his prosthetic hand. Although the artificial limb was somewhat limited in its uses, scratching an itch – depending where it was – was something he could accomplish with it.

'And so this surgery – or *amateur* surgery . . . did this happen pre- or post-mortem?'

'Thankfully after death, without a doubt. If there *is* indeed anything to be thankful about in this case. Although some would say one less prost—'

Swift covered his ears.

'I'm not interested in hearing that sort of talk, thank you, Professor. We'll bid you good day now.' He dug a business card from his wallet, and handed it over. 'If you do think of anything else, you can get me on this extension at Alfred Gelder Street.'

'You ended that rather abruptly, sir,' said Weighton, as they emerged into the fresh air.

'I didn't like his attitude. Although we managed to warm him up and find out what we needed.'

'You don't think he could have really done it, do you?'

Swift stopped dead, and regarded his sergeant with incredulity.

'I don't like him, Weighton. But the fact that he probably has the means and skill to commit the crime, and is someone I wouldn't want to spend any time with, does not make him a murderer. There are small things like opportunity, motive – not to mention that tricky concept called evidence. We've plenty of real work to do. We need to get uniform and forensics on to looking for a murder weapon, a murder locale. We need to interview all her known associates and we need to piece this together bit by bit, as quickly as possible.'

4

Swift knew that trying to persuade his boss, Detective Chief Superintendent Holdridge, that he should be assigned a separate incident room for a murder case in the midst of wartime might be an uphill battle.

The man gave off the mien of a Great War general, sitting upright behind his desk, safely away from the action. As he considered Swift's request, he twirled his ginger moustache – one that Swift had always considered an affectation.

The two men had never really got on. Perhaps it had something to do with the fact that Swift had failed to return his boss's attempt to give him a Masonic handshake on his first day in the job some two years earlier, after Swift had transferred from London's Metropolitan Police Service. Refusing entreaties to join the Freemasons was nothing new to Swift: it had cost him promotions in the past.

That first handshake with his superior officer had been particularly awkward. First, Holdridge had extended his right hand as usual, then almost recoiled when he remembered what he already knew from his briefings: that Swift had a false right arm. The chief superintendent tried again, extending his left arm to grasp Swift's good left hand. But the Masonic grip with his 'wrong' hand had been cartoonish in its over-emphasis of thumb pressure and finger extension. Swift had deliberately kept his own hand as limp as possible. He'd got his message across.

He wasn't *on the level* and had no wish to be. Since that day, the two men had rarely seen eye to eye.

Now, some two years after that uncomfortable first meeting, the detective chief superintendent held Swift's gaze.

'I realise this is your first big murder case up here, and solving it is important, I grant you. But as I understand it, the young woman was a whore. If girls choose that sort of life, it inevitably puts them in danger.'

'With respect, sir, that's irrelevant, and in any case not the whole story. Many people resort to desperate measures to make ends meet in times of war. I want to put as much effort into this as any other murder inquiry.'

His superior sighed wearily. 'But there are brave soldiers, airmen and sailors dying every day, fighting the Nazis, Swift. The people of Hull have suffered their own losses – and continue to do so. Hers wasn't the only body found in that Scarborough Street shelter. We can't be going throwing resources at this.' He paused, gazing at his chief inspector with a grumpy expression. 'Nevertheless, I might be able to find you a small room you can use as an incident room. You'll have to leave it with me.'

'I'll also need some uniform backup, sir, for house-to-house inquiries, that sort of thing.'

'Pah! I'll ask my opposite number, but they're overstretched as it is. You know that. They're always asking *us* for help. A request the other way is likely to get short shrift. But I will ask. Is that all?'

Swift stood up, ready to leave. The negotiations had gone about as well as he could have expected, given the two men's mutual distrust of each other. Was it the refusal of that handshake that had sowed the enmity? Possibly. Or it could simply be that Swift's disdain of the man was too undisguised. However, he suspected the real reason might have been the way he'd been foisted on the Hull force. An investigation down south into a splinter fascist group had turned sour. Its leader had avowed himself – eventually – against Hitler and Nazi Germany once the war broke out. But Swift had made some powerful enemies. Enemies he'd needed to get away from. Enemies who possibly still wanted to do him harm, even though he'd hoped the move to Hull had put enough distance between them.

'There was one other matter, sir.'

'Spit it out then, man. I haven't got all day.'

'I think it would be useful to have a female officer attached to the inquiry, to help with some of the more delicate interviews with Sarah Houghton's friends and acquaintances.'

'You mean to talk to the other prostitutes?'

Swift found himself almost literally biting his tongue. He decided to ignore the comment.

'I just think for some of the more delicate conversations, when we're trying to persuade people to talk about things they might not want to discuss in public, then a woman's touch could be helpful.'

'Did you have anyone in mind? We only have a handful of female officers in the whole force, and none here in CID, thank God.'

'There's someone in the records department whom Sergeant Weighton speaks very highly of, sir. Her name's Kathleen Carver. She's a Women's Police Auxiliary. But bright. Won a scholarship to her school. According to Weighton, she's wasted in the records department.'

'Can't say I know of her, but why would I? Talk to Inspector Wilkinson in records. Tell him I've asked him to release her to help you for a couple of weeks. If he raises any objections, ask him to speak to me.'

Swift made the phone call to Wilkinson. The inspector was initially reluctant to let one of his star workers go.

'The whole force is down on numbers, you know that, Chief Inspector. We're already relying on reserve police officers and auxiliaries.'

Swift told Wilkinson he could turn the request down, but that he'd have to explain himself to Superintendent Holdridge.

'Well, you certainly know how to play a trump card, sir. I don't want to have to go cap in hand to that crusty old bugger. I try to avoid him like the plague anyway. I can let you have her for two weeks, but not a day longer. Don't go messing her around, though, Chief Inspector. She'll work until the cows come home if you let her, so you just have to rein her in a bit. I'll send her up to your office.'

Swift's first impressions of Kathleen Carver, despite Weighton's recommendation, were not that great. The woman appeared timid, nervous and withdrawn. It didn't help that he couldn't, at first, understand a word that she was saying. It was like when he'd first arrived in Hull – and the several weeks it had taken him to understand that 'nerr' meant 'no', 'rerd' was 'road', 'snerr' was 'snow'. Even more baffling was that 'mafting' somehow translated as 'very hot'.

'Sit down, Miss Carver, please,' said Swift. 'Now, did Inspector Wilkinson explain why I wanted to see you?'

Her reply, to Swift, was at first utterly unintelligible. The lilting tones almost sounded like a cross between Geordie and the broadest of Yorkshire accents. Swift had already checked her file and discovered she came from a farming family in Baldersdale, on the very edge of North Yorkshire – in fact, just about as far north as you could go without leaving the county. Only when he asked her to repeat what she'd said a little more slowly, did he finally make out the English meaning of the words.

'He said you wanted me to work with you for a couple of weeks, sir, to help with some interviews.'

'That's correct. What he probably didn't tell you is the nature of those interviews. A young woman's body was found under the rubble of a shelter that was bombed overnight in Scarborough Street. Near the fish dock, to the west of the city centre. Now normally that would be tragic, but not unusual. However, in this case she didn't die at the scene, and not as a consequence of a German bomb.'

Swift let that sink in for a moment. Carver's forehead, under her peaked blue cap, furrowed.

'So what happened, sir?'

'She was strangled. Murdered. There are other more unpleasant details, too.'

'You can tell me, sir. I was raised on a sheep farm. As a bairn, I was taught how to delve into a ewe to deliver a breeched lamb. I've seen enough blood and guts in my time.'

Swift found his brain replaying the image of the gaping wound left in the woman's chest after her heart had been almost surgically excised. He couldn't imagine even the worst emergency lambing would compare.

'All right, well, don't say I didn't warn you.'

He went on to describe what he'd seen when Dr Stephenson had uncovered the body, and the fact that the mutilation had occurred post-mortem. Carver looked revolted, but Swift was impressed when she immediately followed up with a question.

'*Why* would someone do that, sir? And after death, too. Do you think it was some sort of message?'

'Possibly. Or a trophy of the killing. We don't know. The heart often has a symbolic meaning. But let's keep an open mind at this stage. The other slightly delicate thing is that we believe the victim, Sarah Houghton, was involved in selling sexual favours – at least on a part-time basis. That doesn't mean we treat her murder any differently from the murder of any other woman. I must stress that, because you'll find those – some within these walls – who think that because of her activities "she had it coming to her". That's not a phrase or attitude I will tolerate in this investigation.'

'I understand, sir.'

'Your role initially, Carver, will be to help us interview some of Miss Houghton's friends and acquaintances who might more readily talk to a woman. We'll get on to that right away after I introduce you to my sergeant, James Weighton, whom I gather you're already acquainted with.'

Holdridge's promise to find them a space to use as an incident room had been fulfilled – but barely. Swift's heart sank when he realised where they'd be: a windowless side room off the base-ment, with a single bare electric light bulb, four desks, typewriters that looked as though they'd been rescued from the scrap heap, and one telephone. The only concession to luxury: a gas ket-tle with a rusty camping stove, a tide-marked teapot, and four barely clean teacups.

'Well, old ginger nut has certainly pushed the boat out here,' moaned Weighton, as he grabbed one of the desks. 'At least we can make a cup of tea. Put the kettle on, Kathleen, will you.'

'WAPC Carver isn't here to make your tea, Weighton,' said Swift. 'She's here as part of the investigation team. And we're here to work. That thing doesn't look safe, anyway. We can bring teas down from the canteen later, but first I want to sum-marise where we are now, and what we need to do.'

There was a blackboard with chalk on one wall of the room, and Swift used it to start drawing a diagram. In the centre, he wrote Sarah Houghton's name, and radiating out from it, her various known contacts.

He then began to speak, outlining what he'd already asked the uniformed division to do, including a fingertip search of the bomb site, looking for the missing heart – not that he expected them to find anything.

Then he explained what they, as the main investigating team, would be doing. The first thing, and what Carver had been brought on board for, was to go back to Café Prestige – and any other known haunts – to question Sarah Houghton's friends and fellow part-time sex workers. After that, they'd split up, with Weighton detailed to talk to the young woman's relatives in East Hull, and Swift and Carver travelling north-west to Cottingham to check out the dance venue and – if they could get permission – to start interviewing some of the American GIs Sarah had met there.

George Camilleri didn't look best pleased to see them on their return to his café, but Swift could already see they might have more luck this time – various girls who hadn't been there before were now ensconced at the tables, talking in hushed tones to what were probably prospective johns.

'I'm glad to see you took my advice,' said his wife, addressing Weighton rather than Swift, whom she seemed to be studiously ignoring. 'Who's this, then?'

'WAPC Kathleen Carver, Elsie. She's a good sort, so make sure you treat her right. Yorkshire farmer's daughter.'

'Oh aye? From Holderness?'

'No,' said Carver. 'The Dales. Far north of the Dales, next to Teesdale.'

'Well, that's barely still Yorkshire, lass. No wonder you sound more like a Geordie.' Then she dropped her voice. 'Shall I point you in the way of some of the girls Sarah were friendly with? Mind you, go easy on them. News of what's happened to her has fair spooked the lot of them.'

Despite Elsie Camilleri's glare, Swift was determined that Carver shouldn't be going into this on her own. He advised her to begin talking to the women first, then once she'd won their confidence, to persuade them to come into the back room to talk to both her and Swift. The first one he was interested in talking to was the 'Jessica' mentioned earlier by Elsie.

'Is she here tonight?'

Elsie flicked her eyes towards the far corner, where a girl was giggling with a thin, rakish man.

Swift pulled Carver gently towards him and whispered in her ear.

'Try her first. Her name's Jessica. She and Sarah used to go to dances together in Cottingham. There are rumours Sarah had a boyfriend and met him there.'

Meanwhile, he deputed Weighton to get a full list of Sarah Houghton's other contacts and possible clients from the Camilleris.

'What are we looking for, sir?'

'We need the names of as many men who use the services of the girls as possible.'

'I'm not sure Elsie and George will be willing to give names, sir. George's still smarting that we hauled him into court.'

Waiting in the Camilleris' back office area, Swift was pleasantly surprised when Carver brought the girl back with her in a couple of minutes.

'I ain't dobbing anyone in, you know,' Jessica said, as soon as she sat down in front of Swift, with Carver to one side. 'I didn't mind talking to this lass here, but talking to someone official-looking like you is a different kettle of fish.'

Carver had removed her glasses, which had steamed up in the humid café, and was busy wiping them. She raised her eyebrows at Swift, out of sight of Jessica. Swift was glad he'd asked her to change out of uniform into civvy clothes before they'd arrived – it had probably helped win the girl's confidence.

'It's not a question of "dobbing anyone in",' said Swift. 'You were, I believe, friends with Sarah?'

'Yeah. Most of the time. She were all right, she was. Cut above some of the rubbish you get round here. She might have been from a poor area of East Hull, but she'd been brought up right. And it looked like she were just about to turn her life around.'

'What makes you say that, Jessica?' asked Carver.

Swift had to stifle a smile. He was delighted she wasn't just going to sit on the sidelines, listening. He guessed what Jessica was referring to.

'The man she'd met. He were a proper good 'un. I had my eye on him. That's why we both used to go out to Cott.'

'Cottingham?' prompted Swift. 'To the dances?'

'Aye. King Street Rooms. Near to t' Green and bus stop.'

'And what was this man's name?'

'Archibald. Or Archie for short. Archibald Davis.'

Swift had his pencil and notebook poised. 'Can you tell me his address?'

'Well, where the rest of them are in Cott. I dunno the address, like.'

Carver stepped in to explain.

'He's an American GI. Stationed with an all-black unit in Cottingham. From memory, they're housed in those Nissen huts off New Village Road.'

'I can't say I know it,' said Swift.

'It's the road that leads to the north-east of the village – a continuation of Hull Road, just after the main road turns left into Thwaite Street.'

Swift nodded now, getting his bearings in his head.

'I think it's a port battalion,' continued Carver. 'I can't remember which number. They've been detailed to work at the docks.'

Swift cocked his head. 'And this was a fairly new relationship, was it, Jessica?'

''Bout four weeks, I'd say. Give or take a few days.'

'And they hadn't had a falling-out or anything?'

'Oh God, no. She were head over heels. I think he was, too. Mind you, you never know, do you?'

'Know what?'

'With these soldiers, Brits or Americans, when they're away from home. You know, whether there's a wife back home waiting for them and if they're just after a bit of fun. But Archie's genuine, I think. He'll be devastated. Absolutely destroyed. He thought the world of her.'

Carver frowned. 'But did he know about the other side of her life? Here at the Café Prestige, or on the streets?'

'Nerr. I derrn't think so. But Sarah never worked the streets. She was just a part-timer. And she wanted to give it up, poor lass.'

Swift sat back and folded his arms. Then rapidly uncrossed them, belatedly remembering not to give the impression of being closed off to an interviewee you were trying to build a rapport with.

'Could one of her johns have seen her out and about with Archie,' he asked, 'and perhaps become jealous?'

Jessica shrugged. 'It's possible, I suppose. I haven't the foggiest, really.'

'What about anyone at the dances?' asked Carver. 'Had anyone else tried to get fresh with Sarah, and been rebuffed? Someone who might not have liked seeing her walking out with a black man?'

'Not that I can think of, off the top of my head.' Then Jessica paused, and frowned. 'Oh, wait a sec. There was one, now you mention it, who Sarah turned down. And then I did notice him and his mates looking a bit sour-faced when Sarah started dancing with Archie.' Then her face brightened. 'By gum, he can dance, that one. He has all the moves. They all do.'

Jessica became quiet again, as though realising that her friend Sarah wouldn't be taking to the dance floor with Archie, or indeed anyone, anymore.

Swift made a note with his pencil, then looked up at her again.

'This one who you think became jealous. You don't have a name by any chance, do you?'

Jessica shook her head. 'No. Sorry.'

'Would you recognise him if you saw him again?' asked Carver.

'Oh, aye. I don't forget a face. It's an important skill to have in my job. Just so's you know the ones who've treated you bad before, like. After that, I don't give 'em the time of day. No second chances with me, if you know what I mean.'

'Thank you, Jessica,' said Swift, finally. 'You've been very helpful.'

'Well, she were my friend, like. I'll miss her. I want you to catch the bastard who did it, and make him swing for it.'

'We will try,' said Swift, putting away his pencil and notebook. 'One more thing. Would you be prepared to come with us to this dance hall in Cottingham at the next available opportunity?'

'I don't know about that. Being seen with the cops would cramp my style.'

'Come on, Jessica,' said Carver. 'You don't go there for work. No one would know me there. I can dress for the dance, too. When is the next one?'

'Tonight. They're every Wednesday, Friday and Saturday without fail.'

'So will you do it?' Carver persisted.

'Well, I don't mind going wi' you. You don't look much like a police officer, anyroad. More like a little college swot. But they'd smell 'im a mile off. Plain clothes or not, he's a copper as sure as night follows day.'

Swift didn't take offence. 'I'm sure I can do my best to be less police-like, and wear more informal clothes.'

'Tell yer what,' said Jessica, lowering her voice to Carver. 'We could pretend to be sisters. How's about that? And then 'e could be our dad.'

Swift could tell Carver was struggling not to laugh.

5

When Swift and Carver had finished interviewing the young women who used the café for soliciting, they had the grim task of talking to the Houghton family. Uniformed police had already broken the news of Sarah's death to them – her mother had been asked to formally identify the body at the mortuary earlier in the day. But precisely how Sarah had died had, Swift subsequently learned, been kept back from them. Telling a family their much-loved daughter had been found dead after a bombing raid was one thing. Telling them she hadn't in fact died in the air raid, but had been brutally strangled beforehand, then her body mutilated after death, was something else quite entirely. Swift was pleased he had Carver with him, inexperienced though she was. There was nothing like learning on the job.

They headed back to police headquarters in the town centre first. Swift wanted to check what else they knew about the Houghton family – and Carver knew her way around the records department.

He was conscious of her looking at him as he drove.

'Does it give you trouble, sir?'

'Does what give me trouble?'

'Well ... your arm, sir. I saw you rubbing your shoulder. I don't like to pry, and I'm sure you'll tell me about it if you want, but just to let you know I'm able to drive. If you need a rest at any stage.'

Swift felt slightly affronted. It wasn't Carver's place to be asking about it. He liked that she was prepared to speak her mind – but perhaps she needed to choose a little better when to do it.

'I'm perfectly fine, WAPC Carver. Should I ever require any assistance, I'll let you know. But I don't recall asking for any.'

They lapsed into silence.

It was a sore point for Swift, literally and figuratively. When he'd first got the Morris 8 when he was with the Met, he'd resisted efforts to get it specially adapted to make it easier to drive with the prosthetic.

His aluminium arm had once been so foreign to him, as though he was an alien being who'd walked straight out of an H. G. Wells novel. Now it was more like an old friend. An awkward old friend who didn't always do what you wanted or expected. Sometimes he dreamed he still had a fully functioning, flesh and bone forelimb. But he was thankful that he'd been one of the lucky Great War veterans – saying goodbye to the heavy wooden prosthetic he'd first been fitted with had been a joyous moment. Had he got special treatment because his father was on the board at St Mary's Hospital in Roehampton? Or because the medical officer who'd performed the amputation had become a prominent physician to the great and good? If that had resulted in favouritism, he didn't care.

In any case, the trickiest task arms and hands had to accomplish in cars was slam the bloody gearstick into gear – and if anything, because it had had to take over most daily tasks, his left arm was even stronger. The Morris – with only three gears – didn't require a lot of changes anyway.

The Houghtons didn't seem to feature in any large way in police records. Sarah was mentioned – but only in relation to the case in which George Camilleri had been fined for running a disorderly house. Their street, Mulgrave Street – just off Cleveland Street to the east of the River Hull – had suffered a direct hit in a bombing raid the previous summer, destroying a communal shelter, much in the same way as had just happened in Scarborough Street on the other side of the city. Entire families had been wiped out – but the Houghtons didn't appear to have suffered any losses. There was a record for Sarah's unmarried older sister, who'd moved back into the family home – thanks to the fact that her two young children were recorded as having been billeted away from Hull to escape the raids.

When they arrived in Mulgrave Street, the extent of the devastation was clear to see – as was how lucky the Houghtons had been. Their house had clearly once been part of a terrace, but now had been refashioned into a tiny detached dwelling. All the houses either side of it had either been destroyed in the previous year's raid, or rendered unsafe and demolished.

Sarah Houghton had survived all that, thought Swift, but had then been despatched by a murderer. Somehow, it made the act of deliberately burying her body in the rubble of another raid on the other side of the city seem even more perverse. To say nothing of the way she'd been mutilated after death.

The whole family were gathered in the front room. Swift could tell from their raw eyes that plenty of tears had been shed. What he was more surprised about were the two children running around: a girl and a boy, aged about seven and five respectively, who were clearly the offspring of Sarah's sister – the ones who supposedly had been billeted away from the city.

Swift introduced himself and Carver, and turned down Sarah's sister's offer of a cup of tea.

'I'm very sorry for your tragic loss, Mr and Mrs Houghton,' said Swift. 'Thank you for going to the mortuary to identify Sarah's body.'

'It were the least we could do for her,' said Mr Houghton. 'We thought we had a miracle escape a year ago. We thought we were the lucky ones. Then Sarah goes and gets herself blown up by the ruddy Nazi bastards near Hessle Road. What were she doing over that way? Do you know?'

Out of the eyeline of her parents, Swift saw the elder sister grimace and give him a shake of her head. They clearly either weren't aware of Sarah's part-time freelance work or, if they were, they didn't want to be reminded of it. Swift was prepared to play along to that extent. But he had to at least let them know their daughter had been murdered – if only to find out whether the family had any likely suspects in mind.

He cleared his throat, and glanced quickly at Carver, as though he wanted her moral support.

'We're not sure, to be honest. And there are, I'm afraid, other aspects of Sarah's death which are troubling us.'

'Oh aye?' said Mrs Houghton. 'What's that, then? We can't take much more bad news.'

'Although it's correct that your daughter's body was found at the site of last night's Scarborough Street air raid, we don't think that's where she died.'

Swift noticed both parents looking perplexed. The sister, however, who'd sent her children out into the street to play, was simply hugging her mother, a resigned look on her face – as though she already knew what the detective was about to say.

'What do you mean by that?' asked Sarah's father. 'So you're saying she didn't die in the air raid at all?'

'That's exactly what I'm saying, I'm afraid, Mr Houghton. We believe Sarah died elsewhere and then her body was moved.'

'Well, that don't make any sense,' said Mrs Houghton. 'It don't make any sense at all.'

Swift paused, trying to formulate his words in as gentle a way as possible. But there was no getting away from the brutality of what had happened.

'I'm afraid Sarah was attacked. Possibly from behind. While the blackout is necessary, of course, to try to foil German bombing raids, it unfortunately allows criminals to operate with impunity under the cover of darkness. If it's any consolation, we believe Sarah's end was swift.'

'But how?' asked Mr Houghton. 'And why?'

'I'm afraid Sarah was strangled.'

'Oh my God!' cried Mrs Houghton. 'Oh my God!'

She collapsed into the arms of her daughter.

'Well, are you sure about this? Are you sure you haven't made a mistake?'

Swift was slightly lost for words. The image of Sarah Houghton's body on the mortuary trolley – the terrible wound where her heart had been removed – was once again playing like a newsreel in his brain.

Carver stepped in.

'We're sorry to break the news to you all like this. It must be an awful shock for you. I can't imagine what it's like. But we are determined to find Sarah's killer. So we need you all to try to think who might have done this. Did Sarah have a man friend? Were there any old boyfriends who might have been jealous of a new relationship? Anything like that?'

Sarah's father suddenly got to his feet.

'I said he'd be trouble, Doreen. None of you would listen to me.'

'Oh, give over, Fred. He's a lovely lad. You just don't like the fact he's black.'

'Who?' said Swift, feigning ignorance. 'Who are you talking about?'

''Er fancy man,' said Fred Houghton. 'One of them black soldiers billeted out in Cott. He's a nice enough lad, of course,' he added, as though trying to dig himself out of a hole. 'Good manners. Treat her like a lady, he did. Always getting her new stockings and flowers and the like. But I could just tell it would be trouble.'

'Don't you dare speak ill of him, Fred,' said his wife, wiping away the tears from her face. 'Sarah had high hopes for him. She'd been swept off her feet.'

'Aye, well, it's too late now,' said Fred. 'You lot better get down there and take him in for questioning, hadn't you?'

'We'll certainly be talking to him, Mr Houghton,' said Carver. 'As we will with all of Sarah's associates, to try to identify her killer.'

'But let's not jump to conclusions,' said Swift. 'Did Sarah have any former boyfriends who might have been jealous about this new relationship with the soldier?'

'Well, there is one,' said Sarah's sister.

'Shurrup, Betty!' shouted Mrs Houghton.

'I won't shut up, Mam. They need to know. Bobby Stott. Lives in Sherburn Street, off Holderness Road. He were right peeved about her seeing a black soldier – mind you, I don't think it were really Archie's colour that were the problem. Just the fact Sarah weren't interested in Bobby anymore.'

'Archie?' asked Carver, innocently.

Swift had to give her ten out of ten for acting. They'd gone into this interview pretending they knew nothing of Sarah's relationship with the soldier, in order to find out the most information possible from the Houghton family. But, of course, if they didn't know about the soldier boyfriend, they would have been sure to ask for his name.

The sister rolled her eyes slightly, as though she knew the game they were playing.

'Archibald Davis. Works with the others from that black American unit at the docks – I don't think they're allowed to go and fight. It's a port battalion or summat. I don't know if Bobby came across him at the docks, too – 'cause he's a docker. That's how he's avoided being called up.'

'And when you say he'd shown signs of jealousy, how did that manifest itself?'

'How did it what?' asked Doreen Houghton. Then she turned to Carver. 'What's he on about with his posh words, love?'

'How did it show itself, Mrs Houghton?' translated Carver. 'The jealousy.'

'Well, he came round here to have it out with her. Shouting his mouth off. Saying all sorts of filth. Calling her an 'ore and all sorts.'

The despair in the couple's faces had given way to anger – as though it was something for them to cling on to.

'I gave him a good piece of my mind, I can tell you,' said Fred. 'I may be thirty years or so older than the little bastard, but if Doreen hadn't held me back, like, I'd have had a crack at him. Little fucker.'

The burst of animation seemed to tire the couple, and the remainder of the interview yielded little of value.

As they were preparing to go, Swift asked for Bobby Stott's exact address.

'I'll see you out,' said Betty, 'and give it to you outside.'

When they were outside the small house's front door, Betty lowered her voice to Swift.

'Thanks for not mentioning the other stuff in front of me mam and dad.'

'The other stuff?'

'You know. What Sarah got up to at the Café Prestige.'

'They didn't know, then?' asked Swift.

'Well, let's put it this way. If they did, they liked to pretend they didn't. It were never mentioned. Which was why it were such a shock when Bobby came round shooting his mouth off. Here's his address, by the way. I've written it down for you.'

She handed over a piece of paper, with the address written in neat capital letters.

'Do you think this Bobby could have done it?' Carver asked her.

Betty Houghton sniffed. 'Can you ever really tell? You lot would know that better than me. To be honest, I think the reason he was so wound up about it, was that he loved her. Love can make you do the strangest things, can't it? But I don't think Bobby would have wanted to harm her. No way. For my penny-worth, you'll have more luck chasing down some of her punters. I know some of them gave her the creeps.'

'We will do that, as far as we can,' said Swift. 'As you can imagine, a lot of them don't give names – or where they do, they've made them up. You don't have any names for us, do you?'

'Nah. She only ever talked about it in a general way. No specifics, as such. She were embarrassed about having to do it, to be honest.'

Just then, her son and daughter came running past, nearly knocking into Swift.

'Calm down, you two!' she shouted. 'Otherwise you'll be off to bed with no tea.'

Swift held her gaze. 'You never thought about evacuating them from Hull to somewhere safer?'

'They're all I've got other than me mam and dad, officer. I prefer to keep them close. Anyroad, until last night's attack it had all calmed down a bit. Certainly not as bad as last year. That were awful.'

'You didn't think about it then, after the bombing here?'

'Well, I think I looked into it with the corporation, yes. But in the end, I decided not to go ahead. Why do you ask?'

'Oh, nothing,' said Swift. 'I just know a lot of kids have been evacuated, that's all. Anyway, we're sorry for your loss again, Mrs . . .'

'It's still Miss, officer, despite the bairns.'

'Well, thank you for your help, Miss Houghton. We'll let you know if we make any progress.' Swift doffed his hat. 'Good day to you.'

6

Bobby Stott proved more difficult to track down than Swift had hoped. Inquiries at his home, and at Alexandra Dock where he worked, both showed he was on a week's unpaid leave, granted for 'personal reasons'. No one seemed to know what these were, or indeed where he was, which immediately made the detective suspicious.

'Do you think he's our man and he's gone on the run?' asked Weighton.

'I don't think we can conclude that. We can, though, put out an all bulletins alert to other forces just in case he gets stopped at a checkpoint somewhere. We certainly need to question him. We also need to question this Archibald Davis fellow – but we'll need to get the permission of the American military to do that formally. And they might not be very obliging. So let's stake out this dance hall in Cottingham at the first available opportunity – in other words, tonight. Carver can help us. And we'll take Jessica Pickering, too. We may just accidentally run into Private Davis there.'

'Will he be there if his girlfriend's been murdered?'

'We haven't released it to the press yet have we, Weighton? He might not know at all . . . unless . . .'

'Unless he did it?'

Swift gave a small nod.

Swift could see the look of disdain on Jessica's face as they met up near the main bus stop in Cottingham, less than fifty yards or so from the King Street Rooms on the corner of Finkle Street.

'If he's coming in,' she said, 'I hope he's paying for the entrance fee and drinks as agreed. And I don't want him cramping my style.'

Swift lowered his voice. 'We're not really here for fun, Jessica. You're trying to help your friend, remember?'

'I'll stick with her, sir,' said Carver.

'All right. I'll probably stay on the sidelines observing. Jim, can you make sure you stay near the door in case anyone makes a run for it?'

'Of course, sir.'

By the time they got inside, the dancing was already well underway. It was a mid-tempo Glenn Miller tune, popular on both sides of the Atlantic, but Swift knew that in the United States – where they published a hit parade – the tune had topped the chart for several weeks, as many of Miller's dance songs did.

Carver and Jessica got into the action straightaway, accepting the offers of dances, even though Jessica indicated that Davis and his friends didn't look to have arrived yet.

In general, the atmosphere appeared to be fun and friendly, with the black soldiers who were there mixing freely. Swift noticed Jessica and Carver giggling together, whispering, then glancing over at him and whispering again. The detective felt awkward and out of place – and he had a horrible feeling the two women were continuing the 'joke' of their being sisters, with Swift in the role of their 'father'.

His thoughts were interrupted when a busty, dyed-blonde, pompadour-hairstyled woman began trying to talk to him. On a film star, her chosen coiffure might have looked glamorous. With this woman, it just looked as though she was trying too hard. Swift had been concentrating on scanning the room, looking out for any recognition between Jessica and the GIs and local men, or any signs of friction. When he finally tuned in to what the woman was saying, he realised she'd misunderstood what he was doing.

'Seen anyone who takes your fancy?' she asked.

In his two years stationed in the city, Swift had learned that Hull folk were nothing if not direct. He regarded her curiously.

'Those two you've been eyeing up,' she said. 'They're a little young for you, don't you think?'

He laughed then. 'I agree. And I haven't been – as you put it – eyeing them up. They're just some . . . some work colleagues I came with.'

'So you're not spoken for?'

The words were innocent enough. But to Swift, they were like a stab to the centre of his heart. He had been spoken for, of course. Twice. A tragedy and a betrayal. After the second of those, he could barely face life anymore. Only his 'escape' from London to Hull had saved him.

He cleared his throat. Should he lie to put the woman off? She was diverting his attention.

'I'm rather busy, actually,' he finally said. It sounded stuffy. It *was* stuffy.

'Well, you're not too busy for a dance. Come on. I like this one.'

For a second, she pulled him by his false arm. Instantly, she realised her mistake. But he was thankful when she merely adjusted her grip, and lightly pushed him back towards the dance floor. She didn't recoil, as so many would, or – worse still – ask him what had happened. For that he was grateful, and for that he decided to give in and dance with her, rather than continuing to stand on the sidelines.

She was surprisingly light on her feet and after a few moments, Swift found himself enjoying the distraction. He knew, however, he should be concentrating on work – so he resumed his lighthouse scan of the dance hall.

'Some women would be offended,' his dance partner suddenly said.

'I'm sorry?'

'Offended. That you aren't paying them any attention. You haven't even asked my name. You're still too busy watching your young "work friends".'

Swift laughed. 'My apologies. What's your name?'

'Violet.'

'Pleased to meet you, Violet. I'm Ambrose.'

The woman laughed as they continued to move to the music.

'I'm not so sure you are pleased to meet me at all, Ambrose. Your mind's on other things.'

Swift wondered how much to tell her. She may – possibly – be of help.

'That's because I'm working, Violet.' Then he bent and whispered in her ear, 'I'm a police officer.'

'Ooh. I like a man in uniform.' She smiled up at him.

Swift couldn't help thinking she was wearing far too much make-up, even though some of it – like her beetroot-red lips – was the home-made, vegetable-based variety. He preferred his women as natural as possible.

'You're out of luck, then. The nearest I get to a uniform is a suit and hat. I'm a detective.'

He felt the woman suddenly tense up, and the friendly, jokey atmosphere between them evaporated in an instant. Then it was she who began looking round the dance floor.

'Ah, there's my friend, Elsie. I'm going to have to love you and leave you, I'm afraid, Ambrose, but thank you very much.'

Swift was relieved as she moved off. In any normal situation, he'd be suspicious about why she was so nervous to be dancing with a police detective. And perhaps it would be worth a check on her later, in the records department at Alfred Gelder Street. For now, he was concentrating too hard on watching others. He noticed Carver and Jessica had also moved off the dance floor. Jessica was talking to a couple of black GIs, while Carver was sitting at a table, nursing her drink on her own.

A local man appeared to be about to make a move on her, but Swift took the only other seat at the table first.

'You looked to be enjoying yourself, sir,' she said.

'It's not really why we're here, is it? Have you gleaned anything?'

'Not really,' said Carver. 'Jessica says the usual crowd aren't here. No sign of Archie Davis. She's gone over to talk to the others to see what's going on.'

Before Carver had finished her sentence, Swift saw Jessica walking back towards them.

She sat down, and began speaking in a low voice, directing her words towards Swift.

'I don't like it,' she said. 'There seems to be a bit of a nasty atmosphere tonight. And they say there's no chance Archie's coming.'

'Why not?' asked Swift.

'He's disappeared. Gone absent without leave. That's not like him.'

Swift and Carver exchanged glances.

'I'll go and tell Weighton,' said Swift.

Weighton was still standing near the doorway, leafing through that evening's edition of the *Hull Daily Mail*, while a pint of beer stood virtually untouched next to him on a side table. As Swift approached, he looked up from the newspaper.

'Anything doing, sir?' he asked, sotto voce.

Swift gave a small nod. 'Archie Davis won't be coming tonight, I'm afraid.'

'Why not, sir?'

'He's gone absent without leave.'

Weighton blew out his cheeks. 'You think he's our man, then?'

'Possibly, but let's not jump to any conclusions. We'd better get over to their barracks on New Village Road and talk to his commanding officer.'

'Won't we need permission for that, sir?'

'Quite possibly. Where's the nearest police box?'

'I'm not sure, sir. But Cottingham Police Station's just a bit further along this road. Number 90 Finkle Street, I think it is. Not more than a couple of hundred yards at most. There'll be someone on the front desk, at least. They'll let you use the telephone there, sir.'

Swift nodded. 'We could just go straight to the barracks, but I suppose I'd better check in with the detective chief superintendent first. You mind the fort here in the meantime. See if you can find out anything else from those GIs over there.'

'We can't just go barging in there, Swift,' said Holdridge, over a crackly line. *'Maintaining good relations with the Yanks is important to the war effort – that's got to come first. I'm sure you understand.'*

'With respect, sir, this is a murder inquiry. A particularly vicious, sadistic murder. I want to go and talk to them now – before the trail goes cold.'

'Well, I'm not going to authorise that, and you report to me, Swift, and do as I say. This will all have to wait till the morning, until we've got clearance from the War Office. It's half past ten at night, man, for God's sake. I'm already in bed, or rather I was until the telephone rang, and you should be, too.'

'But, sir, it's important that—'

'What's important, Swift, is that I'm ordering you not to go to that barracks or attempt to interview anyone there before we have proper clearance. Do you understand?'

Swift cut the line before giving Holdridge the satisfaction of hearing him accede to his superior's wishes. Then he made another call to the control room at Alfred Gelder Street HQ.

'Detective Chief Inspector Swift here. I'm just about to turn in for the night, but before I do, I wondered if there were any messages for me?'

'I'm glad you called, sir, because yes, there is one. We were wondering about sending a patrol car out to try to find you to deliver it, but I don't have to worry about that now. We've had a call from Scarborough Borough Police for you.'

'Oh yes?' asked Swift, perplexed. 'Did they leave a message?'

'Yes, sir. Apparently, they were responding to an alert you put out about a certain Robert Stott of Sherburn Street in Hull.'

'Bobby Stott. That's right. What about him?'

'Well, he got himself into a bit of a brawl at a pub in the town. He's currently cooling down in a cell at Scarborough nick.'

7

Swift knew it was some forty or so miles to Scarborough. In normal road conditions, that might have taken them a little over an hour. But they would be facing a journey of at least double that. There was a twenty-mile-an-hour night-time speed limit, although as police officers they wouldn't have to adhere to it. But other cars would, and could hold them up as a result. Night-time visibility was reduced because the Morris's headlights had to be shielded due to blackout regulations. Just three narrow slits of headlight beam were permitted. It would make for a gruelling journey. Although he was reluctant to let anyone other than himself drive the Morris, on this occasion he deferred to Weighton. His right shoulder was already aching like sin – it wouldn't stand up to a two-hour-plus drive.

Jessica seemed put out that she wouldn't be getting a lift home. Instead, Swift asked Carver to escort her on the late bus. There was no need to take the WAPC with them to Scarborough, appreciative though he was of her assistance to the inquiry so far. As for Archibald Davis, Swift would – reluctantly – simply have to obey Holdridge's orders and wait until his boss had secured the relevant permissions the following day.

Progress was slow, with Weighton having to hug the white lines in the centre of the country roads to see where he was going. That is, where there actually were white lines. They deliberately skirted Beverley to avoid having to go near RAF Leconfield, and any associated roadblocks. The airfield was currently closed – but there would be tight security around it, as construction teams worked round the clock to convert it from a Spitfire base to one of the main centres for Bomber Command, with all the longer, bigger runways that required. Instead, they skirted Walkington, then followed the Malton road to beyond Bainton, before turning north-east to pick up the main Beverley to Scarborough road again at Driffield. Weighton had to give his boss East Riding geography lessons as they progressed – all of the helpful village signs and signposts had been removed two years earlier when fears of invasion by the Nazis had been all-consuming. Now, that threat of invasion had receded a little. Soviet forces had already turned back Hitler's troops outside Moscow the previous winter, and were putting up fierce resistance in Stalingrad. In the Asian theatre, however, the news was grim, with Burma about to fall to the Japanese, if it hadn't already.

They didn't encounter any roadblocks or checkpoints – but Swift did get the sense at one point that another vehicle was following them. Although the passenger-side wing mirror was adjusted for the driver's line of sight – in other words, Weighton's – Swift could see behind by craning his neck.

Every time he looked, some distance back he could see the shielded lights of another vehicle. Many times before he'd left London, he'd had the same sensation and dismissed it as paranoia. He didn't want that paranoia to overtake his life up here in East Yorkshire, too.

Despite his regular checks in the mirror, Swift eventually found himself struggling to stay awake – until they got to the 1 in 6 gradient of Staxton Hill. By which time the pursuing car – phantom or not – appeared to have given up the chase.

'Do we have to come back this way, too?' asked Swift.

'Yes, sir,' said Weighton, a frown shadowing his darkened face as he concentrated on negotiating their way down the incline. 'Let's hope the brakes on this thing work all right. Have you checked them recently?'

'No.'

'Well, just pray they don't fail, then, sir.'

By the time the two Hull detectives managed to get to interview Bobby Stott, it was well after midnight. Thankfully, according to the custody sergeant, he appeared to have sobered up somewhat.

'He's puked his guts up at least once, so that might have got some of it out of his system. If you'd tried to talk to him a couple of hours ago, you wouldn't have got much sense.'

The sergeant escorted Swift and Weighton down to the cells.

'I'm not sure what the fight was all about. Football or something inane like that, in all probability. Anyway, we're not charging him. Unless that's what you gentlemen are here to do.'

'No, no,' said Swift. 'We just want a quiet word.'

'In his cell, or do you want to use the interview room?'

'The interview room might be a good idea,' replied Swift. 'You couldn't stretch to a couple of teas for me and my sergeant, could you? And perhaps one for your prisoner? We have some news for him which he may find a little difficult to stomach.'

'Of course, sir. How do you both take it?'

'Milk, no sugar for me,' said Swift.

'And I'll go for milk and two sugars if you've got some, please, Sergeant,' said Weighton.

Stott looked dishevelled, as though he'd overslept wearing his clothes, and someone had poured a bucket of water over him to wake him up.

'We'd just like a few words, Mr Stott, if that's all right,' said Swift.

'Who the fuck are you, then?'

'We're detectives from Hull City Police. I'm Chief Inspector Swift, and this is Sergeant Weighton.'

'I ain't done owt. Just had a few too many bevvies, like. What the fuck has that got to do with Hull Police?'

Before Swift could answer, there was a knock on the door, and the custody sergeant entered with a teapot, milk, sugar and cups and saucers balanced on a tray.

'I thought it was easier to make you a pot, then you can help yourselves.' Then he glowered at Stott. 'You watch out, though, you're only getting this service because we've got important visitors from Hull Police. It's not in aid of you, I can assure you, Mr Stott.'

The prisoner threw the sergeant a sarcastic grimace.

As Weighton poured the tea, Swift braced himself for what he was about to tell Stott.

'We've got some rather sad news to tell you, I'm afraid, Bobby, about one of your former girlfriends.'

'Who?' he barked.

'Sarah Houghton.'

'Oh, aye?' Stott looked confused and rubbed his forehead as Weighton passed him a tea. He proceeded to ladle in so many spoonfuls of sugar that Swift lost count. 'It's no good looking at me like that. It doesn't seem rationed for you lot, so I might as well take advantage while I can. So what of Sarah? We'd split up. She were seeing some Yank soldier. A coloured one, an' all.'

'She was found dead in an air-raid shelter that took a direct hit from a Nazi bomb.'

'Er mah God!' exclaimed Scott, the hand stirring his sugar suddenly frozen. He let go of the spoon and the cup and held his head in his hands. 'That's awful. Where'd it happen?'

'The public shelter on Scarborough Street in Hull, off Hessle Road,' said Weighton.

'Good God.'

'When was the last time you saw her?' asked Swift.

'I bumped into her near her folks' place a couple of weeks ago.'

'What were you doing round there?' asked Weighton.

'Well, I work at Alexandra Dock. It's not far away.'

'You weren't called up, then?' asked Swift.

'Dockers are a reserved occupation.'

'We're aware of that, Mr Stott,' said Weighton.

'Well, I wouldn't be called up, then, would I?'

Swift sighed. 'And where were you on Tuesday night, Mr Stott?'

'Here. In Scarborough. Me auntie's got a bed and breakfast. My nerves are a bit shot from all the air raids and the like. I had a few days' leave due, and she let me stay. Been here since the beginning of the week.'

'And your aunt can verify that, can she?' asked Weighton.

'Aye, of course she can.'

'Of course, you could have gone into Hull from here, couldn't you?' said Swift. 'The trains are still running.'

'Why the fuck would I want to go back to Hull in the middle of a week in Scarborough? They haven't had the same number of raids here. There isn't the industry. It's a lot safer here, I can tell you. I don't feel safe in Hull, not working at the docks, like. That's the target. That's what those fucking Nazis are aiming for. Not the bloody police station where you lot are. Anyroad, why are you asking me all this stuff? I didn't fly the bomber that killed Sarah, God rest her soul.'

'I didn't actually say she was killed in the bombing, did I?' responded Swift. 'As it turns out, she wasn't. She was strangled, then her body was moved there, probably to disguise the real cause of death.'

Stott's face – already pale enough, thanks to the amount he'd drunk the previous evening – now blanched almost white as the blood drained out.

'Jesus. Well, it weren't me. I've already told you.'

'You'd had it out with Sarah, though, hadn't you?' said Swift. 'Called her all sorts of names in front of her parents.'

'I were angry.'

'Angry enough to kill?' asked Weighton.

The man banged his muscular forearm down heavily on the table, pulling his shirt sleeve up in the process. Swift quickly examined the tattoos which were revealed: a tiger's head – possibly something to do with the local football club's nickname – and the initials BS next to SH, with an arrow-punctured heart in between.

'I don't have to put up with this. I've told you I was in Scarborough and there are folks who'll vouch for me.'

'Very well, Mr Stott,' said Swift. 'You can provide us with all the details, names and addresses, et cetera, and we'll check out your alibi. Let's hope for your sake it holds water.'

Swift and Weighton eventually got a few hours' sleep, thanks to the desk sergeant sorting out rooms for them at the town's Grand Hotel. Swift was only upset that, given the lateness of the hour, they wouldn't get to enjoy the building's sweeping views of Scarborough Bay until the morning. He was cheered by the thought that Holdridge would no doubt choke on his breakfast if Scarborough Police decided to pass the cost on to their Hull colleagues.

Perhaps because the hotel seemed to double as the billet for a contingent of RAF airmen, breakfast the next morning was one of the best the two had enjoyed in months, if not years, with bacon, eggs, butter, toast and even marmalade – although the latter was the carrot version, first popularised in the previous war.

'Not much sign of rationing here, sir,' said Weighton, under his breath.

'No,' said Swift, smoothing out his starched white napkin, having demolished his scrambled egg and bacon – noting that, thankfully, they were the real thing. Not a hint of ghastly powdered egg had tainted the plate. 'Let's enjoy it while we can.' He glanced at his watch. It was already past half eight. 'We'll have to get going soon, but once you've finished let's stretch our legs and talk things through.'

They didn't have time to go far before returning to Hull in the Morris, but after just a few hours' sleep – and the heavy breakfast – Swift needed a few lungfuls of sea air to get his brain working. They ambled out of the hotel and along the Spa Bridge, which spanned the valley between the town centre above South Bay, and the grand clifftop apartment blocks of The Esplanade. Halfway along, they turned to the sea and admired the view over to the castle.

'Impressive,' said Swift.

'You've not been here before then, sir?'

'No. I've seen this view of the harbour, beach and castle on postcards and calendars, but the furthest I'd got to along the coast until now was Bridlington.'

Weighton laughed. 'Brid's not really a patch on Scarborough, though, is it, sir? And far too many old ladies and maiden aunts for my liking.'

Swift didn't say anything to contradict his sergeant. But he knew *why* there were so many unmarried women and widows in these Yorkshire seaside towns. Many of those who had been married had probably seen their menfolk blown to bits in the killing fields of the Somme and Passchendaele – those huge set-piece battles of the Great War, where millions had been slaughtered, yet the front had often barely advanced. The unmarried? With so many men dead, there had been a dearth of post-war suitors. If they wanted to take solace by spending their widowhood and spinsterhood enjoying the sea air, or listening to big band music in the seafront bandstands, who could blame them?

'I take it we're ruling out Stott as a suspect?' asked Weighton.

'We still need to check his alibi, or ask our Scarborough colleagues for help with that. But no, I can't see it, can you? Hopefully by the time we're back in Hull, Holdridge will have secured us the necessary permission to talk to Archibald Davis's commanding officer in Cottingham. Or indeed, Davis himself, if he's turned up by now.'

8

Theophilus Howard had the rent agreement in his pocket, so it was a big day for him and Bessie. Their first place together, and with the baby on the way it couldn't have come at a better time. Theo knew there could be trouble, of course. There always seemed to be trouble these days. Bessie, Theo and their friends, some of their families – they'd all been lured up to Detroit by the recruiters. Streets paved with gold . . . that sort of thing. Those were the promises.

There'd been jobs all right. Plenty of jobs and good money. But there weren't nowhere to live, at least nowhere half decent. Theo didn't want to be bringing up his new family in a subdivided apartment, crammed in with all the others in one of those hovels in Paradise Valley. So the Sojourner Truth Project seemed like a good solution. It took its name from a good woman, after all – the first black woman to win back custody of her son in a case against a white man. What better start for a newborn could there be than that?

Bessie had warned Theo it wouldn't be easy, and events had borne that out. He'd heard there were new housing projects coming, now the factories were switching from producing cars to weapons and war machines. But when Bessie learned the one he had his eye on was in a white area – bounded by Fenelon Street and Nevada Avenue – she warned him there would be trouble. Already there were incidents almost daily. Whites threatening to walk out of the factories just because a couple of black workers had been promoted. And blacks retaliating for years of oppression and hatred in some of the few ways they could get away with – like deliberately bumping into whites on the sidewalks.

Today was the day they were supposed to be moving in.

They'd taken a look yesterday.

Saw the cross burning in the field. Some welcome message.

But it wasn't just the burning cross. Anyways, the Klan round here weren't always the ones to fear. Their Midwest offshoot had a far worse reputation – and their power base, Highland Park, was only a couple of miles away. They said this splinter group had disbanded, but Bessie didn't believe it. And as well as the cross, there was the picket. White folks – more than a hundred of them – threatening to stop any blacks entering their new homes. When Bessie had seen that, she'd told Theo she wasn't moving after all. It took a whole heap of sweet-talking to win her back round.

'We're blessed, Bessie,' Theo told her that night. 'You're with child and we have the agreement for our new home. Don't let none of what you saw today trouble you. I'll always be here to protect you.'

The next day they drove up early to the project in their battered Ford Coupe, fully intending to move in.

Those 120 white pickets had become a seething mass of more than a thousand.

'I'm not doing this, Theo. I'm not risking my life, and my baby's life, just to make a point.'

'They're not going to beat us, Bessie. The rent's paid. We can't go back to the old place.'

'You'll just have to find someplace else, husband. Or you'll be looking for a new wife an' all.'

When Archie Davis heard what had happened, he whipped Theo into a new state of confusion.

'I'm not one for violence, Theo. But you have a God-given legal right to that new house of yours. You and Bessie deserve it. We ain't gonna let no dumb-ass protesters put a stop to it.'

He fired up Theo good and proper.

'We'll go back there again,' Archie continued. 'Just you and me. Bessie can stay with Dolores until she's happy it's safe. They'll give up in time. It's just a lot of hollerin' and empty threats.'

They went back. Theo wasn't sure, but Archie persuaded him. Normally, Theo was his own man – the voices of others didn't affect him, especially when all that mattered was the future for him, Bessie and the baby in her womb. But Archie was fired up, which was unlike him, and that fired up Theo, too.

What he didn't like was the outline of what he saw in Archie's jacket inside pocket.

'You didn't bring no chiv, did you, Archie? What the fuck are you thinking?'

'Relax, brother. It's just in case. I'm not looking for no trouble.'

When they reached the new housing estate, Theo was relieved to see the numbers of whites standing guard seemed to have dwindled – and a group of young blacks were facing them off.

'What do we do now?' asked Theo.

'You drive up to your house, brother. That sure is your God-given right, and it's the just and lawful thing to do. A man has a right to drive his car to his own house, especially in this here Motor City. We're all making them cars. Might as well use 'em.'

It wasn't really the time to remind Archie that, actually, their work didn't involve motor manufacturing anymore. Both of them worked out at the new Willow Run aircraft factory, on the western edge of Detroit. Which was why it wasn't a very wise move to come here in the Coupe. He needed the car, rust bucket though it was, for the seventy-mile round-trip commute each day. If it got busted up by those white guys, he'd have to queue with everyone else for the bus. And there weren't enough buses, and too many people trying to get them. It had been the same for a while. They'd enticed everyone up here from the South – Archie and Theo had thrown over perfectly good jobs at the local poultry processing plant near their home town of Jackson, Mississippi. Yes, they had been two black workers in an almost entirely white workforce, but most of the time, that didn't prove a problem. Their part of the plant was segregated, and they just kept their heads down. But like many others, they'd been lured up to Michigan by the supposed wealth to be found in the motor industry. It hadn't turned out exactly like that.

'I don't like the look of it,' said Theo. 'Let's turn back.'

'You chicken or something, brother? Like that meat you used to pack in them tins? It's your house now. You don't have no place else to go. You have a *right* to be there. Just drive.'

And so Theo did.

Those white folks jumped out of the way faster than hens being chased by a fox in a farmyard. They scattered in every direction. They didn't look so threatening then.

But a couple of them stood their ground.

They stood their ground and Theo had to stop, staring straight into their faces of hate, else he knew he was heading to jail. To jail – or something worse.

Then the banging on the windows started.

Then the rocking of the car.

Then the wipers were torn off.

Then Theo and Archie were scrambling to try to lock the doors, but before they could, they were wrenched open.

Both of them were dragged out.

That cross, it was still there. That, or another one. And it was still burning.

And then fists flew and they both curled in balls, trying to protect their heads with their arms. All the time, boots were kicking at their heads, their backs, their kidneys.

Theo thought his time had finally come.

But just as he was saying his prayers, his mental goodbyes to Bessie and the baby he'd never meet, he heard the police whistles.

The kicking and punching stopped. They were dragged to their feet.

Then the cops found Archie's knife.

Things were never quite the same again. Theo and Bessie did eventually move into their new home a couple of weeks later, but all the stress had already taken its terrible toll. From day one, they just argued and argued as the baby and Bessie's womb got bigger and bigger.

Without the car, the commute out to Willow Run was hell – too many people trying to get on too few buses. Theo and Archie were forever getting their pay docked for being late.

Trouble at home, and trouble at work.

Bessie packed her bags a few days later, to go back to her mama's in Jackson, taking Theo's baby in her belly with her. The marriage was as good as over.

So when one of the US Army port battalions came to Willow Run looking for recruits to send over to Europe, it wasn't much of a choice for Theo or Archie. They could fight the Nazis and the Jim Crow laws that had driven them from the South at the same time. Even better, they weren't actually having to go into battle. They'd be working. Working to support the war effort.

9

The Morris struggled to make it back up Staxton Hill – this time with Swift at the wheel, even though he'd tried to pick up enough speed at the foot of the incline. As he crashed it into first gear, and pressed the throttle down with his foot as hard as he could, finally it groaned up the steepest part of the gradient. Then, a few moments later, they were on top of the Wolds.

'I wondered if it was going to make it then, sir,' said Weighton. 'I had visions of me having to get out and push.'

Swift smiled and glanced at his deputy's forearms and meaty hands. If you did get stuck on Staxton Hill, who better to have to help than a part-time bare-knuckle boxer who doubled as a giant? He kept his thoughts to himself.

Once they were back at Alfred Gelder Street, Swift went straight to see Holdridge, rather than stopping at the front desk – even though the desk sergeant appeared to be shouting after him.

Only when he reached the detective chief superintendent's office did he discover what the sergeant had been trying to tell him.

Holdridge's secretary broke the news.

'While you were in Scarborough, sir, there was another minor German raid. No one was hurt, but the ice factory by St Andrew's Dock took a direct hit. I think they were just dumping bombs on the way back from somewhere else – Sheffield, perhaps. Anyway, searching through the rubble, the ARP wardens found something that the DCS has had to go and deal with, given you weren't here yourself, sir.'

'What?' asked Swift.

'I don't like to say, sir.'

'Oh, come on, Mary. Spit it out.'

The woman lowered her voice. 'A body part, sir. A severed organ.'

Swift turned, wanting to run back to the Morris, wondering where Weighton had got to.

As he did so, Holdridge's secretary shouted at him, 'Oh, and this arrived for you, Chief Inspector! Some young kid handed it to the desk sergeant – said it was important, and only you should open it.'

She proffered a buff envelope – unmarked, unstamped.

Swift didn't have time to open it, and instead folded it up and stuffed it into his trouser pocket.

He bumped into Weighton coming out of the gents.

'Hurry up, Weighton. With me.'

'Where are we going, sir?'

'The ice factory. St Andrew's Dock. Got hit in a small air raid last night.'

'I didn't hear about that.'

'You wouldn't have done. No one injured, and as far as they know it was just a stray bomb dumped as an afterthought by bombers from a raid elsewhere in Yorkshire.'

'And why the panic, sir?'

'Because the ARP have found someone's severed body part, and I think we know who that someone was, don't we?'

'Sarah Houghton?'

'I assume so, yes.'

Once they reached the dock, a flurry of activity – and the waiting police cars – told them where exactly the ice factory was located.

They parked up, and then set about finding Holdridge.

'Ah, Swift,' said the detective chief superintendent once they found him. 'By name but not always by nature. You're a little late, to say the least.'

'We came as soon as we got back from Scarborough, sir.'

'Hmm. It might have been nice if you'd actually asked if you could go to bloody Scarborough in the first place. Did you arrest him?'

'Who?'

'That Stott chappie. Sweet Sarah's old boyfriend.'

'No, sir, he had a copper-bottomed alibi. Control said they'd found a body part, sir. Presumably Sarah Houghton's?'

Holdridge looked at Swift with an incredulous expression, and rolled his eyes.

'Come with me, Swift, and I'll show you why that can't possibly be the case. You too, Weighton. Thankfully, as you can imagine, the ice has preserved the evidence.'

The superintendent led them to an area where a police photographer was still working, the explosions of his flashgun once again evoking in Swift memories he'd prefer stayed deeply buried in his brain or – better still – that someday he might be able to purge completely. Perhaps that was a forlorn hope. A quarter of a century had passed. If his living nightmares hadn't gone away after that length of time, it was likely they never would.

'Give us a moment, please,' Holdridge said to the photographer.

There – in a chalked-off area on a bed of ice, presumably in the locale it was found – was the severed human flesh in question.

Only now did Swift see how wrong his assumption had been.

He wanted to look away, but he forced himself not to.

What was perfectly obvious was that they were not looking at a woman's heart.

Instead, lying on the ice, severed from the body to which it had once been joined, was a man's scrotum, testicles and penis.

A black man's penis.

Once Holdridge had left the scene, having clearly enjoyed his piece of one-upmanship over Swift, the chief inspector took control. He was surprised to discover his superior hadn't already ordered a full search of the ice factory to try to find the rest of the body.

'Get the uniform team to check every nook and cranny of this place, Weighton.'

'Are we sure the body that was attached to . . .?' He glanced down at the piece of flesh, then seemed to visibly shudder. 'Are we sure the rest of the body this belonged to actually is dead?'

Just the question had Swift's mind going to places he didn't want it to go. He'd seen men with their innards hanging out still somehow surviving, stumbling around the battlefield as though what they were going through was some terrible dream, rather than an even more awful reality. It was amazing, sometimes, what the human body could survive, if only for a few minutes.

'It's possible someone could have survived that, I suppose, if they received immediate medical attention. But for now, let's work on the assumption that whoever did this did it deliberately, and didn't necessarily want the victim to live.'

'Or may have already killed him, as happened with Sweet Sarah.'

'Exactly. But conclusions are to be reached through thorough investigation and the collection of evidence. Not jumped to. Let's get to work.'

'Of course, sir.'

Swift surveyed the scene. The factory was still standing but the roof was badly damaged and a small crater had been formed when the bomb exploded. From the devastation inside, it looked as though it would take weeks, if not months, before it was operational again.

He asked one of the uniformed constables whether any of the factory workers were in attendance.

The PC pointed to the far wall. 'That bloke in the khaki overalls, sir. He's the foreman. He's your best bet.'

Careful not to lose his footing on smaller chunks of ice, or the slush it was fast turning into, Swift made his way over to the man.

'I'm Detective Chief Inspector Swift,' he said, holding up his warrant card. 'I gather you're the foreman here.'

'Well, I was – whether there'll still be a business here after this, I've no idea. We were already on part-time work because of the suspension of the fishing industry.'

'Your name?'

'Walter Skinner. What can I do for you?'

'I presume you've heard what we've found over there?'

'Oh aye. People talk, like.'

'Do you think the victim could have been one of your workers here? Do you even have any black employees?'

'We have had the odd one in the past. Nothing against them meself. They tend to be good workers, not like some of the shirkers we often end up with. But no, we've no black workers at the moment, so I don't think he's one of us. Do you think he's dead, then?'

'Well, we won't know that until we manage to match the dismembered part to a bod—'

At that very moment, Weighton's distinctive East Yorkshire tones echoed through the ruined factory.

'Sir, over here!'

Swift looked over to the other side of the wrecked building and saw his deputy beckoning him.

As Swift strode away, he heard Skinner shout after him.

'It looks like your mate might have the answer!'

'Where was he?' asked Swift.

'Hidden under this mound of ice, sir,' said Weighton.

Two constables were leaning on their shovels. One of them looked slightly shamefaced.

'I'm sorry, Detective Chief Inspector. I think I may have accidentally damaged the body when I struck it with my shovel. After that, we alerted Sergeant Weighton here and were as careful as possible.'

'Not to worry,' said Swift. 'I'm afraid our man looks to be beyond feeling anything. Have you summoned the pathologist yet?' he asked Weighton.

'I'm just about to do that, sir.'

'Ask Skinner, the foreman over there, if there's a telephone you can use. Maybe get Carver down here as well. She'll be feeling like a spare part hidden away in the basement at Alfred Gelder Street. She can help with some of the interviews.'

Swift then kneeled down at the side of the body. The victim was a handsome, well-groomed male. The neat haircut spoke of a military man to Swift. Was it too much of a leap to assume this was the supposedly AWOL Archie Davis? Not really. His local girlfriend had suffered a similar fate, although it was her heart that had been removed. Here, the genitals had been hacked off. Swift forced himself to look. Perhaps 'hacked' wasn't the correct word. The surgery appeared remarkably neat for a criminal's hand. He looked up the naked body to the dead man's neck. Unlike with Sarah's body, the chest was intact, and there was no obvious thin line of bruising from ligature strangulation. But there were darker patches of skin which appeared to Swift to possibly signify the man had met a similar fate to his girlfriend. *If* it was Archie Davis. This time, he wouldn't need to wait for permission to speak to Davis's superior officers. They would have to come here to talk to him – if only to identify the body.

Swift had been half hoping that Professor Jackson might send one of his acolytes rather than taking the job himself, but with much grumbling about how his day had been disturbed, it was indeed Jackson who turned up. After climbing into his medical overalls, he kneeled down by the body.

'You seem to be making a habit of forcing me to examine bodies where organs have been removed, Chief Inspector. Is it a speciality of yours?'

'Not by choice, Professor, I can assure you.'

'Hmm. Are the two killings linked, do you think?'

'This *is* a killing, then?'

Jackson nodded his white-haired head, and pointed to the dead man's neck.

'I should say so. Harder to see the bruising round the neck with darker skin, I grant you. But it's there. Look.'

The professor used his right index finger to draw circles and ovals in the air above the skin of the man's neck.

'Bare hands used this time, not a ligature. You'll be looking for a very strong assailant, judging by the size and muscularity of the victim. It's not easy to strangle someone if they don't want to be strangled.'

'Are the other classic signs of asphyxiation present?' asked Swift.

The professor, who seemed in a better mood today, nodded again. He pointed to the man's eyes.

'You can see the petechiae in the conjunctivae.'

Swift's eyes glanced down to the dead man's crotch.

'What about down below? Before or after death?'

'What's your problem, Chief Inspector? Are you unable to speak plainly? *Down below.* Pah!' Jackson bent down and looked more closely. 'I'll need to examine him back at the lab to be certain, but I'd say – judging by the lack of inflammation in the surrounding tissue – that like our lady yesterday, this bit of butchery was *post*-mortem. And actually, butchery is once again a little unfair on our perpetrator, if it's the same person. He – and I would think to overpower this gentleman it almost certainly was a *he* – seems to have acquired some surgical skill somewhere.'

Jackson got to his feet and sniffed.

'There we are. Not a lot more I can tell you until I've had a good look in the lab.'

'Did it all happen here?' asked Swift.

Jackson crumpled his face as though his nose had just detected a foul smell.

'I doubt it very much indeed.' He kneeled down again, got some rubber gloves from his pocket and snapped them on his hands. Then he lifted the dead man's left foot. 'Rigor mortis hasn't fully set in yet, or at least it hasn't reached his extremities, that's why I can still lift his leg. There's a spare pair of gloves in my doctor's bag there. Be careful when you're rummaging around, though. There they are, in the side compartment.'

Swift found the gloves and put them on each hand in turn.

'Right, you keep his leg lifted.'

The professor, defying his age, and seemingly unconcerned about getting the filth from the floor all over his medical overalls, lay flat on the floor and edged his head under the leg that Swift was holding up. Then he used his gloved fingers to examine it.

'Pass me my torch from the bag, will you?'

Swift was already struggling to hold the leg because of his prosthetic.

'Weighton, take hold of this, please, while I get the professor's torch.'

Once he'd located it and passed it to Jackson, the pathologist used it to highlight the underside of the leg.

'Come and look here,' he urged Swift.

The detective manoeuvred himself with difficulty into position, his head now under the leg too, next to the professor's.

'You can see the abrasions, and once again post-mortem,' said Jackson. 'So it looks like the same modus operandi. Killed somewhere else first, then dragged and dumped here. He's a large man, so I would suspect you are looking for more than one suspect. That's about all you're getting from me here until I've examined the body in the lab.'

'Time of death?' asked Swift.

'Some time in the middle of the night, or very early this morning. As I said earlier, rigor mortis hasn't completely set in, so I'd say perhaps four hours ago or so. Six at the most. Does that help?'

'Possibly. I need to confirm who he is first.'

'You think you know, though, I can tell. Was he a client of the murdered woman?'

'Client, no. Boyfriend, yes. I think she had hopes of starting a new life with him.'

'Oh dear. A pretty unpleasant business all round, then.'

Whether Holdridge had informed the Americans about the new development or not, Swift wasn't sure. What he was sure about was that he didn't like the way they'd arrived – unannounced – trampling all over his crime scene.

The commanding officer saluted, which seemed a trifle unnecessary.

'Lieutenant-Colonel William DeVries, Commander of the 1023rd Port Battalion of the US Army,' said the man. 'And this is Sergeant Roy Mulder of the US Military Police Corps.'

Swift extended his left hand to the senior officer.

'Detective Chief Inspector Swift of Hull Police, and this is my deputy, Detective Sergeant Weighton.'

'I gather you gentlemen have found a body which might be one of ours,' said DeVries.

'Who told you that?' asked Swift.

'Your boss. I forget his name. Hellbridge . . . something like that?'

'Holdridge, I think you mean. Detective Chief Superintendent Holdridge.'

'That's the one. Well, we've had a private from our battalion go missing, AWOL – you know the sort of thing. And your Mister Hellbridge—'

'Holdridge.'

'That's the guy. He said you might have found him. And in a not too pretty state, I believe.'

'You could say that. We'd better show you. The body's about to be taken to the mortuary for a full post-mortem so you're just in time. We're hoping you'll be able to confirm who it is.'

Swift escorted them the few paces to where the body was still lying, in the position it had been found. He asked Weighton to draw away the sheet that had been placed over it.

'Sweet Jesus!' exclaimed the lieutenant-colonel when he saw the mutilated groin. 'What happened there? Was he alive when someone did that? Was that what killed him?'

Swift shook his head. 'We won't know for certain until the pathologist has taken a look in the lab. But as far as we know, no, it wasn't what killed him. He appears to have been strangled. And according to the pathologist's initial examination at the scene a few minutes ago, the wound to his groin happened post-mortem.' The officer looked slightly puzzled. 'After death,' elucidated Swift.

'Gee, I know what that means, thanks. What was troubling me was where "it" is?'

'*It* being his severed penis?'

The lieutenant-colonel nodded.

Weighton pointed to the opposite side of the ice factory.

'The human organ was what was discovered first, and why we were alerted. It was found over there. It's now in an ice-filled box and will be transported to the mortuary along with the body.'

'Aren't we forgetting something?' said Swift, addressing the Americans.

'What's that, Detective?' said the lieutenant-colonel.

'The reason you're here. We need you to identify the body.'

'Of course. Fair shook me, seeing him like that. I think it's our man, but with nigh on a thousand men in the battalion, I can't say I know them all personally. We officers like to keep our distance, I'm sure you understand why.' Then he lowered his voice, talking directly to Swift. 'And you know, when all's said and done, they all look the same, don't they?'

Swift sighed. 'I'm sure *they* don't. So are you saying you can't help us, Colonel DeVries?'

'No, no. Hang on there. Sergeant Mulder, you brought the photos and his file?'

'Yes, sir!' He handed them to the commanding officer.

DeVries shuffled through half a dozen or so black and white photographs, at the same time as looking down at the man's face. He selected one photo, then leaned down for a better comparison.

'Well. Sure looks the same guy to me. Private Archibald Davis. Came over last month with the rest of the guys.' Then he consulted the file. 'According to this, he's originally from Jackson, Mississippi – so way down in the South. That's where his next of kin is. But his most recent address was in Detroit. According to the information we have, before signing up he worked at an aircraft factory. Unmarried, no children.'

'Thank you,' said Swift. 'We'll work on the basis that it is indeed Archibald Davis, but we'll need a formal identification once the body's been moved to the mortuary. Is there someone closer to him who could do that, perhaps? Or do you have dental records?'

'Once I'm back at the base I can ask the medical officer.' DeVries screwed his eyes up in concentration, reading what details the files provided. 'We did have a mighty quick look at his details when he went missing. According to this, he joined up with another soldier from the same area of Detroit, same recruitment drive. Name of Theophilus Howard.' He turned to the military policeman. 'We must have asked Howard about his friend going missing, though there's no note of that here. Do you know Howard, Sergeant Mulder?'

'I can't say I do, sir, although . . . that first name. That's unusual, it sort of rings a bell in my head.'

'A lot of these black soldiers have damn silly names, though,' said DeVries. 'You understand, Detective Inspector.'

Swift didn't react.

'Oh, yeah, I remember now,' continued Mulder. 'There was a bust-up at the local dance hall in Cottingham, where we're based, a week or so back. I think that Theophilus fellow might have been involved. Maybe the dead one, too, God rest his soul. It was about a local girl or something. Some of these blacks think they're God's gift to all women, y'understand me? That don't always go down too well with the local men – those that haven't been called up, anyways. And it don't always sit too well with some of the officers, either.'

Swift nodded. 'We might need to come and talk to you to get more details about that, Sergeant, and to talk to Private Howard.'

'Of course, sir. Happy to oblige.'

'Sergeant Mulder here will also be informing the criminal investigation department of the US Army Military Police, Chief Inspector,' said DeVries. 'I'm sure we can all work together. Nasty business, though. There ain't no way you can put lipstick on a pig.'

'Quite,' said Swift.

'We'll take our leave now. You just holler when that body there is ready for the official identification.'

The lieutenant-colonel snapped his feet together and saluted, while Swift gave a small tip of his hat. Then the two Americans departed.

Once they were out of sight and earshot, Weighton tutted and rolled his eyes.

'And they say people like that are going to win the war for us.'

'Gladdens your heart, doesn't it, Weighton.'

'Not really, sir, no.'

'What they were saying about the dance hall in Cottingham was interesting, though, wasn't it? It kind of backs up what Jessica told us. We need to talk to her again, and to this Theophilus Howard.'

'If they let us.'

'Well, they pretty much gave us permission just then. I'm going to take it as that, anyway. But I don't like the way they talk about some of their own. As though, somehow, some men are less equal than others, just because of the colour of their skin.'

'I noticed that too, sir. It doesn't sit right, does it? Not in a city so closely associated with William Wilberforce.'

Swift raised his eyebrows, surprised at the reference to the Hull politician who had done so much to campaign for the abolition of the slave trade, back in the late eighteenth and early nineteenth centuries. Not that Hull was necessarily a paragon of racial harmony nowadays, despite what appeared to have been a general welcoming of the black GIs, the latest murder notwithstanding. It hadn't been so very long since the Hull race riot – a couple of decades or so. Swift had read about it when preparing for his new job. There were plenty alive who would still remember it. Who might even have played an active part.

'I didn't realise you were such a history buff, Weighton.'

'I'm not, sir. But everyone in Hull knows Wilberforce.'

That might be true, mused Swift – *but did they always uphold his values?*

He kept the thought to himself.

Soon after they'd finally allowed the body to be released to the mortuary, Carver arrived.

'Sorry I'm so late, sir. The trams and trolley buses are still all up the spout after the most recent air raids.'

'Not to worry, Carver. You're here now. Why don't the three of us find a quiet café on Hessle Road, have a cup of tea, and take stock of where we are and what we need to do next?'

10

Swift made sure the café they selected had as few customers as possible. They found one with an extra seating area round the back, beyond the toilets. It was a little grubby and run-down, but would serve their purpose. Swift gave Weighton a shilling and asked him to get the teas at the counter.

Swift invited Carver to sit at a table and then proceeded to fill her in on what she'd missed: the discovery of the severed penis, then the body, and finally the Americans' tentative identification of the dead man as Private Archibald Davis.

'Sarah Houghton's boyfriend,' said Carver.

'Exactly.'

'And what about when you went to Scarborough last night? Did you find anything out from Bobby Stott?'

'Yes . . . and no. Let's wait till Sergeant Weighton's back, and then we can go through everything. Ah, here he comes now.'

Weighton was carrying a tray with a teapot, three cups and saucers, and – much to Swift's surprise – three jam tarts.

'A shilling goes a long way down Hessle Road, it seems.'

'Yes, sir. I'm afraid there's no change, but I thought we could do with some sustenance after seeing all that in the ice factory just now. And I rather suspect the filling may be carrot jam rather than anything more exotic.'

'Nothing wrong with carrot jam, Sergeant,' said Carver. 'Although I doubt it's as good as my mother's recipe.'

Swift laughed. 'I'm sure everything tastes better if you're eating it in the Dales, as opposed to a café in Hull, WAPC Carver.'

Weighton blew out his cheeks. 'Nothing wrong with Hull cafés, sir. Anyway, the proof will be in the eating.'

Having already been told off for assuming that Carver also doubled as the tea girl, Swift was pleased to see that Weighton himself took on the job of pouring their teas this time.

'So,' said Swift, 'we now have two murder victims, both of whom had had body parts removed – after death – and both of whom had been strangled. They were in a relationship, and she sold sexual favours on the side to make ends meet. That gives us plenty of potential suspects. But this morning's discoveries do at least tell us one thing.'

'What's that, sir?' asked Carver.

Weighton supplied the answer. 'That Archie Davis is unlikely to have killed Sarah Houghton.'

'Quite,' said Swift.

'Are you sure you've ruled out Bobby Stott?' asked Carver.

'Well, he had a copper-bottomed alibi, or pretty much copper-bottomed. He was in Scarborough when the first and second murders happened, and as far as we know he still is. So he had a motive, perhaps, but not the opportunity.'

'But he could have got someone else to do his dirty work, couldn't he?'

'True, Carver, he could. Any thoughts, Weighton?'

'If what Sarah's sister said was true, then Stott was very much in love with Sarah.'

'Which could cut either way,' said Swift.

'But she said she didn't think he had it in him,' said Carver.

Swift nodded. 'True. But perhaps we need to check out all his friends and associates. See what they think. See if he mixes with anyone who might be prepared to kill on his behalf. Can you look after that, please, Sergeant?'

'Of course, sir. Judging by the size of our second victim, the killer would have to be big and strong enough to successfully strangle someone. Won't most males like that have already been called up?'

Swift almost wanted to point out that Weighton himself was a shining example of why that wasn't true. You could be as strong as an ox, but have some other condition which rendered you unfit for military service.

'Some of them,' he said, finally. 'Not all of them. Plenty of strong men at the docks, where Stott worked, I should imagine. People who know how to look after themselves, and some of them probably aren't unfamiliar with the inside of a police station. It's a reserved occupation, too, as we know.'

Carver and Weighton both nodded, but remained silent, so Swift continued.

'I suspect, though, we'll need to find out more about this so-called incident at the Cottingham dance hall that the military police sergeant mentioned.'

'What was that?' asked Carver.

Swift filled Carver in on the information that Mulder had imparted to him and Weighton.

'So this Theophilus Howard could be our man?' asked Carver.

'Could be,' said Swift. 'But then, so could anyone else involved who had reason to kill Sarah Houghton and Archie Davis, and had the strength to strangle them, then move the bodies to the bomb sites.'

'And we're certain the two murders *are* linked, are we, sir?'

'Two murders in a short space of time, similar modus operandi in the actual killing, in the mutilation of the bodies afterwards – albeit different parts of the body – and in the disposal of the corpses. And on top of that, the two victims were in a romantic relationship. I should say without doubt they are linked.'

Swift dealt with what he needed to find out from Professor Jackson without actually having to visit the mortuary, which was a relief. He explained on the telephone that someone would be along in due course to formally identify the body, and Swift would ensure they were accompanied by a police officer. Jackson himself was unable to tell Swift much more than he had at the scene – although he did confirm that all his initial suppositions had been borne out by further detailed examination in the laboratory.

Having delegated Weighton to try to make sure that Stott couldn't have orchestrated the killings from his seaside bolthole, Swift drove himself and Carver to Cottingham.

'Aren't you going to ask for permission to speak to this Howard chap first, sir?'

'No, Carver, I'm not. As far as I'm concerned, their military police sergeant gave me that permission in person, whether he meant to or not. Let's strike while the iron's hot, before their military police take him into custody.'

The journey from St Andrew's Dock to Cottingham took them along North Road and past the site planned for Hull City's new football ground. Swift had a passing interest in the game, although he'd never been a fanatic, like some, having moved with his family from his childhood home of Bristol to the rugby-dominated Richmond area of what had once been Surrey, but was now more accurately described as outer London. He remembered, though, the tiger's head etched onto Bobby Stott's forearm, along with the love tattoo inked there permanently – before his relationship to Sarah Houghton proved anything but permanent. Stott was presumably a Hull City fan – their nickname was 'The Tigers', thanks to their usual amber and black playing strip. There were grandiose plans for their ground, but at the moment it was no doubt a mud heap – being used as it was for Home Guard training and tank repairs.

Football wasn't really something he wanted to be reminded of, anyway. Indirectly, that was behind his move from London to Hull – a case down in London that had itself started at a football match a further two years before. Everton's Dixie Dean – in the twilight of his glittering, goal-strewn career – had reacted badly to being racially taunted by a Tottenham fan, leaping into the crowd and punching him.

Although the incident had quickly been defused by a uniformed police officer, Swift had been tasked with investigating the matter further. What he'd uncovered still haunted him to this day: links between the Spurs fan and a British fascist organisation with powerful friends in the upper echelons of British society. Supposedly that organisation, and others like it, had been disbanded at the outbreak of war and their leaders interned – thanks in no small part to Swift and his team's investigation. But there were some powerful individuals who'd never forgiven him. Who'd hired gang members to undermine him, threaten him. Eventually, those threats had become so serious, his bosses at the Met had recommended his transfer. His move to Hull hadn't only been to escape a failed marriage – there was also a much more sinister background.

Swift knew that on some approaches it was hard to see where the city of Hull ended and the village of Cottingham began. Despite being one of several claimants to the title of largest village in England, the settlement was, in effect, a suburb of Hull, which is presumably why it had been chosen to house the American troops. From this direction – heading almost due north from the western side of the city centre along Priory Road – there were actual fields separating the modern housing of the Hull outskirts from some of Cottingham's more historic houses and farms.

Swift hadn't got a good look at the village the previous night when they'd gone to the dance hall. It seemed pleasant enough in the daylight – although not a patch on where Swift had chosen as his home base, just off Beverley's York Road, on the way out to the Westwood and Beverley Racecourse.

The American base was in the grounds of Thwaite Hall – a temporary camp made up of several Nissen huts for the ordinary soldiers, with officers residing in the Georgian-era mansion house, which before the war had been used by Hull's University College.

'Have you telephoned ahead, sir?' asked Carver.

'No. Let's see what they have to say.'

Swift wound down the window of the Morris – not an easy manoeuvre for him, as he had to awkwardly reach across with his left arm, while pushing his prosthetic out of the way. And then, to add insult to injury, he had to fumble to get his warrant card from his inside pocket, nearly dislocating his wrist in the process.

'Can I help, sir?' asked Carver.

'I'm fine,' snapped Swift, then immediately regretted his tone of voice. He was still rattled by remembering the footballer, Dixie Dean, and what had followed.

Once he extricated the ID, he showed it to the guard at the barrier.

'Chief Inspector Swift of Hull Police to see Sergeant Mulder of the US Military Police. He's expecting me.'

'Well, that may be so, sir, but I can't let you through until I've checked. Could you park up over there by the entrance and I'll see if I can raise the sergeant.'

There was a strained silence in the car while they waited. Swift couldn't blame Carver for not wanting to chat – he'd bitten her head off twice now, both times in relation to his war-sustained disability, when she'd only been trying to help. It wasn't a terribly encouraging start to their working relationship – and actually, Swift had been impressed with her so far. She'd do well. If boorish men – and he'd played the part to a T – actually allowed her to.

Eventually, they saw an open-top Jeep approaching from the direction of the hall towards the gatehouse. As it got closer, Swift could tell it was Mulder at the wheel.

He had a quick word with the guard, and then approached the Morris.

He leaned down to speak through the open window.

'Hello again, sir. I understand you want to speak to Theo Howard?'

'If possible, Sergeant Mulder, yes please.'

'Normally a request like that would have to go through my commanding officer, but given Colonel DeVries raised no objection when we were talking earlier at the ice factory, I think I can allow that. I'll just have to ask you to sign the visitors' book here at the gatehouse, and then I'll drive you on up there myself. You're in luck. Normally Howard would be deployed on dock work with the rest of the guys, but he's on compassionate leave today after we broke the news to him about his friend.'

Swift chided himself. He hadn't even considered the possibility that Private Howard wouldn't be on site. At the same time, he was slightly annoyed that he wouldn't get the chance to reveal the news about Archie Davis's fate – it might have unnerved Howard enough to get him to reveal things he didn't want to be revealed.

After settling Swift and Carver down at a long table in one of the rooms in the main house, Mulder went off to look for Howard.

'Sorry I snapped at you earlier, Carver,' said Swift. 'It was rotten of me.'

'That's no problem, sir. I can be a bit of an interferer at the best of times. It must be frustrating for you when people don't just let you get on with life.'

'Still . . .'

'Say no more about it, sir. I understand. Quite a grand old house, this one, isn't it?'

'It certainly is. I don't suppose you see many houses like this up where you're from.'

'Well, Baldersdale itself is a little windswept and bleak, that's true. Although I love it. But yes, not much there apart from farms and sheep. But it's less than ten miles to the Bowes Museum – that's grand enough to put any mansion to shame, sir.'

Swift nodded, and they lapsed back into silence for a few moments until the door reopened and Mulder entered, followed by Private Howard.

Mulder made the introductions, and then the four of them sat down, with the Americans on one side of the table, and Swift and Carver on the other.

'I'll just stay for protocol reasons, you understand, Chief Inspector. Theo here is happy to answer your questions, though you'll all understand he's still mighty upset about the loss of his friend.'

'Of course,' said Swift. 'And our sincerest commiserations, Private Howard. However, I should point out that although the body we've found is strongly thought to be that of Private Davis, and has been initially identified as such by your commanding officer, the body has not been formally identified. I gather from Sergeant Mulder you are prepared to come to the mortuary to help us with the formal identification.'

Howard lowered his eyes and gave a small shudder.

'I will help in any way I can, sir.'

Swift waited a beat for the soldier to compose himself.

'I understand you and Private Davis were very close – you joined up together, I believe?'

'Not just that, sir. He was my best friend. We grew up together, got jobs together in Mississippi, moved up to Motor City together—'

'That's Detroit?'

'Detroit, yes, sir. Detroit, Michigan. We both worked together at the aircraft factory out at Willow Run, and then joined up together and both ended up over here in your fair city. It's a tragedy his life has ended – one so young.'

Swift nodded sympathetically. 'So at this Willow Run factory you were helping with aircraft production. But what about before you went up to Detroit? What was your job in Mississippi?'

'Archie and I both worked in the meat industry.'

Swift leaned forwards, holding the soldier's gaze.

Is this the breakthrough we've been looking for?

'You worked for a butcher's?'

A look of recognition crossed Howard's face, as he suddenly realised where Swift's questioning was headed.

'No, sir. It was just chicken meat we were packing into cans. We didn't get involved in no killing of the birds or butchery, or that kinda stuff.'

'So neither of you were trained butchers?'

'No, sir. Absolutely not.'

Swift nodded slowly. Howard came across as being honest. Perhaps his job in the poultry industry was worth checking out further by booking a transatlantic telephone call. But Swift suspected it would be a waste of time.

Instead, he began a new line of questioning.

'Tell me, Private Howard, were you familiar with Archie's girlfriend, Sarah Houghton?'

'Oh yes, sir. She will be mighty upset. She's as cute as a bug's ear, and he was smitten all right. Wouldn't have surprised me if those two ended up hitched soon. Poor little Sarah. Should I be informing her, sir, or will you folks do that?'

Swift swallowed.

Carver stepped in to fill the void as Howard's face creased in confusion, sensing something else was wrong.

'You hadn't heard, then?' she asked.

'Heard what, lady?'

Swift finally cleared his throat. 'I'm afraid to say, Private Howard, that Sarah Houghton has also been found dead.'

'No! That can't be right, sir, surely? That's awful. They weren't fightin' each other or somethin', were they? I can't believe that.'

'No,' said Swift. 'Nothing like that. They both died separately, on consecutive days.'

'When you say *died*, died how exactly?'

Swift wasn't certain whether Howard was playing them by feigning ignorance. If he'd had to put money on it, though, he'd have said the man's surprise was genuine.

'We'll come to that in a moment. First, tell me more about you, Archie and Sarah. I believe a girl called Jessica Pickering was also involved in your little group. You met the girls at the dances in Cottingham, didn't you? The King Street Rooms?'

'Well, yes, sir. That's about the size of it. My, you do seem to be well informed.'

'That's our job,' said Carver. 'Tell us more about how you all got together, and how Archie came to be walking out with Sarah.'

'Well, it can't have been more than three or four weeks ago or so that we first met up. We ain't been here that long, anyways. And it was wham, bam for Archie, God rest his soul. First time he clapped eyes on Sarah, that was it. That was him done for. And I think she felt the same. Y'all know when that happens. Can almost see those goddamn sparks fly through the air. Poor old Dolores back in Detroit – well, she was a distant memory.'

Swift leaned forwards in his chair.

'So he already had a sweetheart back home?'

'Dolores? Why, yes. She was more than a sweetheart, though. They were engaged to be married, sure as night follows day.'

'Had he broken off the engagement?' asked Carver.

'I don't rightly know, lady. But it was coming, I can tell you, it was coming.' Then Theo Howard seemed to remember that Archie wouldn't be breaking off anything in the future. He shook his head, then lowered his face and held his head in his hands. 'Those poor souls.'

Swift waited a moment for the soldier to regain his composure. Then he leaned forwards once more.

'I understand, though, that everything wasn't always sweet-ness and light at the Cottingham dances. There was some trouble recently, wasn't there?'

Howard glanced quickly at the military policeman, as though asking silent permission to answer. Mulder gave an almost imperceptible nod.

'Last weekend, yeah.'

Swift had to stop himself frowning.

If it was so recent, why didn't Jessica mention it? Unless . . .

'Can you tell us exactly what happened, please?'

'Well, Sarah was there with her friend Jessica.'

'Miss Houghton and Miss Pickering?'

'That's right, sir. Well, all of us – that's all of us regular troops – we knew Sarah was spoken for. I don't mind admitting, I had my eyes on her, too, but Archie's always been a smooth mover, a fast mover. Man, I don't know what sweet words he said to them, but they sure always seemed to work, and they did with Sarah. They'd only been seeing each other a few weeks, but we all knew to back off and leave them to it.'

'So why was there trouble?' asked Carver, frowning.

'Because some of the officers, they didn't like it. Seeing white girls getting all sweet—'

Mulder cleared his throat. It seemed to Swift to be some sort of sign, as Howard had stopped talking.

'So you're saying there was resentment among the white American officers?'

Howard looked at Mulder, who was stony-faced.

Then Mulder intervened. 'With respect, Chief Inspector, I don't think we should be going putting words into the private's mouth. There was a bit of tension, a few punches were thrown, but that's par for the course when soldiers are let loose among local women. It don't mean nothing.'

Swift sighed. 'Are we allowed to hear Private Howard's version of events?'

'Well, I'm here to protect his interests, and the interests of the US Army. We have our own ways of settling these things. If we stick to what actually happened – the facts – and stay away from speculating over whys and wherefores, then maybe we can continue. But I'm not prepared to see the US Army brought into disrepute. You understand what I'm saying, Chief Inspector. I'm sure you do.'

Swift was tempted to get to his feet and end it there. But that was probably the reaction that Mulder was seeking.

He rubbed his chin with his prosthetic hand. It brought a look of surprise from Howard, who probably didn't realise the policeman had a false arm.

'So punches were thrown?' he asked the soldier.

'That's right, sir. As Sergeant Mulder says, really it was nuthin'.'

'Were you involved in the fighting?'

Howard looked at Mulder again. The military policeman gave a little shrug.

'I may have thrown a couple of punches, but I was just defending Sarah and Archie.'

'And what about Archie? Did he throw any punches?'

'One or two, but it was over almost before it had started, sir.'

'And those you were fighting with, they were US Army officers?'

'Yes, sir. Though not the senior officers, y'all understand. There were some local yard dogs, too.'

'Yard dogs?' queried Carver.

Mulder translated. 'Local youths, I think Private Howard means.'

Swift wondered if they were actually getting anywhere. The whole object of this was to try to identify suspects in the killings of Sarah Houghton and Archibald Davis.

'So how did this fight actually start?' he asked.

'Well, we were fruiting with the duchesses – the girls, y'all understand. The joint was jumping so's I don't rightly know *exactly* what happened, but I saw one of the officers grab Archie by the threads, and then it all kicked off. That's about the size of it.'

'Can you give us the names of those involved?'

Howard looked shiftily at Mulder, as though he didn't know if he was permitted to answer the question. In the end, he didn't – at least not directly.

'What you have to understand, sir, is the background.'

'What do you mean?' asked Swift.

'There have been threats,' said Howard.

Swift looked at Mulder. The military policeman was stony-faced. Then he returned his gaze to Howard.

'What threats?'

'The black—'

At this, Mulder intervened once more.

'That's enough, Private,' he ordered. Then he turned to Swift. 'We've done an official report. I can check with the colonel to see if we can let you have a copy. I want to stress to you guys no one was put on a charge, it's all done and dusted. Now I think we can all agree that Private Howard has had one heck of a shock today in finding out about his friend's demise. Fact is, the whole camp's in shock. We've been welcomed with open arms here in Cottingham – cute little village – and in Hull, too. There ain't been no trouble, other than that two-bit slap around. But I think Private Howard has been open and honest with you, and we better just leave it there. OK with you folks?'

Mulder phrased it as though it was a question, but Swift could tell it wasn't. He glanced quickly at Carver, and rolled his eyes out of sight of the military policeman. Then he put away his notebook and started to get to his feet, while extending his hand to Howard.

'Quite. You've been very helpful, Private Howard, and once again, our sincere condolences for your loss.'

'He was a good friend, sir. I loved him with all my heart. And Sarah was a good girl, too. I know she'd been a bit wayward at times, but who isn't? Archie knew that, too, but to him she wasn't cut-rate. She was a classy gal and he loved her. But if she mixed with the wrong sorts in the past, maybe that's where you should be looking, sir.' Howard ended his handshake with Swift, and accepted Carver's hand in turn. 'And you, lady.'

Mulder escorted them from the room and into the hallway.

'I hope you don't think I was interfering too much in there,' he said.

'You've got your job to do, Sergeant, as we have ours. But Private Howard seemed to be implying there was some racial tension between the officers and the men. Would you agree?'

Mulder lowered his voice. 'I wouldn't put it like that, sir. Let's just say, we have our way of doing things, and you have yours. The important thing is we're all on the same side. We just wanna get Hitler whupped as soon as possible, then skedaddle back home. I'm sure you agree with that, sir, don't you?'

'I certainly do. But I will need the names of all those involved in that fight, please. And I'd like to see that report you mentioned.'

'Of course, Chief Inspector. I'll send a motorcycle messenger to your police headquarters with them later today, once I've got a secretary to type up the copies. Remind me where that is again.'

'Alfred Gelder Street in Hull. Just mark them for my attention. One other thing, while we're here. I take it you have a medical officer attached to the battalion?'

Mulder nodded. 'We have a team of three non-combat medics, sir. Much smaller than for a fighting battalion.'

'Could I talk to the chief medical officer?' asked Swift.

'I don't see no reason why not, sir. But that's something I'm gonna have to get Colonel DeVries's OK for, I'm afraid.'

DeVries was clearly annoyed that Mulder had allowed Swift and Carver to interview Theophilus Howard without his express prior agreement. After asking the two police officers to stay outside his room, Swift could hear the raised voices of an argument between the sergeant and his commanding officer.

Nevertheless, a few moments later, DeVries emerged all smiles, though Mulder – trailing behind him – looked a little chastened.

'We'll take you over to the medical station now, Chief Inspector. Captain Floyd Sanders, MD, is our chief medical officer. What exactly did you want to talk to him about?'

'Information,' said Swift, non-committally.

DeVries laughed. 'That's not particularly forthcoming, Chief Inspector. But I do have to check. You're not planning to interview him as a suspect, are you? Otherwise I'd have to refer it up the chain to the Military Police command.'

'No,' said Swift. 'Not as a suspect. Yet. I'll let you know if that changes.'

Swift half expected DeVries to insist that he or Mulder sit in on the interview. But once they'd escorted him to Sanders' domain, they left Swift and Carver to their own devices – although DeVries did have his own short discussion with Sanders in private first.

'Captain Sanders will let us know when you've finished your chat,' said DeVries. 'Either Sergeant Mulder or I will come to escort you to the gatehouse.'

'Thank you, Colonel DeVries.'

Swift and Carver entered the room, the latter closing the door behind her. Swift could tell from the discoloration of the cream paint on the walls that the room had previously housed a number of beds and bedside tables. The majority had been removed. It looked as though it was a former student dorm, or perhaps had been the sanatorium of University College, until the Americans had taken it over.

Sanders rose from his chair and extended his hand to Swift and Carver in turn as they introduced themselves. Swift thought the man looked remarkably young – fresh-faced, and with a full head of dark hair – as though he was possibly newly graduated from medical school.

'Pleased to meet you,' he said. 'Colonel DeVries says you're investigating the murder of Private Davis. Nasty business, if you don't mind me saying so.'

'Did you know him?' asked Swift.

'In passing, nothing more. He'd come in for treatment once or twice.'

Swift frowned. 'Oh yes? What for?'

Sanders pointed to the wall behind the pair. They turned their heads, and Swift saw the poster. A Snow White lookalike, all pure and innocent, with the accompanying words:

SHE MAY LOOK CLEAN –
Pick-ups
"Good Time" Girls
Prostitutes
spread Syphilis and Gonorrhea
You can't beat the Axis if you get VD

'The clap. A few doses of penicillin soon cleared it up. I hear the girl he was walking out with put it about a bit.' Then the young doctor looked at Carver. 'Sorry, lady. I didn't mean to cause offence.'

'None taken,' said Carver.

'That girl – or young woman – has unfortunately been murdered, too,' said Swift.

'So I'd heard, Chief Inspector. A goddamn awful business.'

'It certainly is,' agreed Swift. 'Where we think you might be able to help us, is in connection with some of the methods used in the killings – or rather, after the killings.'

The young army doctor frowned. 'How so?'

'The bodies were mutilated after death. Now I don't want that spread around, please – it's not information that we've released to the newspapers, for example. But we believe the killer had some sort of medical, or possibly veterinary, training. Surgical training.'

The doctor gave a strange, strangled laugh. 'OK. I get where you're coming from. You wanna know if I've got an alibi?'

Swift cocked his head. 'Well, I didn't actually ask that, Captain. However, if you're volunteering one – or rather two, as the killings happened at different times in differing locales – then that would certainly be useful.'

Captain Sanders rolled his eyes. 'You'd better tell me when they both happened, then.'

Carver produced her notebook and, after checking with Swift, gave the approximate times of death.

Sanders consulted what looked like a diary on his desk.

'Looks like I'm in the clear, Chief Inspector,' he smirked. 'As you can see here, both of the evenings in question, Tuesday and yesterday, Wednesday – and through the night – I was on call, here at the base. That means I have to stay actually within its confines, and account for my movements so I can be roused if necessary. As you can see, on the first occasion it was indeed necessary. A soldier with suspected appendicitis. Turned out it was nothing more than a bad dose of food poisoning, but you can't take no chances with appendicitis. Anyways, you can see here there's a note of my attending him, right here at the medical centre.' He turned the page of the log book. 'And here's the note detailing that I was on call here at the base last night, too. So, I'm sorry to disappoint—'

'It's not a disappointment, Captain Sanders, I assure you,' interrupted Swift. 'I didn't for a moment suspect you, and I assured your commanding officer I was not interviewing you as a suspect. And your alibis are something *you* volunteered. What I was actually going to ask you is, who else on the base has any form of surgical training? However rudimentary.'

Sanders breathed in slowly. 'Well, there's my two assistants, but they're not here presently. Every day they accompany the men to the docks, in case of accidents there, which as you can imagine, aren't a rarity. As to where they were on the two nights in question, I don't rightly know. I was the medical officer on duty, so they weren't. That's about as much as I know straight off. But I can find out for you.'

Swift nodded, and began to collect his hat from the table.

'Well, look, if you do that, it would be much appreciated. And perhaps I could trouble you to draw up a list, however short, of people here on the base who have had medical training, aside from those two. Perhaps you could pass it to your Sergeant Mulder, who's forwarding some other information to my office.'

Swift and Carver rose to their feet and extended their hands in farewell.

'What do you think, sir?' asked Carver, as they began the drive back to Hull, after Mulder had escorted them to the Morris.

'I don't know what to think. From talking to Howard, it's clear Jessica Pickering certainly wasn't telling us the full story. She was happy enough to go with us to the Cottingham dance hall, yet neglected to tell us there had been a huge rumpus the previous week involving Sarah Houghton and her American GI sweetheart, both of whom are now dead.'

'What about the white versus black thing, sir? Sergeant Mulder was quick to cut the private off when he was talking about certain threats. What do you think he meant? After all, segregation between whites and blacks is still practised in the USA, isn't it?'

'It certainly is.' Swift changed gear and the Morris juddered forwards. 'But they're not in America now. When in Rome . . .'

'I get the feeling they may not see it quite the same way, sir. And do you think either of those other medics could be involved, or even Sanders himself?'

'Sanders? No. His alibi seemed solid. The others? Let's wait and see.'

Swift was only half concentrating on the conversation. As they'd left the US base, he'd noticed a car behind them set off at the same time. A black car. Two occupants. He made sure Carver didn't notice his checks in the mirrors. It appeared, however, that they were being followed. The question was – why? Was it simply the interaction with the Americans? That would be of interest to many. Or was it something more worrying from Swift's past which had followed him from London and had now re-emerged – right in the middle of his first major murder inquiry?

11

Once they were back in their incident room at Alfred Gelder Street, Swift was pleased to see Weighton had returned, too. He was boiling a kettle on the camping stove.

'Are you sure that thing's safe, Weighton?'

'There's only one way to find out, sir. I can't be doing with traipsing back and forth to the canteen all the time. Do you two want a cup?'

'It might help stimulate the thought processes, I suppose.'

'Yes please, Sergeant Weighton,' said Carver. 'Milk, two sugars.'

'Did you get anywhere, Weighton?' asked Swift.

'Well, I've identified a couple of characters who have police records for violence and intimidation who were thick as thieves with Stott. As for actual hit men? He doesn't seem to have hung out with that crowd. We don't have the same level of gang violence as you'd get down in London, for example, as you well know.'

'All right. Who are the ones you've identified?'

'There's a guy called Reg Dalby – he's a shop steward at Alexandra Dock. But as well as being involved in legitimate union activities, he's also got a number of convictions for assault occasioning actual bodily harm.'

'And they were more than just pub fights, you think?'

'Seems so. There were suggestions blackmail was involved, forced evictions, possibly even a protection racket going on. It was George Camilleri at the Café Prestige who pointed me in his direction.'

'Have you talked to him yet?'

'Not yet, sir. I thought it was something you would like to be involved in.'

'You indicated there was someone else?'

'Yes, sir, but I'd rather talk about him in private, if that's all right.'

Swift frowned. 'We are in private.'

Weighton glanced at Carver.

'It's all right, sir,' she said. 'I can make myself scarce for a quarter of an hour or so. I'll get a tea from the canteen after all.'

'Thank you, WAPC Carver,' said Swift. 'Although you shouldn't have to. If we're working as a team, which we should be, there shouldn't be any secrets between us.'

Weighton looked shamefaced. 'It's just a little delicate, sir.'

'All right. We'll see you in a few minutes, then, Carver. Thank you.'

Once Carver had left, Swift sighed.

'We shouldn't be excluding her, you know, Weighton. She has the makings of a very fine police officer, even though this force doesn't seem to actively encourage female recruits.'

'I know, sir. And I agree. But this concerns – shall we say – some of my extracurricular activities, which you're aware of, but Carver isn't necessarily, and I don't want her getting the wrong impression.'

'All right. I understand what you're referring to. But you ought to ask yourself whether there's a correct impression those *extracurricular activities* could give. Somehow, I don't think so.'

'It's a family tradition, sir. It's part of our heritage.'

'So you keep telling me, Weighton. But I don't think family traditions that involve beating someone half to death with your bare fists are ones that are worthy of preserving, still less when you're a serving police officer. And not just any police officer – *my* detective sergeant.'

'I thought you understood, sir.'

'Well, you thought wrong, Weighton. It's something I've tolerated so far because you insist you're not going to stop. I've told you it's dangerous, barbaric, and not becoming of a police officer. You seem ashamed enough of it that you don't want to mention it in front of Carver, and as a result you've chosen to exclude her from this conversation. That, Weighton, is a problem that needs dealing with. I'm trusting you to deal with it before I have to. Do I make myself clear?'

'Yes, sir. Quite clear.'

'That being said, if through mixing in those circles you've come across information that might help with the inquiry, I need to hear it. So spit it out.'

Weighton's face had crumpled while Swift had been giving his lecture. From strong but friendly giant, he'd taken on the look of an awkward, overgrown schoolboy, thrust into adulthood too soon. But Swift wasn't sorry he'd made his position clear – it was something he should have done earlier. Bare-knuckle boxing, even though some – especially in Weighton's 'community' – regarded it as sport, was to Swift little more than semi-organised savagery.

'Well, one of the other boxers I'm friendly with has some connections with what you might term "shadier" characters. They're friends from childhood, nothing more. My boxer friend himself is totally straight.'

'As far as you know.'

'As far as I know. Anyway, I was asking around, and my friend said this guy knew Stott. Not only that . . . My friend said he'd heard a story recently about a Hull lad who'd had his girl "stolen" from him by one of the black GIs out at Cottingham. The other boxer – this shady one – works at the docks with Stott. That's why he's not been called up. He was intending, apparently, along with some of his friends, to teach the pair a lesson.'

'The pair being Sarah Houghton and Archie Davis?'

'I assume so, sir, yes.'

It all sounded to Swift a little like gossip twice removed. And probably as unreliable as that, too. Nevertheless, it needed to be followed up.

'Do you have a name for this *shady* character?' Swift hoped he wasn't being too sarcastic as he said it. 'An address?'

'His name is Ron Lewis. He lives just off Holderness Road, very near Stott. That's probably how they became friends. That, and the fact they both work at Alexandra Dock. I expect that's where we'll find him.'

Swift got to his feet, and picked up his coat and hat.

'We can pick up Carver from the canteen on the way. And on the way to the docks you can explain to her how you choose to spend your spare time.'

'Yes, sir,' mumbled Weighton.

'What's wrong, Sergeant? It's part of your "heritage", isn't it? I'm sure you're not suddenly ashamed of it.'

Alexandra Dock was such a hive of activity, it was almost difficult to imagine there was a war on. Evidence of the various bombing raids was still all around, however. Although the infrastructure had been repaired sufficiently to allow the dock to keep operating, everywhere there were signs of damage. Buildings reduced to rubble and shells, stumps of mangled metal where once cranes had stood, and a general feeling of half-builtness – a sort of purgatory between regeneration and desolation. But amid all that, there was the noise of shouting, the clanging of metal, the groaning of machinery and repeated shouts of both anger and laughter.

They'd already dropped Carver off at the Houghtons' house on the way. Her job was to break to them the news about Archie Davis. His identity had now been confirmed – Swift had received a call from the mortuary before they'd set off. After that, Swift had asked her to doorstep Bobby Stott's neighbours to see what she could find out. Strictly speaking, it should have been a job delegated to the uniformed division, but they were short on numbers, too – and Swift had grown to trust Carver in the short time they'd been working together.

Once they'd got permission from the dock authorities to question people, Swift decided their first port of call should be the union office. On the way, they spotted what looked like a Russian freighter tied up at the quayside, with some of the black soldiers from the US port battalion involved in unloading its cargo of timber.

The dockworkers' union office was a small, semicircular corrugated iron building. It looked a little like a miniature version of the Nissen huts of the port battalion in Cottingham. In fact, thought Swift, it probably was – either that or an overgrown, above-ground version of an Anderson shelter. A temporary structure, possibly built after the Blitz of the previous year. But like many similar temporary buildings, it would become semi-permanent until there was the will and the money to properly replace it with brick or concrete. There seemed little point at the present, when Nazi bombers could return at any moment. Though thankfully, with the Germans bogged down on the Eastern Front with the Soviet Union, raids this year had been far fewer.

They entered the office, and approached a desk where a swarthy-looking middle-aged man was hunched over some papers.

'Could you tell me where we might find a union official by the name of Reg Dalby?' asked Swift.

'Who wants him?' replied the man, gruffly.

Swift flashed his warrant card. He immediately noticed the look of apprehension in the man's face.

'I'm Detective Chief Inspector Swift of Hull Police, and this is Detective Sergeant Weighton.'

The man looked up at Weighton, seemingly amazed by the sergeant's size.

'Oh aye? Well, I'm Reg Dalby. What do you lot want?' Then he lowered his voice, even though there was no one in earshot. 'I've stayed out of trouble these last couple of years, and that's the way I want to keep it, thank you very much.'

Weighton leaned down, getting his face close to the union official's.

'No one's suggesting you are in any trouble, Mr Dalby. But we do want to ask you some questions, and if you want to stay out of trouble, you'd do well to answer them, and answer them honestly.'

The man snarled back, 'Is that a threat?'

Swift drew up a chair and sat down opposite the man, without being invited.

'Take it how you like, Mr Dalby. We're investigating a murder – well, two murders, in fact, which we believe are connected. So it's a serious matter.'

'Murder? I ain't never murdered no one.'

'No one said you had, did they?' replied Swift. 'But you've a criminal record for violent behaviour. Surely you're not now pretending you're some sort of guardian angel all of a sudden, are you?'

'There's no need to take that tone, officer. I didn't say I wouldn't answer your questions, did I? But make it quick. There's a war on, and we're involved in valuable war work here.'

Swift exhaled slowly. 'I'm quite aware of the war, thank you, Mr Dalby. Now, what can you tell me about Bobby Stott?'

'Stott? Is he involved in these murders, then?'

Weighton slapped his meaty hand down on the table. Dalby jerked his head backwards.

'Just answer the question,' said Swift's deputy.

'Well, I know of him. Can't say we're that close.'

'When was the last time you spoke to him?' asked Swift.

'I don't rightly know. Perhaps a couple of weeks or so, maybe a tad longer. He's a good worker, and a good union member. That's about it really.'

Weighton leaned forwards again. 'We heard you are a bit closer than that. Where is he at the moment?'

'He was given a week's compassionate leave or summat. Split up with his girl. I heard she'd run off with one of them black Yank soldiers – you know, the ones out at Cott. Some of 'em work here. There's a lot over there.' Dalby pointed vaguely in the direction from which Swift and Weighton had just arrived. 'They're unloading the timber from that Soviet tub.'

Swift drummed his fingers on the table. Either Dalby knew very little, or he was playing them.

'Did he ask you to do anything about it?'

'Do anything about what? You're not making any sense.'

Weighton intervened. 'Did he ask you to try to sort out his girlfriend situation?'

'Eh? Why the heck would he do that? Sort it out? What do you mean? Is that what these here murders are, then?'

'We're the ones asking the questions, Mr Dalby,' said Swift. 'Let me make it plain. Did Bobby Stott – while he was away on compassionate leave, or before he left work – ask you to take any action to try to get his girlfriend back, or punish those responsible for the end of the relationship? Yes or no?'

'No. Absolutely not. As I said, all I knew was he was upset about it, as any folk would be. But other than that, I know nothing.'

Swift gave a weary sigh. 'All right, Mr Dalby, thank you. One more thing before we go. Where would we find Ron Lewis?'

Dalby's face darkened. 'What the fuck do you want wi' him? I'd steer well clear if I was you.'

'And why's that?'

'He's a nasty fucker, if you'll pardon my French. Best avoided. And not a good union man. In fact, very much the opposite.'

'What do you mean by that?' asked Swift.

'Just what I say. Used to try and recruit in the docks for Mosley's lot.'

The mention of Oswald Mosley had Swift's internal antennae twitching. He'd had quite enough of the various British fascist groups down south – he didn't want to get involved in any of that again. It figured, though. Mosley's organisation was very much working-class-based – as opposed to the group Swift had been investigating in London and the Home Counties, which enjoyed widespread support among Britain's upper classes.

He saw that Weighton, too, was frowning.

'Recruiting for the British Union of Fascists? But they've been a proscribed organisation since the start of the war. Mosley's still in jail.'

Dalby snorted. 'I said *used* to. Anyway, leopards rarely change their spots. I'm just giving you both a friendly warning. And if you do have to speak to him, keep a few paces back – at least not in range of his fists. He's very handy with them. Does a bit of bare-knuckle fighting for wagers on the side. I went to watch him once. It were like watching a rabid dog tear someone apart.' Then Dalby looked up at Weighton again, his eyes widening. 'Hang on. I thought you looked familiar. You were there, too, and fighting. A bloody copper.' He turned to Swift. 'Did you know that, officer? Why do you allow that in your ranks?'

'None of that is your concern, Mr Dalby. I expect Sergeant Weighton was undercover at the time, so don't repeat what you've said outside here, otherwise you could be facing a charge of obstructing the police.'

Dalby's angry expression relaxed into more one of contrition.

'Oh aye, right, sorry. None of my business, of course.'

'Now,' said Swift, 'where exactly will we find Mr Lewis?'

'At the rail depot. He's involved in loading timber onto the railway. Pit props – timber for the mining industry, that sort of thing.'

'And where is this depot?' asked Weighton.

'Here, I'll show you.'

Dalby got to his feet eagerly, as if delighted his part in the questioning was over, and he could pass the two detectives on to let someone else suffer. He led them back to the entrance to the office, then outside and round the corner. He pointed out the steam coming from the funnel of one of the locomotives working on the docks.

'Ask anyone there. They'll probably try to run a mile at the sound of his name, but they'll know where he is. Mark my words, though. Don't mess with him. He's evil through and through.'

'What do you make of all these dire warnings, sir?'

'Well, you say you know him, Weighton. You don't seem scared. Mind you, not much puts the wind up you, which is why I recruited you as my deputy.'

'I wish I could say I was flattered, sir. However, I'd hoped it was my detective skills you valued, rather than my physical prowess.'

'Those too, Weighton, of course,' laughed Swift. 'You're a man of many talents.'

They could see a number of workers loading timber onto small cranes, which were then swinging round over to the railway goods wagons, where more dockers – or railway workers – unloaded them.

'Do you see him?' asked Swift.

'Not at the moment,' replied Weighton. They walked a little closer. 'Ah, there he is. The tall dark-haired one.'

Swift could see the man Weighton meant. His physique was similar to his sergeant's. As they got nearer still, someone seemed to have alerted Lewis. He turned round, appraised them for a couple of seconds, then broke into a run.

'He's trying to make a getaway, sir,' shouted Weighton.

'You follow him, Weighton. I'll try and cut him off the other side of the railway track.'

Swift ran as fast as he could towards the locomotive at the head of the goods train. He ducked his head down and could see two pairs of legs running on the other side of the train. The first pair of legs, belonging presumably to Lewis, were some fifty yards or so behind him, with Weighton another twenty yards back. If Swift could get across to the other side of the track quickly enough, he might be able to cut Lewis off.

His pace was slowed by having to hold on to his prosthetic at the shoulder to prevent it becoming detached. Lewis was gaining on him all the time.

But he got to the front of the train just in time, crossed the tracks, and then stood right in front of Lewis's line of sight.

'Police! Stop! You're under arrest!'

Swift held his good arm up, outstretched with palm facing out, as though he was a traffic policeman. There could be no mistaking the instruction. But Lewis ignored the warning, and instead ran right at Swift, then fended him off a little like a rugby league player might. Swift lost his balance, but as he fell, he managed to grab at Lewis's leg with his good arm.

He couldn't hold him, but it was enough to throw the man off balance in turn.

Lewis stumbled, slowed, and in the next few seconds Weighton was on him, bringing him crashing to the ground.

Before Lewis could react, Weighton had him in an armlock, and then managed to cuff him as a now upright Swift placed his boot on the back of the man's neck and pressed down hard.

'Aargh!' Lewis shouted. 'What the fuck are you doing? I've done nowt wrong.'

'Why were you running, then?' asked Weighton.

'You can explain at the station,' shouted Swift. 'Ronald Lewis, you are under arrest, and you will be questioned on suspicion of assaulting a police officer with the intention of resisting arrest. Now get up.'

Swift wondered why the man had indeed taken flight when he saw them. He must have realised they were policemen. Even in plain clothes, two men wearing suits and hats in the middle of a dockland working environment probably spelled trouble. Did it mean they had got their man? That Ron Lewis was responsible for killing Sarah Houghton and Archie Davis? That was a mental leap too far. What was certain, though, judging by the size and strength of the man – not to mention his reputation – was that if Mr Lewis was of the inclination to strangle someone, he had the physical wherewithal to do it. And probably to do it with relative ease.

When they got back to Alfred Gelder Street, Carver was nowhere to be seen. No doubt she had finished with the Houghtons, and had moved on to Holderness Road under her own steam, catching a trolley bus or tram. The whole tram network was being replaced by electric trolley buses – but for the moment, trams still ran on some lines. If she was doorstepping Stott's neighbours, she might be a good while yet.

Another thing missing on the way to and from the docks was the car he was convinced had started to follow them outside the US base in Cottingham. Perhaps they'd become bored and given up.

Swift and Weighton got the custody sergeant to place Lewis in a cell, and then decided to let him sweat a little.

'There's no rush,' said Swift. 'Let him think we've got something on him, which of course we don't, then he might be more willing to talk.'

'Well, we do have something on him, sir. He assaulted you.'

Swift shrugged. 'We don't want him for that, though, do we? Our only interest is if he's our man.'

'Shall I make us a cup of tea while he thinks things over?'

'Good idea, Weighton. We never really got to enjoy that last one.'

Before Weighton could turn his attention to the tea-making, the incident room telephone rang. Weighton picked up the receiver.

'It's the control room, sir,' he said. 'They're asking for you in person.'

Swift ambled over to the phone.

'Detective Chief Inspector Swift here.'

'*Good day, sir. There's a reporter from the* Hull Daily Mail *on the line for you. Name of Bert Feather. Says he's heard there's been an incident at the docks, and he'd like a word.*'

Swift had come across Feather several times before. As the local newspaper's crime reporter, he was occasionally the source of good tip-offs, although most of the information tended to go from Swift to Feather, rather than vice versa. This current investigation was a horribly delicate one, given the involvement of the Americans. For that reason, Swift wasn't really at the stage where he wanted to involve the press. Would stalling Feather work? The man was incredibly persistent. It might depend on how detailed his information was from the fracas at the docks. But they could have been arresting Lewis for any number of things.

'Tell him I'm busy on an inquiry at the moment, but I'll ring him back as soon as I'm able to.'

'*Right ho, sir. Will do, of course.*'

Swift knew Feather would be back sniffing around before too long. But stalling might just buy them a little time. Having everything splashed over the *Hull Daily Mail* wouldn't be to their advantage at the moment. Hopefully, the mere fact of an arrest at Alexandra Dock of a known thug wouldn't give Feather enough to construct his story without more from Swift, and that wouldn't be forthcoming any time soon.

Just then, there was a knock on the incident room door. Weighton opened it to find a slightly out of breath uniformed constable.

'Sorry to bother you, sir,' said the PC, addressing Swift. 'Detective Chief Superintendent Holdridge has asked that you be brought to his office. Immediately.'

'*Brought to his office*? That's a rather strange way of putting it, Constable. I'm perfectly well aware of where DCS Holdridge's office is, and I don't need an escort.'

'Well, I'm sorry, sir. But those are my instructions. To escort you to his office.'

Swift looked at Weighton and mimicked a lah-de-dah expression.

'Oh well, if that's what DCS Holdridge has said, who am I to disobey? Looks like you're boiling that kettle just for yourself, Weighton. I won't be long – I hope.'

Swift allowed the constable to knock on Holdridge's dark oak door, rather than do it himself, as that was what the young policeman seemed determined to do.

'Come,' echoed the unmistakably haughty tones of Swift's commanding officer.

The constable entered, followed by Swift.

'I've located Detective Chief Inspector Swift and brought him to you, sir,' said the PC.

Swift had to give him full marks for stating the obvious.

'Ah, yes, thank you, Constable. That will be all. Swift, sit down, please.'

It was immediately apparent that Holdridge wasn't alone. Two men in dark suits, whom Swift had never seen before, were also there. He had no idea who they were, but they gave off an official, governmental air. A third visitor was also present in full dress uniform. It was Lieutenant-Colonel DeVries, and Swift didn't like the look of what was almost a small smirk plastered on his face.

'Thank you for coming, Swift,' said Holdridge.

'I wasn't aware I had much choice, sir.'

'Hmm. Well, we've some good news for you. There's been a development in your case which I'm sure you'll be pleased about.'

'Oh yes?' said Swift, hastily translating anything Holdridge said through his own Alice-in-Wonderland-style translator. What it almost certainly meant was that Swift would be livid. 'Just before you give me that news, could you perhaps introduce me to your other guests? I've already had the pleasure of meeting Colonel DeVries earlier today, but these other two gentlemen . . .?

'Their names and who they exactly are is no concern of yours, Swift. They are here merely to observe. It is Colonel DeVries who you have to thank for making your life easier.'

'Oh yes? How so?'

DeVries leaned forwards, with his arms on the desk.

'We've arrested Private Theophilus Howard, who I believe you talked to earlier today, Chief Inspector, for the murder of his friend, Private Archibald Davis. We expect to get a full confession. We believe Private Howard was also responsible for the death of your victim, Sarah Houghton, who was romantically involved with Private Davis.'

Swift ignored the American once he'd finished speaking and looked hard at Holdridge.

'You are aware, sir, that both murders happened in our jurisdiction, and therefore it is we who should be investigating them, not the American military.'

'Don't take that tone with me, Swift. There are matters of national security at stake here, matters far more important than the death of some two-bob Hull prostitute. From now on, I shall take personal charge of liaising with the American military.'

'So you're saying I'm off the case, sir?'

'I am, Swift, yes.'

'Well then, I'll bid you good day, sir, and you, gentlemen. You know my address, sir, if you need me for anything.'

Swift nodded at each of the men, then turned on his heel and slammed the door shut behind him. He could hear Holdridge still shouting out his name through the heavy door, but he had no interest in listening.

12

A new day dawned, and for the first time in a while, Swift could take a leisurely breakfast and enjoy a day off. Holdridge hadn't actually suspended him – simply taken him off the case. It had been Swift himself who'd taken umbrage and decided to stay at home until the detective chief superintendent saw sense. It was a risk, of course, but Swift was convinced he was in the right.

When he'd arrived in Hull two years earlier, he'd managed to rent a house in Beverley, on the edge of the Westwood – a large area of common land at the western edge of the market town, and home to the racecourse. Swift was unsure whether it had, at one time, been completely wooded. But now the woods themselves were just small pockets in a huge expanse of rolling pastureland. It was his lung – his escape from Hull and work. Soon after transferring to Hull Police, he'd managed to pull a few strings and get his horse sent up from where it was usually stabled off Petersham Meadows near his parents' home. He'd found stabling just off the Westwood, and at least once a week he took her out for a gallop. The stable hands usually exercised her on at least two other days, so the animal – a white mare he'd unimaginatively called Blanche – was in good fettle. At fifteen years old, she was getting to an age where perhaps Swift should consider putting her out to pasture. But it was his one link back to his cavalry days. Riding his first horse after the Great War had helped in his recovery. Although with just one good arm he still found mounting and dismounting difficult, it was a pastime that he could continue to enjoy despite his disability.

He took the horse on a gallop to the north side of the Westwood, along the outer rails of the racecourse. Inside, there was no racing now – instead the railed course itself was used for military drills and exercises, with the land bounded by the interior rail given over to cultivation. He slowed to a trot to cross the York Road, and then cantered Blanche round the edge of the small wood known as Burton Bushes, avoiding the fenced-off areas of turf which had been ploughed for crop growing, then brought the horse to a halt by the golf green.

He'd never played the Westwood course, but was fascinated by the fact that golf was still being enjoyed in the middle of a world war. He'd even started practising one-handed in his back garden. Mostly chipping, but he'd also begun trying some drives and longer shots with hollow, perforated rubber practice balls, designed to fly about a tenth of the distance. One day, perhaps early in the morning or at dusk to limit the amount of spectators there to witness his embarrassment, he might feel ready to try a few shots on the course itself.

This was the game in its most basic form. Each green, like this one – the ninth, the furthest reach of the course – was surrounded by wires and poles to keep off the cows and sheep. There were no bunkers; the only defences were the natural bumps and hollows of the Westwood pasture. That, and what looked like punishing rough away from the animal-grazed fairways.

He watched as a middle-aged man fluffed his chip approach right into one of the wire surrounds, then picked the ball up and tried again. The man's second attempt wasn't much better – barely creeping onto the green – but at least he'd missed the fence. Swift wasn't sure if that was a penalty shot, or if replaying after hitting the fence was allowed under some special local rule. He'd only played one similar golf course before – a moorland nine-holer with his father, while on holiday in South Devon before the first war. Again, there had been wire surrounds to stop sheep getting on to the greens and ruining them. Here, the Westwood was pastureland, rather than high moor – so the fences were to keep out cattle, too. But with some of the pasture turned over to vegetable plots, that provided an extra hazard. The other golfer of the pair seemed to have lost his ball in among the cultivated area.

The scene was pastoral, peaceful. A whole world away from this new war. Swift and many of his generation – especially those who'd fought and suffered life-changing injuries – found it almost inexplicable. How, little more than twenty years after the nightmare slaughter of the Western Front, it had all started over again.

After returning Blanche to her stables, and settling her weekly keep, Swift returned to the house.

When he'd been out riding the horse, something had been pricking lightly into his leg. At first, he thought it must be a thorn or similar from one of the Westwood's many gorse bushes that he and Blanche had brushed against without realising.

But as he opened the front door, he realised it was something in his pocket – and remembered the small package which had been handed to him by Holdridge's secretary before he and Weighton had set off for the ice factory.

He pulled out the folded envelope. Something sharp was sticking out: the end of a brass pin.

Frowning, he placed the envelope temporarily on the hall shelf, then picked up his leather driving gloves and – using his teeth to help compensate for his lack of dexterity – pulled them onto both his good hand and his prosthetic.

Then he picked up the envelope again and, gingerly, tore it open.

He saw the back of it first. A brass lapel badge. The pin had worked free of the clasp, which was why it had broken through its paper covering.

His heart started pounding, drumming in his ears, even before he turned the item over to see the emblem on the other side. Almost as though he knew what it was going to be.

He wasn't wrong.

A golden lion, lying *couchant* atop an enamel emblem.

The outer ring design was innocent enough. Almost like a circular lifebuoy decorated in the colours of the Union flag.

It was what was in the centre that chilled his blood, and found him dropping the object on the floor in horror and disgust.

On a white background, a black hooked cross.

A swastika.

13

Swift knew all too well what the emblem signified, of course. Which was why he'd dropped it in shock, as though it was a piece of red-hot metal. Not the swastika itself, which had been a perfectly innocent Asian religious symbol until it had been subverted by Hitler and his bloodthirsty cronies. It was the way it was used here which made Swift shiver, even in the mild early-summer temperatures.

Encircled by the colours and design of the Union flag, with the golden lion at its apex, this was the emblem of the Imperial Fascist League. It was the British fascist offshoot Swift had helped to expose, and eventually bring down, in a long investigation which had started with those racial insults yelled at Dixie Dean at the Spurs game four years earlier. What was it the 'fan' had shouted? *We'll get you yet, you black bastard!* Something along those lines, anyway.

The arrival of the lapel badge meant one thing. Hull, or rather Beverley, wasn't far enough away from the group's Home Counties stronghold.

And now it was Swift in their sights.

* * *

He knew the best way to get over his shock and calm his nerves. A cup of tea. It always worked wonders. But after boiling the kettle on the stove, he was just about to pour the water into the pot when the doorbell rang.

Swift wasn't expecting visitors. He approached the door warily, ensuring the safety chain was in place. Just in case whoever had hand-delivered the lapel badge to Alfred Gelder Street, or whoever had got a young lad to do their dirty work for them, had now decided to reinforce their little 'message' with an in-person visit.

Swift felt his face relax in relief when he saw who was on the doorstep: Weighton. And his sergeant had brought WAPC Carver with him.

'Ah, welcome, you two. Won't you come in? You'll join me for a cup of tea at least, I hope.'

Swift hoped his voice didn't betray the fact that, until a moment ago, his nerves had been on edge, his mind imagining all sorts of things. He needed to get a grip.

'Thank you, sir. That would go down a treat. And Kathleen has brought along a chocolate cake, too.'

'Splendid!' said Swift, with an almost forced jollity. 'Come in, come in.'

'It's not much, I'm afraid, sir. It's my mother's egg-free recipe. Still quite yummy and moist, though.'

Swift led them into the parlour. 'Sit yourselves down. I'll just get the tea.'

'Shall I bring the cake, sir?' asked Carver.

'No, don't trouble yourself. Here, I'll take it through and cut us some slices.'

He returned with teapot, milk jug, cups, saucers, sugar, slices of cake and plates all balanced on a tray.

'Are you all right with that, sir?' asked Weighton.

'Just about. The right arm's not good for much, but it seems to come into its own for balancing tea trays.'

He nearly regretted his words as he tried to place the tray on the table, almost upsetting the whole thing. Unbidden, Weighton stood to take over, and Swift sat down in his armchair, moving his pipe away from the side table.

'So,' he said, 'to what do I owe the honour of this visit?'

'Well, we heard what happened, sir,' said Weighton. 'Thought perhaps you could do with cheering up.'

'I'm fine, Weighton. You know me. Holdridge and I are rarely on the best of terms. I'm only sorry for Carver here. Does this all mean you're having to go back to the records department, Carver?'

''Fraid so, sir. Back there on Monday morning.'

'What about you, Weighton?'

'Well, it was partly at the behest of the chief super that I'm here, sir. He wants you back at work. First thing Monday.'

'Does he now? And what work am I supposed to be doing exactly, given I've been taken off the most important case?'

'He says there are still loose ends to tie up around Houghton's murder. And there's one more thing, sir.'

'What's that?'

'I was curious about the meeting you had with DCS Hold-ridge, and the fact that that American officer wasn't the only gentleman present.'

'That's right. There were another two there. Looked like ministry types to me. I wasn't introduced. And to be honest, they just sat there.'

'You didn't recognise them then, sir?'

'Should I have done?'

'Well, I was chatting to the desk sergeant – Whitehead. He's been around the block a few times. Knows what's what in Hull. He says he signed in two local bigwigs at DCS Holdridge's request.'

'Hmm. So not ministry men?'

'No, sir. One of them was Ernest Bethell, the MP for Holderness. He's a Conservative. The other was Audley Smethwick, the deputy leader of Hull Corporation. He's Labour.'

Swift frowned. 'I should have recognised them, shouldn't I?'

'Not necessarily, sir. WAPC Carver, would you know them?'

Carver swallowed her piece of cake quickly, and then washed it down with a gulp of tea to avoid speaking with her mouth full.

'I can't say I've heard of either of them.'

'*I* would have done,' continued Weighton, 'but only because I'm a local, and I'm forever reading the *Mail*, mainly for the football.'

'There are only friendly matches at the moment, Weighton. I shouldn't think they're anything to get too excited about. But I agree, it seems slightly curious these two men were involved. Any thoughts as to why?'

'I'm afraid not, sir. I just thought you'd like to know.'

'Perhaps we should look into their backgrounds a little? Strictly off the record, of course.'

Carver leaned forwards in her chair. 'I just cannot believe the man we interviewed in Cottingham strangled and mutilated his best friend. Let alone his best friend's girlfriend. He seemed genuinely distraught about Archie Davis's killing – and his surprise that Sarah Houghton had been killed, too, and in a similar way, also seemed genuine.'

'I agree,' said Swift. 'And perhaps I was a little hasty storming out of Holdridge's office.'

'I can't say I blame you, sir. I think I'd have done the same.'

'Well, look . . . tell Holdridge I'll come back. You can also tell him that as far as I'm concerned the Americans have no jurisdiction whatsoever over Sarah Houghton's murder, and that we shall continue to investigate it. There's not a lot we can do about Private Howard's arrest, but circumstances can change quickly. Perhaps we need to get back on the horse straightaway. I can always pretend I misunderstood the purpose of this visit – and that my understanding from you, Weighton, was that the DCS had asked me to resume the investigation into Sarah's murder.'

Weighton frowned. 'Well, he didn't really say that, sir.'

'No, perhaps not. But that's what I've understood you to have said. I must have got the wrong end of the stick. All my fault, Weighton, don't worry. And Carver, don't you worry either. I'll ring Inspector Wilkinson in records right away and explain there's been a misunderstanding and you won't be returning to the records department after all.'

Swift rubbed his good hand and his prosthetic hand together gleefully.

'Your mood seems transformed, sir,' said Carver.

'It is, WAPC Carver. It's amazing what some fresh air, tea and chocolate cake can achieve. Your mother's recipe is very good, by the way. You'll have to write me out a copy. Eggs or no eggs.'

'So I can tell DCS Holdridge you'll be back on Monday, sir?'

'No, Weighton. I'm back as of now. I'll come in to tell him myself. I'm afraid one downside is both of you might have been hoping for the weekend off. You can forget that. We have a murder to solve. Well, two murders – it's just that one of them, temporarily, has been taken out of our hands.'

Swift didn't need to tell his two colleagues what had transpired just before they arrived. If those he'd hoped to escape from in London were now trying to target him once more, he didn't want any of that spilling over into this investigation. The less Weighton and Carver knew about it, the better. He just hoped they wouldn't be targeted by the mind games, too. At present, there was no sign they had been.

Holdridge seemed surprised to see Swift.

'I thought I told Weighton that I wanted to see you back at work on Monday.'

'Ah, sorry, I must have misunderstood, sir. I assumed you simply wanted me back at work as soon as possible, given we have a murder to solve – well, two murders, although our American colleagues have made an arrest in the case of one of them.'

'And I've taken you off the case.'

'In respect of the murder of Archie Davis.'

'Yes.'

'But not in respect of Sarah Houghton – a case over which the Americans have no jurisdiction.'

'Don't try my patience, Swift.'

'Should I take things higher, sir? To the chief constable, perhaps?'

Holdridge banged his fist down on the table. 'No, Swift. Continue to investigate the Houghton murder if you must.'

'Thank you, sir. I've also told Inspector Wilkinson I still want WAPC Carver working with me.'

'If you insist, Swift. Now, if that's all . . .'

'There was one other thing, sir. Why were those politicians in here yesterday when we were discussing a sensitive murder case? The American colonel I can understand – just about. But the Conservative MP for Holderness? The deputy leader of Hull Corporation, a councillor affiliated to the Labour Party? It was none of their business, and it makes me look like a fool.'

'It's not my fault if you didn't know who they were, Swift. You live and work in the Hull area now. Sometimes we in the police have to stay on the right side of politicians to make our lives easier.'

'What possible interest do they have in this case?'

'The Holderness constituency covers Cottingham, so the local MP has a perfectly valid interest in how well our American guests are integrating into the community. Clearly, when one of them has been murdered, the local MP is going to want to be kept informed. And as the police force for the city of Hull, we have to maintain good relations with Hull Corporation, too. When a citizen of Hull is murdered, then clearly the council will be concerned. But I don't have to justify myself to you, Swift. Just get on with your job, and don't – whatever you do – go upsetting the Americans any more than you have already. They'll help win the war for us, you mark my words. And that is the most important thing. Not your bloody prostitute murder.'

Having literally been back on his equine mount that morning, Swift now felt very much back on the proverbial horse, too.

He gathered himself, Weighton and Carver together in the incident room.

'Weighton, can you do some digging into the backgrounds of that MP and the councillor? See if they've crossed swords with the police at any stage before. It might even be worth asking if any of your underworld contacts have had dealings with them. I can't put my finger on it, but there's something not right about all this. Carver, you're coming with me. Let's see if we can find Miss Jessica Pickering and see what she has to say for herself.'

George and Elsie Camilleri looked as pleased to see the police as they usually did.

Swift approached the café counter.

'Is Jessica around, George?'

'You've just missed her,' he said. 'Literally by a few seconds.'

'Do you know where she was off to?'

'Elsie, any idea where Jessica was off to?'

'I don't know. She sometimes hangs around in the Holderness Tavern.'

'Which way's that?' asked Swift.

'I know, sir,' said Carver. 'Not far from here, in Witham, a few hundred yards back towards the city centre.'

'Don't be causing her any trouble!' shouted Elsie. 'She's fragile enough after what happened to Sweet Sarah. She doesn't need you lot making her life a misery.'

14

Theo and Archie didn't rightly know where Hull was on a map. Somewhere in the north-east of England, people said. Big enough city, but nowhere near as big as Detroit. It had taken a hell of a hammering from Hitler's bombers the previous year. Much of the city centre was in ruins, but the docks the Nazi bombers had been aiming for were back in action, and that's where the two friends and the rest of the battalion would be detailed to work.

The officers kept their distance, of course. It was as though the Jim Crow laws they thought had been left behind had been bundled up in a kitbag and brought along with them. So the white officers got the nice big house at the end of the drive, and the only time Theo, Archie or their colleagues were allowed up there was if they were on a charge.

The regular soldiers got the tin shacks. They weren't too bad, though. On the edge of a pretty enough English village,

Cottingham, which was itself almost part of Hull. But the best thing for Theo and Archie was that Hitler's bombs had rarely reached these outer edges of the greater Hull area. They were playing their part in the war effort but, for the time being at least, they were relatively safe.

This was a new start for both of them. The last few weeks in Detroit had been hard. When Bessie packed up and headed back down south, it wasn't just Theo who was hurting about her and the forthcoming baby. Without her best friend, Dolores kept on itching to leave Detroit, too. Theo and Bessie's relationship was over, but it looked as though Archie and Dolores were heading the same way.

So when they found the local white girls didn't look down on them, didn't deliberately cross to the other side of the road as though to get away from a bad smell, well, it was as though they'd arrived in a land of milk and honey. It wasn't just the girls, either – although they were starved of attention, with so many of their menfolk away at war. All the folk in Cottingham and Hull went out of their way to be friendly, and Theo and Archie soon found a small amount of politeness and kindness went a long, long way. They'd heard folks in some parts of England didn't like GIs flashing their money around, showing they got better pay than their English counterparts. But if you were respectful in Hull, you got respect back.

You also got respect for your dance moves. Dance moves and smooth talking. That's how Archie had snared Sarah. But then, Archie always was a smooth talker.

They met the girls on their first night at the King Street dance hall. Both of them made a beeline for Sarah and Jessica – and both of them wanted Sarah over Jessica. That girl just had something about her. Theo soon realised, though, he was going to be playing second banjo.

'I feel bad for you,' said Archie. 'You know I do. I got a good woman back home in Dolores, but she's a coal-scuttle blonde. This one's the real thing. I can feel it in my bones.'

'Well, you go and bust your conk, then,' said Theo. 'I'm not stopping you. I know when I'm beat.'

'You're not sweet on that Jessica, then?'

'Well, maybe. She's fine dinner, all right. But I'm not sure she's sweet on me.'

But when Archie started smooching up close to Sarah, Theo wasn't doing the same with Jessica. He was watching the folks watching. He was getting the feeling some on the sidelines weren't too happy – including some of the lower-ranking officers. White officers, of course. All the officers were white. They wouldn't like to see Archie coming on like a gangbuster with a white girl. There was some tension in the air.

Archie didn't seem to notice all that.

When they got back to the base, Sarah was all he could talk about. He talked and talked and talked until in the end Theo had to tell him to shut it.

'You need your sweet dreams, and I gotta catch some cups.'

So Archie fell heavily. Straightaway, he and Sarah were walking out. Then he was meeting her parents, her sister, her sister's kids. Giving Sarah and her sister nylons, buying the kids toys.

He didn't like that the family never had any money, and that Sarah was supporting them with her 'work' at the Café Prestige.

Then one of those jealous white officers told Archie exactly what 'work' Sarah did.

It was like Archie's world had come crashing down.

15

Swift and Carver managed to spot Jessica walking along the pavement before she reached the Holderness Tavern. Swift stopped the Morris a few yards in front of her, and then wound down the car window. Jessica hadn't recognised the car, and at first leaned down to talk to Swift, obviously thinking he was a punter, then backed away quickly when she realised her mistake.

Carver and Swift leaped out of the car.

Jessica had increased the pace of her walk.

Swift shouted after her. 'We just want a quick word, Jessica! We can either do it formally, or informally – whichever you'd prefer.'

The young woman turned round, giving him what almost looked like a snarl.

Swift opened the rear door of the car, waiting for her to decide. After a moment's hesitation, she began walking back towards them.

'I don't like the way you lot cramp my style,' she said. 'A girl's got to earn a living. It's hard enough these days as it is.'

'We don't want to stop you earning a living,' said Carver. 'We just want a little more help.'

Jessica ducked her head, climbed in, and Swift slammed the door shut.

He adjusted the rear-view mirror so he could see the young woman's expression.

'Can't you drive somewhere out of the way so's any customers don't see us nattering? They won't take too kindly to me blabbing to the cops.'

'All right,' said Swift. 'Let's do that.'

He did a U-turn, and began driving eastwards. After a couple of miles, they reached East Park. Swift turned left through the park gates, and after a hundred yards or so stopped in the car park.

They'd been silent throughout the short journey, but now Swift turned in his seat.

'Have you heard about Archie Davis?'

Jessica nodded, bowing her head. 'I'm scared, Mr Swift. First Sarah, then Archie. Who's to say I won't be next?'

'Someone's been arrested, Jessica. If he is indeed the culprit, then you've no longer anything to fear.'

'Who?'

'Theophilus Howard.'

'Theo? You've got to be kidding. Theo wouldn't hurt a fly. He loved Archie. They were like brothers. You've got the wrong man there, you must have.'

Carver joined the fray. 'Have you been fully honest with us so far, Jessica?'

'What's that supposed to mean?'

'You told us there was a bit of an argument at the dance hall last week,' said Swift. 'You didn't tell us there was a full-on fight involving Archie and Theo.'

'I didn't want to get either of them into trouble. But yes, it was a bit more serious than I made out.'

Swift sighed. 'Do you think this fight could have had anything to do with Sarah's and Archie's murders?'

Jessica shrugged. 'Mebbe. You're the detective, aren't you?'

'Yes, but you can help us, Jessica,' said Carver. 'Did you get the sense that the level of resentment against Sarah and Archie's relationship was enough to make someone want to kill them?'

The young woman shook her head. 'I just don't know. Possibly. Archie had a heart of gold, as has Theo. They couldn't do too much for you. But unlike Theo, Archie also had a bit of a mouth on him.'

'What do you mean by that?' asked Swift.

'Well, I could imagine him talking himself into trouble. He was very angry about the poverty the Houghtons were facing. He thought that was what had driven Sarah to sell her body. He had a go at the corporation about it. Got himself into a right tizz.'

Swift frowned. 'What did the way Sarah earned her money have to do with Hull Corporation?'

'That's not what I mean. He was angry about how much money she was providing for the family – how much she felt she had to pass on. It was something to do with having to support Betty's two children as well.'

'But they would get school meals, surely?' asked Carver.

'Not all kids. And not all councils. But that wasn't the point. Archie had a go at the corporation, and discovered something. I didn't really understand it.'

'What?' asked Swift.

'Well, he reckoned when he moaned to them, asked them why they couldn't do any more, they said the kids shouldn't be there anyway.'

This chimed with Swift. He remembered thinking the same about Betty's children. The Houghtons' street had been so badly damaged by the bombs of the previous year. Why hadn't the children been evacuated like so many others? Could that be really what this was all about? Had they – had he, Swift – been too blinded by the overt racism displayed by the white American officers, and just assumed that was what lay at the heart of all this? When in fact it might be something altogether different.

'And what had Archie tried to do about it?'

'He'd kicked up a big fuss. Said the Houghtons should write to their MP, lobby their local councillors, that sort of thing.'

'And did they?' asked Swift.

His mind immediately turned to the two suited men in that meeting with Holdridge. The Tory MP for Holderness, and the deputy leader of Hull Corporation, a Labour man.

'I don't know. It weren't really my business, were it? What I do know is Betty didn't want no fuss. She liked her bains close to her. I don't think she really fully realised what Sarah was having to do with her body to make that happen.'

Carver interjected now. 'But surely Archie himself could have helped out with money? Those American GIs are said to get paid enough. What is it? Five times as much as British soldiers.'

Swift frowned. 'Steady on, WAPC Carver. I know they get paid more, but I'm sure it's not as much as that.'

'I think you'll find it is, sir.'

'She's right, yer nerr.' Swift noticed Jessica was sounding more Hull-like all of a sudden – not bothering to try to mimic the posh English of the BBC news announcers from the wireless as so many young women did these days. Why? Was it that she felt more comfortable with the police? Or was she lying, concentrating too much on her lies, and letting her natural accent slip out? 'And he did help them,' she continued. 'He said Sarah could give it all up – and I think she would have. If she'd lived, like. But that weren't his point. His point was Sarah had sold her body, got into prostitution, *because* the Houghtons had no money. And his view was they had no money because of funny goings-on at the council.'

'Do you think that's right?' asked Swift.

'Do I? As it happens, no. I don't want to be crude wi' you two. But giving a hand job or blow job is easy money. And Sarah wouldn't do much more than that. She might have laid back and thought of England once or twice, but she certainly didn't do owt like take it up the—'

'Thank you, Jessica,' Swift quickly interrupted. 'We don't need that level of detail. You've been a great help. Can we give you a lift anywhere?'

'Aye. You can take me back towards the 'Olderness Tavern. But dern't drop me right outside. Drop us off up a nearby side street. As I've already said, you two cramp my style.'

Once they got to a suitable location, Swift turned the engine off, then climbed out of the car and opened the rear door of the Morris.

'Well, you certainly know how to treat a lady, officer,' said Jessica as she climbed out. 'I wish there were a few more like you in the world.'

'Don't mention it, Miss Pickering. And thank you for your help.'

'Well, much as I was 'appy to talk to you this time, I hope that's an end to it. Although if you wanted to offer me police protection, I wouldn't say no.'

'We don't have the resources for that, Miss Pickering. Not when there's a war on. But just because your friends have been killed, it doesn't mean you're in any immediate danger. If I really thought you were, I would of course make an exception.'

'Aye, well, I hope you don't live to regret those words, officer. I'll be seeing you.'

Swift watched her walk away towards the pub, no doubt to pick up her next john. The offhand way she'd described selling herself had revolted him. But then, who was he to judge? He just hoped that his confident assertion that she wasn't in need of protection was actually rooted in reality.

He wasn't at all sure it was.

16

By the time they got back to Alfred Gelder Street, Swift was ready for another cup of tea. He was delighted to see that Weighton had arrived back with the same thought. The revolting-looking kettle had already started whistling on the camp stove, in a strange, intermittent way, like an overenthusiastic amateur football referee blowing for a penalty.

'Can't we sort out a better system that that, Weighton?'

'I'll leave that for you to arrange with your friend Mr Hold-ridge, sir.'

'Well, we're almost midway through the twentieth century. One would have thought an electric one wasn't beyond the limited parameters of Hull City Police's budget.'

'Personally,' said Carver, 'I rather prefer a whistling kettle on gas. It makes the tea taste better and adds to the experience.'

Swift raised his eyebrows. 'If you say so, WAPC Carver. If you say so. Anyway, Weighton, any progress?'

'Some, sir. Not a lot. How about you?'

'Snap. Some. Not a lot. Do you want to go first?'

'All right. Well, you remember our friend Ron Lewis?'

'Ah yes, of course. I'd rather forgotten about him.'

'Well, after you had your little falling-out with DCS Holdridge, we had to release him. We didn't have anything on him – other than the fact he'd resisted arrest.'

'And assaulted a police officer. Me, as I recall.'

'Yes. Well, we could have charged him, of course. But I rather thought it might be nice to leave that hanging over him. To have him owing us, rather than simply banged up in a cell.'

Swift shrugged. 'Makes sense I suppose, Sergeant.'

'But a member of our uniform team lives out his way. I asked him to keep an eye on him. Not a full-scale surveillance operation, you understand. Just a little part-time work when he had the opportunity.'

'All right. Interesting.'

'He was on a day off today, so this time I decided to join him on his spying adventures. You know how it is. Often you need at least two people to set up a proper tail.'

Swift nodded. 'Don't keep us in suspense, Weighton.'

'Well, you'll never guess who we saw him meeting.'

'I think perhaps I might,' said Swift. 'Did it happen to be either the local councillor or the MP who sat in on my meeting with Holdridge and the American colonel?'

'It did indeed, sir.'

'Which one?'

'Both. And we managed to get photos.'

'Excellent, Weighton. Excellent. And where was this, may I ask?'

'In East Park.'

Carver gasped in astonishment. 'That's where *we* were. Just a few minutes ago, Weighton.'

'Well, I'm glad you two didn't blow our cover, then. Anyway, those same two bigwigs hired a rowing boat on the boating lake, rowed to the other side, and then picked up Lewis.'

'You're sure it was him?'

'Quite sure, sir. We've got a photograph of them handing him a brown envelope. A rather thick brown envelope.'

'Filled with notes, you think?'

'I've no idea, sir. But that's a strong possibility.'

'It is indeed. I think it's time we paid Mr Lewis another visit, don't you? If he was swanning around on a boating lake up to no good, there's a chance he's on a day off, so we might catch him in.'

Swift also wondered whether Lewis's links to Bethell and Smethwick had any other significance. The union man at the docks, Dalby, had mentioned Lewis's fascist connections – did they possibly extend to Bethell, a Conservative politician? Many Conservative MPs had shown sympathy for the fascists, if not outright support. Mosley himself, after all, had started out as a Tory MP immediately after the Great War. Swift was less inclined to think that the Labour councillor, Smethwick, had fascist tendencies. But stranger things had happened. Before Mosley's eventual disillusionment with mainstream politics, he'd served in a Labour government.

Weighton turned the gas off on the stove.

'Tea had better wait, then?'

'Well, let's you and I go and see Lewis. WAPC Carver, could you perhaps do some more digging about this MP and the councillor – and Lewis, too? Use your contacts in the police records department, and anything else you can think of. By all means make a tea for yourself first. We would take you with us, but this Lewis chap is a nasty piece of work.'

'You said he lives just round the corner from Stott?' said Swift, as they headed out once more to the eastern half of the city.

'That's right, sir. Stott's in Sherburn Street, Lewis is one street further along off Holderness Road – Morrill Street. You might remember it – it was caught up in the first raid on the city a couple of years ago. Around the time you arrived on the force. Half a dozen killed – Morrill and Rustenburg Streets on this side of the city, and Carlton and Eastbourne Streets on the western side. Not far from where Hull City's new ground will be, if they ever get it finished.'

'I wonder if the new ground will bring them more success. You're a bit of a fan, aren't you, Weighton?'

'I am, sir. We've never done very much, to be honest. An FA Cup semi-final is probably our best achievement. Took the mighty Arsenal to a replay. They narrowly pipped us, though. My dad managed to get us tickets for the second game. Should never have lost. The ref sent our centre-half off for no good reason, so we played most of the second half with ten men.'

'Do you think they'll ever get to the final? Or up to the first division? That would be a big thing for the city.'

'I doubt it, sir.'

'Tigers by name, but not by nature, eh?'

'The trouble is half the city are rugby league fanatics, so there's not the supporter base a city of this size ought to have. Are you a rugby league man, sir?'

'No. Strictly union. Although I don't really follow team sports – golf is more my sort of thing.' He looked down sadly at his prosthetic arm. 'Well, it was.'

'Brentford must be your nearest football team, though, sir. They're pretty handy.'

'I used to go to a few games. Not since they've been in the first division.'

'Who's that Scottish forward of theirs? I keep on seeing him in the top scorers' charts in the papers.'

Swift changed gear in the Morris as they turned right into Morrill Street.

'McCulloch, do you mean? He's gone now. But yes, he was very popular with the fans. Anyway, enough of idle football chat.' Thinking of football reminded Swift too much of the Dean incident, the subsequent investigation, and the 'gift' of the lapel badge – all things he wasn't planning to enlighten Weighton about, unless he couldn't avoid it. They needed their minds on the actual job in hand. 'Which number house does Lewis live in?'

Weighton pointed to the house, part of a turn-of-the-century terrace, although the terrace was only partially complete because of the 1940 bombing. Lewis's house had survived.

Weighton knocked hard on the door, as Swift stood to one side.

A thin-faced woman wearing a dirty, threadbare housecoat opened the door, and then stood guard at it.

'Who are you? What do you want?'

Swift showed his warrant card. 'Detective Chief Inspector Swift, Hull City Police. This is Detective Sergeant Weighton. We're looking for Ronald Lewis.'

'Oh aye? What the fuck has he done now?'

'He's your husband, I take it?'

'Aye. For all the good it does me. You'll not find him here. Try the Crown Inn opposite East Park. Mind you, by now he'll probably be plastered. You'll not get much sense out of him. Then again, he doesn't talk much sense at the best of times.'

The Crown was a modern affair – a large art deco pub, probably completed just before the war, Swift thought. With its wide facade flanked by faux twin towers with slit windows, if you didn't know better you could have almost mistaken it for a cinema.

They scanned the bar, peering through the fog of cigarette fumes. Swift found himself almost choking. He limited his own smoking to an occasional pipe at home – and neither Weighton nor Carver indulged, or at least not at the office. But they were the exception rather than the rule: their incident room at Alfred Gelder Street must have been one of the few in the building that was smoke-free.

The pub was relatively crowded. Today was Friday – so wages day. Dockers who'd managed to evade their wives demanding they hand over their housekeeping money were probably oiling their gullets with ale as quickly as possible. But there seemed to be no sign of Lewis. The noise level had quietened as soon as they'd entered, as though people could tell they were outsiders.

'Have you been here before, Weighton?' said Swift, sotto voce.

'Once or twice, sir. Not for leisure, you understand. When I've been looking for people – people of interest, shall we say.'

'So you might be recognised?'

'Possibly.'

They approached the bar.

'Can I have a word with the landlord?' Swift asked the barmaid.

'Fred!' the woman shouted. 'Someone's here to see you.'

'Who is it?' a man shouted.

'Police,' the woman replied, even though Swift and Weighton hadn't introduced themselves. The noise level in the pub quietened still further, and Swift was conscious of heads turning to look towards them. The barmaid, too, turned back to them. 'You are police, aren't you?'

'We are indeed.'

'Ah, here he is.'

An overweight man with a pot belly straining the buttons on his shirt was wiping his hands with a beer towel. He sniffed at them.

'Well?' he asked, gruffly.

'I'm Chief Inspector Swift, this is Sergeant Weighton. Hull CID. We believe a certain Ron Lewis of Morrill Street is a regular of yours.'

'He is.' The man flicked his head backwards. 'Try the back bar. I daresay you won't get much sense out of him. He's been knocking 'em back and buying rounds in like he's won the bloody football pools. 'Appen he has, for all I know.'

As they opened the saloon doors to the rear bar, their entrance had the same effect it had had at the front, but to an even greater degree.

They were met with menacing glares, as though they'd intruded on a private party.

Lewis was perched on a chair, swaying slightly, holding a hand of cards.

'Oh heck!' he exclaimed. 'Look what the cat's dragged in.'

'Well, it's lovely to see you as well, Mr Lewis,' said Swift.

'I hope you're not expecting me to include you two in the next round. You can buy your own bloody booze.'

'We're not here to have a drink, Mr Lewis,' said Weighton. 'A word, please. Outside.'

One of Lewis's acolytes started to get to his feet threateningly, but Lewis waved him to sit down again.

'It's all right, Bill. No harm in speaking to them, even if they are fucking coppers.'

As he rose unsteadily, he towered over Swift – and almost matched the height and build of Weighton. The three of them exited the back door of the bar and went into the pub yard.

'What the fuck do you two want, then? You said I were free to go, Sergeant, and you weren't pressing charges.'

'We're not, Mr Lewis,' said Weighton, adding, 'at the moment. But we'll keep that one up our sleeve just in case. And just a reminder, you're on police bail. We can bring you back in at any time we want.'

Swift let the meaning of Weighton's words sink in with the half-inebriated giant of a man before he started speaking.

'You seem to have come into some money, Mr Lewis. Buying rounds for everyone, I'd heard.'

'No crime in that, officer. I'm a generous man. It's payday and we got off after finishing the work.'

'And you didn't come by the money from other sources?'

'What the fuck do you mean by that?'

'Show him the photographs, will you, Sergeant?'

'Certainly, sir.' Weighton pulled a set of prints from his pocket, which he'd had developed in the police dark room. 'Recognise yourself in these, Mr Lewis?'

The man sniffed. A look of apprehension fleetingly crossed his face, but soon disappeared.

'You can't tell who it is, it ain't clear enough.'

'It's you, Mr Lewis,' said Swift.

'Happen it is, happen it isn't. So bloody what? Going boating in East Park isn't a crime. Yet. You buggers'll probably make it one before too long, though.'

'Well, we know it's you,' said Weighton. 'I took the photographs.'

'What the fuck are you spying on me for?'

'I'm sure you know the answer to that, Mr Lewis,' said Swift. 'Who are the other gentlemen in the photograph?'

'No idea.'

Weighton grabbed the man by his work overalls.

'Oh, come off it, Ron. Why would you get into a rowing boat with two strangers?'

'Perhaps we were re-enacting *Three Men in a Boat*. You see, you lot probably think I'm pig-ignorant, don't you? But I like a bit of reading. Keeps my mind active. Who were that one by? That Jules Verne bloke, weren't it?'

'Jerome K. Jerome, actually,' said Swift, as Weighton released his hold on their suspect.

'Aye, well, I knew it began with a "*J*".'

'What was in the envelope they gave you?' asked Weighton.

Lewis tapped his finger on the side of his nose. 'That's my business, Mr Weighton. It's nowt to do wi' you.'

'Unless what was in that envelope was the proceeds of crime,' said Swift. 'Then it's very much our business. Especially as you were meeting a local Member of Parliament and a leading light at Hull Corporation.'

The revelation that they knew the identities of the other two men seemed to bring Lewis up short. His shoulders had slumped, as though he knew the game was almost up. The trouble was, in reality Swift was aware that he, Weighton and Carver had barely scratched the surface of what was going on. He suspected the part played by Lewis was at best a minor one. Employed by the others for his thuggery, no doubt. But to do what? Was it something to do with the murders of Sarah Houghton and Archie Davis? And if so, what?

'I can see you know we're on to you,' Swift continued. 'We're also on to your more eminent partners in crime. We also know you have an unhealthy regard for a jailed right-wing politician.'

'Thoughts and beliefs aren't fucking crimes,' snarled Lewis.

At this Weighton moved forwards again, grabbing Lewis by the neck, slamming his back against the pub wall and squeezing his windpipe.

'Now my sergeant here,' continued Swift, 'is very useful with his hands, as I think you're aware. So far we've played things by the book. But we don't have to. I want you to get a message to those other two.'

'I . . . don't . . . know . . . who . . . you mean.' Lewis struggled to get the words out as he gasped for breath.

'Let me remind you of their names, then,' said Swift, as Weighton kept up his neck hold on the man. 'Ernest Bethell, the Tory MP for Holderness, and Councillor Audley Smethwick. Tell them Detective Chief Inspector Swift of Hull CID is on to their case. They can either wait till we bring them down publicly, or they can come voluntarily to Hull Police Station to make a statement. Do that, and as long as your part in all this is relatively minor, Lewis, you might just escape a jail sentence. Do you understand?'

The man gave a small nod, and Weighton released his hold.

Lewis doubled over, gasping for air.

'Fucking doing things by the book. You could have fooled me.'

'Do you think he'll pass that message on, sir?' asked Weighton, once they were safely back in the Morris, returning to the city centre.

'I suspect he probably will. Whether the other two will pay any notice is quite another matter. They may just call our bluff. Or they might be so chummy with DCS Holdridge that it's we who find ourselves in trouble.'

'You don't strike me as the sort of person who would be worried by that, sir.'

'I'm not, Weighton. I just want to crack this case – or cases, if we've stumbled on something else by accident.'

Once they were back in the incident room, they finally managed to sit down and have the cups of tea they'd been on the point of making earlier in the day. There was no sign of Carver, other than her dirty teacup and the teapot, neither of which she'd deigned to wash up.

'I'll do that, sir,' said Weighton, taking them out to the sink in the gents, while Swift watched the kettle.

He tried to get his thoughts in order. The fact that the two local politicians had met and handed something – presumably cash – to Lewis was not necessarily connected in any way to the murders of Houghton and Davis. And yet . . .

Why had it been those same two politicians in the meeting with Holdridge and the American commanding officer?

The coincidence was too great to be accidental, especially as the two men were from opposite sides of the political spectrum and should – by rights – be sworn enemies. One spending his time protecting wealthy East Riding farmers and businessmen, the other fighting for the oppressed and poor of Hull, while no doubt giving succour to good old 'Uncle Joe' in the Kremlin. It was an alliance that made no sense. And then there was the arrest of Theophilus Howard. Swift's instincts told him the man was innocent and the victim of a set-up. But why? And would the Americans let him and Weighton back to interview Howard again?

His thoughts were interrupted by Weighton returning with the newly washed teapot, cup and saucer, dripping water on the floor. Not that it mattered down in here in their basement room. The plaster on the walls was already blown in several places, with salt bloom from the damp. A few drops more wouldn't do any harm.

Almost as soon as Weighton had entered, an out-of-breath Carver followed him, as though she'd been dashing to get back.

'Ah, sir. I hoped I'd catch you.'

'You've got something for us, WAPC Carver?'

'I think so, possibly.'

Swift noticed she was carrying a sheaf of papers.

'What have you got there?'

'My notes on the financial background of Ernest Bethell.'

'Oh yes? Sounds intriguing. Weighton's just making the tea. You sort yourself out and I'll pop and see if I can get some cake from the canteen.'

'No need for that, sir. I've still got some of that egg-free chocolate cake in my bag. There's enough for all three of us.'

As Carver spread out her papers on the table, Weighton finished brewing the tea, and then poured each of them a cup.

'So,' said Swift, 'take us through it all.'

'Well, you may or may not know where the Bethell family money comes from.'

'Fish, isn't it?' said Weighton. 'Or it was, I know that much.'

'Fish meal, to be precise. Bethell's Fish Meal and Oil Company Ltd – a thriving business before the war broke out.'

'But not now?' asked Swift.

'Absolutely not,' said Carver. 'The fishing industry has been decimated by the war. Especially out of Hull, which relied on North Sea fishing – which is now far too dangerous. I was able to get a copy of their accounts filed at Companies House. For the last two years, Bethell's has traded at a loss.'

'I'm sure they're not alone in that,' said Weighton. 'There'll be winners and losers in the war. The winners are mostly those companies that have been able to convert to arms production.'

'I can't imagine that happening to a fish meal processing plant,' said Swift. 'Unless we're planning to fire fertiliser pellets at the Nazis.'

'No. As well as the accounts, showing Bethell's is possibly in financial trouble, I've got a contact at Martins Bank in Whitefriargate, which handles both the Bethell's company bank account and Ernest Bethell's personal account.'

'A *contact*?' said Swift. 'Who?'

'I'd rather not say, sir. It's personal.'

'You haven't done anything illegal to acquire this information, have you, Carver? I'm all for using initiative, but we're supposed to be upholding the law, not breaking it.'

'*I* haven't, sir, no.'

'Why don't we just hear what Kathleen has to say, sir?' intervened Weighton.

Swift gave a shrug and raised his eyebrows. 'Go on then, WAPC Carver.'

'Well, approximately a year ago, apparently to try to stop his family's fish processing firm from going bankrupt, he took out a rather large loan, with the family's stately home – Burstwick Hall, a medieval manor house in Holderness – as security. The trouble is, he hasn't been keeping up repayments properly. According to my source, unless he finds some money quickly, Ernest Bethell stands to lose the lot. The family firm, the family stately home, not to mention his reputation as an upstanding, important member of the community.'

'For people like that,' said Weighton, 'that's what they care about most. That's what they'd be most afraid of losing. Their *reputation*. Their *standing*.'

Swift was silent for a few moments. What Carver was saying was intriguing. But how did it tie in to their murders? Were they in danger of getting sidetracked into something which, while distinctly dubious-sounding, was possibly more of a case for the fraud specialists?

'All right,' he said, finally. 'Let's say all this is correct, and I've no reason to doubt its veracity, although I do have some questions about how you've come by this information, Carver. Where does this take us? If we investigate it further, why are we investigating it?'

'But, sir,' said Weighton, 'surely the relevant questions are, what is the link between these two politicians and the murders of Houghton and Davis? Did they play any part in the arrest of Private Howard by the Americans? And why were they giving money to Ron Lewis? Because I'm sure that was what was in that envelope. Why else would he suddenly be so flush as to be able to stand everyone round after round at the Crown?'

Weighton is right, of course, thought Swift. *They* were *the questions.*

Carver's information had given a glimmer of an answer, but the case or cases were still a conundrum. And then, of course, there was Jessica Pickering's account of Davis making trouble at the corporation. Was that where Audley Smethwick's involvement came in?

'That's all very useful information, Carver. Did you manage to get anything on the Labour councillor, this Smethwick character?'

'I haven't had a chance yet, sir, no.'

'Well, it sounds like you've been busy enough. Well done, good work. As long as none of the information was illegally obtained.'

Swift noticed Carver was looking a little sheepish, but Weighton came to her rescue.

'Perhaps I might be able to help with Smethwick. He represents the Southcoates ward, which is where I live. I can ask around some of my contacts and see what I come up with.'

'Good idea, Weighton. I was feeling very despondent this morning. It's never nice to have the rug pulled out from under your feet. But we've made good progress today. Let's call it a day and I'll see you both on Monday.'

'Thank you, sir,' said Weighton. 'I'll use the weekend to make a few inquiries about Smethwick.'

'I was thinking about possibly popping back home for the weekend,' asked Carver. 'Would that be all right with you, sir?'

'Of course, Carver. By home, do you mean North Yorkshire?'

'Yes, sir. My mother's not been too well.'

'I'm sorry to hear that. Do you need some extra leave?'

'I don't think so, sir. With a bit of luck, I should still be able to get the Hull to York train, and change there for Darlington.

If I'm too late for the bus to Barnard Castle, I'll splash out on a taxi.'

Swift reached into his pocket, and brought out a ten-shilling note from his wallet.

'I'm not sure if Baldersdale has any public houses, Carver, but if it does, have one on me.'

'Ten bob, sir? Are you sure? I'd be pretty damn squiffy if I bought ten bob's worth of beer. What would that get me – about twenty pints? I'm not really a beer drinker, and I doubt even the thirstiest farmer could manage that.'

'Well, get a present for your mother then, if she's been under the weather. Or put it towards your train and taxi fare. It won't often happen, so don't look a gift horse in the mouth, and I know you auxiliaries don't get paid a great deal. Weighton, I've got your telephone number in case there are any developments over the weekend. Do your parents have a telephone connection, Carver?'

'They don't, sir. But the next-but-one farm has a phone. I'll write down the number for you. They'll know where to get me.'

Swift could sense something was wrong as soon as he opened his front door. A feeling that something had been disturbed – again. The house was far too big for one person, but these days he rather liked his own company. After his former wife Margaret's betrayal, he doubted he'd ever share his life or home with anyone ever again. But the corollary of living on your own was that everything had its place, you knew where everything should be, and just so much as a small disturbance of that routine was enough to set one on edge. Nevertheless, it took a few seconds for him to realise *what* it was that was different. Normally, at the end of a day's work the first thing he'd do was check his mail – the postman never normally arrived before he'd left in the Morris for Alfred Gelder Street. But earlier, after his spat with Holdridge, he'd been rather distracted by the hand delivery of the lapel pin badge. And now he was just pleased to be home. He didn't think to look down at the doormat. So, he didn't notice it until his foot crunched the envelope – another envelope.

Again, it was unmarked – no name of addressee or sender, no postage stamps – but this time it had been hand-delivered actually to his home, rather than to the front desk of Hull Police. And if – as he suspected – it was another missive from that damned fascist group or its supporters, that was taking things to a whole new level.

This time, it was a larger brown paper envelope. Again, there was an object inside, but it looked bigger, bulking out the envelope more.

He picked it up. It had a meaty smell.

Then he noticed some liquid had leached from the packet and stained the paper. It looked remarkably like blood. He smelled his fingers where they'd touched the paper.

It *was* blood.

He placed the package down again.

He opened his work bag and extracted his pair of rubber gloves, placing them over both hands – his prosthetic included – using his teeth, as he had earlier that day, to help stretch them over his real and artificial wrists.

Then he opened the package to find out what was inside.

When he saw what it was, he almost dropped the envelope again in disgust.

An animal's severed ear, and from the almost snow-white fur on the outside of the organ, he immediately knew which animal it had been cut from.

How could they?

This time they had gone too far.

He rushed out to the Morris, locking the door behind him, with the envelope in his hands. A maelstrom of thoughts raced through his head as he ran to the car. He jumped in, started it up, and then drove off towards the stables.

He just hoped that whoever had done this knew what they were doing, whether it was Lewis or one of his cronies, or someone else entirely. That they had some surgical training and hadn't caused too much suffering to his beloved horse. Perhaps that was a forlorn hope.

There was no message with the ear. But its arrival, so soon after the badge, was message enough.

They were targeting him.

The meaning was twofold – they now knew where he lived, and he was therefore vulnerable.

And they obviously knew where his horse was stabled. If they were prepared to maim Blanche, they might be prepared to kill her, too.

They must have been watching him. What had gone on in London had followed him here.

Will I ever escape from it?

The thought made his heart race, the drumming of it hammering in his ears once more.

The stables were obviously shut up for the day, but there was a light on in the adjoining farmhouse. Swift rapped on the farmhouse door.

The door was opened by Molly, the farmer's daughter and stable girl.

'Someone's attacked Blanche!' he yelled.

'What do you mean, Mr Swift? The doors are padlocked. No one's ever managed to force their way in.'

'Well, they have, I tell you. I've got the evidence in this envelope. Quickly – she might be bleeding to death.'

Molly went back into the house to fetch a set of keys, and then followed Swift, who was already running round to the stables.

'See, Mr Swift,' she said, rotating the padlock in the door's staple, the hasp still locked in place. 'No one's been in here. We've never had a break-in yet. They'd have trouble forcing this lock, I tell you.'

She opened it, switched an electric light on, and the stable was suddenly illuminated. Swift rushed over to Blanche's stall. She was standing serenely, munching some hay.

Both her ears were still intact.

Molly looked at him oddly.

Swift frowned. 'I don't understand.'

Molly grabbed the envelope from his gloved hand, with Swift still worried that forensic evidence was being destroyed. She opened it, and brought out the ear.

'You're not much of a horseman, Mr Swift, if you can't tell the difference between a sow's hide and that of a beautiful mare like Blanche. This isn't a horse's ear at all. It's a pig's – probably from the local abattoir. Someone's played a prank on you. Not a particularly pleasant prank, but a prank nonetheless. Nothing more, nothing less.'

Swift could feel the blood pulsing in his face.

He'd been made to look a fool, but the important thing was that Blanche was all right.

And, even if it wasn't Blanche's ear, this was more than just a prank – of that he had no doubt. It was another message, the second in a day. It was too coincidental to have come from a separate source, though Swift knew he should keep an open mind. But he'd seen the film *Gaslight* a couple of years earlier – he knew the power of psychological terror.

There was little he could realistically do to stop it, save for asking forensics to look for fingerprints on the two envelopes. But he knew they wouldn't find any. If someone was clever enough to know just how to push his buttons, then they wouldn't have been stupid enough not to wear gloves.

He decided to go to bed early, even forgoing the BBC news on the wireless. He didn't want to be hearing about war and killings, not after the shock he'd had – the second in less than twenty-four hours.

But he slept fitfully. His dreams were full of severed organs, mutilated bodies and explosions which turned out to be police flash cameras. In many of them, Margaret appeared, along with

Richard – his once-best friend whom she'd run off with. She was taunting him that he was less of a man than his friend because he only had one good arm – something that, to be fair, she never did in real life. If anything, she went too far the other way. Swift didn't like people making allowances for his disability, but Margaret completely ignored it – almost as though she refused to recognise that he even had a prosthetic arm.

Finally, he decided to get up and make himself a cup of tea. The caffeine would probably work against him getting back to sleep. But sometimes just the mere act of getting up and putting the kettle on, then spooning the tea leaves into the pot and pouring the hot water over them, was mundane enough to calm his mind.

Sure enough, when he went back to bed with the intention of reading a book for an hour or so, he drifted off almost immediately.

His sleep, though, was disturbed by terrible dreams and memories, all muddled together so that he was never quite sure when he was awake and remembering the awful truth, or asleep and having nightmares that were equally terrifying. Mixed up in all of it was the day he lost his arm – and the aftermath.

The fight to keep him alive.

And the fact that he had been saved was a debt of gratitude he owed to one man.

When the whistle came to go over the top, it had almost been a relief, after the tension had ratcheted up minute by minute. The noise had been deafening as the British artillery opened up ahead of the advance, and the Germans responded. As he went over the top to secure a position with his machine gun, about halfway to the Boche front line, he didn't see any signs of life. But perhaps that wasn't surprising – visibility was almost nil. Choking fumes from the dust of summer-baked mud had been sent high into the sky by the exploding shells.

Then the rifle and machine gun fire had come out of nowhere. Swift had tried to respond but he was scared of hitting his own troops – dropping like flies around him. One soldier had his jaw blown right off yards from Swift but continued to advance until he, too, was mown down. Someone shouted 'Down, down!' and Swift had tried to move with his gun to a shell hole. But as he did, he heard the whistle of another shell coming, and froze that instant – instinctively. His arm reached up towards the top of the crater, but as it did there was a sudden explosive pain in his shoulder. Then he felt the terrible numbness in his arm, and made the mistake of looking at it – or what was left of it. That was the moment he blacked out.

The next thing he remembered, someone was speaking to him in soft, consoling Yorkshire tones, in what looked like a tent. There was blood everywhere. Bloody dressings everywhere. But all he could hear were these posh Yorkshire tones, trying to lull him. Then he saw it. The guillotine. He tried to yank his arm away, but it was too late. It sliced down, severing his useless, destroyed arm at his shoulder. The arm that he could still feel – until he woke up.

That young doctor, Charles McMoran Wilson – who must have been little more than thirty years old – had helped to save his life.

But for months afterwards, that wasn't how Swift had seen it. Dr Wilson had mutilated him. He blamed him for the excruciating pain he had suffered in his shoulder ever since. Only as the years passed did Swift come to view him more kindly.

Dr Wilson didn't abandon him. It was he who'd managed to recommend Swift for a new aluminium prosthetic arm – and then Swift's father who'd finally pulled the strings. The two of them together were a powerful force. Swift knew Wilson felt slightly guilty for using the guillotine on him. That was the accepted way they performed amputations then. Only later, with advances in science and medicine, did surgeons come to realise the terrible damage the guillotine did to men's nerve endings. Shoulder stumps like Swift's were left with the severed nerves exposed.

Dr Wilson – who'd become an eminent physician with a practice on Harley Street – wouldn't abandon Swift. The doctor rather regarded the 'boy', as he called him – even though Swift was little more than ten years younger – as his pet project. Several times he'd re-operated on Swift's stump, trying to cover up those nerve endings with more flesh, to ease his discomfort when wearing the prosthesis and harness.

He'd always told Swift that he could call on him, day or night, and he had never charged a fee. And not just to talk about the physical pain. Dr Wilson had received the Military Cross for his medical services on the battlefield; he'd witnessed at first hand the terrible psychological trauma of war and he knew Swift had suffered that, too. And there had been times, working for the Metropolitan Police, when Swift had made that detour to Harley Street – times when he felt he just couldn't go on.

Getting up here to Hull was supposed to be a breath of fresh air. How was he to know he'd be going from one blitzed city to another? And then this case, with the horrific mutilation of Sarah Houghton's and Archie Davis's bodies. That had brought the war memories all rushing back.

Then last night and the pig's ear – almost certainly meant to represent Blanche's ear – when he'd already been unnerved by the arrival of the lapel badge.

He couldn't get the thoughts of bodies and severed flesh out of his head.

In his dreams, Blanche became a pig; the pig needed to have one of its limbs amputated, and it was Swift having to do it, on the battlefield. Everything was mixed up, messed up.

A melange of horrific images he would rather forget.

Finally, he must have dozed off. He was woken by a harsh knocking at the front door, then the bell being pushed repeatedly.

He put on his dressing gown and slippers, barely awake, and went to open the door.

Once again, he took the precaution of engaging the safety chain first. Once he had, he opened the door the six inches or so it allowed.

There were two men in suits and hats on his doorstep. If he didn't know better, he might have mistaken them for fellow detectives.

'Detective Chief Inspector Swift?'

'Yes. Who are you? I'm not fully dressed yet.'

'Why would you be, sir? It's the weekend, and we're sorry we've disturbed you so early.' The man hitched up his suit sleeve and consulted his wristwatch. 'Although actually, it is already past nine o'clock.'

'And?'

'And we're going for a walk, and we thought you might like to accompany us.'

'And why would I do that when I don't even know who or what you are?'

'A fair point, sir.'

The man delved into his pocket and produced an ID. As he showed it to Swift, the detective noticed that while the man's photograph was on display, he'd placed his fingers in such a way that his name – and rank, if he had one – remained hidden. As did the name of the organisation he served. But the address was revealed, and that told Swift all he needed to know.

PO Box 500.

The address of the Military Intelligence Service, Section 5.

MI5.

'I'll just need to get dressed,' said Swift. 'I won't be a moment.'

17

'I notice you still haven't properly introduced yourselves,' said Swift, from his seat in the back of the pair's Humber Pullman. The car was a popular choice for the Army and RAF, and while those were usually in khaki and blue-grey respectively, this was an all-black model. Perhaps the government had bought a job lot, and some had found their way to the security services. 'You know my name, I don't know yours, and you told me we were going for a walk, but we seem to be taking a drive.'

'We are going for a walk,' said the man in the passenger seat – the one who'd partially shown Swift his ID. 'We're just going a little way out of Beverley first, so there's less chance of us being overheard. Are there any favourite walks you'd like to suggest?'

They'd turned off the main Beverley to York trunk road, and were following the Newbald Road across the Westwood.

'If you park up here on the left – there, by the seventh green. We can walk back along the fairway towards the tee.'

The driver, who so far had been the silent partner of the two, indicated with the hand signal for turning left, and pulled over onto the verge. He was obviously old school, thought

Swift, learning to drive before flipper indicators had become *de rigueur*. That, or the left-hand flipper of the Humber had become stuck, which was a common fault.

They left the car and began to walk.

'The golfers are used to walkers, cattle and all sorts, quite frankly,' said Swift. 'But it might be an idea to keep half an eye out for stray balls flying over.'

The talkative member of the pair sniffed.

'Why anyone would want to play golf in the middle of a cow field is a mystery to me.'

'The course has a very good reputation, actually,' countered Swift. 'And I'd very much like to play here – but the arm rather precludes that.'

'Ah, yes. Unfortunate. Anyway, enough golf talk. Let's get down to business, as it were. You're involved in a murder case which has come to our attention.'

'Oh yes? Why's that?'

'Don't play the innocent, Chief Inspector. You're an intelligent man – you know very well why. It is vitally important to the British government that our American allies are not embarrassed in any way.'

'I understand that. But presumably His Majesty's Government are equally keen that justice prevails, and that the American army doesn't subvert the judicial process.'

'Is there any suggestion they're doing that?'

'Well, they've arrested the friend of a victim, who they regard as a suspect, on very flimsy evidence. That makes my job very difficult. Yes, that victim was an American soldier, but he was found murdered and mutilated in the city of Hull, which is very much my jurisdiction. Not theirs.'

'Nevertheless,' the man replied, 'we can't have you causing trouble with the Americans.'

'I wasn't aware I had.'

'Let me put it another way,' said the man. 'At the moment, we're simply having a friendly chat. That's the way we'd prefer to keep it. You, more than anyone, perhaps, understand the horrors of war.' He looked pointedly at Swift's prosthetic hand. 'People are dying on the battlefields, Mr Swift. In Europe, Asia, the Middle East. That is the government's priority – winning the war. The Americans are absolutely essential for that. It took them long enough to arrive, after all. So, we're hoping this conversation will help to crystallise your thoughts.'

'There seems to be an implied threat there.'

'There is. If you don't take heed of this conversation – if we haven't managed to persuade you – then should your investigation continue to cause embarrassment to His Majesty's Government, we will take steps to remove you.'

Swift raised his eyebrows.

'Not, not like that, Chief Inspector. We're not actors in a spy film. But we will ensure you are removed from CID and placed out of harm's way. Is that clear?'

'Perfectly,' said Swift. 'And as a result, much as I'm enjoying the company on this walk, you've said what you wanted to say, so shall we turn back?'

Once they'd driven back to Swift's York Road house, the talkative one turned in his seat and stretched out his hand.

'So, we have an understanding, Mr Swift?'

Swift shook the man's hand limply.

'I wouldn't go as far as to say that, Mr . . .? Forgive me, you still haven't given me your name, and your driver friend hasn't said a word.'

'He's more of a listener and a doer than a talker, Mr Swift.' He reached into his inside pocket, pulled his wallet free, and then slid out a printed business card. Although it wasn't much of a business card. Just a name – Terrence Haughtree – and a phone number in Woodstock, Oxfordshire. 'If you need to discuss anything, don't hesitate to call me.'

'You're not based in London, then?'

'No, though don't let the number fool you. We're not holed up in some country village pub. And it's a step up from London. There we were at Wormwood Scrubs prison till it was bombed in the Blitz. Now we're housed in Blenheim Palace. Much more pleasant, I assure you.'

'I'll bid you good day, then,' said Swift, pocketing the card. 'I would say cheerio to your driver, too, but he doesn't seem the friendly sort.'

'Good day, Mr Swift. Let's hope we won't have to meet again.'

Then the man raised his eyebrows, and opened his mouth, as though he'd forgotten one of the things he wanted to say. Swift was convinced it was theatrics, rather than forgetfulness.

'Oh, one more thing before you go, Mr Swift. I'd keep your eyes peeled, if I were you. We know about your bit of trouble before you came up to Hull. You put some rather powerful noses out of joint. In fact, you seem to make a habit of it. If anything out of the ordinary happens . . . you know . . . you feel yourself being followed, anything like that, you will let us know, won't you?'

For a second, Swift considered mentioning his two recent unwanted deliveries through the letter box. And the sense that he had, indeed, been followed on more than one occasion. Then he thought better of it. In any case, he wasn't sure Haughtree was actually alerting him to a possible threat, or making it clear that he would or already had been tailed . . . by the security services themselves.

The meeting had been curious, with as much left unsaid as said. But it didn't particularly concern Swift, and he wouldn't be paying any heed to the warning, either. He found the previous day's unwanted 'gifts' much more troubling. Not so much for himself. But if he had been made a target, or was being given a warning, what about Carver and Weighton? Weighton was a family man, with young children – even if some of his family traditions were a little unorthodox. And Carver was a young woman with her whole career in front of her – bright, determined, inquisitive. All the attributes for a good detective, if police forces would actually give the fairer sex a decent crack of the whip. Perhaps the war would change everything. Women had proved they could do what was traditionally regarded as men's work: driving lorries, working the fields, even – no doubt – working for the security services, although both of Swift's recent visitors had been male. He didn't want Carver to get caught up in anything which might mean that promising career was over almost before it had begun.

For the time being, Swift knew what he wanted to do – have a leisurely breakfast. His weekend routine – and he was only getting a weekend routine at all because Holdridge had removed him from at least fifty per cent of the case – had been rudely interrupted by the two men in suits.

Swift still had some spare petrol coupons from getting reimbursed for the visit to Scarborough, but the question was what he could usefully do with them. On previous weekends off, when they weren't interrupted, and when he had enough petrol coupons available, he would go for a walk or drive in the Wolds when he wasn't exercising Blanche on the Westwood. His embarrassment of the previous evening meant he'd probably leave going back to the stables until tomorrow. Although he wasn't an avid reader of the *Hull Daily Mail*, like Weighton, he did like to pick up a copy on a Friday evening in case there were any weekend events worth attending, or even just for the cinema listings. He didn't fancy sitting in a dark cinema on his own. Down in London, he might have gone to a rugby game in the winter, or cricket now that summer was almost here. He leafed through the paper and his eyes settled on an article about Driffield Show – Driffield was a drive of less than half an hour, and at twelve miles distant, wouldn't use up too much petrol. The show was normally held in high summer, but because of the war, for some reason this year May had been chosen. He quickly made himself a corned beef sandwich and a flask of tea, and then decided to set off.

This time he did go via Leconfield, trying to see what he could as he drove past the works going on to convert it to a bomber base. The road north beyond that was mostly flat – the Wolds skirted Driffield to the west in a crescent shape from the west Hull villages, swinging out to Market Weighton, and then curving round to the north-east to form the spectacular coastal cliffs between Bridlington and Scarborough. The land to the east and south of the low-lying hills was almost unremittingly flat, coming to a point at Spurn Head, a narrow, constantly shifting spit of sand arching out into the Humber and the North Sea. It was the first line of defence for the port of Hull – with a gun battery that had existed since the Great War, though upgraded for this one.

All the time, Swift was conscious of Haughtree's warning, constantly checking his rear-view and side mirrors. At one point, a black car with two men in it seemed to be staying close to his tail for mile after mile, and he felt the hairs prickle on the back of his neck. But then it turned off – and wasn't replaced.

There was already a queue for the car park once he reached the showground – a perfect target should any German bombers choose to mount a daylight raid. But there had been far fewer raids of any sort this year – and the bombers rarely reached East Yorkshire's countryside towns and villages anyway.

Swift parked the Morris, admiring the way its maroon paint-work shone in the sun, then began to take a look around the showground.

He realised his mistake early on. This was a mainly agricultural show for farmers and those who worked in the farming industry. There was various parading of prize sheep, cattle and even pigs – although many of the pigs themselves didn't seem to want to be paraded anywhere.

He looked around the side stalls to see if there was anything of more general interest.

Behind one of the tents, in front of what looked like some traveller caravans, he could see a crowd had gathered, and there were outbreaks of boisterous cheering. Two uniformed constables were at the back of the crowd, presumably checking things didn't get out of hand. Swift tried to make his way through to see what was going on. Then he realised. It was a boxing match, and it looked to be Weighton's favourite variant of the sport – the bare-knuckle version.

'Is this actually legal?' he asked one of the constables in a low voice.

'And who are you, sir, may I ask?' the PC replied.

'Detective Chief Inspector Swift, Hull Police.'

The PC looked chastened. 'Oh, sorry, sir. I didn't realise.'

'Why would you?'

'Are you involved in some sort of undercover operation, sir?'

'No. I'm simply on a day off, having a look round the show, and I came to see what all the fuss was about. So, Constable. *Is* this actually legal?'

'Believe it or not, it is, sir. Unregulated, yes. But not against the law, so there's nothing we can do about it.'

A loud cheer went up, as one of the boxers had obviously landed a particularly critical punch, or even a knockout blow. Swift wondered if Weighton was anywhere among the spectators – presumably this would be quite a big event in the bare-knuckle boxing calendar. Swift couldn't see much through the crowd, so decided to move to try to get a better vantage point.

'Well, thanks for that,' he said to the PC. 'I suppose I ought to get somewhere where I can actually see.'

'You do that, sir. We're more interested in making sure the crowd don't get out of control than watching the action.'

Swift finally found a vantage point with an unobstructed view of the ring.

Evidently one bout had just finished, but another was just about to begin as there was a man in the centre of the ring with a loud hailer, apparently about to announce the new contestants.

'Ladies and gentlemen, give a warm Driffield welcome, please, to two literal giants of the East Riding bare-knuckle boxing world. You might have seen them at Hull Fair, you might have paid a tanner to try and take them on, and got whupped into the bargain. But here they are in the flesh. Both hailing from east Hull, on my left . . .'

A bare-chested man emerged from one part of the throng, with his back to Swift, then turned to each side of the crowd as the announcer introduced him.

'Our first giant of the ring, someone who, despite his name, you wouldn't want to meet in Toytown – it's Larry "the Lamb" Lawton.'

A huge cheer rang out for the man, who was a similar giant size to Weighton.

The mental comparison to his deputy made Swift wonder, and in the next few seconds, his thought was confirmed.

'But we don't just have one monster fighter here today, we have two. Because on my right . . .'

A second giant of a man emerged, again with his back to Swift. But from his gait, his hairstyle and build, Swift already knew who it was, even though he couldn't see the man's face yet.

'Another *big* name, and previous champion here, Jim "Little" Weighton.'

The cheer for Weighton was – if anything – even bigger than the one Lawton had received.

Now Swift was beginning to regret his decision to come here.

It was one thing hearing about Weighton's dubious boxing exploits; it was quite another seeing them in the flesh. Swift almost wondered about moving off, and leaving them to it. But a horrible fascination kept him watching as the two men prepared to square up to each other.

Weighton had insisted to him that the sport was safe – safer, in fact, than boxing with gloves. Swift found it hard to believe, but there was a certain logic to it. Weighton always claimed that the punches with bare knuckles weren't as hard as those with gloves. The term 'punch drunk' hadn't been coined for nothing, but according to Weighton, it applied mainly to regular gloved boxers. Sustaining repeated heavy blows to the head could do – and had done – permanent brain damage to many. Yes, bare-knuckle pugilists sustained cuts to the face – which Weighton was often having to cover up at work by borrowing his wife's make-up kit. But they weren't suffering concussion or broken bones. That was his argument, anyway.

As the two men prepared for the fight, Swift remembered how Weighton had described it to him.

'Imagine you're hitting a brick wall with your bare fists. You're going to punch it fairly lightly, aren't you, otherwise you cause unnecessary damage to yourself. The wall will still be all right. Now imagine putting heavy boxing gloves on. You're going to be able to punch that wall much, much harder. That's the difference. I'm not saying people don't get hurt, but I originally came from a traveller community. It's part of our tradition, that's all.'

Despite Weighton's reassuring words, Swift found himself having to look away when the fighting actually began, especially when Lawton landed a particularly un-lamb-like punch that crunched into Weighton's body, sending his deputy reeling backwards. Perhaps it was a result of what he and millions of others had been through less than a quarter of a century earlier. After the slaughter he'd witnessed, he couldn't stand seeing knuckles crash into flesh and bone in the name of sport. To him, it was barbaric – whatever Weighton claimed.

He moved back away from the ring, and took refuge in the prize vegetable tent. Somehow, watching Mr Peacock from Wetwang win a rosette for his huge marrow was more like the peace his brain craved. He still kept half an ear open for the roars from the boxing ring behind the tent.

When the biggest roar went up, and it appeared the contest was over, he decided to risk going back to the ring.

He half expected to see Weighton lying flat on his back, knocked out. He'd vowed that if that was the case, he would pull rank and prevent his deputy from boxing in the future. In fact, he was tempted to do that whatever the outcome.

But instead, it was Lawton lying prostrate. Weighton, blood-ied in the face, but otherwise seemingly undamaged, was hav-ing his arm raised in the air by the announcer, and accepting the cheers.

After a few spongefuls of cold water were wrung out over his face, Lawton groggily came round and was helped to his feet.

Weighton and Swift locked eyes.

Swift's sergeant immediately dropped his gaze guiltily, then turned away so he didn't have to see his boss's disapproving glare.

'You should have told me you were coming,' said Weighton when they met up in the boxers' tent a few minutes later.

'I wasn't intending coming to see you box, I can assure you,' said Swift.

'What's happened, then? Are we needed at Alfred Gelder Street?'

'No, not that either. I came to spend a few hours at Driffield Show, hoping to calm my nerves, and then I discover you here. Don't get too excited, though, I didn't watch you smash Lawton's face in. And all this in the name of sport? No. Sorry. It's not for me. I went to look at the prize marrows instead.'

'Each to his own, I suppose,' said Weighton.

'Anyway, I'm pleased you survived. But I'm very surprised your wife lets you do this of a weekend. Shouldn't you be taking the kids to the beach, or something like that?'

'Beaches aren't very welcoming when they're covered with barbed wire to stop the Nazi invasion.'

'They won't invade now,' said Swift. 'They missed their chance. Too tied up on the Eastern Front. If they opened another, that would be it. And Hitler knows that, I'm sure. He may be mad, but he's not a fool. Anyway, at least I've seen you fighting with my own two eyes now, rather than hearing about it. It'll have to stop, you know.'

'You can't do that, sir.'

'We'll see, shall we?'

Once Weighton had been patched up, Swift invited him for a restorative cup of tea at the tea tent.

'Wouldn't you rather have a beer, sir? I'll buy, out of my winnings.'

'No, but you have one if you must. I can't stand beer in the middle of the day – makes me go to sleep. I'll get myself a pot of tea, you get your beer, and we can meet in the tea tent. I might just check in with Alfred Gelder Street at the police box over there first, just in case.'

In the end, Weighton managed only a couple of sips of his pint of mild.

He could see Swift hadn't even bothered to get his tea, and his face fell.

'Sorry,' said Swift. 'You'd better leave that, or donate it to someone sharpish. We need to race back. Another body's been discovered.'

18

'Isn't it quicker to go by the Hull Road?' asked Weighton, when they got to Beverley and saw Swift seemed to be following directions to his own house on York Road.

'I didn't say the body had been found in Hull itself, did I, Weighton? It hasn't.'

But instead of turning right into York Road, Swift went straight on through North Bar, then took the Walkington Road out towards the Westwood. Just before it joined the Keldgate Road near the golf clubhouse, Swift parked the Morris alongside various other police and army vehicles.

'Eh?' said Weighton, confused. 'This is the East Riding force's patch, isn't it?'

'It is indeed. Strangely though, Sergeant, killers don't seem to pay any attention to police force administrative boundaries.'

They walked swiftly across the rough pasture, already grown knee-length in the spring and early-summer growing conditions, heading towards the old windmill known as Black Mill. They could see a handful of other people already there, and police tape fluttering against the Westwood skyline, punctuated as it was by concrete bollards – designed to prevent any would-be Nazi invasion glider force from landing.

'Careful where you put your feet,' said Swift, narrowly missing a cowpat himself.

When they got to the mill, Swift was unsurprised to find Holdridge there, along with Lieutenant-Colonel DeVries, Sergeant Mulder and a number of East Riding uniformed officers and detectives.

'Ah, Swift. I thought you'd be here quicker than that, given that you can't live more than a couple of miles away.'

'I don't spend all my time at home on my days off, sir. Weighton and I were enjoying the delights of Driffield Show. We got here as fast as we could.'

'Well, I've already agreed with the East Riding lads that we'll be leading the case, even though it's on their patch – given the other two murders happened in Hull, and it's clearly linked.'

'Why's it clearly linked, sir?'

'I'll show you both. Come inside the old mill. And, Weighton, what the hell's happened to your face? Has your wife been slapping you about?'

Weighton gave a false laugh. 'Something like that, sir.'

The two detectives followed Holdridge through the mill entrance.

'It's used by the pasture masters now – people from Beverley with rights to tend the common land. Mainly for storing tools and things. Anyway, the duty pasture master arrived a couple of hours ago and found this.'

Holdridge theatrically pulled back the sheet used to cover what to Swift was obviously – from its small size – just part of a corpse. He was still slightly shocked to see a severed head. Male, early to mid-twenties if he had to guess, his eyes still open and staring in shock. Swift put on his gloves, kneeled down, and gently closed the eyelids. It seemed more respectful somehow.

'I'm assuming,' he said, 'as DeVries and Mulder are here, that it's one of theirs?'

'Correct assumption. They had another private go AWOL last night, but neglected to tell us. I'm not too happy about that, you understand. They've since identified him as that soldier – Private Ulysses Delaney.'

Swift nodded. 'Presumably you're taking charge, though, sir . . . as I'm off the case.'

'I'll have none of your cheek, Swift. Obviously, given this development, you're very much on the case again.'

'What about Private Theo Howard?'

'What about him?' said Holdridge.

'Well, I presume he's been released.'

'That's something you'll have to take up with DeVries and Mulder. As you can imagine, there's a modicum of embarrass-ment.' Then Holdridge lowered his voice. 'Not as much as there should be, mind you.'

'All right, thank you, sir. Has a search been ordered of the Westwood in case the rest of the body's here somewhere?'

'Not yet, no. I'll have a word with my opposite number in the East Riding force, and see if they can spare you a uniform team and some dog handlers.'

Swift's plan for searching the 500-plus acres of the Westwood – a monumental task – was to divide the area into quadrants bounded by the various roads which criss-crossed the common land. The largest of these was approximately where they stood – with Black Mill in the centre. It was so big, Swift split the team into two, with himself heading one team and Weighton the other. Weighton's team began a sweep in a north-easterly direction, while Swift's team looked after the west and south-west. Only when they started did he realise Weighton's team had the tougher task, as most of the pasture between Black Mill and Beverley had been cultivated for the war effort.

Swift couldn't help thinking in terms of the golf course. His ambition of playing there one day – once he'd perfected his one-armed back garden practice routine – was what tended to rule his gallops on Blanche. He decided to keep reasonably close to Black Mill to begin with, covering the ground between it and the small wood that separated the sixth tee from the sixth green. Golfers played over the wood, a blind par three, with the tee high above the green, and the ground falling away sharply at the wood's edge. Swift tried to think like someone trying to hide a body – not that their killer, if it was the same person or persons, had made much of an effort to hide his victims' corpses so far. Yes, there was the opportunistic use of the bombing raids, but there hadn't been any real effort to disguise the deaths as being a result of Hitler's bombs. For one thing, bombs didn't tend to selectively remove hearts or sever sexual organs.

He felt something in his bones about the wood, though. There were various dips and hollows inside it. Old chalk pits, he seemed to remember someone telling him.

At the same time, throughout the search, part of him was feeling he should be somewhere else. Back at that Cottingham US base, making sure an innocent man – in the shape of Theophilus Howard – was set free.

It was just on the edge of the wood that the dogs stopped, and one of them began scrabbling at the ground, being pulled back fiercely by his handler. It was trying to paw at the earth and tree-bark track that encircled this area of the pasture, and was normally used to train racehorses. Swift had followed it with Blanche a couple of times, but she seemed happier when they were on proper turf.

'Is it just the racehorses he's smelling?' Swift asked the handler.

'I don't think so, sir. They're highly trained, these animals. We gave them the scent from the severed head. That's what they'll be looking for.'

And then Swift realised why this would make such an excellent place to hide a body. The ground was already disturbed – the very nature of the bark and earth mixture (or peat and bark, he wasn't sure) meant that the track looked as though it had almost been newly cut. A shallow grave could be easily covered by the mixture and no one would be any the wiser. That said, this was equally true of the cultivated area where Weighton and his team were searching.

'All right,' he said to the sergeant in charge of the East Riding uniformed team. 'Let's dig where the dog is indicating. Go carefully, though, please. We don't want to damage the body and any possible forensic evidence we might find.'

A group of half a dozen constables began shovelling away first the bark and peat covering, and then the earth below.

Suddenly there was a shout.

'Sir! Here!'

Gingerly, the constable scraped away more earth, with Swift looking on. Slowly, a hand emerged, then a shoulder, and finally the severed neck. It was clearly the body that belonged to the head.

The black soldier, Ulysses Delaney.

Swift first tried to use semaphore to attract the attention of Weighton's team, now probably some five hundred yards or more away from them towards Beverley. It was too far, and it looked as though they had their backs turned anyway.

Instead, he picked out the youngest PC and told him to run and tell the other team, as fast as he could.

When the two teams finally rendezvoused, Weighton had a discovery of his own to announce. In the cultivated area, they'd found a hastily buried axe, with what clearly looked like blood on the bit. A possible murder or mutilation weapon, which they could now check for fingerprints.

By rights, according to where the body had been found, the post-mortem should have been carried out in Beverley by the East Riding pathologist, but Swift called in a few favours to ensure that it was transferred to Hull mortuary under the care of Professor Jackson. And that it took place almost immediately – that same afternoon. Swift wasn't the professor's greatest fan, but it still made sense for the same pathologist to be in charge of the official examination of all three bodies.

Even without Jackson's help, Swift knew there were similarities with the Archibald Davis killing. Not least because, once again, the sexual organs had been sliced off the body. This time, though, the man's penis and testicles had been buried in the same grave, along with the rest of the torso. Only the head had been displaced.

The mutilation of each of the three bodies was bizarre – almost ritualistic.

They had two black soldiers and one white woman as victims. Two of them had been lovers. What was their link to the third? Or was there another body yet to find?

Professor Jackson had arranged the body like a complete jigsaw – the head and sexual parts in their correct places, give or take a few eighths of an inch.

'Do you think a multiple murderer is on the loose, Swift?' he asked. 'I was hoping, as the others were a pair, that that was the end of it.'

'It's a strange one,' said Swift.

Not just the actual killings, but the involvement of other agencies. Why had MI5 agents come all the way from Blenheim Palace in Oxfordshire to give him what amounted to little more than a friendly warning? Couldn't they have telephoned? It seemed a ludicrous waste of fuel and man-hours, given both were in short supply. And there was still the strange connection between the Conservative MP, the Labour councillor and a dockland thug.

But the strangest thing of all for Swift was the unseemly speed with which Theophilus Howard had been arrested – on the flimsiest evidence. As far as Swift was concerned, that had to be where the answer to this case lay – at the US base in Cottingham. Something was being covered up, he was sure.

'*A strange one* doesn't seem to really do things justice. So I take it you *don't* think it's a multiple murderer?'

'Not a traditional one, no. If there is such a thing. Anyway, I'm not really here to discuss my theories. I'm here to find out what you can tell *me.*'

'All right. Well, the most horrific injuries – or at least the ones that look the most horrific – both occurred post-mortem. The decapitation and the removal of the sexual organs. So you have a similarity with the other killings there, although obviously in the first murder it was the heart that was removed. And the other two didn't have their heads chopped off – *chopped* being the operative word. Some sort of axe.'

'The uniform team found a wood axe hastily buried near Black Mill on the Westwood where the head was found. So that makes sense. What about cause of death?'

'Because of the post-mortem decapitation, it's harder to tell. I'm still checking things. But I think strangulation again. So pretty much the same as your other victims.'

Swift and Weighton decided they needed some extra authority from Holdridge for what they wanted to do next. They drove from the mortuary down Beverley Road, and then turned left at its corner with Cottingham and Clough Roads, heading towards Hull University College. Holdridge lived in a large house in Newland Park. Whether he'd afforded that on his chief superintendent's salary, or whether it was the result of family money, Swift wasn't sure. It was certainly one of the wealthiest parts of Hull.

They caught Holdridge in his driveway, loading his golf clubs into his car, about to set off for a round – no doubt at somewhere swankier than Beverley Westwood – taking advantage of the extra evening light that the wartime doubling of summer time would bring.

Swift deliberately parked in such a way that the chief superintendent wouldn't be able to drive away until they did.

'What is it, Swift? I thought you had another murder to investigate?'

'We do, sir. But we need some help from you.'

'What?'

'We need the whole of the US base in Cottingham locked down. No one to come in, no one to go out. Then we need the authority to question them all. And I need your help to do that.'

'We can't do that.' Holdridge scanned his head around, as though checking none of the neighbours were witnessing the exchange. 'Oh, blast. I'm late for this bloody round of golf as it is. You'd better come in, Swift. You too, Weighton. I've only got a couple of minutes, mind.'

'Sit down,' said Holdridge, gesturing to two dining room chairs. 'What you're asking for is impossible. Certainly impossible for me to authorise.'

'But, sir,' said Weighton, 'we know that's where two of the victims are from, and the first victim was in a relationship with a soldier from there. The likelihood is the killer may be one of their troops. Even if not, it seems as though they are targets and therefore in danger.'

'I don't need the obvious facts stating to me, thank you, Sergeant. None of that makes a blind bit of difference. The over-riding issue is that the Americans are our allies. We invited them here, we're bloody glad they're here, and we can't go upsetting relations with them. In any case, even if it were possible, some-thing like that needs to come from the chief constable. Probably higher still. The Home Office, even.'

'Do you want us to approach the chief constable, sir?' asked Swift.

'No, Swift, I don't. I want you to drop the idea immediately, and that's an order. The best I can do for you is to put in a request to Colonel DeVries *asking* if you can interview his men. But there are more than a thousand of them. You need all your ducks in a row first – you can't just go barging in and asking to speak to them all. You need to present me with some evidence.'

Swift sighed.

'It's no good making faces at me, either. It's just the way it is.'

Swift got to his feet, and Weighton followed.

'I wasn't asking to interview all the men there,' said Swift. 'My concern is more to stop the killer striking again. We've had three murders – and we're no closer to solving them. How many more are you going to tolerate?'

'The answer to that, Swift, is that I'm not. You're the one tasked with finding this killer. I suggest you get on and do it.'

'What next, sir?' asked Weighton, as they drove back towards Alfred Gelder Street.

From this approach, the devastation the city had suffered in the previous year's Blitz was all too apparent – bombed and burned-out buildings hadn't yet been repaired. There were simply too many of them. Swift paused before he answered, remembering that night – little more than a year earlier – when he'd first met Weighton at the Wyke Street bombing. It had been a clear, moonlit night, but soon the sky had turned orange from the fires blazing all over the city – more than 150 at one stage. Here, on the corner of Queen's Gardens and King Edward Street, in the shadow of the Zeppelin-like barrage balloons that were supposed to protect it, Hull had briefly been left with its own version of the Leaning Tower of Pisa. The iconic Prudential Tower, the only part of the Prudential Building left standing, but tilting. They'd demolished it the next day for safety reasons. Half the shops in the city centre had been destroyed or damaged by a series of high-explosive bombs dropped on Paragon and Jameson Streets. The next day, Swift had been amazed to see that the statue to Hull's other famous son, the poet Andrew Marvell, had survived undamaged in front of the burned-out ruins of the Co-op. So many shop windows had been boarded up that the shops themselves had put up notices saying: 'Our window displays are reversed. Come and see them from the inside!'

'Sir?' prompted Weighton again, aware that Swift had disappeared into his own thoughts.

'Sorry, Weighton. Whenever I see the city centre now, my mind goes back to last year.'

Finally, he answered his sergeant's question, as they drove past their Alfred Gelder Street headquarters, with Swift failing to stop as Weighton had perhaps expected.

'I'm at a bit of a loss, to be honest. I'd hoped we might have got a little more co-operation out of Holdridge. Perhaps that was a forlorn hope. Forensics are taking a look at the axe your team found on the Westwood. If whoever decapitated Ulysses Delaney was stupid enough not to wear gloves, then we might get somewhere. Until then, perhaps we need to go back to where this all started.'

'The King Street Rooms in Cottingham? Aren't you driving the wrong way, sir?'

'Well, who was at the King Street Rooms with our first two victims?'

'Jessica Pickering?'

'Exactly.'

The Café Prestige had just shut its doors as they arrived.

Weighton shouted through the glass door at George Camilleri.

'Let us in, George, it's urgent!'

'We're closed,' the man said. 'We do Saturday breakfasts and lunch, then that's it. We've got to have some time off, Mr Weighton.'

'We're looking for Jessica Pickering, Mr Camilleri,' said Swift.

The man cupped his hand to his ear, as though he couldn't hear.

'Open the door, then!' yelled Weighton. 'Otherwise we'll break it down.'

George opened the door a crack, but clearly wasn't going to allow the two detectives inside.

'We've not seen her today,' he said.

So he did hear us after all, thought Swift.

'We didn't see her last night either, mind you. As we told you before, she's often out at Cott on a Friday night at the dances.'

'What about on Saturdays?' asked Weighton. 'Any idea where we might find her?'

'You could try the Holderness Tavern if she's indulging in a bit of the hair of the dog or working early. Or home, if she's sleeping last night off.'

'And where is "home"?' asked Swift. As the words left his mouth, he realised this was something they really ought to have established before now.

'Elsie knows – hang on.'

He locked the door again, and moved to the back of the café, shouting for his wife. After a couple of minutes, he was back.

'She lives wi' her folks in the Garden Village. Elm Avenue, near the Club House. Elsie isn't sure of the number of the house, but it's one of the semis. I guess you'll just have to try knocking on a few doors.'

'Do you know where we're going, Weighton?'

'Elm Avenue, sir? Yes, I know that. And the Club House.'

'I didn't even realise Hull had a garden village. I thought that was the sort of thing you got on the outskirts of London – the Home Counties and what not.'

'You're right up to a point, sir. I think Letchworth in Hertfordshire was the first, wasn't it? This one in Hull was built for workers in the nearby Reckitt's factory. I think actually not so long after Letchworth – certainly before the Great War. Well before I was born, anyway.'

They turned into Elm Avenue. Swift could see that *all* the houses were semi-detached here.

'The Club House is just up there on the left,' said Weighton. 'I guess we're just going to have to knock on the doors either side of it. Someone will know which is the Pickerings' house.'

'It's rather nice round here, Weighton.'

'Not quite as posh as where you are in Beverley, sir. Or where Mr Holdridge is. But it does have a sort of village green. There used to be bowling and a tennis court in the middle, surrounded by railings. But now they grow vegetables there, and the railings have been taken away and melted down.'

'Everyone has to do their bit, Weighton.'

'Of course, sir.'

They parked the car by the Club House, and then tried the house immediately to the left. Weighton knocked on the door. A middle-aged woman answered.

'We're looking for the Pickerings,' he asked. 'We believe they live in one of the houses near the Club House, is that correct?'

The woman looked at the detectives quizzically for a moment.

'And who are you?'

'We're from Hull City Police,' said Weighton, pulling out his warrant card.

'Oh, blimey. Nothing's happened to their lad, has it? He's out in North Africa with the Royal Engineers.'

'No, it's nothing like that,' said Weighton. 'We're actually looking for Jessica Pickering.'

Swift noticed the woman's face cloud over at the mention of Jessica's name – as though she wasn't particularly welcome round here.

'And she's not in trouble, if that's what you were thinking,' added Weighton.

'Aye, well, they live in one of the pair of semis the other side of the Club House – the far one.'

This time, it was Swift who rapped on the door. Again, it was a middle-aged woman who opened it.

'We're looking for Jessica Pickering,' said Swift. 'I believe she lives here with you?'

The woman looked slightly alarmed, as though she could tell they were from the police.

'That's right. She's not in any trouble, is she?'

'No, not at all, Mrs . . .'

'Pickering. Same as my daughter.'

'Can we have a word with her?' asked Swift.

'Well, you could, except she's not here at the moment. She's an adult woman. Comes and goes as she pleases. And who are you two, then?'

This time, Swift produced his warrant card.

'Detective Chief Inspector Swift, Hull City Police. This is my sergeant. You don't know where we might find her, do you, Mrs Pickering?'

The woman looked left and right up the street, as though checking no one could see.

'You'd better come inside. She didn't come back last night, and we haven't seen her. As a matter of fact, we're starting to get a bit worried.'

Mrs Pickering led the two detectives into the front parlour.

'I'll just get my husband. He's out the back doing the garden.'

Swift had a quick look round the room. There were the obligatory wedding and baby photos, and then a photograph of a young man in uniform, presumably posing just after signing up. But nothing obvious of Jessica herself as an adult.

The Pickerings returned, the husband still dressed in his gardening overalls.

'I understand you two gentlemen are looking for our Jessica?'

'That's right, Mr Pickering. Any ideas where we might find her?' asked Swift.

'I'm afraid not. She sometimes hangs around the Café Prestige and the Holderness Tavern, we're given to understand, though we wish she wouldn't. Neither of them are particularly suitable for a young lady on her own.'

'Your wife said you were a little worried she hadn't come home,' said Swift.

'Well, aye, but it's early days yet. She's a grown woman.'

'But she normally comes home each night?' asked Weighton.

'Normally,' said Mr Pickering. 'Eventually,' he added.

'Reg!' said his wife. 'She's a good girl, really. Just led astray by a few of her friends.'

'You can say that again,' said her husband.

Swift frowned. 'But do you know where she was last night? Or who she might have been meeting?'

'She'd started going dancing in Cottingham. She and her friend . . .' The words died in the woman's mouth. 'We heard about it. Awful thing.'

'But Jessica still insisted on going to the dances?' asked Weighton. 'How did you feel about that?'

'We had words,' said Jessica's father. 'Strong words.'

'A row?' asked Swift. 'Is that why she hasn't come home?'

Mrs Pickering suddenly burst into tears, and slumped down into an armchair.

'I said you were too hard on her, Reg.'

'I'm only interested in her well-being, Maud. She's putting herself in danger.'

'What exactly was said, Mr Pickering?' asked Swift.

'I said to her if she were going out seeing those soldiers in Cottingham again, not to bother coming home.'

At that, Maud Pickering's sobbing intensified.

'Why did you have to say that, Reg? She's our only daughter, whatever she's done. She'll always be welcome here. Always.'

'Do you know which soldiers she was friendly with, Mr Pickering?' Swift continued.

'Does the name Ulysses Delaney ring any bells?' added Weighton.

Reg Pickering shook his head. 'No. She never really talked about it. All I know is it were some of those black ones stationed out at Cott. You know, the ones who work at the docks.'

'And was that a particular problem for you, Mr Pickering?' asked Swift. 'That they were black?' He raised his eyebrows at the man, challenging him.

'What are you asking me questions like that for? I've not done anything wrong.'

'No, you haven't,' admitted Swift. 'And we're not here to judge, in any case. We simply want to find Jessica and ask her a few questions which may or may not help our inquiries.'

'Inquiries into what?' asked Maud Pickering.

Swift was aware that, somehow, the murders had so far managed to evade the local and national press. Even Bert Feather seemed to have lost interest in the Ron Lewis fracas at the docks. Perhaps that was par for the course in a time of war. Holdridge had been keen that there be no leaks to reporters because of the sensibilities involving the Americans. But it was one thing bodies being found in bomb sites – police would have expected to have been active there in any case. It was quite another, all the activity and searches on Beverley Westwood earlier that day. Without doubt, that would get into Monday's papers, even if it happened too late for the Sundays.

'Well, you seemed to imply just now, Mrs Pickering, that you were aware of what had happened to Jessica's friend, Sarah Houghton.'

'Yes. It was terrible.'

'So you'll understand that we are murder detectives.'

'Murder!' shrieked the woman. 'What are you talking about? You're not saying Jessica's been murdered, are you?'

'It's all right, love,' said Reg, wrapping his arm round his wife's shoulder. 'I don't think they're saying that at all.' He turned his eyes on Swift. 'Are you?' He looked accusingly at the chief inspector.

Swift realised he'd blundered. Jessica's parents had probably simply been told by their daughter that her friend was one of those whose bodies had been discovered after the Scarborough Street air raid. But not actually *how* she died.

He looked at Weighton, hoping his sergeant might rescue him. Weighton was studiously looking down at his shoes.

'No, I'm not saying that at all, Mrs Pickering. But I'm afraid to say Jessica's friend *was* murdered. That's why it's important we speak to Jessica as soon as possible.'

He wasn't going to let on that they'd already spoken to her before – at least twice – and that they'd even taken her to one of the Cottingham dances to try and get her to identify any likely suspects in the killing of her friend. Neither was he going to reveal that two black soldiers had also been murdered – one of whom was her friend's boyfriend. He'd already put his foot in it enough.

'So you're saying the last time you saw her, she indicated she was going dancing in Cottingham?'

'That's right, officer,' Maud replied. 'If you do find her, please get her to telephone, at least to tell us that she's all right.'

'We will do, of course. In the meantime, do you have a recent photograph of Jessica we could borrow? We will, of course, return it to you.'

Swift and Weighton weren't sure if there would be anyone at the King Street Rooms, but there was a chance they would already be preparing for that evening's dancing, or if not, a noticeboard outside might have the contact details for the caretaker.

They were fortunate to find the rooms were open, with cleaning and tidying up going on. The main room was a large hall with a stage, which was where the dance had taken place the other night when they'd been with Jessica.

Swift approached the woman who appeared to be in charge.

'I'm looking for the caretaker.'

'You've found her. Elsie Goodman. What do you two gentlemen want?'

Swift took out his warrant card. 'We're detectives with Hull City Police. I'm Chief Inspector Swift and this is Sergeant Weighton. We want to talk to the people involved in organising last night's dance, and also to anyone who was there.'

'Oh yes? Has there been some trouble, then?'

'Not at the dance as such,' said Swift. 'But we're making inquiries into a case – and those who were at the dance may be able to help us. We're particularly looking for a young woman from Hull by the name of Jessica Pickering, of Elm Avenue in the Garden Village.'

'She's come a long way, then. The dances must be getting popular. Well, in terms of organising, such as it is, that's me. That's to say, I sort out the letting of the place.' The woman looked round the room. 'I'm just trying to see if there's anyone here who would have been here last night. Oh aye, there's Dot. Dorothy Middleton. She looks after the cloakroom tickets on dance nights. She'd be your best bet.'

Swift and Weighton approached the young woman. She was a slight, nervous-looking thing, late teens or early twenties, Swift estimated, wearing round wire spectacles, and with her mousy-coloured hair pulled into a tight bun high on her head.

'Could we have a word, Miss Middleton?' said Swift.

'It's Mrs Middleton, actually, but certainly.' Swift realised that – close up – she was older than he'd estimated. Perhaps more late twenties, early thirties, but the way she'd pulled her hair back tightly had had the effect of smoothing out her skin. 'I can spare you a few moments. Who are you?'

'We're policemen. The name's Swift, this is Sergeant Weighton.'

'Pleased to meet you,' said the woman. 'What can I do for you?'

Swift realised that not just his assessment of her age had been erroneous. While she might look as though she wouldn't say boo to a goose, that belied an inner confidence.

'I understand you look after the cloakroom on dance nights?' asked Swift.

'That's right.'

Weighton stepped a pace towards her. 'So that means you'd see pretty much everyone who comes into the dance hall.'

'Pretty much, yes, although only if they were wanting to leave their coats. On warmer nights many wouldn't bother, especially the men if they were wearing jackets. Most of the lasses, though. Most of them would come in with coats over their dresses.'

'And do you recognise this woman?'

Swift brought out the photograph of Jessica that he'd borrowed from the Pickerings. Dot studied it for a moment, then her face widened in recognition.

'Oh, yes. I do, actually. I noticed her when she left. She'd got friendly with one of those soldiers. You know, the black ones stationed in the grounds of Thwaite Hall. She left with him.'

'Just those two on their own?' said Weighton.

'Yeah. Although there was another group went out soon after them. Other American soldiers, but white.'

Swift was ferreting in his pocket to get out another photo he'd been given by Sergeant Mulder up at Black Mill. He showed it to Dot.

'Was this the soldier?'

'Yes, that's him. Why? Nothing's happened, has it?'

'We're just making a few inquiries,' said Weighton, non-committally.

'And,' continued Swift, 'did you recognise any of the others in the group that followed them out?'

'No, I don't think so.' Dot frowned, then raised her eyebrows and a single finger at the same time. 'Ah yes, actually. It weren't just the Yank soldiers, now I remember. There were a couple of local lads, too. We shouldn't really let them in because they're underage, but sometimes we turn a blind eye and those two look older than they are, anyway.'

Swift cocked his head. 'Those two?'

'Well, I don't know both their names, actually, but one of them was Joe Barchard. He lives on South Street. Next to the nursing home.'

Swift nodded. 'Well, thank you very much, Mrs Middleton. You've been most helpful.' He tipped his hat to her, as Weighton gave a small nod. 'Good day.'

Luckily for the two detectives, Joe Barchard was at home – though his mother seemed very suspicious about why they wanted to talk to him.

'It's nothing serious, Mrs Barchard,' lied Weighton. 'Joe's not in any trouble, if that's what you're thinking.'

'It's just a little chat about something he may have seen last night.'

'Joe!' she shouted up the stairs. 'Come down at once! There's two policemen here to see you. You'd better not have been getting up to any mischief again.'

An overgrown youth slowly made his way down the stairs.

'Is there anywhere quiet we can take Joe where we won't be disturbed, Mrs Barchard?' asked Swift. 'We just want to show him a couple of photographs and see if he can help us to identify certain individuals.'

Mrs Barchard eyed the two detectives suspiciously.

'I suppose you can use the dining room.' Then she eyeballed her son. 'If you've been up to no good, there'll be trouble, mark my words.'

'I haven't done nothing, Mum. Honestly.'

'It's true, Mrs Barchard. We just think Joe can help us with a sensitive matter.'

'Now then, Joe,' opened Swift once they'd settled down with the boy at the dining room table. 'As we said, you haven't done anything wrong. We're just looking for a little help and a few answers to our questions. Now I believe you were at the dance in the King Street Rooms last night?'

'Yeah.'

'What we're particularly interested in is when you left. I understand you followed out some American soldiers.'

'Yeah. The junior officers. They're all right. They buy us b—'
He suddenly clammed up.

'It's all right,' said Weighton. 'We know you're under eighteen.
That doesn't interest us, we've already said that. So they sometimes buy you beers?'

'Yeah. The barman knows us so he won't serve us if we go up
direct.'

'So what happened when you left?' asked Swift.

'They told us to follow them. Said we might see something
interesting. Something disgusting.'

'And,' said Swift, 'I understand they in turn were following a
couple – a soldier and a young woman.'

'Yeah. The American officers were saying stuff like, "Why do
you let them negroes steal your white women? That wouldn't
ever happen where we come from. You should do something
about it."'

'They were trying to egg you on – get you angry?' asked
Weighton.

'Maybe,' said the boy. 'But that were earlier. When those
two – the white woman and the black soldier – started dancing together. Just after they'd brought us our next round of
beer. The main reason we followed them was they said we'd see
something exciting.'

'Do you know any of their names?' Weighton continued.
'Would you recognise them and be able to point them out if we
showed you some photographs?'

'I don't know names, no.' He screwed his face up. 'At least,
I don't think so, off the top of my head. I can try to remember.

But yeah, if you had photos I reckon I'd be able to recognise most of them.'

Swift leaned forwards and brought out his photos of Jessica Pickering and Ulysses Delaney, just to make sure no wires were crossed.

'Were these two the couple you were following?'

'Yeah. That's them.'

'So after you left the dance hall, where did you all go?'

'We followed that couple. They climbed into the grounds of Elm Tree House – you know, the big posh one just round the corner.'

'Between Finkle Street and South Street?' asked Weighton.

'Yeah. Well, it's got big grounds with loads of bushes and stuff. We always used to sneak in there as kids to play hide-and-seek.'

Swift cocked his head. 'So they climbed in – what, through the fence?'

'No. The hedge. There's a gap in it. Everyone knows about it, like. They all go in there after the dancing. You know, kissing and cuddling, like. Lasses and the soldiers. Especially if they're a bit beered up.'

'Did it look like these two had been drinking?' asked Weighton.

'I dunno. If he had, it didn't seem to affect his performance. He was at it like a rabbit. Gave her a right good hammering. She wasn't complaining, mind. Moaning her head off. So loud I thought the cops might come. It isn't far from the cop shop.'

Swift shrugged. 'And what were the other Americans doing – the officers, you said?'

'Yeah, well, I think they are. All the ordinary soldiers here in Cott are black, and the officers are white. Dunno why. Maybe that's how they do things over there.'

'So. Were they just watching, too?'

'Yeah. We only stayed about five minutes, mind. Me and my mate Bill Griffin. Then we skedaddled. He went back to his place in Hallgate, so just the way we came, and I came back here, but there's a short cut through to South Street. You just have to climb over the fence. It's easy to get through now because they've taken the railings away to be melted down.'

'And when you left,' said Weighton, 'the group of white Americans was still there watching the couple?'

'Yeah. That's it, really. Can I go now?'

'One more thing,' said Swift. 'I'm going to get a pen and paper from your mother. What I want you to do is draw me a map of Elm Tree House gardens, showing exactly where you climbed in and got out again, and exactly where the couple were carrying on, and where the group who were watching were positioned. Can you do that for me?'

'Well, I'm not too good at drawing. But I'm happy to try.'

'What do you think, sir?' Weighton asked once they were back in the Morris. 'Do you think he's telling the truth?'

'I don't see why not,' said Swift. 'He was honest with us about drinking beer, and that's what he seemed to be most worried about.'

'Should we have told him about the murders?'

'Why worry the lad? We just wanted information from him. It'll be dark soon. Let's take a look at this Elm Tree House garden quickly, and then detail uniform to do a thorough search tomorrow morning. Someone may have dropped a lighter, something like that. You never know.'

It was only a short drive in the Morris to the South Street entrance of Elm Tree House. Swift wondered about doing things properly and knocking on the house's front door, but there were no lights on. It didn't look as though anyone was home.

Instead, they found the gap in the hedge which Joe Barchard had used for his short cut, and squeezed through.

Dusk had fallen by now, and with the canopy of several large horse chestnut trees shadowing the gardens, Swift was forced to bring out his torch to study Barchard's hand-drawn map.

From his crude drawing, he managed to work out which were the bushes where Ulysses Delaney and Jessica Pickering had supposedly become amorous.

'Don't you think we should be careful, sir, not to disturb anything before uniform have had a chance to comb the area? If Joe's story is correct, and he and his friend disappeared after ten minutes or so, then we don't know what happened afterwards. This could even be the murder scene. If there are boot prints, things like that, we don't want to be contaminating the crime scene.'

'You're right, of course,' said Swift. 'But let's at least have a look with the torch. See if we can see any signs of anything in the bushes without going in there.'

They identified the bushes, and drew closer. Swift shone the torch inside, as none of the fast-dwindling daylight was penetrating. What they could see though, underneath the arched branches of one of the larger bushes, was a natural void – almost the shape of a small cave under the tight foliage.

'Do you think it was there?' asked Swift. 'There's certainly enough room, and you wouldn't easily be seen, from Elm Tree House or the road.'

'What was the weather like last night though, sir? Was it a clear sky?' Weighton had got his own torch out now and was consulting his pocket diary. 'Full moon isn't till next week. Last night would only have been a half-moon.'

'What's your point, Sergeant?' asked Swift, as he continued to swing his own torch left to right under the bushes.

'My point is, sir, even if it was a clear night, there's a black-out. It's almost pitch-black now and the sun hasn't even fully set. Unless there *was* a lot of moonlight last night, which there wasn't, how on earth did Joe Barchard and his mate see anything? How did the other, white, American soldiers see anything?'

'So you're saying Barchard was lying?'

'Not necessarily lying, sir. Just gilding the lily a little, the way teenagers telling stories about sex often do.'

'From the way Joe described it, with the amount of noise Miss Pickering was making you wouldn't have had to see anything to know what was going on.'

'Unless those weren't the sounds of sex, sir.'

'Hmm. I think it's possibly your imagination that's running wild, Weighton. Hang on! What's that?'

Swift's torch beam had picked out a torn piece of what looked like orange cardboard.

'My eyes aren't good enough, Weighton. Come here and take a look.'

Weighton used his own beam, too, so that there were two shafts of light trained on the piece of discarded litter.

'Is that what I think it is?' asked Swift.

Weighton got down on his knees.

'I can't see all the writing, sir. But I can see the trademark. It says Dur—'

Just then, Swift felt an almighty thump in the back, and his legs taken from under him.

'What the—?'

'Gotcha!' a voice shouted from behind him.

He tumbled to the floor, crying out in agony as his prosthetic harness dug into his shoulder.

'What the hell's going on?' shouted Weighton as he clambered back to his feet.

Swift couldn't see anything, but could feel the weight of a man on top of him.

'Gotcha. I saw you breaking the blackout with your bloody torches. I'll have you for that.'

'You will not!' shouted Weighton, pulling the man away. 'Get off him! We're detectives in the middle of a murder inquiry. And it's not even fully dark yet. The blackout hasn't started.'

Swift felt the man release him, and then Weighton helped him to his feet.

'Explain yourself!' shouted Swift.

'Well ... I ... er ... I saw you breaking the blackout with your torches. Nobody told me about any murder.'

Swift shone his torch over the man, illuminating his blue uniform, white helmet and ARP badge. Then he got his own warrant card out, and held it up for the man, illuminated by the torch.

'Ah, sorry, sir. Looks like I may have overstepped the mark.'

'Hmm,' said Swift, dusting himself down, and rearranging his harness. 'Well, I suppose you were only doing your duty, if a little overzealously. Now tell me, were you on duty here last night, and did you see anything suspicious going on here?'

'No, sir. I'm afraid last night wasn't my duty turn.'

'All right. Well, you can do something useful for us now. We need to get this area sealed off for a fingertip inspection. Can you stay here and guard it, please, while we go to Cottingham Police Station to arrange everything?'

'Of course, sir. Will do, sir. And my apologies once again.'

'Not to worry, warden. No harm done. I appreciate you were only trying to do your best. Now you stay here, and one of us or a uniform colleague will be back in a few minutes.'

The next day, Sunday, Swift took charge of the daylight search of Elm Tree House gardens. The discarded piece of orange cardboard or paper turned out to be exactly what he and Weighton had suspected – an empty condom packet. But they didn't find the used condom to go with it. In any case, if what Joe Barchard had said was correct, the hideaway had probably been used by plenty of other lovers in the past. The only other firm evidence of human activity under the bushes was that the foliage void or cave that was a lovers' corner at night, had been used in the day-time by children as a den. There was a broken toy wooden sword and a torn piece of a Jolly Roger flag – presumably this had been the children's pretend 'pirate' base. Swift had it all labelled and placed in evidence bags just in case. But he was frustrated. The forensics lab had already checked the handle of the axe used to decapitate Ulysses Delaney after death for fingerprints.

There were none.

The inquiry had another murder victim – but they were no further forwards.

All that changed early on Monday morning.

19

Dawn had barely broken when Swift got the telephone call from the Alfred Gelder Street control room. The body of a young woman had been washed up at Spurn Point, on the northern side of the mouth of the Humber.

'Had the body been mutilated?'

'*What do you mean, sir?*'

'Did the local police notice any signs that the body had been mutilated?'

'*We don't have a lot of detail, sir. But no specific mention of that. Just that the naked body of a young woman has been found on the beach near Spurn Point Military Battery. Uniform constables from the East Riding force are in attendance. DCS Holdridge told me to contact you. Shall I tell them you're on your way, sir?*'

'I am, yes,' said Swift, trying to get dressed as he talked, which was difficult with a gammy arm. 'But it's an hour and a half's drive at the best of times, and I'll have to collect my sergeant and auxiliary constable on the way.'

Carver was in digs in Marlborough Avenue, without a telephone – which was something Swift would have to get sorted – so he had to wait for her to quickly throw on some clothes. At least Weighton's home in Southcoates was pretty much en route. Even so, Swift's ninety-minute estimate turned into more like two hours.

On the way, Swift and Weighton told Carver about the developments over the weekend, and the discovery of the third body – that of Private Ulysses Delaney.

'So are you saying this is likely to be Jessica Pickering's body, sir? That's awfully sad if so – it seems so much worse when the victim is someone you know. And she'd been good enough to help us, too.'

Swift couldn't disagree. He felt a horrible weight of guilt. He could picture the faces of Reg and Maud Pickering – the anguish that their daughter was missing, the hope that it was nothing except a small family spat. Was their world about to come tumbling down? They didn't know yet, of course. But Swift had an awful feeling they would as soon as they arrived at Spurn. The length of the journey somehow made things that much worse – he could feel nausea increasingly grip his insides as they ticked off the Holderness towns and villages: first Hedon, then Thorngumbald, Keyingham, Ottringham and Patrington, with its magnificent Gothic church spire. Each village they passed was taking them nearer to what – to Swift – was inevitable. The discovery of Jessica Pickering's body – the fourth victim of this grisly series.

It didn't help that – thanks to surreptitious glances in the rear-view and wing mirrors – he could tell the two men in their black car were back on their tail. Should he alert Weighton and

Carver? Even to warn them just to be on their guard? Perhaps there was no point in worrying them. And, when he checked again a few moments later, the car was nowhere to be seen. Was it all just his imagination?

'What I don't understand, sir,' said Carver, 'is why Theo Howard is still under arrest.'

'I agree, it's concerning,' said Swift. 'But DCS Holdridge insists the matter is out of our hands.'

'But it stands to reason, sir. If we have four murders, and two of them were committed while Howard was in custody, he can't be the guilty party. Don't the Americans have to abide by English law?'

'They're a law unto themselves,' said Weighton.

'Sadly,' agreed Swift, 'that seems to be the case. But we need them for the war effort. And you're rather jumping the gun, WAPC Carver, in assuming we have four murders. At the moment, the count stands at three homicides and a dead body – and until we reach Spurn, we don't know if this is Jessica, or indeed if whoever it is has been murdered, or has drowned accidentally, or has committed suicide. Some people are so fed up of this bloody war they just can't take it anymore. Especially if a loved one has been killed.'

When they got to Spurn, the three of them had to show their warrant cards at various army checkpoints, and then again to soldiers who were guarding the beach.

On the beach itself – which looked more like a mudflat, as this was the inland or Humber side of the narrow spit of land

– there were another couple of soldiers and a handful of East Riding constables. There were also a couple of men in suits and hats, like Swift and Weighton. The Hull detectives assumed these were their East Yorkshire counterparts.

'DCI Swift?' asked one of them.

'That's right,' said Swift. 'This is Sergeant Weighton and WAPC Carver.'

The man nodded. 'I'm Detective Inspector Poskitt, this is Sergeant Verrill.'

'So what makes you think the body's one of ours?' asked Swift.

'Well, we don't necessarily. But we'd seen in the police logs about the murders in Hull, and the body on the Westwood linked to them. There was also mention that a woman had gone missing. So, woman goes missing, woman's body found. It may be linked.'

'If it's our one,' said Swift, 'then I'm sad to say I've met her. In fact, all three of us spent the evening with her the other day, when she was helping us with our inquiries into the first murder.'

'You'd be able to identify her, then, sir?' asked Poskitt.

'Unfortunately, yes. Unless the fish have already been feeding on her face.'

'No,' said Poskitt. 'The body's in pretty good condition. That's why we didn't think it had been in the water that long and could be your missing woman.'

The body had been covered with some sort of tarpaulin. Poskitt kneeled down and drew it away as far as the shoulders.

Swift heard Carver's gasp, and at the same time felt a rush of emotion himself. It was Jessica Pickering, as they had suspected.

He could feel his eyes prickling. Sometimes this job was too cruel, and here he felt a huge weight of personal responsibility. Just a couple of days earlier, they'd been talking to Jessica in person. Swift had even rejected her request for police protection. Now here she was, her life extinguished. He'd let her down, badly.

Her facial expression was one almost of surprise – but other than that, and a little bloating, the flesh looked well preserved. He noticed, too, the telltale narrow bruising round the neck of ligature strangulation.

'May I?' asked Swift, taking hold of the tarpaulin and removing it further. It seemed wrong to do so, somehow, when the dead woman was unclothed. But he had to know. He drew the tarpaulin fully away, exposing the rest of her flesh.

Jessica's body was naked, as Sarah Houghton's had been.

Once her chest was revealed, Swift was slightly taken by surprise. He would almost say pleasantly surprised, but that seemed inappropriate.

'Not the same then, sir?' said Weighton from behind him.

'No, Weighton. Not the same.'

This time there was no mutilation – her heart had stopped beating many hours before, but at least it was still where it should be. Then he thought of Davis and Delaney, and had a horrible thought.

He pulled the tarpaulin back still further.

But her genitals were intact, too, or appeared to be. Possibly some bruising, but Swift felt it indecent to look for too long. The body would be taken to the mortuary in Hull for a proper examination.

He quickly covered her again – her face, too. When the eyes were hidden, he breathed a silent sigh of relief. Lifeless they may be, but Swift didn't want them staring back at him. He felt guilty enough already that they hadn't managed to prevent this outcome.

'I take it she is your missing one, then?' asked Poskitt.

'I'm afraid so,' said Weighton.

'Who was she?' asked Verrill.

Swift almost answered that she was a part-time prostitute, but stopped himself just in time.

'She was a much-loved daughter. A young woman with everything to live for. Her name is – or rather was – Jessica Pickering. From Summergangs in Hull.'

'The Garden Village there?' asked Poskitt.

Swift nodded.

'Poor lass,' said Verrill.

Swift looked out over the beach, up the Humber back towards Hull. Visibility was quite poor, with drizzle and a light mist. But he could imagine how it all looked when it was clearer – the muddy waters of the Humber, lapping at the shore here where they'd be mixed with the salt water of the North Sea. Not many miles of river estuary – the start of the Humber wasn't far beyond New Holland, just a few miles to the west, where the Trent and Ouse met to become this great silted divide, that looked so menacing whether you were on the north bank, in Yorkshire, or the south, in Lincolnshire. Jessica Pickering's body would have been dumped somewhere upstream – in all probability, from the north bank.

Or perhaps in the River Hull itself, the waterway which divided the west and centre of the city from the eastern side. Perhaps that's where she'd met her end, before being flushed into the Humber and then washed up here by the tide, like a piece of human jetsam.

How could some people take another's life so easily, ending their hopes and dreams?

It didn't bear thinking about.

And now Swift was faced with the grim task of telling Jessica's parents.

It was still more than an hour's drive back through the flat, featureless landscape of Holderness to reach the Pickerings' house. Not for nothing was one of the areas around here called Sunk Island – low-lying land which had been reclaimed from the Humber, a little like the polders and dykes of the now Nazi-occupied Holland.

The long drive gave them more opportunities to discuss the case. And more chances for Swift to check for their 'tail'. But there was no sign they were being followed on the return journey.

'What I don't understand,' said Weighton, 'is why – if they left the dance in Cottingham together – Jessica's and Delaney's bodies were found so far apart. One buried on the Westwood – the other dumped in the Humber.'

'Or in the River Hull and then washed into the Humber,' said Swift. 'Carver, could you, perhaps, once we're back at Alfred Gelder Street, get in touch with University College? See if they've got any experts in physical geography or anything similar, who could estimate where the body could have been thrown into the water? They might be able to estimate river flows, tidal flows at this time of year. The River Hull skirts Beverley to the east, and at that point it's tidal. The body could have been washed down by the tide – the geography isn't necessarily so far apart.'

'Of course, sir,' said Carver. 'I'll get on to that as soon as we're back. Did we get any further with our two politicians?'

Swift frowned. 'Good point. With the new murders, we've rather neglected that side of things. Weighton, did you get any further with your investigations into Bethell and Smethwick?'

'I'm afraid the discovery of Delaney's body rather put paid to that, sir. I was planning to do it over the weekend.'

Carver leaned forwards from her position in the rear of the car, resting her elbows on the backs of Weighton's and Swift's seats.

'I can take that up again, sir, as well as the tidal flow query.'

'Thank you, Carver.'

Weighton turned towards Swift.

'So do we think they could have been killed under those bushes in Elm Tree House?'

'In flagrante, you mean, Weighton?'

'Exactly, sir.'

'Well, we can only go by what we found there, which was precious little. That condom packet could have been anyone's from any time – unless we manage to lift some fingerprints from it, and getting fingerprints from paper and card isn't always easy.'

'Doesn't it depend on how porous the surface is, sir? I would have thought cardboard is more porous, so it might be easier.'

'Perhaps,' said Swift. 'We'll see. But whatever, they were thin pickings from under that bush.'

They'd reached the outskirts of the eastern part of Hull by now, and Swift checked with his sergeant – who knew this part of the city better than him – where they needed to go to get to the Pickerings' house.

'Take a right here, sir, then left, then right again and you'll be on Holderness Road. Then I can point out the turning.'

Swift had half expected Mr and Mrs Pickering to be out at work – it being a Monday. But when they knocked on the door, Jessica's father answered.

As soon as he saw the three of them and their grim expressions, his face fell, and his hands began quivering.

'Can we come in, Mr Pickering?' said Swift in his most gentle, caring voice possible. 'There have been some developments.'

The man simply nodded, opened the door fully and stood back, as though he couldn't trust himself to speak.

He led them into the parlour, where his wife was sitting in an armchair, nervously wringing her hands together.

'No!' she began screaming. 'God, no! Reg, tell me this isn't happening.'

'I'm sorry, Mrs Pickering,' said Swift. 'Could we sit down?'

He didn't bother introducing Carver, but was pleased when she went to try and comfort the woman, because her husband was simply standing – as though shell-shocked – in front of the fireplace, his hands clasped tightly together in front of him. So tightly, Swift could see the whites of his knuckles.

'I'm afraid, Mr and Mrs Pickering, that the body—'

'No! Please, no,' whimpered the woman.

'That the body of a young woman matching the age and appearance of your daughter—'

Reg Pickering burst into tears now. 'Oh God, Maud. Our daughter. Our beautiful daughter. Our little baby Jessica.'

'—has been found at Spurn Point. Now, we will need one of you to formally identify her later at the mortuary, if that's possible.'

'So it might not be her?' asked Maud, in almost hysterical, misplaced hope.

'Love . . .' said her husband, in a resigned voice.

'In many cases, we couldn't swear to a victim's identity, but in this case I saw the body myself, as did Sergeant Weighton and Auxiliary Constable Carver. I'm terribly sorry, but there is no room for doubt. The identification at the mortuary will be merely a formality, but I'm afraid it has to be done. It will be awful for you both, and I am again most terribly sorry. From what I know of Jessica, she seemed a lovely girl.'

Swift wasn't lying. He knew the girl had taken a wrong turn somewhere to get involved in the goings-on at the Café Prestige as she had. But to him, she'd been a character: intelligent, one who could have flourished had the hand she'd been dealt turned out a little better.

As Maud Pickering continued to sob in Carver's arms, her husband had begun to frown through his own tears.

'You . . . you . . . you said v-v-victim?' he stammered.

Swift realised he'd erred.

'I meant nothing by that, Mr Pickering. We have no indication of cause of death.' The lie came easily. 'It could have been a tragic accident. Jessica may have slipped into the river by accident, fallen from the bank or a quayside. We just don't know. And we won't until the post-mortem is complete.'

'But you're a senior detective, aren't you? They don't send folk like you out for nothing. Someone's done her in, haven't they?'

Swift didn't answer. But his silence told the couple all they needed to know.

In the end, it was Weighton who accompanied Reg Pickering for the formal identification. Once that was out of the way, the post-mortem could begin – with Swift again managing to agree the formalities with the East Riding authorities to allow it to be carried out in Hull, by Professor Jackson.

'So what do you know about this woman, Chief Inspector?' he asked Swift, after having his assistant wheel in the body. 'By the way, ligature strangulation again – like the first. I think you already knew that.'

'Thank you, yes. I noticed the bruising on the beach. Her name is – or was – Jessica Pickering, from the Garden Village estate. She was a friend of the first victim, Sarah Houghton. And as you know, her body was recovered from the mouth of the Humber at Spurn Point. She and Sarah were both acquainted with the two other victims – or at least, Jessica knew both of the soldiers. We haven't yet established whether Sarah knew the second GI.'

Jackson frowned. 'And when you say she was a "friend" of Houghton's, do you mean she was in the same line of work?'

'Is that really relevant?' asked Swift, pointedly.

Jackson looked slightly shamefaced, which – for him – was an unusual turn of events.

'Sorry, I know my choice of words before was somewhat inappropriate. This is a nasty business, I agree. But yes, in this case it is relevant.'

'Well then, yes. She was involved – at least on a part-time basis, as with Sarah – in selling sexual favours. To what extent, I don't know.'

'All right. Thank you. The reason is that there is evidence she had had multiple sexual partners recently, and some force may have been used. See here?'

Swift breathed deeply. Always a mistake in a mortuary. The fact that Jackson was manipulating Jessica's lifeless vagina with his rubber-gloved hands didn't help.

'There's bruising – ante-mortem bruising – redness, and swelling not associated with the normal swelling you get from a body having been immersed in water. Judging by that bruising and some tearing of the tissue, it almost certainly wasn't consensual. In other words, Chief Inspector, she'd been raped – multiple times.'

In one way, the words Jackson was saying were just words, and the lifeless quality of the flesh in front of him meant it was hard for Swift to envisage what had happened to what once had been a living human. But he only had to conjure up the image of Jessica happily dancing with Kathleen Carver at the Cottingham dance hall from a few days earlier, for everything to become shockingly real and visceral.

He hunched his chin into his chest, feeling the guilt almost overwhelm him.

Then he swallowed, trying to compose himself.

'Anything else?'

'Yes. A fingernail ripped off – evidence she tried to fight back. Also some fibres under the other fingernails. She might have managed to tear someone's clothing during the rapes.'

'Ah,' said Swift, his mind fully back on the job. 'Did the fibres look military, from an army uniform or one of the other services? Particularly the US Army?'

He was still convinced that must be where the answer to this case lay – despite the difficulties of actually getting into the American base and obtaining permission to question any suspects.

Jackson shook his head. 'I'm afraid not. Black and white fibres, that's all. White shirt, black trousers possibly. Anyway, we'll extricate them all and bag them up for you. Your forensic people can then take a look.'

Back at Alfred Gelder Street, Swift again tackled Holdridge in his office.

'Is there any news on whether the Americans have released Private Theo Howard yet, sir?'

'I did try to follow it up, Swift. They said he'd already been transferred. Down to Somerset or something.'

'"Transferred" as in released and transferred to another unit, or what?'

'As you can imagine, Swift, with two of their number having been murdered, dealing with them is like walking on eggshells.

And as you can well understand, the police and the American military are not the only two agencies involved. In fact, I have information that you know that very well. You were given a friendly warning, I believe?'

'By whom?'

Holdridge banged his fist down on the table. 'If you want my co-operation, don't play the clever dick all the time. You know very well who I mean. My information is they took you on a walk on Beverley Westwood to explain the situation.'

'That is true, but I didn't make any deal with them and I equally made my feelings on the matter perfectly clear.' Swift leaned forwards in his chair, holding Holdridge's gaze. The man might be his superior in rank, but Swift had precious little respect for him. 'Now, let me spell something out to you, sir. Unless you secure permission for us to begin questioning the soldiers and officers at the Cottingham port battalion base, there is absolutely no prospect of this case being solved. That means a vicious, sadistic killer and – as we now know – rapist remains on the loose. In fact, the likelihood is that there is more than one of them, working as a pair or a gang. That threatens the people of this city, and all the surrounding towns and villages. I realise there are sensitivities when it comes to dealing with the Americans, but that cannot be allowed to ride roughshod over the upholding of the law. That is our job. To uphold the law and bring criminals to justice, and the perpetrators in this case are some of the most vile I have come across in my career.'

Holdridge had edged his chair back slightly during Swift's invective. He was fiddling with his moustache repeatedly. Then he opened his arms theatrically, and laid his palms stretched outwards on the desk.

'So what do you suggest I do?'

'I have a witness. A youth who saw the last two victims leave the dance hall in Cottingham, and actually followed them with a group of American officers.'

'Good grief, Swift. Why didn't you say this before?'

'Things have been moving rapidly, sir, and I only came by this witness last night.' Holdridge didn't need to know that Swift had been sitting on it since Saturday evening.

'All right, then. As I asked before, what do you suggest?'

'You need to obtain permission from the Americans for us to hold an identity parade. We need information from them about exactly who was at Friday night's dance, and then I will bring along my witness and get him to identify who followed Jessica Pickering and Ulysses Delaney out of the dance.'

'Is he reliable, this witness of yours?'

Swift remembered Weighton's theory about the blackout, the lack of light under the bushes, and his questioning of whether some youthful exuberance and fevered imagination had played their part in Barchard's account. Holdridge didn't need to know that.

'Yes, sir. Absolutely reliable.'

While he was waiting for Holdridge to secure clearance for his identity parade plan, Swift asked for an update from Carver. He'd already despatched Weighton to check with the Barchard family that Joe would be willing to comply should they get the go-ahead.

He and Carver were sitting in the incident room with a cup of tea – one that Swift himself had made a point of making, just to hammer it home to Carver that he didn't expect her to play the role of tea girl.

'I didn't get very far with University College, I'm afraid, sir,' she said. 'They did have an expert, but he said the currents – although fast-moving – were quite unpredictable. He said it was almost impossible to predict where a body that washed up on the estuary side of Spurn Point would have entered the river. Strangely, he might have been able to tell us something in reverse.'

'What do you mean by that?'

'Well, if we'd known where and when the body entered the water, the size and weight of the body, then he might have been able to estimate when and where it might be washed up. But not the other way round.'

'So nothing that's of help.'

'Basically, no. Sorry, sir. But I did have more luck with our two politicians.'

'Oh yes?'

Swift started to top up his tea, then realised there wasn't enough left in the pot. He ambled over to the camping stove, lifted the kettle and decanted some more hot water. Then he left it to brew for a minute or so.

'Remember when we went to the Houghtons' to tell them about Sarah's death?'

'Yes.'

'And you were remarking that it was odd her sister's children hadn't been evacuated? Then we had Jessica – God rest her soul – telling us Archie Davis had been kicking up a stink at Hull Corporation about the selfsame issue. And she implied he'd uncovered something that he thought was pretty important.'

'Something along those lines, yes, I remember. It's only a couple of days ago, after all, Carver! I might seem to be getting on a bit in your eyes, but I haven't gone gaga yet. Well, not quite.'

Carver took a sip of her tea, then topped it up from the pot.

'Well, what I managed to find out is that our esteemed councillor—'

'Audley Smethwick?'

'Exactly. Well, he's not just deputy leader of the council – he's also the man responsible for the whole evacuation and billeting programme of children from Hull.'

'Interesting.'

'Well, he was out when I called, but I started questioning his secretary gently. She didn't want to talk at first. But given it was lunchtime, I said I'd stand her lunch at the British Restaurant nearby. I got the feeling she'd open up if I managed to get her away from the corporation offices in the Guildhall.'

'And did she?'

'As a matter of fact, she jolly well did, sir. Turns out she can't stand Smethwick. I think he turned her down for a promotion or something, so she was happy to stab the knife in, as it were. She reckons there's definitely some funny business been going on between him and Ernest Bethell.'

'The Tory MP.'

'Yes,' said Carver, taking another gulp of tea. 'It turns out he's on the national committee tasked with funding the billeting and evacuation programme. Now, as well as Archie Davis's complaints, she says another black American soldier turned up the other day demanding to see Smethwick. He was saying he had evidence he was a crook and that he'd be taking that evidence to the police. He went further, too, according to Smethwick's secretary, claiming Smethwick had ordered the murder of his friend Archie Davis.'

'That doesn't make sense,' said Swift. 'Are we saying Smethwick also killed Jessica Pickering and Ulysses Delaney?'

Carver held her hands up as though she was surrendering.

'I'm not saying anything, sir. Just repeating what the secretary told me. The other interesting thing was, I showed her a photograph of Ron Lewis. She said Lewis had definitely met Smethwick in his offices within the last week. In fact, there was one meeting between the three of them – Smethwick, Bethell and Lewis.'

'So did she have any idea exactly what Davis and Howard – if we assume it *was* Howard – were accusing Smethwick of?'

'She didn't know that, sir. But it turns out it wasn't just the two American soldiers who'd been kicking up a fuss. There's been a string of complaints from mothers claiming their children have been denied school meals.'

Swift frowned. 'What's the relevance of that?'

'The relevance,' said Carver, 'is the reason *why* they were being denied school meals. And that's because the schools were telling them their children shouldn't have even been there. They were registered as having been evacuated and billeted away from Hull. And therefore the mothers must have brought their children back to Hull illegally. But all the mothers insisted that wasn't true.'

'And what did Smethwick do?'

'Well, according to his secretary, he's a powerful man. He simply pulled a few strings to ensure school meals were restored to these children, and just claimed there had been a misunderstanding.'

'Will this secretary give us a signed statement?'

'That's the trouble, sir. She's frightened of losing her job. She says she's prepared to try to help us. But she won't do anything official. Not until we can guarantee there will be no comeback against her. In other words, only if we can guarantee Smethwick's downfall.'

'Well, we can't do that. We don't have the evidence if she won't give a statement.'

'Ah, well, that might not be the case, sir. She says *she* has the evidence. She's found the files with all the figures that prove the fraud. She says it's massive – and she's prepared to hand those files to us – as long as we keep her name out of it.'

20

Weighton was all for moving in straightaway against Bethell and Smethwick, but Swift urged caution.

'First, we need to actually see this evidence that Smethwick's secretary has, and evaluate it. I'm sure what WAPC Carver has uncovered is significant, but Bethell is still a powerful man nationally, as is Smethwick locally. If we—'

There was a knock on the incident room door.

'Come!' shouted Swift.

In strode Holdridge, puffed up with self-importance. He beckoned Swift to come and talk to him out in the corridor, then lowered his voice.

'Don't say I never try to help you, Chief Inspector. I've managed to pull some strings. The Americans aren't happy about it, but you can have your identity parade. They've given us a list of the soldiers and officers who were at the dance in question in Cottingham. If, as you claim, this youth you have as a witness is reliable, then I see no reason why we can't clear this matter up. All right? Colonel DeVries and Sergeant Mulder will assist you.'

'Thank you, sir,' said Swift.

Then Holdridge frowned, and twisted the left-hand side of his ginger moustache.

'Don't mess this up, Swift. Remember, under the Allied Forces Act, the Americans have jurisdiction over the disciplining of their own soldiers.'

'That may be so, sir. But at present, that doesn't exclude our jurisdiction over *criminal* proceedings.'

'You might find that may be about to change, Swift. There are moves in Parliament. So *if* you manage to find the guilty parties, and *if* you want to get any of them in front of a British court – as opposed to an American military court martial – you'd better get a move on. Just remember, that base in Cottingham is as good as United States soil. So, treat them with respect.'

Swift went with Weighton to round up their witnesses – Joe Barchard and his friend Bill Griffin – while he delegated Carver to collect as much hard evidence as she could from Councillor Smethwick's secretary.

'Be careful, though, please, WAPC Carver. We need to make sure our case against Bethell and Smethwick is as copper-bottomed as possible. But that doesn't mean putting yourself in danger. We know for certain they're associated with Ron Lewis, who is a very nasty piece of work. There's also a possibility – given their run-ins with Archibald Davis – they may be linked somehow to the murders.'

'Don't worry, sir,' said Carver. 'Us Dales folk know how to look after ourselves.'

As he watched the slender young woman turn away, Swift admired her guts. She was intelligent, too. But she'd also shown by how she'd acquired the information about Bethell's money troubles that she didn't always do things by the book.

Sometimes, that was useful.

Sometimes, it was nothing more than foolhardy.

They'd already telephoned ahead to make arrangements with the Barchard family to pick up Joe, but his friend Bill Griffin was more of an unknown quantity. They really should have interviewed this second youth before now. But the oversight might have its advantages. So far, it was only Barchard who'd agreed to try and identify the American soldiers involved. Despite what he'd insisted to Holdridge, Swift didn't fully trust the youth. Something nagged at the back of his mind. Not least, Weighton's insistence that – in the blackout, and under the darkness of those bushes in Elm Tree House gardens – it would have been nigh on impossible for Barchard and his friend to have witnessed anything at all. What was beyond doubt, however, was that they had followed the American officers out of the King Street Rooms. The Americans had, in turn, been following Ulysses Delaney and Jessica Pickering. And both Pickering and Delaney had been murdered – the former after multiple rapes and sexual assaults. Barchard and Griffin were therefore vital witnesses, but that nagging doubt made Swift wonder if they were perhaps even more than that. Were the two youths suspects, too?

'This is the address we have for Griffin,' said Weighton, as Swift brought the Morris to a halt outside the terraced house he'd pointed to, approximately halfway between Cottingham railway station and the village centre.

Swift rang the bell, and then stepped back.

A plump, rosy-faced woman wearing a multicoloured floral headscarf opened the door, wiping her hands on her apron as she did so. She looked at the two detectives quizzically.

'Yes?' she asked.

'We're detectives with Hull Police,' said Swift. 'Is Bill at home?'

The woman's brow furrowed. 'What do you want with him? He's not in any trouble, is he?'

'Not at all, Mrs Griffin,' Swift replied. 'We have information that he may have been a witness to an incident we're investigating. We just need a quick word, if he's got a moment.'

'Well, you won't find him here, not during the daytime. He works at the baker's.' She pointed down the road. 'Just follow Hallgate, past the junction with King Street, and it's on the right-hand side. You can't miss it. He works at the back, lugging stuff around.'

Once they'd got Bill Griffin in the Morris, Swift and Weighton began to question him – both men struggling to turn in their seats, Swift due to his arm, and Weighton just because of his overall size.

'You're not in any trouble, Bill,' said Swift, noticing the youth would barely look at him. 'We simply want you to help us with something.'

'What?' the youth replied, sullenly. 'I ain't done nothing.'

Weighton shuffled as though he was trying to get comfortable as he swivelled his neck.

'The chief inspector's already explained we're not talking to you as a suspect. But you and Joe Barchard were at the dance hall in Cottingham the other night. We gather you followed some American soldiers, who were in turn following a couple – a white woman and a black American soldier.'

'So?'

Swift sighed. 'So we want to ask you a few questions about that. You were with your friend, Joe Barchard, as I understand it?'

'That's right.'

'And you and he followed the group of American soldiers into the gardens of Elm Tree House, just off Finkle Street in Cottingham. Not far from the dance hall.'

'Yeah. What of it?'

'What did you see?' asked Weighton.

'Not a lot. I only stayed there a few minutes. And it's the blackout. You can't see bugger all in the blackout, anyroad, so it were a waste of time.'

'Waste of time?' echoed Swift.

'Aye. Joe reckoned the GIs had said the couple were gonna start messing around. You know.'

'What?' asked Weighton.

'Sex stuff. In the bushes. But I couldn't see owt. And I was peggered. So I told Joe I was off home. That's all I can tell you, really. Can I go back to work now? Otherwise they'll dock me wages.'

'We won't keep you long,' said Swift. 'So given it was the blackout, Joe wouldn't have been able to see anything either?'

'I reckon not. Unless his mam's been feeding him too many carrots.'

Swift took a long, slow breath. 'All right. Cast your mind back to when you left the dance hall itself. Would you recognise any of the American soldiers you were following? They were officers, I believe.'

'Well, they were white. And the white ones are the officers. The black ones are the ordinary soldiers. If you showed me photos, I might be able to pick them out, like.'

Swift pulled two photographs from his inside pocket.

'Was this the black soldier?' he asked, showing Griffin a photograph of Ulysses Delaney.

'Looks like him, aye. I can't be a hundred per cent, like.'

Swift produced the other photograph – of Jessica.

'And this was the woman he was with?'

'Yep. That's her, all right. Why are you so interested in them two, anyroad?'

'We're just looking into something,' said Weighton. 'Now we also want to try to identify the officers who you followed out of the dance hall.'

'Oh aye? Have you photos of them, too, then?'

'I'm afraid not,' said Swift. 'We'd like you to come and identify them at the American base.'

The youth looked alarmed. 'What, like stand in front of them and pick them out? They'll have my guts for garters if I do that.'

'Don't worry,' said Swift. 'We're arranging it in such a way that you'll be able to see them, but they won't be able to see you. You'll be behind a curtain with peepholes.'

'Well, I don't know about that. I told you. I need to get back to work. Can't afford to have me wages docked, like.'

'So are you refusing to help the police with their inquiries?' asked Weighton, with a hint of menace.

'Er . . . no, officer. I didn't say that, did I? Of course I'll help you.'

As soon as Swift and Weighton picked up Barchard, Swift started to realise something was wrong. Barchard seemed particularly cowed and – while he didn't talk as such to his friend – Swift thought he saw him communicating with the other youth with hand signals.

Once they were in the US base, waiting in a room with their two witnesses, Swift leaned over and whispered in Weighton's ear, having to lift himself up in his seat slightly, even though Weighton had bent his head down towards his superior's mouth.

'I don't like the feeling I'm getting here,' he said. 'Barchard seemed to be giving Griffin signals with his fingers of some sort.'

Weighton shrugged, and cupped his mouth over Swift's ear.

'He was sitting directly behind me, I'm afraid, sir. I didn't see anything. You might have misread things. They may simply be nervous.'

The door opened and DeVries and Mulder entered, then asked Swift and Weighton to come outside into the corridor.

'We've done what you asked, Chief Inspector,' said DeVries. 'We've attempted to identify everyone who was at the dance night in question, but it means there are some twenty individuals.'

'So many?' queried Swift.

'The dances are popular, with officers and men. We've used a large tarpaulin to divide the room where the identity parade will take place. At strategic points there are eyeholes, so your witnesses will easily be able to see the officers concerned, without being seen themselves. That should allow them to identify any suspects without fear of reprisal. Each of the officers will be wearing a numbered bib for identification purposes.'

'And you haven't included any officers or men who weren't at the dances?' asked Weighton.

'Your Chief Superintendent Holdridge explained what he and you wanted. As I understand it, this isn't a line-up which is going to be used evidentially.'

'Correct,' replied Swift. 'Our witnesses didn't actually see any crime or crimes committed. It's simply a case of identifying those in the group that left just after Jessica Pickering and Ulysses Delaney. We want to pinpoint those men, and then question them about what they saw.'

DeVries nodded. 'That's understood. Sergeant Mulder here will be helping to make sure it all passes off smoothly.'

Swift was somewhat mollified when DeVries's promises were borne out. From the lieutenant-colonel's description, he'd expected some kind of Heath Robinson affair – but in fact, the tarpaulin screen served its purpose. Without looking through the eyeholes, it was impossible to see the soldiers on the other side, and vice versa. Swift made sure by checking both sides of the screen.

Mulder armed both youths with pads and pencils. The idea was that they should note down the bib numbers of those whom they could positively identify as having followed Jessica Pickering and Ulysses Delaney out of the dance hall.

First to make his way down the line was Griffin. He wouldn't meet Swift's eyes before he started, and the suspicion again grew in Swift's mind that they were wasting their time with this.

When he got to the end of the screen, having looked through all the peepholes, he passed his marked pad to Swift.

Immediately, the detective knew he'd been right to be apprehensive. There were twenty-two serving men behind the screen, all of them white. Griffin had noted down ten of them – but the pattern with which he'd done so was immediately suspicious. Every other officer on parade bar one, in a strict sequence. All the noted numbers were odd – 1, 3, 5, and so on – right up to the last number noted down – 19. The only odd number not chosen was 21.

After handing in his paper, he shuffled off to the corner of the room, and again wouldn't look Swift in the eye.

Next up, it was Barchard.

Again, at the end of the line, he handed his pad to Swift, but unlike his friend, he stared the detective chief inspector down – as though he was silently challenging Swift to contradict him. Then he joined his friend in the corner, with a little smirk on his face.

Swift almost didn't need to look at the pad to know what would be there, but he did anyway. Again, a perfect sequence of numbers – 2, 4, 6, and so on – with the last number being twenty.

Griffin had 'identified' all those – bar one – with odd-numbered bibs.

Barchard's selection were all of the even-numbered bib wearers.

Only the officers wearing the numbers 21 and 22 had failed to be picked out by either of the youths.

Without saying anything for a moment, Swift showed the pads to Weighton. It took a moment or two for his sergeant to grasp the meaning of the almost perfect mismatch between them. Then he looked up at the two youths and glowered.

'You two!' shouted Swift. 'Come with us.'

As he did so, he could hear sniggering break out from behind the tarpaulin curtain. He thought he saw a smirk on DeVries's face, too, until the American commander quickly disguised it.

Swift and Weighton took the two youths back into the original room where they had waited for the identity parade to be readied.

Swift indicated to the two to sit down at one side of a long oak dining table, while he and Weighton installed themselves on the opposite side.

Then he turned the two pads round so Griffin and Barchard could see each other's 'work'.

'What the hell is the meaning of this?' he thundered.

Griffin looked shamefaced, but Joe Barchard shrugged.

'Perhaps we didn't get as good a look at them as we thought.'

Weighton leaned over the table, putting his own face right up to the youth's.

'If you've been leading us on a wild goose chase, Barchard, we'll throw the book at you, mark my words. Every step you take in this village will be watched. Any little thing you do wrong, we'll come down on you like a ton of bricks, I can assure you. This is a murder inquiry we're conducting, not some schoolboy playground game.'

Despite Weighton's invective, during which spit almost flew into Barchard's face, the youth's expression was challenging, almost mocking. The two youths had obviously concocted some sort of plan. And before that, they'd probably been leaned on by the American officers.

'We said we'd try to help you, and that's what we did,' said Barchard. 'It's not our fault if we didn't identify the same ones as each other. Can we go now?'

'All in good time,' said Swift.

'Will you give me a lift back to work?' asked Griffin.

'No,' replied Weighton, 'we bloody well won't. Perhaps your American friends could sort something out for you. After all, one good turn, eh?'

Swift and Weighton left the two youths to stew in the room, and then went to try to find DeVries and Mulder again.

The two American officers were overseeing the taking down of the tarpaulin partition in the room they'd used for the abortive identity parade.

'Ah, Chief Inspector,' said DeVries. 'Not the outcome you were hoping for, then?'

Swift was determined to try to stay polite.

'Not exactly, Colonel DeVries. But no matter. We'll simply have to interview all twenty or so that you and Sergeant Mulder identified as having been at the dance. Could you arrange that for us immediately, please?'

'It's not as easy as that, I'm afraid, Chief Inspector. As you're no doubt aware, the United States Army is pushing for sole jurisdiction over alleged offences involving its troops on British soil. The issue could be decided by your parliament within a matter of weeks. In those circumstances, any request such as that has to be referred up the chain of command. I'm sorry, but I don't have the authority to compel the officers to talk to you. I will ask, however. But I don't think you can expect the answer today. These things take time, especially when they're so sensitive.'

As Mulder smirked on the sidelines, Weighton intervened, moving to stand threateningly in front of the American commanding officer.

'Don't you believe in upholding the rule of law, then, Colonel DeVries?'

Swift tugged at his arm. 'That's quite enough, Weighton.' Then he held DeVries's gaze. 'I fully understand your position, Colonel DeVries.'

'Thank you, Chief Inspector. It's unfortunate. But there it is.'

'May I use your telephone to speak to my own superior about this matter?' asked Swift.

'Of course, be my guest. Sergeant Mulder, could you please show the chief inspector my room? He can use the telephone in there.'

When Swift asked to be put through to DCI Holdridge by Hull Police control room, he was given a message which meant that – even if DeVries had relented and given them permission – any interviews with the US officers would have to wait.

WAPC Kathleen Carver hadn't checked in with control at the time she'd been supposed to.

What's more, a report had been made about a female in a Women's Auxiliary Police Corps uniform being bundled into a car, apparently against her will, near Ron Lewis's hangout opposite East Park – the Crown Inn. Swift immediately thought of Haughtree's warning, the fascist lapel badge and the severed animal ear. He'd thought he was the one being watched, and possibly targeted. Instead, they'd struck against Carver. And he hadn't even warned her. He would never forgive himself if she came to any harm.

21

Thankfully, the witness to Carver's apparent abduction had noted down the registration of the vehicle – a blue-black Singer Bantam. When they did a check on the number plate – CRH 425 – with Hull Corporation, Swift was unsurprised when the clerk told him it was registered to a certain Ronald Arthur Lewis of Morrill Street, Hull. Perhaps he was simply doing Bethell and Smethwick's dirty work again. But this time, by apparently abducting a member of the WAPC, he'd gone too far.

Holdridge came on the line, and sounded furious.

'*There's been a sighting of the car by a police patrol at the White Cross, where the Hull to Bridlington and Beverley to Bridlington roads meet. It was heading north, towards Brid. Get yourselves to Beverley Police Station as soon as possible – it'll be quicker than coming back here. The East Riding Constabulary have agreed to lend us a fast Wolseley patrol car – and a driver who actually knows how to use it. You'd better make sure she gets back to Hull safe and sound, Swift. Why the hell did you allow an auxiliary to conduct an inquiry on her own? Good God, man, it beggars belief. Make sure you sort out your own mess. And as soon as you've found her, report to me immediately. You understand, Swift?'*

It clearly wasn't the time for Swift to try to fight his corner. In any case, for once, Holdridge was absolutely right. Swift had put Carver in danger – he just hoped he didn't live to regret it.

'Yes, sir. We're on our way.'

The Wolseley, a 14/56 model, was fast indeed. Swift, in the front, and Weighton, cramped in the rear, found themselves having to cling on to the handholds as the driver regularly nudged seventy miles per hour. They seemed to be spending almost as much time on the right-hand side of the road as the left. Traffic was thin because of petrol rationing, but there were regular overtaking manoeuvres of farm and military vehicles.

Although it was a radio-equipped patrol car, they found they couldn't get a signal out in the countryside, and so stopped briefly at a police box in Brandesburton.

Swift got an update from the East Riding force's control room in Beverley.

'They've just been spotted on the outskirts of Brid. One of our patrols tried to cut them off, but they swerved round him. You're twenty minutes or so behind them. They looked to be heading towards Flamborough. Ron Lewis keeps an old fishing boat there. At North Landing. Perhaps try heading there. A radio car from Brid is giving—'

Swift didn't wait for any more. He leaped back into the Wolseley, and the driver, who'd kept the engine running, roared off along the A165 towards Bridlington.

Within twenty minutes, they'd reached the outskirts of the coastal town, skirted the centre, and were ignoring the thirty-mile-per-hour speed limit, racing along the mostly straight Marton Road.

Swift clung on to the passenger door grab handle for dear life, watching the speedometer on the Wolseley being pushed to its maximum.

They had to slow down through Flamborough village itself, but then Swift instructed the driver to get to North Landing as quickly as he could.

It was another dead straight road, and the driver took Swift at his word, throwing him back against his seat with the force of acceleration. Although straight, taking the road's switchback of humps and dips at speed made Swift feel nauseous. As they reached the end, and the driver slammed on the brakes, Swift could see at least two East Riding patrol cars waiting, with uniformed constables being directed by plain-clothes officers.

Swift and Weighton got out as quickly as they could. Swift prepared to introduce himself and his sergeant, then realised the detectives were the same two officers who had been at Spurn Head – DCI Poskitt and DS Verrill. The East Riding force was a relatively small one – perhaps it wasn't a surprise – although the two locales where Swift had now encountered the pair stretched almost the entire length of the East Yorkshire coastline. Some fifty miles in total. A few miles to the north-west, at the end of Filey Bay, it would be North Yorkshire's patch.

'It looks like Lewis's boat has been taken out,' said Poskitt. 'There are recent drag marks on the sand and shingle.'

'Do we know where to?' asked Swift. 'And any sign of WAPC Carver?'

'Four sets of footprints in the sand, sir,' said Verrill. 'And one set was much smaller than the others. If I had to lay money on it, I'd say they were from a woman's shoes or boots. Trouble is, the sand is very coarse here. Come along, I'll show you.'

'Also,' added Poskitt, 'we've commandeered a boat from one of the fishermen here. He's going to take us out in it. We'd heard you were just a few minutes behind us, so we thought we'd wait till you arrived, given the kidnapped officer – if she has indeed been kidnapped – is one of yours.'

Swift nodded his thanks.

'So no one's actually sighted Lewis's boat from the land, sir?' asked Weighton.

'No, Sergeant,' replied Poskitt. 'But it's not surprising, really. Steep cliffs, as I'm sure you know. Flamborough Head's a favourite suicide spot, I'm afraid. Not only that, it's made of chalk, which the North Sea erodes fairly easily. So the cliffs are riddled with sea caves – many of them big enough to hide a boat in. They could be anywhere.'

The climb down to the beach was a steep one. The uniformed police had already prepared the way, placing what looked like scaffolding boards over flattened sections of the barbed wire barricades. Though Swift couldn't imagine the Nazis would choose this narrow bay and its surrounding cliffs as the site for an invasion. The south coast, with its proximity to France, was a much more likely site. Or even the almost endless stretch of beach between Bridlington and Spurn. In any case, since the previous year, the threat of invasion had faded. Unfortunately, the prospects of a swift end to the war with the entrance of the Americans didn't seem that likely, either. There was no doubt their arrival had been a huge fillip to the beleaguered British – but the news from North Africa and the Far East was not good.

Once they reached the beach, Swift could see preparations to launch the boat they were borrowing were well underway, with the police helping the local fisherman. It seemed a labour-intensive task, with the large coble being half pushed, half pulled down the slope of the beach, with wooden beams placed in front of it over the sand and shingle to prevent the vessel getting stuck halfway down.

'Not the easiest of boats to launch,' said Poskitt.

'How would they have done it with just the four of them?' asked Swift.

He breathed in the sea air and its pungent mix of the tang of salt and stench of rotting bladderwrack. Weighton was amusing himself by popping the seaweed's air bladders under his size twelve boots as they waited for the boat to be readied.

'Lewis's is much smaller,' said Verrill. 'This one's a proper fishing coble. His is little more than a rowing boat. In fact, I wouldn't fancy going out in it at all. The cross-currents and tides here are treacherous.'

The warning didn't do much to help Swift's overwhelming feeling of guilt at having allowed Carver to be put in danger in the first place.

'It's a good thing it's calm today, then,' he said.

'Aye, there is that,' said Poskitt.

Weighton was frowning as he watched the police constables and fishermen pushing with their backs against the rear of the boat, trying to get it sufficiently into the water to float.

'Doesn't it damage the propeller? I assume it has got a propeller?'

'Oh aye, Sergeant,' said Poskitt. 'They're designed like that. The propeller's in a recess under the boat, a sort of bubble, if you like, formed by the boards of the vessel. That way they can sit flat on the beach, and be dragged down to the sea, as you saw. I'm afraid you're both going to get your feet wet climbing in.'

Weighton managed to haul himself in unaided, but had to help Swift by pulling him up by his good arm.

'What's the plan?' Swift asked Poskitt.

'I thought we could try some of the larger caves first – the ones that are big enough to get a boat into. Mind you, theirs is smaller, so they'll be able to hide more easily. If they are hiding. I'm not sure what they're up to. Is it linked in any way to these murders of yours, Chief Inspector?'

'There does seem to be a link, yes,' said Swift. 'One of the victims had uncovered what he thought was some sort of fraud at the council. My auxiliary policewoman, Kathleen Carver, had uncovered more evidence of that fraud.'

Poskitt frowned. 'You let the auxiliaries actually investigate, then? At Beverley, they're only allowed to help with administrative tasks.'

'That may be true,' said Swift, 'but don't you have a fully-fledged WPC in CID? Which is more than can be said for us in

Hull. Anyway, she's a bright girl. Tough, too. My decision, I'm afraid. I just hope she's all right.'

He looked warily out to the grey expanse of the North Sea, as the fisherman fired up the boat's engine.

There was a series of caves in the cliff face to the north-west, and that's where Poskitt directed the boat.

'Let's try this side first,' he said. 'The fisherman agrees. The caves are bigger this way.'

Swift shielded his eyes with his prosthetic hand, scanning the horizon. There was nothing to be seen. Fishing – even close to the shore like this – was not exactly encouraged during the war, though not banned outright. In the bigger fishing ports, such as Hull and Grimsby, the trade had been decimated because it was just too dangerous for deepwater vessels to put to sea – a U-boat could blow them to smithereens in seconds.

The fisherman cut the engine as they edged into the first of the caves that was big enough to take a boat.

'I can't take her much further in,' he said.

Poskitt had brought a police megaphone with him.

'Do you want to try with this?' he asked Swift.

Swift brought the narrow end to his mouth with his good hand.

'This is the police!' he shouted. 'WAPC Carver, are you here?'

The only response was the sound of his own shouts echoing round the cave. That, and the gentle slapping of the seawater against the rock face.

Swift shrugged at the fisherman, who restarted the engine and backed out.

'How many caves are there?' he asked Poskitt.

'God knows. Lots. But we can only get in the bigger ones, so let's just concentrate on those.'

Weighton looked dubiously over the side of the boat.

'What state's the tide?'

'We're about midway between high and low tide,' said Poskitt. 'At the lowest tide you wouldn't be able to get a boat in some of these.'

'How much more to rise?' asked Swift.

Poskitt referred the question on to the fisherman at the helm.

'A good six, seven foot at least,' he said.

More than enough to drown a man – or a woman.

They'd had to duck entering the last cave. Another seven feet of water in there, and the water would have virtually reached the roof.

If Carver was being held in one of these caves against her will, her time was running out.

The next few caves were smaller – too small for the coble. The fisherman was now steering them round the headland towards Thornwick Bay.

Then they spotted Lewis's boat, coming out of the cliff on the far side of the cove.

'There he is!' shouted Poskitt.

'That's Smuggler's Cave, that one – one of the biggest. It goes more than two hundred foot under the cliffs.'

'I don't see Carver, sir,' said Weighton.

Swift screwed his eyes up, squinting to try to see better.

'That's just Lewis on his own, isn't it?'

'I think so.'

'What do you want to do?' asked Poskitt. 'Give chase to him, or see if he's dropped Carver off in the cave?'

It was an agonising choice.

'How long till high tide?' asked Swift.

'Three or four hours or so, and it's a big one today.'

'Will it submerge the cave totally?'

Poskitt shouted the same question to the fisherman.

'No, mebbe not. But I wouldn't want to be stuck on a ledge in there, worried I was about to be washed off. Can this lass swim?'

Swift had no idea. He looked at Weighton, who shrugged.

'Sorry, sir. I just don't know. But Carver's a tough one. Surely we can't let Lewis get away?'

Swift came to a decision. It was no choice, really.

'Get him to take us into the cave!' he yelled at Poskitt. 'We'll have to deal with Lewis later. Anyway, it's Smethwick and Bethell we really want. Where the hell are they?'

Swift was struggling to understand what was going on. Presumably Carver had somehow challenged Smethwick and Bethell – perhaps they had realised the game was up. But why Flamborough? Unless they'd been planning to flee the country? But it was a long way, through treacherous U-boat-infested waters, to neutral Sweden. And they were on the wrong side of the country for getting to Ireland.

As they entered the cave, Swift immediately yelled through the megaphone to try to attract Carver's attention. To let her know they were coming to her aid. But again, he received no reply.

Poskitt had pulled a torch from his pocket and used it now like a searchlight, scanning it left and right in a slow arc, highlighting the damp, glistening cave interior. The beam settled on a shape on a ledge that looked like a huddled figure, but as they edged closer they realised it was just a small boulder, thrown up there, no doubt, in a winter storm.

Swift tried shouting again. 'Carver! It's DCI Swift here! Are you all right?'

This time, as well as the echo of his own voice, Swift thought he heard something else. He put his index finger to his mouth, urging the others to be silent. The fisherman navigating the boat had, in any case, cut the engine, and was advancing slowly by using a wooden oar like a punt.

'There!' shouted Weighton.

Poskitt's torch settled again. This time on a shape in the water. At first, he thought it was just a seal or other sea animal flapping around. Then he realised. It was some sort of tarpaulin, with something underneath. But the water was rising fast, threatening to submerge it.

The fisherman quickly manoeuvred alongside, and Weighton went over the side of the boat. At first, Swift didn't understand why his deputy hadn't sunk into the water. Then he realised he was standing on some sort of submerged ledge – and the bundle was balanced on it, too.

But before Weighton could reach it, the tarpaulin was suddenly thrown aside, and Carver emerged like a butterfly from its chrysalis, staggering to her feet, hands still tied together and mouth taped shut.

Weighton quickly held her to make sure she didn't fall from the ledge, then cut her wrist ties with a pocket knife, and gingerly removed the mouth tape.

'You're all right now, Kathleen,' he said as he held her.

Carver started gasping for air, as though she was hyperventilating. Swift could see her whole body shaking under the beam of Poskitt's light. Either from the cold, and her unwanted bath, or from sheer terror.

'They ... they ...' Carver was taking in huge gulps of air, trying to get her words out but failing. After a couple of moments, she managed to pull herself together. 'They've only just left. There was an argument with Lewis. Something about money. Then Smethwick and Bethell started arguing, too. Something's gone wrong with their plan – I think they were planning some sort of rendezvous with a ship in Filey Bay.'

'But there was only Lewis in the boat,' said Weighton.

'That we saw,' pointed out Swift. 'The other two could have been lying in the bottom of his boat to keep out of sight.'

'No! He took off without them after the argument,' said Carver. 'I couldn't see, but I heard them talking about a chimney or something. I think it was the Devil's Chimney. And it sounded from the echoes of their voices as though they were going further into the cave, rather than towards the entrance.'

'That doesn't make sense,' said Swift.

The fisherman suddenly interjected, 'Aye, it does, sir. The lass has it correct. There's another smaller cave system, and that's what it's called, right enough – the Devil's Chimney. They say smugglers used to use it to get down here, even at high tide. It goes right up through a fissure in the chalk. Hundred feet or more tall, it is. Comes out right at the top of High Holme – the headland above us. But there's said to be a chamber about half-way up. They could be hiding out in that. I'll see if I can remember where the entrance is.'

Once Weighton had gingerly helped Carver into the coble, and had levered himself back in, too, the fisherman began to punt with his oar more frantically, taking them further into the cave system.

'Are you all right, Kathleen?' he asked.

'I'm fine, sir. But soaked. I'd managed to free my leg ties and get to my feet just as you arrived. I was starting to panic, though, I'll admit. The water's rising.'

Swift had already noticed. He hoped the fisherman wasn't going to get them stuck. Carver was probably suffering from the equivalent of shell shock at least – if not hypothermia as well. Really, they ought to be turning around and getting her to hospital for a check-up as a priority, despite her insistence that she was fine.

Poskitt's torch now highlighted a darker area, high in the cave.

'There she is,' said the fisherman. 'The Devil's Chimney. I don't know how safe it is. It hasn't really been used regularly for hundreds of years, but the locals know about it. They say there are parts where you have to crawl down on all fours. It's a good thing it's nearly summer and fairly dry. There's been lads tried to do it in the winter who've drowned when it gets filled with rainwater.'

From the description, Swift knew that with his arm he might have difficulty getting through. But Carver looked in a bad way. And Weighton was obviously too big.

'Verrill and I can go, if you like, Chief Inspector.'

Swift knew he would be having to confront his terror of confined spaces – a hangover from the trenches. But he didn't want the East Riding force to wrest control of this investigation from him.

'No, I'm going. Though if you or Verrill, or one of your uniformed officers, was able to accompany me, I'd be grateful.'

'I'm not sure that's a good idea, sir,' said the fisherman. 'What with your arm, and all that.'

Swift ignored him, and gestured to Weighton to help him out of the boat.

'Shouldn't I come with you, sir?'

'No, Weighton. If it's narrow, you're going to get stuck. In any case, I want you to get Carver to hospital as soon as possible. You can do more good staying with her.'

'I don't need to go to hospital, sir,' said Carver. 'I'm feeling much better now.'

'You do, WAPC Carver,' insisted Swift. 'And that's an order.'

In the end, Poskitt decided to go with his Hull colleague. It meant the two oldest men would be struggling through the cave system, although Poskitt also selected an agile and younger uniformed officer to accompany them. The remaining members of the party were instructed to return to the police vehicles at

North Landing as soon as possible, and get Carver looked at in the nearest hospital in Bridlington.

Poskitt went first, with Swift in the middle, and the younger uniformed PC taking up the rear.

As soon as he was inside the confined darkness, the memories and images crowded in on Swift. Shuffling on his stomach through the mud, under shell and mortar fire, not knowing whether the debris raining down, and its dampness on his face, was wet earth, wet shit from the horses, or wet body tissue – the torn-asunder flesh of colleagues and comrades. Here, it was drips of water from the sides of the narrow rock fissure, but Swift had to keep reminding himself of that. He tried to keep his eyes focused on Poskitt's torch beam ahead. Was it his imagination, or was it weakening? Squeezing through the narrow gaps in the rock wasn't doing his prosthetic arm much good, either, and where the harness joined it to his shoulder, the throbbing was more intense than ever.

'Are you sure we're going the right way?' he asked Poskitt.

'There is only one way. In winter, it must be some sort of underground stream.' Then Poskitt swore under his breath. 'Pardon my French. We're just coming to the narrow bit the boatman mentioned. You'll need to get down on all fours.'

As they'd already had to crouch and shuffle along some bits of the way, Swift's heart was not filled with joy. He tried to control his breathing, tried not to let the mounting sense of panic take over his brain.

'Ready?' asked Poskitt.

'As ready as I'll ever be.' He turned to the constable behind him. 'What about you, Armitage?'

'I'm fine, sir. Bit knackered, but the quicker we do this, the quicker we'll be out in the fresh air again.'

Poskitt had already gone on ahead.

Swift again just tried to follow the light, and attempted to ignore the pain in his shoulder, or the thought that – at any moment – he could get stuck, with only one good arm with which to try to wrench himself free.

Thankfully, the confined space was short-lived, and immediately afterwards they were in a larger chamber. Swift was about to say something when – in the torchlight – he saw Poskitt hold his left-hand index finger to his mouth, while cupping his right ear with his other hand. When Armitage emerged from the tunnel, Poskitt repeated the gesture in an even more exaggerated way.

Swift wanted to breathe in deeply, and stretch his body. Instead, he tried to still everything and listen.

Then he heard it.

Distantly, indistinctly, echoing down from the next part of the tunnel, the sound of voices. Arguing. He tried to make out what they were saying, but couldn't.

Poskitt leaned over to whisper in his ear.

'Sounds like we're gaining on them, though I can't imagine there's much further to go. Have you got a truncheon with you, or any other sort of weapon?'

In the ghostly light of Poskitt's fading torch, Swift nodded. He didn't elucidate what exactly his weapon was, but – partly as a Pavlovian response – he felt for the outline of his Belgian-made

Baby Browning in his pocket. The gun was highly illegal – he wasn't about to pull it out and wave it in front of the East Riding detective.

They set off again in the same order, squeezing themselves into the next narrow passageway, climbing all the time up through the mass of chalk that made up these giant cliffs. Chalk that was gradually being eroded and turned into a honeycomb by the seawater below and the rainwater above. In parts, though, this small tunnel or fissure felt too regular – as though the work initially done by nature had at some stage been given a helping hand by man.

Every now and again they caught the occasional snatch of shouting. If it was indeed Smethwick and Bethell, they didn't appear to have made up their differences.

Finally, the dank air of the small cave changed perceptibly, and Swift realised that instead of following the light of Poskitt's torch, his eyes were trained on a growing patch of natural light. They were nearly out.

Swift had to shield his eyes from the light as he finally squeezed above ground. The entrance here was well disguised, overgrown with long grasses. As he became accustomed to the glare, he realised Bethell and Smethwick's shouting match still hadn't calmed. They were standing over by the cliff edge, grappling with each other, too consumed by their own private anger to notice the police officers stealthily approaching from behind.

They turned in shock as Swift shouted out.

'Ernest Bethell! Audley Smethwick! Don't move. You're under arrest for the abduction of a serving police officer and for suspected fraud and embezzlement. Put your hands above your heads. Slowly.'

Smethwick moved to obey, raising his arms and clasping his hands behind his head as instructed.

But Bethell turned, and began to run.

Towards the cliff edge.

Swift pulled out the Baby Browning with his left hand, released the safety catch with his thumb and brought it up to aim at Bethell's legs.

'Stop there, Bethell!' shouted Swift. 'We're armed. I won't hesitate to shoot.'

But the MP ran on, then launched himself with a scream and disappeared into thin air.

'Jesus!' exclaimed Poskitt, looking first at the space which Bethell had occupied, now just an expanse of grass, then sea, then sky. Stripes of colour so vivid in the moment, they almost looked as though they belonged on the national flag of some faraway island nation. Then he stared at the tiny pistol in Swift's hand, still aiming at that empty space.

Swift slid the catch back, and re-pocketed the gun.

'You didn't see that,' he hissed. 'Not a word.'

Poskitt sort of nodded and shrugged at the same time.

While Armitage busied himself cuffing Smethwick, Swift and Poskitt made their way to the cliff edge, just to double-check Bethell hadn't miraculously broken his fall on an intervening ledge.

They reached the edge, and gingerly peered over. Swift felt horribly giddy doing so.

And there was nothing to see.

Nothing except a precipitous drop, and the sea gently slapping the rocks far below.

No one could survive that.

Bethell's body wasn't visible, but Swift could imagine what it looked like. He'd seen the results of suicides from high buildings in London before. From this height, if anything, the results would be even worse.

Ernest Bethell MP had taken his shame, the reasons he'd besmirched the family name and his own reputation in a desperate attempt to stave off bankruptcy, to the grave.

A watery, rock-strewn grave far below.

From the self-important pomp of a local VIP, someone who even had a national profile, he'd transformed himself into food for the fishes and seagulls in an instant.

The question was, was the reason for his suicide simply the uncovering by Carver of the billeting fraud – massive and career-ending though that was? Or was there something more sinister, linked to the deaths of Sarah Houghton, Archie Davis, Jessica Pickering and Ulysses Delaney?

22

Once they got back to Hull, Swift decided to leave Smethwick to stew in a cell for an hour or so before they interviewed him. Carver had insisted to Weighton that if she was going to hospital, she would rather it was the Royal Infirmary in Hull rather than Bridlington's smaller hospital, but she was soon seen and pronounced fit and well.

It still left Swift having to deal with Holdridge's ire.

'You've made us look like fools, Swift, and in front of our colleagues from the East Riding force, too.'

Swift shuffled in his chair opposite the detective chief superintendent.

'I don't think that's entirely fair, sir. We've caught the culprits. Well . . . one chose to commit suicide rather than face justice, but that's certainly not my fault. And we rescued Carver unharmed.'

'More by luck than good judgement, by all accounts. Bethell's death is an embarrassment, too.'

'The man was corrupt, and had used violence and threats to try to cover up his corruption.'

'Well, I just hope you make something stick on Smethwick, and that he admits to the fraud and Bethell's part in it. Otherwise, you'll be for the high jump. You've already got four unsolved murders on your account, Swift. Now get out.'

In the interview, Audley Smethwick gave a good impression of a deflated balloon. Swift could imagine his usual mien, lording it over his council fiefdom, hobnobbing with his MP friend – even though that friend was from the opposite end of the political spectrum. Now that self-importance was gone. Smethwick knew Carver's documents would be his undoing.

'You're in a lot of trouble, Mr Smethwick. The Crown takes a dim view of special wartime schemes set up to help keep British citizens safe from Hitler being defrauded by people such as you.'

'It were Bethell's idea. He were the architect of it.'

'Aha,' said Swift. 'That will be your tactic, will it? Blame everything on the dead man because he can't answer back. There's one small problem with that line of defence.'

'Oh, aye?' said the man, smirking.

Weighton banged his fist down on the table, making Smethwick flinch.

'I wouldn't take this lightly, Councillor Smethwick. Whichever way you look at it, your career as a local politician is over. Your name will be mud. Not only that – there is the not so trivial matter of the person who first complained about your activities ending up dead.'

'And murder,' added Swift, 'as I'm sure you know, is a capital offence.'

Alarm suddenly swept over Smethwick's features.

'I haven't murdered any bugger. I don't know what you're on about.'

'I'm on about an American soldier, Archibald Davis,' said Swift. 'We know he came to your office complaining his girl-friend's sister's children had been wrongly recorded as being billeted away from Hull. That's how our Women's Auxiliary Police Constable Kathleen Carver managed to uncover Bethell's and your squalid scheme.'

'And,' added Weighton, 'Sarah Houghton – the girlfriend – was murdered, too. Convenient to get them both out of the way, wasn't it, Councillor?'

'I had nothing to do with either of these bloody murders. I know nowt about either of them.'

Weighton opened the evidence folder, brought out a series of photographs, and turned them round on the desk so they sat squarely in Smethwick's eyeline.

'Do you recognise any of the people in these photographs, Councillor Smethwick?'

The man was refusing to look. Weighton picked the top one off the table and thrust it right in front of his nose.

'I can help you identify them if you like,' said Swift's deputy. 'The man rowing here on East Park boating lake is Ron Lewis – a well-known local thug. The two gentlemen with him in the boat are you, and the late MP for Holderness, Ernest Bethell.'

Swift cocked his head. 'Ring any bells, Mr Smethwick?'

Weighton leafed through to the next photo. 'And here's you, handing an envelope to Mr Lewis.'

'That don't prove nowt!' spat Smethwick.

Swift shrugged. 'No. Unless Mr Lewis has admitted to us that what was in the envelope was money – a considerable amount of money – paid to him for certain acts of thuggery and violence.'

'Acts,' added Weighton, 'designed to frighten off Archibald Davis, to stop him bothering you and uncovering your nasty not-so-little fraud.'

'Well, what of it? We didn't ask him to murder no one.'

Swift rubbed his chin with his prosthetic hand. As well as its actual function of scratching an itch, the action often had a side benefit of unnerving interviewees.

As Smethwick watched him warily, it gave an opportunity for Weighton to turn the screw.

'You were aware, though, presumably, that Lewis had links to Mosley's fascists? That he actually recruited for them at the docks? How will that go down with your Labour colleagues?'

'Mosley's lot? Nerr, I didn't nerr. He were Bethell's man, not mine. Nowt to do wi' me.'

Aside from letting his native Hull accent slip out, Smethwick seemed to have found renewed mettle from somewhere. Swift decided he needed to up the ante. 'Ron Lewis's politics are the least of your problems, Mr Smethwick. Now, you're an intelligent man. You wouldn't have risen so high in Hull Corporation if that wasn't the case. I'm sure, therefore, you're aware of the felony murder rule.'

This time it was Smethwick banging his fist on the table.

'I've already told you. There weren't no murders, at least not on my behalf. Nor Bethell's, that I know of. But he's not here to answer for himself.'

'As I was saying,' continued Swift, 'the felony murder rule provides that where a criminal kills in the act of committing a dangerous crime, the offender *and the offender's co-conspirators* may be found guilty of murder.'

'No!' shouted Smethwick.

'Yes!' Weighton yelled back into his face. 'Yes, Councillor Smethwick. That is the seriousness of the charges you are facing. Not just financial crimes. A potential murder charge.'

Swift spoke softly now. 'And therefore, a charge for which you could be hanged.'

He watched the blood drain from Smethwick's face.

Weighton and Swift stayed silent for a few moments. Silence itself was an excellent weapon in interviews. It made the suspect uncomfortable. It encouraged them to want to talk. To enhance the effect, Hull Police had deliberately installed noisy pendulum clocks on the walls of each interview room, so that the rhythmic tick-tock of the pendulum would sound to the interviewee like the sound of his or her time running out. That was all they could hear now: a rhythmic tick-tock.

Tick-tock.

Tick-tock.

Tick-tock.

After perhaps a minute, or a little more, Swift cleared his throat.

'However, we do have certain latitude in choosing which charges to press. I would stress to you, therefore, that it's in your interests to make a full and frank confession.'

'Well, I didn't commit any murders, and I didn't conspire to commit any murders.'

'In which case,' said Swift, 'a full statement of what exactly you did do may well help your case.' He got a sheaf of documents from the evidence folder. 'But remember, we have all these documents provided by your personal secretary at Hull Corporation.'

Swift turned them round to face Smethwick, then flicked through them a little like the flicker books of photographs, so popular before the advent of 8mm cine film – although that was the preserve of the rich. In the backstreets of Hull, no doubt, boys and girls would still be leafing through their flicker books of cartoons and sports stories. Perhaps even war comics these days.

'We have all the evidence we need,' said Swift, as he flicked through the bundle once more.

The flicker movie for Smethwick was a collection of his misdeeds – like his old life draining before his eyes.

He knew the game was up.

'All right,' he said. 'What do you want to know?'

23

Three days earlier

Theo Howard couldn't really understand why this court martial was going ahead, and so quickly too. He'd not been given any chance to mount a defence. No sooner had he tried to help that Hull policeman, than he'd found himself being arrested by the snowdrops, and the very next day here he was.

He knew he didn't kill Archie Davis. Archie was his best friend – they were buddies from way back when in Jackson, Mississippi. More than that, they were as good as brothers. Surely they didn't have no evidence against him? And accused of killing Sarah Houghton, Archie's sweetheart, too. Why, that was a goddamn lie.

But people were lining up, seemingly hell-bent on sending him down.

There were the white officers who went to the dances in Cottingham, saying he had hit on Sarah first. That he was jealous of Archie for stealing his girl. That was a goddamn lie. Yes, he'd had his eyes on her at first, like everyone else. She was fine dinner. But as soon as Archie made a move, and he saw the love in Sarah's eyes, he knew he'd been beat. Archie had that chick locked up, fair and square. Theo, he was pleased for Archie, not jealous – though he was a mite worried about what Dolores back in Detroit might make of it. But Dolores wasn't about to jump in port, anyways.

Theo tried to butt in, to counter their accusations, but the military judge – or whatever he was – just slapped him down.

Time after time after time.

It was just like the time the English detective interviewed him, when he'd tried to tell the cop what had been occurring, and Mulder had jumped in and stopped him before the word 'black' was even halfway out of his mouth. That Englishman probably left with the wrong impression – that he was talking 'bout *black soldiers*. Well, that wasn't it at all. Nothing could have been further from the truth.

Now, here at the court martial, they were just lining up to bad-mouth him, like they'd been biding their time, full of hatred and bile. Almost as though they wanted to nix him out. Maybe they did. Saying they'd seen things they hadn't seen.

Lie, after lie, after lie.

It was like each and every damn one of them wanted to turn the twister to the slammer.

And why was he being tried by the goddamn American military anyways? Everyone knew it was full of Klansmen. All the officers hated the black soldiers. There was hatred in their hearts. And that Lieutenant-Colonel DeVries? Well, he just let 'em get away with it.

But this was goddamn England. They weren't in the United States now. The accusations against him were all lies, and a jury full of good English men and women . . . well, they would have seen through all that. They saw the heart of a man first, not the colour of his skin. That's why the Houghtons had welcomed Archie like a long-lost son. And a bit of politeness went a long, long way with the English.

Well, that's what Theo was thinking. But then they brought in their English so-called 'witnesses' and they proved to be even bigger liars.

The first one was some goddamn councillor. He had a thick Hull accent, you know, it sounds like they can't be bothered to pronounce their words properly.

Said he'd seen Theo with Sarah somewhere off Hessle Road in Hull the night she was killed. That they'd been arguing. That Theo seemed to be gripping her tightly, forcing her somewhere against her will. Well, that weren't true, for starters. Theo knew he'd been in Cottingham, at that pub on West Green – what's it called? The Blue Bell Inn, that's the one. He hadn't been anywhere near Hessle Road.

Then the next goddamn liar they wheeled in, well, he took the goddamn biscuit – in fact, the whole fucking biscuit barrel. He didn't talk in a Hull accent. Oh no, sir. He was all high and mighty, and hoity-toity, spoke like his lips never moved a goddamn inch. Well, this one had them eating out of the palm of his hand, as soon as he said he was a Member of Parliament. Not just any Member of Parliament, either. He was the 'Right Honourable' Member of Parliament for Holderness – and that included this here good village of Cottingham. But as far as Theo was concerned, there weren't nothing 'right honourable' about this man, if you could even call him a man. Because he was another goddamn liar.

What was his fairy story? Only that he'd visited the site of the Scarborough Street bombing off Hessle Road as soon as he heard about the tragedy. Not only that, but in the dim light of dawn – that's the sort of flowery words he was using – he'd seen a black man dragging a woman's body through the debris. At first, he thought he was one of the black soldiers from Cottingham, helping with the rescue work. But now, he said, looking Theo straight in the eyes, he recognised the man as the defendant, one Theophilus Howard, and he was sure the woman's body was that of the murdered girl, Sarah Houghton.

Well, that just about finished Theo. He knew then he was heading for a long stretch in the slammer. He wouldn't have to go crawlin' back to Bessie down in Jackson no more, asking if she'd take him back, asking if he might spend some time with the baby daughter or son he'd never seen. No, sir. He wouldn't be seeing the outside of a jailhouse for an awful long time.

There were one curious thing, though.

Theo never got to hear about his sentence. Not a squeak.

The sentencing hearing, they said, was being held in camera. Well, that wasn't English – no English he understood, anyways. They only explained to him later that it meant 'in secret'.

He just assumed he'd been handed down a long old jail term.

Everyone he asked, they wouldn't tell him. Said it was none of his concern.

He'd been found guilty, he'd done the deed.

Eventually, he just gave up asking.

It weren't more than a day or so later that he was saying good-bye to Cottingham in the back of a snowdrop prison van. The journey took hours and hours, and they wouldn't tell Theo where he was going. Only by looking out the back door could he try to get some semblance of the geography, but geography wasn't his strong point, and all the road signs had been taken down anyways. They didn't want Hitler to find his way around too easily, should he ever decide to take an excursion here with Nazi soldiers.

Eventually, one of the MPs told him he was being taken to Shepton Mallet – some strange-sounding hicksville town beyond the city of Bristol. Way, way down to the south-west. About as far from Hull as you could get. The English had apparently given their American friends the use of a jail there.

Theo could imagine the colour of all the prisoners.

Black.

And he could imagine the colour of all the jailers.

White.

And when he got there, he wasn't wrong.

His cellmate was in there for raping a white woman. An English woman. Theo assumed he must be innocent, too, and framed. But no. First night they were together, he only went and admitted he'd goddamn done it. Theo wasn't happy about that. He didn't want to be locked up with no cut-rate rapist.

Then Theo asked him what length jail term he'd been handed down.

At that, the soldier just laughed and laughed and laughed, as though Theo had just told the best, the dirtiest joke in the whole wide world.

He'd slapped his thighs, and then stared with this horrible stare straight into Theo's eyes.

'Don't you know what this goddamn place is, man? Oh my God! You don't, do you? Jesus wept!'

Then he started laughing again. This godawful cackle that just went on, and on, and on.

Trouble was, Theo just didn't get the joke.

24

Extracting the confession from Smethwick had – in the end – been like shelling peas. Swift was convinced that, in any case, he, Bethell and Lewis were not the guilty parties in respect of the murders. The trouble was, on that front they were no further forwards – the two youths involved in the identity parade had clearly been got at by someone. So much of the two cases didn't make any sense. Why had Bethell and Smethwick abducted Carver – and why take her to Flamborough? Even after Smethwick had told all in the interview, Swift wasn't a lot clearer in his head. There seemed to be some half-baked plan to rendezvous with a fishing boat from Scarborough in Filey Bay, and escape to Iceland. Even before they'd been confronted by Carver with her evidence, they'd realised the game was up. Carver had just got in the way.

'You left a police officer tied and bound in a tidal cave,' Swift told Smethwick. 'You must have known that when the tide rose, she would drown. If she hadn't managed to work herself free, and we hadn't got there, you would have been facing a murder charge. We could still have you for attempted murder.'

'That wasn't our intention,' pleaded Smethwick. 'We just needed her out of the way. Lewis was told to ring the police anonymously once he'd got us to the fishing boat.'

'So what went wrong?' asked Weighton. 'Why aren't you and Bethell safely on your way to neutral Iceland? Not that a trip to Iceland would be in any way safe.'

'Lewis started blackmailing us – saying we weren't paying enough for his services. He left us high and dry in the cave, then just motored off in his boat. In fact, I'm not sure there ever was a Scarborough trawler waiting for us. That's what Lewis *said*. But he's just a con man and a thug. We should never have got involved with him.'

Swift snorted. 'It sounds as though there are plenty of things you shouldn't have got involved with, Smethwick. But you'll have plenty of time to reflect on that in prison. You won't be seeing the outside of a jail again for a long, long time.'

Now, gathered round in the incident room the next morning sipping a freshly brewed cup of tea, Swift was considering where to take the investigation next. Without the authority to question the American soldiers at the Cottingham base, they seemed to have hit a dead end. If Smethwick's statement was the truth, and there seemed no solid reason to doubt it – other than the fact that the man was, of course, a fraudster – then the link to the murders only went as far as asking Ron Lewis to frighten off Archibald Davis. Even if that 'frightening off' had gone too far, that didn't explain the deaths of Sarah Houghton,

Jessica Pickering and Ulysses Delaney. Not to mention the mutilation of several of the bodies, and the multiple rapes Jessica had suffered.

'We still need to track down Lewis and arrest him,' said Weighton.

'True,' admitted Swift. 'How's that progressing?'

'I've had uniform stake out his house, but since the Flamborough incident he hasn't returned. The East Riding force say his boat is still missing from North Landing, and he's not returned to work in the docks either. In short, he's disappeared.'

Swift watched Carver rifling through the contents of the evidence room, which they'd laid out on the incident room table to try to give themselves inspiration.

'Are you feeling all right now, WAPC Carver?' asked Swift.

Holdridge had ordered that she be kept away from any active side of the investigation. From now on, she would be limited to research and administrative tasks. Swift hadn't had the heart to tell her yet.

'I'm fine, sir. I was fine all along. Didn't really need to go to hospital. It was just a bit of a shock, you know, at the time.'

He saw her toying with the Durex packet, recovered from underneath the Elm Tree House garden bushes, with her gloved hands – almost as though she wasn't sure what it was. Then she discarded it, and picked up the Jolly Roger flag instead.

'I see we've labelled this up as a child's pirate flag, sir.'

Swift frowned. 'Yes. That's what it is, isn't it?'

'I'm not so sure, sir. Look at this stitching, and the hole here.'

Before Swift could get at the piece of material, Weighton put on a pair of protective rubber gloves and picked it up.

He wrapped the hole a few times round his finger, then held the material up and waved it around as though he was flying a flag.

'Seems to work as a flag to me,' he said.

Carver took it back. 'But the skull and crossbones is the wrong way up, and look at the stitching around the hole. It's curved.'

'And?' asked Swift.

Carver placed the material against her own uniform, rotating it so the skull was horizontal.

'I don't think that hole is designed to go round a flagpole, or even a child's makeshift flagpole, like a bamboo cane. It's a sleeve hole.'

'Aha, Carver,' said Swift. 'Excellent work.'

'So what are you saying?' asked Weighton.

'I'm saying this is part of a pirate uniform.'

Swift frowned. 'But even if we establish it's a child's pirate costume, that doesn't really take us any further, does it? We know that space was used as a children's play den, but almost certainly during the daytime. It doesn't mean we'll be able to find new witnesses—'

'Sorry to interrupt, sir,' said Carver. 'But I don't think it *is* part of a child's costume at all.' She held it up against herself again. 'The sleeve hole is too big. It's clearly designed for—'

Swift slapped his left hand against his forehead. 'Hang on! We're forgetting something, aren't we? Those fibres Professor Jackson found. The ones under Jessica Pickering's fingernails. They were black and white, weren't they? We thought a suit, or white shirt and black trousers. But what if it's this?' He, too, rolled on some protective rubber gloves and picked up the material, holding it up to the light, looking particularly at the edges. 'It looks like it's torn from something, doesn't it? What if Jessica's attacker was wearing this, and in the struggle she managed to tear part of it off?'

'I agree with you. Seems possible, sir,' said Weighton. 'Well done, Kathleen.'

'Yes. Great work, Carver. Weighton, you and I had better take this over to Professor Jackson right now and see if he can tell us whether the fibres match. Carver, I want you first to get it photographed by the in-house photographer here, get the images developed immediately, and then take the photos round any fancy-dress hire shops there are in Hull. Or perhaps we should be looking in Cottingham, though I wouldn't have thought the shopping parade there is big enough.'

'There's a toy shop there, sir,' said Weighton. 'My wife and I have taken the kids there occasionally. But no, I agree, more likely to have been hired in Hull.'

Carver's face lit up. 'I can think of one place, sir. The joke shop in Hepworth Arcade. Dinsdales, I think it's called. That does fancy dress, too. It's less than a quarter-of-a-mile walk. I could start there.'

'Good idea, Carver. You do that. If the shopkeeper recognises it, get any details you can of recent hires. And well done again.'

'Do you think that was wise, sir?' Weighton asked, once they were in the Morris, on the short drive to the mortuary at Hull Royal Infirmary.

Swift felt himself bristling. 'What do you mean, Sergeant?'

'Allowing Carver to investigate on her own again, sir. And joke shops don't always limit their products to children and, shall we say, family fun. Under the counter, you can sometimes get more salacious things. You know – "what the butler saw"-type stuff. Sometimes worse.'

'It's research, Weighton,' said Swift, huffily. 'Holdridge said she was allowed to do research. I'm sure she won't be asking for anything from under the counter, will she? Although you seem to be remarkably well informed about it.'

Nevertheless, he knew Weighton had a point. And his sergeant wasn't even aware of the not-so-subtle 'threats' Swift had received in the form of the lapel badge and the pig's ear. Not to mention Haughtree's 'advice'.

Having an inconsequential tiff with Weighton wasn't the best preparation for a meeting with the pathologist, Professor Jackson – a man capable of inciting anger in Swift by his mere presence. To be fair, though, in his recent dealings the professor seemed to have mellowed somewhat. And today, he was positively eager to try to help his police colleagues.

'What is it?' asked Jackson, when he saw the skull and crossbones material.

'We're not entirely sure,' replied Swift. 'We thought it was a child's pirate flag. But we've now decided it isn't. And it seems too big to be a child's pirate costume either.'

'How can you tell from this scrap of material?'

Swift pointed out the sleeve hole, as established by Carver a little earlier.

'So our best guess is it's some sort of adult pirate fancy-dress costume.'

'And why is it relevant to your inquiry?'

'It was found at a locale where we know Jessica Pickering and Ulysses Delaney were seen together before they were murdered.'

'And?'

'And we remembered, rather belatedly it has to be acknowledged, about the black and white fibres you said had been found beneath Jessica's fingernails – as though she'd been in some sort of struggle and ripped some material, possibly the clothing of her attacker or attackers.'

'Ah, yes.'

'You've still got those fibres, I take it?'

'Of course. Filed away. I was waiting for your forensic people to collect them. I'll get my assistant to bring the evidence bag and we can take a look under the microscope.'

Once the assistant had retrieved the relevant file, and Jackson had extricated the evidence pouch, he proceeded to set up two microscopes side by side. Then he used a pair of tweezers to carefully tease out both black and white fibres from the torn material – the white from the felt skull and crossbones design, the black from the background material the felt skull had been stitched onto.

When he was satisfied, he adjusted the focus on both microscopes, examined them himself, and then invited Swift and Weighton to take a look in turn, with Swift going first.

'Notice anything, Chief Inspector?'

'Well, I'm not an expert. But the fibres on each slide look remarkably similar.'

'They do indeed,' said Jackson. 'It's not really my field of expertise either, and you might want to send both samples off to one of your police forensic laboratories. However, I know enough to tell you the fibres are not just similar. They are identical.'

'And what does that tell us?' asked Weighton.

'It tells us, Sergeant, that unless there are lots of people going a round in home-made pirate costumes – which I very much doubt – then whoever was wearing this was the person, or one of the people, who attacked Jessica Pickering. Find the owner of this garment, and you have your killer.'

Carver was delighted that the chief inspector had trusted her with this side of the investigation, and she intended not to mess it up. She knew his superior, DCS Holdridge, would have hauled Swift over the coals about the Flamborough affair. Carver had been frightened. She had genuinely feared for her life in that sea cave. But it wasn't going to put her off police work, and she was determined not to get sent back to the records department again.

She and Swift had something in common, anyway. They were both a little like fish out of water here in Hull. Swift with his plummy voice, his occasionally posh airs, and the war wound which he never mentioned – but which still clearly caused him problems in his day-to-day life. She wondered what had brought him to Hull in the first place. He wasn't one for small talk, and she'd never summoned up the courage to ask him. But there seemed to be an air of sadness about him – the fact that he lived alone in that lovely house on the edge of Beverley Westwood, rattling around in a place far too big for one person, just added to the sense of melancholy. He clearly needed somebody to love, but didn't seem to ever make much effort in that direction.

He was also obviously escaping from something or someone, and that was what he and she had in common. Carver had been like her brother – desperate to escape from the stifling confines of Baldersdale. That a place so windswept and desolate could at the same time feel claustrophobic was a strange juxtaposition. It wasn't that she didn't love being out on the moors and the Pennine fells, breathing the smell of heather and peat, and revelling in their untamed beauty. It was just that if she didn't get away, she knew her life would be mapped out for her. She'd be married off to a local farmer's son; they'd have lots of children, some of whom would be similarly bound to the land. She wanted something else, and she knew her brother, Richard, did, too. That's why he'd enlisted with the Royal Navy at the first opportunity. He just couldn't wait to get away either.

She was walking along Lowgate, not far from where it transformed into Market Place, at the corner of Silver Street and Scale Lane. This was the best bit of Hull – the Old Town. Grand historic buildings, and hidden alleyways with exotic names like The Land of Green Ginger. How had anyone managed to come up with that one? There were various theories. That it had perhaps been the centre of the ginger and spice trade in the Middle Ages. Or that it had been named after a Dutch family, the Lindegreens, that Hullensians possibly mispronounced. And that the 'ginger' really referred to Mr and Mrs Lindegreen's son – and somehow Lindegreen Junior had transformed into its almost fairy-tale-like modern name.

She reached the arcade. This part of the city had been relatively undamaged by the Blitz of the previous year, although two high-explosive bombs had fallen further down Market Place Street, beyond the King Billy statue.

Carver entered the joke shop and waited to be served.

The young assistant referred her to the shop's owner, and she showed him the photograph of what they now believed to be part of a pirate fancy-dress outfit, rather than a pirate flag.

'Well, I wouldn't be in business long if I hired out or sold tat like that, would I?'

'What do you mean?' asked Carver.

'You can tell it's all handmade. The skull and crossbones is very naive and childlike. It's not been made by machine or mass-produced.'

Carver frowned. She was sure it was an adult costume.

'So you're saying you think it *is* a child's costume?'

'That's not what I said, love, is it? It's childlike in its design. Just not very good. Have you got the actual thing, or just the photo?'

'For now, just the photo, although I could come back later.'

'Well, I wouldn't bother if I were you. As I say, it wasn't bought or hired here.'

'But it's a pirate costume, do you think?'

'Why do you say that?'

'The skull and crossbones.'

'Aye. Well, you'd get that on a flag, I grant you that. But have you ever seen any pirates dressed in a Jolly Roger flag? Look, over there. There's the pirate costume we hire out, and we sell a similar one, too. Looks nowt like it, does it?'

Carver had to agree it didn't. It looked to have more in common with an eighteenth-century dandy's outfit, with its bright colours, puffed-out materials, knee breeches and headdress.

The man had another look at the photograph.

'Who are you with, anyway – the police?'

'That's right.'

'Are you investigating summat?'

Carver felt she was getting out of her depth. Would Swift be angry if she told the man they were investigating a series of murders? The killings still hadn't been released to the local press for fear of frightening a community already at its wits' end after three years of war. But then she didn't want to go back to him completely empty-handed. She lowered her voice.

'We're investigating a murder.' One murder sounded much better than four. Surely Swift couldn't be angered by that. 'But please don't mention that to anyone else.'

'Don't worry, I'm not a blabbermouth, miss. I'd say rather than trailing round fancy-dress shops, you'd be better off in the library or at University College. If this is linked to your murder, then . . . Well, I don't rightly know, this is a bit of a stab in the dark . . . but perhaps it's some sort of club uniform. Would that tie in with anything else you've discovered?'

Carver was non-committal in her reply. It was clear the man was almost as much in the dark as she was. Nevertheless, she thanked him and said her goodbyes.

25

Before Swift had time to catch up with Carver to let her know their findings in respect of the black and white fibres, he found himself faced with another serious problem. Bert Feather, the local newspaper's crime reporter, was waiting for him in the reception of Alfred Gelder Street police headquarters – this time in person. He'd called the control room several times already. Each time, he'd been faithfully assured of a return call from Swift – one the detective had never made.

'Ah, Detective Chief Inspector Swift. Any chance of a quick word? You never did return my calls as promised.'

'I'm rather busy, I'm afraid, Mr Feather.'

'Won't take long, sir, I assure you. And I may just have some information that might interest you for once, rather than vice versa.'

Feather was an old-school reporter. The broken blood vessels and bulbous nose on his face had prematurely aged him – that, and his balding pate. But his florid features were a telltale sign that most of his tips he got by standing his contacts drinks in the pub. Swift knew that with the downfall of Councillor Smethwick and the suicide of the local MP, his attempts to keep his current investigations out of the local press couldn't last.

'All right, Mr Feather. I can spare you a few moments, I suppose. Let's go into the interview room.' Then he turned to his deputy. 'I'll see you later, Weighton. See if you can catch up with Carver.'

'Will do, sir.'

They sat down opposite each other in the same room where Swift and Weighton had questioned Smethwick just a few hours earlier. Feather got out his notebook and pencil, and then sat there as the pendulum clock tick tocked away in the background.

Swift was in no hurry to break the near silence, and in the end it was Feather who made the first move, licking the end of his pencil and preparing to write.

'So, I was waiting for you to ring me back, Chief Inspector.'

'As I said, Mr Feather, I've been very busy.'

'So I'd heard.'

Swift wondered what exactly Feather *had* heard.

'Anything we want to say to the press, Mr Feather, we'll issue in a press release.'

'That's not very friendly, Chief Inspector. I thought we might be able to trade a little information.'

'You go first, Mr Feather. Then we'll see.'

Feather smiled and winked. 'Can't say fairer than that, Chief Inspector. All right. Here's what I know. I know you've been investigating a series of murders in Hull involving prostitutes and American GIs based at Cottingham. *Black* American GIs.'

Swift was silent, his face poker-straight.

'Are you confirming that, Chief Inspector?'

Swift sighed. 'I thought we agreed you were going first, Mr Feather.'

'Aha. There's no tricking you, is there, Mr Swift. All right, here's what I've found out. The Americans have already court-martialled someone for at least one of your murders.'

'Really?' asked Swift. 'Who?'

'A black soldier by the name of Theophilus Howard. He was found guilty and transferred to Shepton Mallet prison in Somerset – a jail that's been given over entirely to the American military to do with what they wish.'

'Well then, you do know something I don't, Mr Feather. If it's true. When did this happen?'

'Just a couple of days or so ago. And yes, it is true. The hearing was held in camera – no press were allowed to attend.'

'I do know what in camera means, Mr Feather.'

The journalist smiled slyly. 'Touché, Mr Swift. But I also know something else.'

Feather tapped the side of his nose with his finger, winked, and cocked his head. The combined effect made him look like one of Dickens' most untrustworthy characters.

'And what's that, Mr Feather?'

'Well, if you'll excuse me, sir, I should just point out this has been a very one-sided conversation so far.' He leaned forwards in his chair, close enough that Swift could smell the beer fumes on his breath. 'However, here's an extra little nugget for you. The sentencing hearing was also held in camera and the accused wasn't even allowed to attend. In fact, my sources tell me he doesn't even *know* the verdict.'

'Which was?' asked Swift.

'Aha. Well, I can't give you everything, Mr Swift, can I? Not without something in return. But I will tell you this. Two of the key witnesses who helped secure the court martial verdict have since been unmasked as charlatans and frauds – by your team, I believe.'

Swift sighed. 'Go on.'

'None other than our late esteemed MP for Holderness, the Right Honourable Ernest Bethell – although whether you're still right and honourable after you've topped yourself just before being arrested for fraud and embezzlement, I'm not quite sure. Aided and abetted by another fallen local political giant, the deputy leader of Hull Corporation, Audley Smethwick, who I gather is currently banged up in these four walls for his part in the scandal.'

Swift took a long breath, and steepled his good hand and his prosthetic one together in front of his face. Or at least as steepled as he was able to make with his false hand. Feather appeared to know everything, and more. Quite how, Swift wasn't sure. He'd have to try and check up on that later. But for the time being, he needed to decide how to deal with this. He could deny everything, and be made to look stupid by Feather. Or he could co-operate, and try to control Feather's news story as much as possible. He really ought to run that by Holdridge. But Hold-ridge had on several occasions been less than helpful in dealing with the Americans and ensuring access for Swift and his team. He owed the DCS nothing.

Finally, Swift smiled. 'Your sources are very good, Mr Feather. I can see it's time for me to co-operate with you, and I'd be happy to. You presumably know we're investigating four murders.'

'Four?' exclaimed Feather.

'That's correct. And two of them happened *after* Theophilus Howard was taken into custody. It's Hull Police's view, however, that all four murders were carried out by the same man or men.'

Feather's face creased into a severe frown.

'Hang on. So you're saying Howard isn't guilty?'

'That's precisely what I'm saying, Mr Feather. On top of that, the fourth victim, Jessica Pickering, suffered a series of violent sexual assaults before being strangled. In short, she was gang-raped. And I can give you more details that even the *Hull Daily Mail* would probably find too revolting to print. However, while it's true that the two female victims did occasionally sell sexual favours, they were very much part-time sex workers, and if there's any way you can keep that aspect out of the newspaper, I'd be grateful, for their families' sakes. And I don't think it's particularly relevant. We don't believe that's why they were killed.'

'Well, I can't promise anything, Mr Swift, but you know how it is. You scratch my back, I'll scratch yours. *Four* victims?'

'That's right. The bodies of the first three had been mutilated, too. Sarah Houghton's heart had been excised and the two GIs both had their genitals surgically removed by the attackers, all of the mutilation happening *post-mortem*.'

'Good God!'

'Good God indeed, Mr Feather.'

'Well, better than ante-mortem, I suppose.'

'There is that. The body of the second GI, Ulysses Delaney, was also decapitated – again, post-mortem.'

Feather sniffed loudly. 'Jesus. It's revolting. But you're absolutely sure all four victims were killed by the same person or persons?'

'As far as we can be, yes.'

Swift went on to give the reporter the full details of the billeting scandal involving Bethell and Smethwick, and how it had been uncovered by WAPC Carver, playing up her role as much as possible. How she had been kidnapped by Bethell, Smethwick and Lewis – and left to drown in the sea cave at Flamborough Head.

'Good grief. Are you charging Smethwick with attempted murder, too?'

Swift sighed. 'It might be too difficult to prove his intent was to kill her. He claims that wasn't the case. He's fully admitted to the fraud. That will get him a long enough sentence. And his partner in crime is no longer around.'

'Well, I don't know where to start with this story. Each aspect of it is probably worth the lead story in the nationals, never mind the bloody *Hull Daily Mail*.'

'You should be able to sell it to the nationals, then, shouldn't you? That would keep you in beer money for a while.'

'Ha!' guffawed Feather. 'My reputation for liking one or two obviously precedes me, Mr Swift. Doesn't stop me doing my job, though. I'm a bloody good reporter, though I say it myself. I have to say, though, I'm a little wary about trying to sell this to the nationals before we've got it out in the *Mail*. With an MP involved *and* the American military, the government would probably slap a bloody great big D-notice on it, and I'd be able to report bugger all. I'm still not sure what the best story is, though. "Police heroine saved from imminent drowning". "Shamed MP plunges hundreds of feet to his death rather than face jail over billeting fraud". Or "Hull Ripper gang terrorises the city's women and US GIs". Blimey. I've never dealt with anything like it before.'

Swift smiled. He could imagine Holdridge's face when he read it in the paper – his features would be redder than his ginger moustache.

'You indicated there was something else, however, Mr Feather?'

Feather breathed in deeply. 'Well, there is, yes. Going back to what we were talking about earlier – the fact that Theo Howard has already been convicted by the Americans.'

'I will try my utmost to make sure that's overturned,' said Swift. 'It's clearly a miscarriage of justice – and you can quote me on that.'

Feather made a quick scribbled note. 'Well, that's very kind of you, Chief Inspector. It's just I fear you might be too late.'

Swift frowned. 'Why's that?'

'Because, in secret – without even his knowledge – Theophilus Howard has been sentenced to death.'

26

Weighton and Carver bumped into each other in the incident room.

'Is the chief inspector around, Sergeant Weighton?' asked Carver.

'He's not, I'm afraid, Kathleen. Not for a while, anyway. That crime reporter from the *Mail* who's been ringing up all the time has finally collared him.'

Carver had sudden visions of the joke shop owner ringing the newspaper as soon as she'd left his shop. She hoped that wasn't the case. She was *sure* that wasn't the case. He'd given her his word. Although the word of someone who made his living through people playing tricks on one another possibly wasn't the most copper-bottomed in the world.

'That's a shame. I've found out a little more about our so-called "pirate costume". Not much, but a little. I wanted to talk to him about what I should do next.'

'Can I help?' asked Weighton.

Carver stared up at the giant of a man. There was something terribly reassuring about having someone like Weighton on your side. You kind of always knew you were going to end up safe. Whether it was true or not, that was the air he portrayed.

'Perhaps. The joke shop owner was insistent that there's no way our bit of material is actually from a pirate costume. He showed me some real ones in his shop, and I tend to agree.'

'Oh yes?' said Weighton. 'Why's that?'

'Well, pirates might *fly* the Jolly Roger flag, but they never *wear* the skull and crossbones, do they? It's never part of their clothing.'

'I can't say I've ever thought about it too deeply.'

'Well, I'm telling you it's not, and the joke shop owner agreed. His theory was that it was more likely to be the costume of some sort of club or something.'

'Or gang?' suggested Weighton.

'Possibly. Anyway, his suggestion was that I either go to the municipal library, or the one at Hull University College, and see if I can find out more. I thought I might try University College first. I could get the trolley bus. But now with the newspapers on to the case, everything seems a lot more urgent, doesn't it? I was just wondering if there was any way you could give me a lift over to Cottingham Road?'

'Well, the chief inspector asked me to look after you, so I don't see why not. I don't suppose he'll mind if we borrow the Morris.'

'Rather you than me, sir. He seems to love that motor car, though I can't think why. It's not the most comfortable thing, is it?'

'It isn't, Carver. But as you say, it's probably quicker than the trolley bus.'

Weighton picked up Swift's car keys from the key hook, and then collected his coat and hat. Carver couldn't help the feeling that they were acting like naughty schoolchildren while their teacher was out of the room.

'So, is this a fully-fledged university, or what?' asked Weighton, as they indicated to turn off Cottingham Road into the college campus.

'No,' replied Carver. 'I think that's why it's called University College, sir, rather than Hull University. I don't think they can award their own degrees. I'm not sure how it works, but I think it's somehow linked to the University of London.'

'You never fancied going to university, then? You're bright enough, I'd have thought.'

'Is that a compliment, sir?' laughed Carver. 'I just wanted to do my bit for the war effort, to be honest. And get away from farming. Joining the Women's Auxiliary Police Corps seemed as good a way as any.'

Weighton showed his police warrant card at the entrance gate, and asked the way to the college library.

'It's that large building on the right, officer, the Cohen Building, opposite the main reception. If you put this permit on the dashboard of your car and then park over there, you won't have any problems. We don't often get visits from the police. Anything amiss?'

'No, no. We're just here to do a bit of research.'

'Well, if you just go to the library reception, I'm sure they'll help you.'

Carver had brought the photo of the material, but Weighton had also taken the precaution of bringing the actual piece of evidence in its evidence bag. After they introduced themselves, Carver took charge and showed it to the librarian.

'We're from Hull Police, and we've got this piece of evidence which may be crucial to our inquiry. We're just not sure what it is. I know it's a long shot, but we wondered if someone in the library might be able to help.'

Weighton had made sure the material was protected in a cellophane wrapper.

'Can I take it out?' asked the librarian.

Carver handed her some rubber gloves. The woman put them on and then held up the material and examined it.

'What do you *think* it is?' she asked Carver.

'Well, at first we thought it might be a child's pirate flag. But it's clearly part of a piece of clothing. You can tell by the stitching at the sleeve. So then we wondered if it was some sort of pirate fancy-dress costume, but we've pretty much discounted that. That's why we came here, to be honest. Just on the off-chance it might be some sort of club or cult uniform, and you might recognise it.'

The woman screwed up her face. 'To be honest, it does ring a bell. But I can't remember why.' She called over to her assistant, who was busy cataloguing some books. 'Janet, any ideas what this might be?'

The younger woman looked carefully at the piece of material, then shook her head.

'No idea. Why?'

'This lady and gentleman are from the police. They want to know. Something's in the back of my mind, I just can't remember what.' Then she turned back to Carver and Weighton. 'Can you perhaps tell me a little more about the case it's connected to? That might jog my memory.'

Carver wasn't sure how much she could say, but Weighton came to her aid.

'It concerns a series of attacks on American GIs stationed near here, and local girls they were going out with.'

'Oh dear,' said the librarian. 'I didn't read about that in the paper.'

'It hasn't been in the papers,' said Weighton. 'Not yet.'

'Sounds nasty. My impression's always been that the American troops – I assume you mean the ones stationed at Cottingham – have been welcomed with open arms.' She frowned again, as though she was still trying to recall something. 'Humour me a little. I know you won't want to reveal too much detail about your case, but the American thing is jogging my memory. Where in America were these GIs from who were attacked?'

'Originally?' replied Carver. 'I think they came from near Jackson in Mississippi.'

The woman's face fell. 'No, no. That's not it.'

'But most recently they'd lived in Det—'

'That's it! Detroit!' shouted the woman, forgetting herself for a moment. A chorus of shushing came from academics and students ensconced at various desks around the library. 'Oops, sorry,' she said, dropping her voice to a whisper again. 'I'm usually the one telling other people off. But that's it. That's where I remember it. A film about Detroit starring Humphrey Bogart.' She turned to her assistant again. 'Janet, you remember,' she hissed. 'That one starring Bogart we went to see. It must have been three or four years ago. What the devil was it called?'

The other woman looked at her blankly and shrugged.

'Damn! Whoops, sorry. I still can't remember its name, but I'm sure that's where I saw a costume similar to that. If you come over here, we've got an archive of the *Hull Daily Mail*. We're just going to have to go through the film review section. Now which years do we need? It was definitely before the war. So perhaps '37, '38, and part of '39 should do it.'

'That's going to be nearly a thousand editions of the paper to work through,' said Weighton. 'Certainly hundreds.'

'No, no, Sergeant,' said the librarian. 'Don't despair. They only do the film reviews once a week. So at most 150, probably fewer. Ah, here we are. The files are very heavy, Sergeant. Can you pull out those three, and we can take them to the table over there. If one of you does 1937, the other 1939, and I'll look through 1938, because if my memory serves me correctly that's approximately when the film is most likely to have been shown.'

The librarian's enthusiasm for the task was catching, and Carver found herself quickly thumbing through the heavy files, getting into a rhythm and working out via the thickness of the newsprint where each Friday's art section of the newspaper would be. But all three of them seemed to be getting nowhere, and Carver found her arms aching from holding up the heavy pages. Her fingers, too, were soon covered in the sooty black ink of the newsprint.

'Yes!' the librarian suddenly shouted, to another chorus of shushing and stern looks.

Carver and Weighton gathered round her.

'Here you go. Friday, February 11th 1938.'

Carver looked at the review over the librarian's shoulder. There was a picture of Humphrey Bogart – looking a little younger than in *The Maltese Falcon* – the review itself, but also another photograph.

The one that sealed the deal.

It was taken from the trial on which the film was based – a murder and kidnapping in Detroit, the last city in which Archie Davis and Theo Howard had lived.

A murder and kidnapping committed by a sinister group. The *Hull Daily Mail* had reproduced a photograph showing police dressed up in the group's members' uniforms.

And there they were, as clear as night and day.

The sinister black hoods and hats, with only eye and mouth holes.

And breaking up the black of the headdress and robes, the pure white skull and crossbones.

A uniform enough to make you shudder.

The uniform of a Ku Klux Klan offshoot known as the Black Legion, which was also the title of the film.

An offshoot, according to the paper, which was even more hate-filled.

Even more evil.

And even more deadly.

27

Swift had been steeling himself to confront Detective Chief Superintendent Holdridge. He was half tempted to let his boss read everything in the newspaper, but he knew that would send Holdridge apoplectic. And with Feather's revelation about the death sentence hanging over Theo Howard, Swift now needed the DCS on his side. He couldn't let an innocent man be executed on his watch.

Carver and Weighton's return now gave him further ammunition.

As soon as they arrived back at the incident room, Carver got out the relevant copy of the *Hull Daily Mail*. The college librarian had allowed them to borrow it on the strict under-standing it was returned once the police photographer had taken photographs for the evidence file.

When Swift saw the image of the Detroit policemen dressed up in the uniform of the Black Legion, and Carver explained its significance, he knew they had to act.

The trouble was, could they?

He also knew that Theo Howard had tried to warn him and Weighton about this, when Mulder had cut him off mid-sentence.

The word 'black' – that he'd only manage to start before being silenced by the military policeman – wasn't an adjective applying to another soldier, as Swift had assumed. It was the first part of the name of this sinister white supremacist offshoot. They'd been given half the answer – they just hadn't seen it.

'Carver, I want you to contact Detroit police. You'll need to book a transatlantic call. I can give you any authority you need. I want you to try to find out from them if this Black Legion group is still active, and whether they have any details on suspected members. Particularly any members who are thought to have joined the US Army and been stationed in the United Kingdom. Get their names, backgrounds, any details of suspected offences, even if they weren't charged . . . that sort of thing. Meanwhile, Weighton and I are going to see DCS Holdridge.'

Swift watched Holdridge's face progressively redden with anger as he apprised him of his conversation with Feather, although – for now – he omitted the part about the sentence passed on Private Howard.

'What the devil do you think you're playing at, Swift? Talking to the press without my express authority.'

'I'm afraid it was a damage limitation exercise, sir. We probably should have gone to the press sooner – everything was bound to get out at some stage, especially with someone as persistent as Feather. He already knew pretty much everything. He was going to print it all, and would have made us out to be fools had I not intervened.'

'How on earth do you work that one out?'

'Because, sir, in some respects Feather actually knew *more* than we did. For example, were you aware that the court martial for Theophilus Howard had already taken place?'

'I'd heard something to that effect, yes.'

'But he's an innocent man, sir.'

'Do you know that for certain?' thundered Holdridge.

Swift nodded at Weighton, and his deputy produced the copy of the *Hull Daily Mail* and the fragment of the Black Legion uniform from behind his back. He opened the paper at the relevant page, and turned it round for Holdridge. Swift came round to Holdridge's side of the desk to point everything out.

'This,' he said, holding up the piece of material, 'was found at the scene in Cottingham where we believe Jessica Pickering was engaged in sexual activity. As you can see, it's almost identical to part of the uniform being modelled in this photograph by Detroit police officers following the arrest of members of a white suprema-cist group known as the Black Legion for a particularly gruesome murder and kidnapping in their city. That case then became a film starring Humphrey Bogart – that's how it came to be in the *Mail*, and how it was recognised by the librarian at University College, thanks again to excellent work by WAPC Carver and Sergeant Weighton here. Now we also found fibres under Jessica Pickering's fingernails which are an exact match to this piece of the Black Legion uniform, indicating she tore it from one of her attackers while she was trying to defend herself from a vicious sexual assault.'

Swift could tell that it was starting to sink in with Holdridge what everything meant, but his boss wasn't quite ready to give in just yet.

'That still doesn't prove the court-martialled soldier didn't commit the first two murders – those of Sarah Houghton and Archie Davis.'

'It doesn't prove it, no. But it provides a bloody great question mark over his conviction, and if this evidence had been shown by us at his court martial then I'm confident he would not have been convicted. What's more, his conviction was partly secured thanks to false evidence from the late Ernest Bethell MP and Councillor Audley Smethwick – both of whom we've now unmasked as fraudsters.'

Holdridge gave a long sigh. 'Well, what do you want me to do about it? As you know, the Americans are a law unto themselves. And I told you about the bill going through Parliament which will give them sole jurisdiction over any crimes their soldiers commit.'

'Yes, but it hasn't gone through Parliament yet, has it? The crimes weren't committed on an American base. Two of the victims aren't even American soldiers. We have to uphold the justice of the United Kingdom, not the United States. And there's one more reason why we need to act straightaway. Something that Feather managed to find out from his sources.'

'What?' asked Holdridge, clearly losing patience.

'Private Theo Howard has been sentenced to death. He could have a noose round his neck at this very moment, for all we know. We have to act now.'

28

They decided to go in mob-handed, enlisting the help of the East Riding force, whose patch it was officially. Holdridge insisted on accompanying Swift, Weighton and Carver. In fact, he tried to keep Carver out of the loop, but Swift was adamant she be present as she'd done so much to crack the case.

The City of Detroit Police Department had come good – providing them with a list of names of people still suspected of being active in the Black Legion, several of whom had been asterisked as having gone on to join the US Army. They'd also provided background information on the Legion's activities – suspected as they were of killing some fifty people in the US Midwest in the previous decade.

The notorious case of the murder of Charles Poole, that had formed the basis for the Humphrey Bogart film, and the trial that followed, was thought to have seen the Legion disband. But the Detroit Police Department weren't so sure – they believed some former members were still active, and new members had been recruited in the Highland Park area of Detroit – where the group was first formed. A key twisted motivation for Legion members seemed to be to *protect the sanctity of white Protestant women.*

That wasn't the end of it. The American police had imparted one piece of information that suddenly made everything fall into place. One of the suspected Black Legion members had a particular reason to want vengeance against white women who'd become involved with black men.

The mother of the Legion member in question, who'd now become a soldier, had run off with a black man.

When his father found out his wife had betrayed him, and who with, he'd hunted the pair down and killed them both by strangulation. Not only that, but the husband – in a bizarre post-death ritual – had cut out his wife's heart and hacked off her lover's penis.

When Swift read that in Carver's notes of the telephone conversation, he realised that could be the group's bizarre justification for the Hull crimes – the son mimicking the crimes of the father. Perhaps he'd had his nose put out of joint by Sarah Houghton or Jessica Pickering each walking out with a black American GI.

If so, his revenge – if that's what it was – was not just brutal, but verging on madness.

The soldier's name: John Rushing.

The police cars all assembled outside the Cottingham barracks. Poskitt and Verrill were there, too, drafted in to help with interviewing suspects.

At first, there was a stand-off.

Sergeant Mulder refused to let the police enter. Lieutenant-Colonel DeVries backed him, even ordering the gatehouse guards to aim their weapons at the police squad.

In the end, Holdridge managed to talk him down.

'It won't look good for you, Colonel DeVries, if you're seen to be obstructing the British police in the course of their duty. This base may, technically, be American soil while your troops are here, but we have solid evidence that people here are suspects in the murders of two British women and two American soldiers, committed on British soil – *outside* your jurisdiction. We need your co-operation to search your officers' quarters.'

Holdridge outlined the evidence that Swift had presented to him a short time earlier: the fragment of Black Legion uniform and a photograph of the relevant *Hull Daily Mail* article – proving beyond doubt what the torn material was. The deciding factor, though, was the information from Detroit Police – and the list of names of suspected Black Legion members who'd gone on to join the military.

All of them were from the Highland Park area of Detroit.

DeVries read out a selection of the names.

Lowell Dean.

Herschell Vincent.

Dayton Gill.

And last, but not least, John Rushing.

'Well, I'll be damned,' said DeVries. 'Those are all officers with my battalion. Rushing is even a captain. Dean's a lieutenant. Gill and Vincent are first lieutenants.'

'Where are they at the moment?' asked Swift.

'Well, they're all at work – at the docks, supervising soldiers. Loading and unloading. That's what we're here for.'

'We need to search their quarters,' said Swift.

DeVries eyeballed him. 'Normally, I'd say no, Chief Inspector.' Then he waved the incriminating police photo reproduced from the *Hull Daily Mail*. 'But this puts a whole different light on things. Guards, lower your weapons, and open the barrier. We're to give these gentlemen here every assistance they need. You hear that, Sergeant Mulder? Some of these men may be your friends, but they're no friends of mine. I'm not having the name of this battalion besmirched by scum like this. We help the British police. And if necessary, we help the British police nail these guys.'

'There's one other thing,' said Swift. 'You realise what this means for Private Theo Howard? You need to contact Shepton Mallet prison straightaway, and make sure he's released before it's too late.'

Mulder showed Swift, Weighton and the East Riding detectives to the officers' quarters, while Holdridge completed formalities with DeVries.

While the soldiers were housed in Nissen huts in the grounds, the officers were sharing grand rooms in the main house – Thwaite Hall.

The detectives took a room each, with a couple of uniformed constables to help with the search. Carver stayed by Swift's side. He couldn't allow her to conduct a search herself – but equally, he didn't want to her to miss the denouement of the investigation.

At first, none of the searches turned up anything incriminating. Swift ordered them to start all over again, his team included.

It was on the second pass in his own room – Captain John Rushing's quarters – that Swift discovered the loose floorboard.

'Here,' he said to the constables. 'Lift this up, please.'

When they had, Swift lay flat to the floor, then reached around in the void with his good hand. Immediately, he grabbed hold of some smooth, satin-feel material. Then more. He pulled it all out, then struggled to his feet. Four black robes, each adorned with a white felt skull and crossbones, one of which looked as though it had been hastily, and badly, repaired.

'Can one of you see if you can either take up more of the floorboards, or reach your hand in further? I was struggling a little.' Swift didn't have to explain why – the two PCs could see his prosthetic hand.

'Of course, sir,' one of them said, and then imitated Swift by lying flat to the floor then reaching into the void with his arm. This time he pulled out a length of rubber-covered wire, with handholds at each end, and handed it to Swift. The chief inspector showed it to Carver, who gave a grim smile. He was prepared to bet his Beverley house on them finding Sarah Houghton's blood on it – the final proof they would need that Theo Howard was innocent.

Swift told the others what he'd found, then went downstairs again to inform Holdridge and DeVries.

The lieutenant-colonel bowed his head and held it in his hands.

'Good God! These men have dragged the name of the US Army through the mud. Whose room did you find it in?'

'Rushing's.'

'The most senior of them. Well, that's just sick, Chief Inspector. They must be sick in the head. They'll pay for this, you can be certain.'

'They will,' said Swift. 'Because we will put them on trial. What time do they return from the docks?'

DeVries looked up at the clock on the wall of his office.

'In about half an hour or so. I'll make sure the four of them are arrested immediately and brought to you in Hull.'

'If it's all the same to you, sir, we'll stay here and make the arrests ourselves.'

When the US Army trucks arrived back at the barracks, DeVries was as good as his word in making sure the military assisted the police in the arrests.

The only one who tried to resist was Rushing himself, turning to run and pulling out his gun. It was DeVries himself who warned him off.

'I'd drop that weapon if I were you, Captain!' he shouted. 'You're heading for a long, long jail term anyways. But you fire that goddamn gun, and you're going to swing for it, boy, so help me God!'

Rushing seemed to belatedly come to his senses, let his gun fall to the floor and raised his hands above his head.

Once the four of them had been put in separate rooms under armed guard, the detectives prepared to interview each one individually. First, Swift went to DeVries's office with Holdridge. He knew the lieutenant-colonel had already put in one call to his superiors, and had also rung Shepton Mallet prison.

'I'll do everything I can to make sure he's freed,' he'd said. 'Or at least to make sure sentence is stayed until everything is sorted out. Then we can work on getting Howard an official pardon.'

Virtually as soon as they were back in DeVries's office, the telephone rang.

As the lieutenant-colonel answered, Swift could see his frown deepening by the second.

'Well, that can't be right, sir!' he bellowed down the line. 'Makes us look to be fools and barbarians. And no, I won't watch my language. Good day to you.' He slammed down the handset.

'I don't need to tell you, Chief Inspector. That wasn't good news.'

'What did they say?' asked Swift.

Perhaps it's already too late for Howard. If so, I'll never be able to live with myself.

'Your executioner – Thomas Pierrepoint, I believe – is already on his way. The sentence is being carried out tomorrow morning.'

Swift felt everything crowding in on him.

He couldn't let this happen.

Theo Howard was innocent. Not only that – his best friend had already been killed by these vicious white supremacists, sheltered by the US Army.

He was not going to let that man lose his life, too, for a crime he did not commit.

He gestured to Holdridge, indicating he wanted to speak to him in the corridor, out of earshot of the American commanding officer.

'I'm sorry, Swift, truly I am. But I don't see that there's anything we can do.'

'With respect, there is, sir. And I intend to do it. I need you to wrap up the interviews here, helped by Poskitt and Verrill. Carver can act as your assistant, and fill you in on any background to the case that you're uncertain of. I need to take Weighton with me.'

'Take him where?'

Swift didn't have time to answer the question. He turned on his heel and went to find his sergeant.

There wasn't any time left to lose.

29

Theo Howard only learned the truth the night before it was all due to happen.

It was his cellmate who put him out of his misery, or threw him into his misery, whichever way you wanted to look at it.

'You still don't know, do you, brother?' he asked just before they tried to get some sleep. 'Goddamn it, you still don't know. You're as blissfully ignorant as a little babe.'

Then the man started laughing, a godawful cackle.

Theo knew the man was strong, but he was stronger. He got up, towered over him, then grabbed him round the neck with his forearm and started to squeeze.

'You don't laugh at me, punk.'

'Well, why ever not?' The man spluttered as he struggled to breathe. 'Ain't you ever asked yourself why we're in this cell together, me being a rapist and all?'

Theo released his grip slightly to allow his fellow prisoner to talk more easily.

'What the fuck do you mean?'

'Well, man, it's like your mama gave you shit for brains. Don't you know the penalty for rape in the US Army?'

'No,' admitted Theo.

'Well, let me tell you something, then. It's the same as for murder, and you're in here for murder, ain't you?'

'I didn't murder no one. I was fixed up.'

'Well, it's too late for you now, Private. And it's too late for me. This is our last night on this earth. Tomorrow, we go to meet our maker. But if it's as you say, and you's innocent, well then, you're heading up to Heaven, brother. Don't think they'll be making any room up there for me.'

Theo started to squeeze the man's neck again.

'Tell me you lying, brother. You must be lying.'

'I admit, I'm not always the most honest guy. But this is no word of a lie. Enjoy your last night of dreams, brother. Tomorrow we'll be swinging by the neck.'

30

Swift and Weighton managed to persuade Mulder to assign them some fuel – enough to ensure they wouldn't have to stop at a petrol station to fill up, although Swift knew the tank was almost full. The Morris could do well over forty miles per gallon if driven carefully, but they would be thrashing it. He wished he had a more powerful car with a bigger fuel tank – for example, he could have tried to persuade Holdridge to lend him his. But the time wasted arguing with him would have probably negated its value.

Weighton offered to drive first – but they both knew that, where they were going, they would have to regularly swap at the wheel.

The smell of fuel from the jerry cans on the back seat and boot was overpowering.

'Are you sure that's safe, sir?' asked Weighton, as Mulder helped Swift load up the fuel cans.

'No. But do you have a better idea, Sergeant?'

Before they set off, Swift made one telephone call.

He managed to speak to the man concerned, who agreed to meet him and talk to him in a village pub. But that was all. Swift didn't want to give details of his request over an open phone line in any case.

For as much of the journey as they could, they both kept the Morris's speedometer as near as possible to its maximum – just under sixty miles an hour. The rattling and noise meant the journey was more tiring than it ought to have been, but with so few private vehicles on the road because of petrol rationing, at least they weren't held up by other traffic.

They struck out south-west towards Doncaster but then skirted to the south, picking up the Great North Road near Bawtry. At Newark, they turned off and again headed south-west, this time along the Fosse Way, south of Nottingham, then following the route of the old Roman road towards Leicester.

The road, in common with many that originated in Roman times, was almost dead straight. The lack of bends helped to alert Swift. Once again, he got the sense they were being followed. A car he'd first noticed near Bawtry – a Humber, so without doubt faster than the Morris – seemed to be making no effort to overtake them, just keeping on their tail.

Weighton obviously noticed him checking regularly in his mirrors.

'Something wrong, sir?' he asked.

Swift shrugged. 'I don't think so.'

'Then why do you keep on checking in your mirrors?' Weighton turned in his seat. 'If it's that car behind, I noticed it earlier, soon after we joined the A63, not long after we left Cottingham.'

Cottingham?

Then if it was following them, it had been with them nearly all the way. Swift sighed. How much should he tell Weighton?

'Is there something you're not telling me, sir?'

Swift shrugged. 'If I tell you, it's not to go any further.'

'You can rely on me, sir.'

What Weighton said was true. In the year or so they'd worked as a pair, Swift had never known him to be loose-lipped.

'All right, Sergeant. I don't *know* we're being followed. But we might be. And I've had that sense before. Since virtually the start of this inquiry. On the way to the Driffield Show. Another time in Cottingham, after visiting the US base there. And then on the way to Spurn Head. Up until now, I've dismissed it. But I was given a friendly warning something like this might happen.'

'From whom?'

'I had a visit from the security services. MI5. At the Beverley house. They took me on a little walk. Some unsolicited advice about not upsetting the Americans, that sort of thing.'

'You think it could be MI5 following us?' asked Weighton, an element of excitement, almost, in his voice.

'I don't know. There's a couple of other strange things have happened during the investigation. But they're more linked to an investigation that got me into a spot of bother when I used to be with the Met.'

'Strange things?'

'Threats. Or at least, implied threats. I ruffled a few feathers, shall we say – the feathers of some quite important people. I thought I'd left it all behind me. But something was sent to me that made it clear I hadn't. That they hadn't forgotten.'

'What exactly was that?'

'Exactly? A metal badge from an anonymous sender. Innocent enough, you might think, Weighton.'

'Well, it's hardly like receiving a hand grenade in the post, sir.'

Swift gave a hollow laugh. Then he checked his mirrors again. Bizarrely, since they began their conversation, the Humber seemed to have turned off. Perhaps he was becoming paranoid after all. But then Weighton claimed to have noticed the car, too. The trouble was, so many government-issue Humbers looked the same these days – in a strictly limited range of colours.

'The car's gone.'

Weighton turned to double-check.

'So it has. Perhaps the one I saw earlier wasn't the same one after all. But come on, sir, what was the relevance of this badge?'

'It was an insignia. A Nazi insignia.'

'Good grief!' exclaimed Weighton. 'I hope you logged it and put it in an evidence bag. You don't want to be caught with that, sir.'

Swift didn't answer, but he knew his deputy was correct. Stupidly, he'd simply hidden it away in a locked drawer at the Beverley house.

'I have to confess, sir,' continued Weighton, 'I still don't fully understand.'

'It was a membership badge of the Imperial Fascist League. With the Met, I was involved in a case where I was responsible for tracking down as many of them as possible, and making sure they ended up in jail when war broke out.'

'Isn't that MI5's job, sir?'

'I worked with them.'

'So what do you think was the significance of the badge?'

'I think it was a warning, Weighton. They were letting me know that they know where I am. And one day, no doubt, their supporters will try to get their revenge. At first, I wondered if it was directly connected to this current investigation. The London case involved race, too . . . that was my thinking. But to be honest, I think it was just coincidence.'

'Worrying though, sir. I wish you'd told me earlier.'

'Well, when Carver was kidnapped, you can imagine what I thought. But it's me they're after, if anyone. I don't think you and Carver have anything to worry about. It wasn't your argument.'

'Perhaps not, sir. But I want you to know you should always tell me about things like that. I'll always cover your back, but I can't protect you against things you don't tell me about.'

Weighton was right, of course.

But if it came to it, Swift wasn't sure his deputy would be any protection at all.

At Coventry – a city that had been devastated by Hitler's bombers some six months before the height of Hull's own blitz – they turned south, heading towards Banbury. All the time, because of the lack of road and town signs, Weighton was having to ask his boss where they were, almost like a small child on his or her first long journey in the family car.

'What I don't understand precisely, sir, is where we are going, and why?' asked Weighton, after several minutes of silence.

'You'll see, Weighton.'

'I hope it's going to be worth it, sir.'

'I hope so, too. An innocent man's life depends on it.'

Eventually, in a village somewhere north of Oxford, Swift parked the car outside a country inn called the Bear.

'Is this where we're staying the night, sir?'

Swift snorted. 'I doubt we could afford it, Weighton. And no, it isn't. Wait here.'

Terrence Haughtree was waiting for him, as promised, in the hotel lobby. This time his silent sidekick was nowhere to be seen.

'Chief Inspector,' he said, getting up from his armchair and extending his hand. 'I half wondered if I might see you again before too long. Good journey, I hope?'

'I've had better,' said Swift.

They sat down opposite each other, separated by a low coffee table.

'Will you join me for a cup of tea? Or something stronger, if you prefer?'

'I won't, Mr Haughtree, no. And I don't intend to keep you long. I need some help.'

'Oh yes?'

'The case you came to see me about. We've pretty much wrapped it up.'

'So I understand.'

Swift rolled his eyes. Why was he not surprised that MI5 knew about everything almost before he himself did?

'But there's a loose end – a rather serious loose end, which in my view reflects very badly on this country. And I'm not prepared to let it happen, at least not without a fight.'

Haughtree lowered his voice. 'You're talking about Private Howard, I presume?'

Swift nodded.

'Well, I don't see there's anything I can do to help you. And I don't think it should be your concern.'

'But there's been a terrible miscarriage of—'

Haughtree held his hand up, palm outwards.

'Let me stop you there, Chief Inspector. It's not up to us to say how the American military police should or should not conduct their courts martial.'

'But the crime happened on British soil, under my jurisdiction, and one of his alleged victims is a British subject.'

'Ah, well, on that you seem to be misinformed, Mr Swift. My information is that Howard was found guilty and sentenced solely in respect of the murder of his fellow GI, Archibald Davis – and not in relation to the British woman. Therefore, the US Army was within its rights. Now, we have made representations to the Americans asking that his sentence be commuted, but so far those representations have fallen on deaf ears. And His Majesty's Government does not want to push things too far. As I explained to you before, keeping the Americans on side is vital to the war effort. That is what is of paramount importance here. Not the fate of one soldier. Not when thousands are dying on the battlefields every day. You have to be able to see the wood for the trees, Mr Swift.'

Swift could feel the anger and resentment boiling up inside him as the man continued his condescending little speech.

'You do realise the sentence is being carried out at dawn tomorrow morning?'

Haughtree looked genuinely surprised. 'I didn't, no. Where did you get that information from?'

'A reliable source.'

'Well, that is disappointing. We were led to believe our entreaties were still under consideration, even though so far they had failed to get any traction. However, it doesn't change the overall picture. We've done what we can, and we have bigger fish to fry. I'm sorry, Mr Swift.'

Swift got up from his chair and turned on his heel.

He didn't say goodbye to the man. He didn't see any point.

Outside, Weighton was in the car reading the sports pages of the *Hull Daily Mail*. For some reason, that irked Swift, especially as there was no meaningful competitive sport being played these days.

'Have you used the jerry cans to refill the petrol tank, Weighton?'

'Um . . . no, sir. I didn't realise—'

'Well, do it now, man. Quickly!'

The next leg of the journey started with Weighton driving, and both men in a foul mood – silent other than occasional barked directions from Swift.

Eventually, Swift decided he ought to break the ice.

'I'm sorry I snapped at you, Sergeant.'

'That's quite all right, sir. I was out of order – I should have anticipated we'd need to fill up. Where are we off to now?'

'London, Weighton. And put your foot down. We're running out of time.'

Once they picked up the A40, they made rapid progress past High Wycombe and Beaconsfield, and were soon in the outskirts of the capital.

This leg of the journey was little more than ninety minutes or so – but with darkness having fallen, and the Morris's headlight beam restricted by its blackout covers, it was likely to take up to two hours. As a result, Swift decided to let Weighton keep driving, rather than swapping round halfway as they had before. In any case, his shoulder where the harness joined his body to the prosthetic arm was hurting like hell. Weighton was a younger man, anyway. He could manage.

'Where are we going this time, sir?'

'Marylebone in central London. When we get to the new Western Avenue bypass, it should be quite quick.'

They passed some of the construction work for the last section of the road, near Denham, and then picked up the completed part.

Soon after passing Madame Tussauds, Swift instructed Weighton to turn right. The waxworks had been damaged by a high-explosive bomb during London's Blitz, but the facade was untouched. Swift knew many of the wax figures themselves had been destroyed, however. He'd read it in the newspapers. Evidently Weighton had, too, and seemed to know what Swift was thinking about.

'You know, of course, which waxwork didn't get destroyed by the bomb, don't you, sir?'

'Hitler's?'

'That's right, sir. You must have read the report, too. His figure moved a bit to one side, and a small lump was chipped out of his face by shrapnel, but that was it. Ironic, isn't it?'

'You could say that, Weighton. Let's hope our bombers do better on Berlin and manage to blow up the man himself.'

'They say he's not often in Berlin, though, sir. Doesn't he prefer it at the Wolf's Lair in East Prussia, and the Eagle's Nest at Berchtesgaden?'

'I wouldn't know, Weighton. I'm not an expert on Hitler's movements, thank God. Now, keep your eyes peeled. It's not easy to see in the blackout, but we're looking for number 129.'

'Aren't these mostly posh doctors' practices, sir? Will there be anyone here at this time?'

'I hope so, Weighton. This is the last card I've got to play. Let's pray it's a trump.'

Swift rapped the door knocker and rang the bell at the same time. The house was in darkness – but then that wasn't a surprise when you could be fined several shillings for an accidental sliver of light showing through the blackout curtains and screens.

Eventually, Swift heard the sound of footsteps, then the front door being opened.

In the dim light from the stars and moon, he could make out the features of the housekeeper, Mrs Curtis, as she opened the door a crack but kept the safety chain on.

'I'm sorry, we're closed,' she said.

'It's me, Mrs Curtis. Ambrose Swift.'

'Ah, Ambrose. We haven't seen you for a good long while,' she said, taking the safety chain off and opening the door fully.

'Come in, come in. I'm afraid he's not here, though. He was called away by Winnie, I'm afraid. You know how it is. They might almost as well be married. I'm expecting him back for a late supper, though, perhaps in as soon as half an hour's time. Can you wait till then? I can make you a cup of tea, and some supper for yourself, if you haven't eaten.'

'I haven't actually, Mrs Curtis. That's very kind of you. Would it be all right if my sergeant came in as well? He's in the car over there.'

'Of course, of course, Ambrose. The more the merrier. You know you're always welcome here.'

Mrs Curtis had managed to prepare a cold supper fit for a king, with meats, pies, sandwiches and cakes which seemed to bear little resemblance to the usual ration-restricted wartime fare. Perhaps Dr Wilson's now elevated position secured him preferential ration books and supplies.

Swift was getting nervous about how long they were having to wait. Time was slipping away, and if this mission was to prove more than a wild goose chase, the good doctor needed to turn up soon.

Eventually, Dr Wilson did return – not long after Mrs Curtis's estimated arrival time. To Swift the minutes had seemed to drag, though there were certainly worse ways to while away time than eating sandwiches, pies and cakes washed down with lashings of strong tea.

The doctor seemed genuinely delighted to see Swift.

'Ah, the boy returns. We haven't seen you for a long while, which I might say is a jolly good thing. And who is this giant of a man you've brought with you?'

'This is my sergeant, Dr Wilson. James Weighton – he's my deputy in the CID in Hull.'

'Ah, Hull. A rather delightful city, I must say, but then it is in God's own country, so it would be. Sounds like it suffered rather dreadfully from Hitler's bombs, though.'

'Pleased to meet you, sir,' said Weighton, rising to his feet. 'And you're not wrong. We did get quite a pasting, and the rest of the country rarely hears about it.'

'I'm well aware of that. However, I can tell you, Sergeant, whenever I hear the news announcers say "a north-east coastal town" has been badly hit, I know exactly where that is, even if others don't. I'm a Yorkshireman myself, you see, although the accent's not as strong as yours, Sergeant. Spent too long down here for that. I've become a southern softie.' He turned back to Swift. 'Anyway, I'm sure you've not come all this way unannounced for idle chit-chat, Ambrose. What is it I can do for you? The shoulder isn't playing up again, is it?'

'No, no. It's not that, Doctor. To be honest, I need a favour. A rather big favour.'

'Oh dear. That sounds ominous.'

'You're my last hope, actually. It's in your power to help save an innocent man's life.'

'Well, then. I swore a version of the Hippocratic Oath when I graduated from St Mary's Hospital here in London. I can hardly refuse.'

'The only trouble is, it means you using your most important connection, and there is not a moment to lose.' Swift glanced at his watch. 'In as little as eight hours' time, an innocent man may be put to death.'

'And you're certain this man is innocent?'

'Without a doubt.'

'Well, then, I'll do everything I can to help you.'

He picked up a slice of pork pie from the spread laid out by his housekeeper and wrapped it in a napkin. Then he shouted through to the kitchen.

'Mrs Curtis, I'm afraid I have to go straight out again. Duty calls. But I've taken a piece of your excellent pie with me, and I shall avail myself of more of your delightful repast when I return.'

'Where are we going?' asked Swift.

'Well, I'm presuming you want me to appeal to Winston's better nature. There's no point trying to do that over the telephone. He'll just come up with some sort of excuse. If we lay the facts in front of him in person, then you may just have half a chance, Ambrose. I'm not promising anything, though. The fate of one man when a war is going on, and we're not even winning it yet, might not be seen as a priority. And I have to warn you, he's not in the best of moods today.'

Dr Wilson allowed Weighton to drive them in the Morris, with Swift squeezed into the back seat. As they drove along, the doctor munched on his slice of pie as Swift filled him in on more details.

'Get your story straight, Ambrose,' he said between mouthfuls, 'and make sure it is as strong as possible. Be concise and precise. He doesn't suffer fools gladly, as you probably know, and he has a surgical mind that can cut an argument to shreds in no time. So, make sure he doesn't have chance to refuse you. What you're asking for is the right thing, I'm sure of that. But I would just counsel

you not to be overconfident of success. Winnie has certain . . .
how shall I put it? . . . slightly archaic views. If your soldier was a
white man, well . . .'

'Then he almost certainly wouldn't be facing the noose,' said
Swift.

'I grant you that,' said Dr Wilson. 'But the Prime Minister
does not necessarily view things the same way as you or I.'

Weighton pulled up on Victoria Embankment, and Dr Wilson
told the two detectives to wait in the car while he checked how
the land lay at 10 Downing Street. Soldiers guarding Downing
Street immediately took an interest in the Morris, and Swift was
forced to show them his and Weighton's police warrant cards to
avoid being moved along.

The minutes ticked by, with Swift becoming ever more
anxious.

'What exactly is your plan, sir?' asked Weighton.

'Well, as you've probably gathered by now, Weighton, as you
haven't asked, Dr Wilson is Winston Churchill's personal physician. He also happens to be the medical officer who amputated
my arm and saved me when I was dragged half-dead from the
killing fields of the Somme in summer 1916. Since then, he's
occasionally continued to treat me for complications following
the amputation, and the fitting of my prosthesis.'

'A useful connection to have, sir.'

'It is, but I'd still rather my arm was intact.'

'Sorry, sir. I didn't mean any offence.'

'None taken, Sergeant. This is the last throw of the dice, though. The meeting in Woodstock was with a contact in MI5 – the home security service. I thought that might work, but it didn't. If Dr Wilson comes back in the next few minutes saying Churchill has refused to see me, then we'll have failed.'

'But we found the real killers, sir.'

'That won't matter a damn, Weighton, if an innocent man goes to the gallows. I would never be able to live with myself.'

A few minutes later, Dr Wilson was back. Swift had by now moved into the passenger seat. The doctor leaned down and spoke through the open window.

'You're lucky, Ambrose. He *is* in a bad mood, but your story – or at least my garbled account of it – distracted him somewhat. He's agreed to give you five minutes. Don't waste it.'

Both Swift and Weighton started to get out of the car.

'Just you, I'm afraid, Ambrose,' said Dr Wilson. 'He made that quite clear. Sorry, Sergeant.'

Swift nodded. 'You need to stay with the car anyway, Weighton, sorry. Otherwise these soldiers here will probably try to blow it up as a security threat.'

They walked along Downing Street, past number 10, to the far end junction with Horse Guards Road.

'You can see why I took a little time, I'm afraid, Ambrose. He's not actually in Downing Street at the moment, he's in the Cabinet War Rooms.'

There was a wait at the entrance while Dr Wilson sought clearance for Swift, and then they were escorted down to the basement rooms. Swift and Wilson were taken to a small room, little more than a cupboard.

'The transatlantic telephone room,' whispered the doctor. 'Perhaps he's going to go to the very top on your behalf.'

Churchill was sitting there, on a mahogany and green leather chair, puffing away on one of his trademark cigars and leafing through some papers.

Dr Wilson coughed to attract the Prime Minister's attention.

'This is Chief Inspector Swift, Prime Minister. The detective from Hull.'

Churchill gave the impression he hadn't heard at first, still leafing through his papers, with his back to them. The cigar fumes were overwhelming, and Swift found himself having to dig his fingernail into the flesh of his thumb on his good hand to stop it coming up and wafting away the smoke. Eventually, the Prime Minister deigned to reply.

'Ah yes, Charles. Just a moment.'

Then he placed down his papers, and turned in his chair.

'You're a fortunate man, Chief Inspector, in two respects. Firstly, to have a trusted friend in Charles McMoran Wilson – my personal physician, whom I gather treated you at the Battle of the Somme. And secondly, that I'm at this very moment waiting for a call to be put through to President Roosevelt. I'm aware of the background to your investigation – you came to the attention of MI5. You caused them some extra work, but nevertheless they spoke highly of you. But you must understand this is a sensitive matter. So, state your case, man.'

Swift suddenly found his throat had constricted and that he was struggling to say anything, never mind anything remotely cogent. Eventually, though, he pulled himself together, and as succinctly as possible, outlined the facts.

'In conclusion, sir,' he said, wrapping up his short statement, 'should we as a country allow an innocent man to hang, when he should by rights have been tried under our jurisdiction, then we are as a country diminished. The British sense of fair play, the British justice system, is renowned the world over. If we allow this atrocity to happen, we have allowed ourselves to descend to little more than savages.'

Churchill didn't speak for a moment, instead taking another few puffs on his cigar. Then he placed it down in his ashtray.

'Fine words, Chief Inspector. But in the years to come, history will not judge us on what we did or didn't do in respect of a murder investigation in Kingston-upon-Hull. It will judge whether inviting in our American allies helped to foreshorten Hitler's reign of terror. Nevertheless, I owe Dr Wilson here a great deal, and he has spoken eloquently on your behalf. Here is what I can do for you. I will give you a letter, signed by me, asking the authorities for clemency for this man. If you wish, you can take that with you to Shepton Mallet prison, though I cannot promise it will do any good, but it may just help delay matters.'

'Could you not send a telegram to the jail to that effect, sir? I'm worried we won't get there in time.'

'No, Chief Inspector, I cannot. The letter will have to suffice. I'm not prepared to risk angering our American allies further by interfering in their affairs. However, I shall also raise the matter at the end of my telephone call with the American president, simply because he is a personal friend. Again, I cannot promise it will do any good. That's all, Chief Inspector. I have already dictated the said letter to my secretary, based on what Dr Wilson told me, and I have signed it. You may collect it on your way out. I bid you good evening.'

31

After dropping Dr Wilson back at Harley Street and saying their thanks and goodbyes, Swift realised he and Weighton now had a race against time on their hands. It was almost midnight. In the daytime, the 130 miles or so to Shepton Mallet might have been achievable in perhaps three hours. With the restrictions of the blackout, and the difficulties of night-time driving in the war, they were looking at more like four or five hours – even if they didn't stop for a break. At least this time Weighton had taken the initiative and refilled with what remained in the Americans' jerry cans while he'd been waiting outside Downing Street. By Swift's calculations, they had just enough petrol to get to Shepton Mallet.

Weighton said he was happy to drive to start with, even though both of them were dog-tired and struggling to keep their eyes open. The dull ache in Swift's shoulder had now become a throbbing pain – he really needed to rest it. Nevertheless, when Weighton nearly swerved into a ditch near Andover, having obviously fallen asleep momentarily at the wheel, Swift insisted he would take over. Virtually as soon as they set off again, Weighton slumped in the passenger seat, snoring loudly. Swift opened the driver's-side window, hoping the fresh air would keep him awake.

But the other thing keeping him alert was every other vehicle's shielded headlights in the rear-view mirror, rare though they were at this time of night. On this occasion, though, there was nothing suspicious enough to make him think they were being followed.

They continued to make good progress until they reached Salisbury Plain.

Then, suddenly, the Morris started juddering and Swift struggled to keep control.

Weighton immediately woke up.

'What's happened, sir?'

'Puncture, I think, Weighton. The last thing we need.'

He checked his watch. They were perhaps an hour's drive from Shepton Mallet if this hadn't happened, with dawn due to break in around an hour's time. Swift knew that Thomas Pierrepoint had a reputation for getting his day's work out of the way as early as possible. He didn't like his victims to have too much time to think about their fate. They had to get a move on.

'You've got a spare, though, sir, haven't you?'

'Yes. Are you any good changing tyres? I'm not much use with this.' He pointed apologetically to his false arm.

'Yes, I'm a dab hand,' said Weighton. 'We'll be back underway in no time.'

They both got out of the car and Weighton removed the spare wheel.

'Where's the jack in this thing, sir?'

Swift got out his torch and looked in the boot. The jack was nowhere to be seen. Then he looked in the glove compartment – again, nothing.

Finally, he remembered.

'Oh, God! I totally forgot. I lent it to a neighbour in Beverley when they had a puncture. They never returned it and I forgot to ask for it back.'

Weighton sighed, and looked around.

Swift wondered if they could jack the car up with stones, or if Weighton might even be able to hold it up, while Swift fixed the wheel on – his sergeant was probably strong enough. But he knew that with his bad arm, he wouldn't be able to fulfil his part of the task.

'Look,' said Weighton. 'There's a pair of cottages there on the horizon. You wait here, I'll run there and try to wake them up. Someone's bound to have a jack.'

It seemed like half an hour before Weighton was back at the car with the jack, although in all probability it was nearer to twenty minutes.

Nevertheless, by the time they got back on the road, the standing stones of Stonehenge were much more visible than before. It wouldn't be long before dawn broke.

By the time the sun came up, they were still some half an hour or so from the prison. Swift put his foot right to the floor on the accelerator, but the Morris stubbornly refused to go more than its rather sedate top speed of fifty-eight miles per hour.

When they finally got to the prison gatehouse, Swift showed the guard their authority from Churchill.

'Mr Churchill himself. Gee! What's he really like?'

'I don't have time for this, officer. I need to be taken to the commanding officer or governor urgently.'

'Of course, sir. I was only passing the time of day.'

'Has Thomas Pierrepoint arrived yet?'

'You mean the hangman? I'm not rightly sure I should be telling you that, sir. But you look over your shoulder, that's him and his assistant in their car.'

Swift realised the pair were about to drive off.

'What's happening?' he asked, alarmed.

'He's always an early riser, sir, so he is. You wouldn't believe it, would you, sir? Mighty fine work if you can get it, I'd say. He's on his way home – finished his work for the day already.'

Swift covered his eyes with his hands.

'No!' he cried.

Then he beat his good fist into the wood of the guardhouse, again and again.

Weighton, behind him, put his arm on his boss's shoulder to comfort him.

They were too late.

Just as Swift had feared, they had let Theophilus Howard down.

Swift had felt such empathy with the man. His fate was simply an affront to human decency. An affront to the British justice Swift and Weighton had sworn to uphold.

An innocent man had gone to the gallows in a case in which Swift was the lead detective.

Swift would never, ever forgive himself.

32

A few hours earlier

Theo knew he wouldn't be getting much sleep on his last night. There were too many things running around his brain. He tried to think what had caused all this. Pictured those white officers in his mind. Trying to remember their faces, one by one.

Then, suddenly, he remembered.

Captain Rushing. His face had always seemed familiar. So had that of Lieutenant Dean. When he arrived in Cottingham, he was sure he'd seen them before, but he just couldn't remember where. They sure treated him and Archie mean, right from the start. They couldn't do no right. Those two were always picking holes in their work at the docks, even though Archie and he were among the best goddamn workers there were.

The thing that triggered his memory was thinking of Bessie, and where it had all started to go so wrong. Back in Detroit, when they'd been due to move into their dream home at the Sojourner Truth project. Theo regretted signing for that house now. That was supposed to be their for ever home – him, Bessie and the baby. That day they were supposed to move in.

Running the gauntlet of the crowd.

The crosses burning in the field.

They were nearly there. And then those two white guys stood in their path, and Theo had slammed on the brakes just in time.

Then all hell had broken loose when the cops discovered Archie's knife.

But now he knew. That's where it all began. Thousands of miles away in Detroit. Because he could see their faces now, through the windshield.

Creased up in hatred.

Hatred of his and Archie's black skin.

That was who they were.

Rushing and Dean.

Faces of hate.

In Detroit and in Hull.

'What you thinking about, brother? Not long till dawn now, is there?'

Theo didn't want to talk to no rapist punk. How could a man do that to a woman against her will? That was against the Lord's word, as sure as night follows day.

'You know, I thought she wanted it,' the man said.

Theo could hear he was sobbing away. Maybe Theo shouldn't be too hard on him.

'I thought you said you went and raped her. That's what you told me, straight out. That's what you said.'

'That's what she said. When her man came home. I thought she loved me. I thought that was what she wanted. She said her man wouldn't be home for hours and hours. We met when we were dancing. Those white girls, they love to see a black soldier dance.'

'They sure do,' said Theo. 'Didn't you tell them at the trial you thought she wanted it?'

The other man laughed. An evil cackle.

'You sure are a joker. Who'd you think they gonna believe, those white officers in charge of the court martials? A good English white woman – or a no-good punk black soldier boy? I didn't stand a chance.'

'So is you saying you ain't done it, after all?'

'I don't rightly know, soldier. I stopped when she started hollerin'. But she only started hollerin' when her man came back. Before that, the only noises she were making were the noises of sweet love. That's what I'm going to think about, when they put that rope round my neck.'

'Brother, you gotta tell someone. If you don't think you did it, it ain't right you swing for it.'

'That's not how it works, though, is it? We thought we'd left them Jim Crow laws behind when we left the South. But they followed us, all the way up North, and all the way over here.'

'You from Detroit, too?'

'No, sir. I'm from New Orleans. But yes, I went north after the jobs and money. You?'

'From Jackson, Mississippi. But yup, the same. Brother, you've got to say something, though.'

'There ain't no fighting against Jim Crow. He's over here now, too. It must be the Lord's work. Maybe it's my time to go and meet my maker.'

'I don't even know your name, brother.'

'I'm Private Augustus Booker, at your service, sir. And you?'

'Private Theophilus Howard. But you can call me Theo.'

'Weren't we supposed to get some sort of special meal before we go?'

'If we were, they ain't asked me.'

'Me neither. What you going to be thinking about, Theo, when they put that rope round your neck?'

'I'll be thinking about my good woman back home – Bessie. And our baby.'

'What's your baby's name, brother?'

'I don't rightly know. Bessie and me, we split before the baby was born. I don't even know if it's a girl or boy.'

'Well, that's a crying shame she'll never see her father. I'll pray for you, boy, just before I swing.'

'I'll do the same for you, Augustus. I'm mighty sorry you're going to hang for something you didn't do.'

33

The guard looked at Swift curiously, not understanding what was going on.

'You still wanting to see the commanding officer, sir? Or you gone and changed your mind?'

Swift thought there was little point. They had come all this way, to no avail. He had done his best, but it just hadn't been good enough.

'We still might as well, sir,' said Weighton. 'If only to show them the letter from Churchill and watch them squirm.'

'That won't be any consolation, Weighton, I can assure you.'

They were escorted to what had obviously once been the prison governor's office – indeed, that designation could still faintly be seen on the repainted door, underneath the new name sign. It now read LTC James P. Smith, 707th Military Police Battalion.

The guard knocked on the door.

'I've brought the visiting British detectives, sir, the ones we called about from the guardhouse.'

'Thank you, Private,' said Smith, showing Swift and Weighton inside.

After the introductions, Smith invited them to sit down in front of his desk. Swift declined.

'We won't be staying long. It appears we've arrived too late anyway. We saw Thomas Pierrepoint leaving.'

'Ah, yes, he always insists on starting at an ungodly hour, Chief Inspector. And that means I have to get up, too, to oversee things. Normally, as you can imagine, even though I'm an early riser, you wouldn't catch me here at this time.'

Swift had to bite his tongue. That the commanding officer seemed to be complaining about having to get up early to oversee executions beggared belief.

He handed over the letter from Churchill.

'We brought you this. But it appears our Prime Minister's entreaties have been delivered too late.'

Smith read the letter with what appeared to be a slight smirk on his face. That made Swift so angry, he wanted to get up and punch the man. His knuckles whitened on his good hand where he was grabbing his chair arm, trying to prevent himself doing something he'd regret.

When he'd finished, Smith didn't say anything, but simply picked up the telephone handset on his desk and dialled an extension number.

'They're here,' was all he said.

Then he sat back in his chair and folded his arms.

Swift was astonished, and livid into the bargain.

'Don't you have anything to say for yourself? Aren't you even going to say sorry?'

'Goddammit, don't take that tone with me, sir! You are a guest here, and I can just click my fingers and get you thrown out if I wish. While we're here, this is American territory, and the justice of the United States of America is what holds sway. Now we don't have to be friends, but I'm not having you insulting either myself or the US Army. Is that clear?'

This time it was Swift's turn to stay silent. He refused to even recognise what the lieutenant-colonel had said. Instead, he collected his hat from the table and rose to his feet, indicating Weighton should do the same with a quick nod of his head. Then he turned on his heel.

There was no point staying here. Their mission had failed, and that was that.

Just then, there was another knock on the door.

'Enter!' bellowed Smith.

The door opened, and Swift felt a rush of astonishment and delight flood his body.

There, in his uniform, carrying his kitbag, and accompanied by an armed military police guard, stood Theo Howard.

Swift turned to Smith. 'But I thought—'

'You just went and jumped to the wrong conclusion, Chief Inspector.' Then he turned his gaze on the soldier. 'Private Howard, you've got a lot to thank Chief Inspector Swift and Sergeant Weighton here for. They've just gone and saved your goddamn life – and your army career to boot. You're being released back to your battalion in East Yorkshire.'

'I don't understand,' said Swift.

Lieutenant-Colonel Smith waved the letter from Churchill.

'This here letter wouldn't have done the trick, though I'm mighty impressed you managed to secure it.' Then he picked up another piece of paper. 'But when I receive an urgent telegram from the President of the United States of America, well then, that's a whole different ball game. I don't know how you persuaded your Prime Minister to talk to President Roosevelt, but whatever you did, it goddamn worked. Well done, mister policeman.'

The sea change of emotions was almost too much for Swift to bear. He could feel his eyes prickling.

He turned, and could see Weighton's massive hand pumping Theo Howard's, as though he was trying to squeeze the life out of it.

When it was Swift's turn, he used his prosthetic in a gentler handshake, congratulating the soldier, despite the throbbing pain in his shoulder.

'I'm delighted, Private Howard. Absolutely delighted. But you should never have been put through all this.'

'I tried to tell you, sir, when you first interviewed me. I tried to tell you who the real culprits were. But Sergeant Mulder, goddammit, he shut me up before I could get the words outta my mouth.'

'Well, I'm sorry, Private Howard, for all you've been put through. Truly sorry.'

'There's no need for you and Sergeant Weighton here to apologise, Chief Inspector. You got nothing to feel sorry for. You goddamn saved my life, saved my skin, and I will be forever grateful. You can be sure of that.'

Once they'd finished their hugs, Lieutenant-Colonel Smith cleared his throat.

'Aren't you forgetting something, Chief Inspector?'

Swift frowned. What did the American officer mean?

Then he saw him proffer the Churchill letter.

'I would guard this with your life, Mr Swift. I shouldn't think many folks have managed to acquire something like this. Something to show the grandkids one day.'

Swift smiled his thanks, and pocketed the document. He wasn't going to let his sadness about his lack of children, never mind grandchildren, spoil such a happy moment.

34

The Americans had been planning to send Howard back to Cottingham by train, via Bristol. But when Lieutenant-Colonel Smith learned that Weighton and Swift were going back there anyway, it was agreed that the two detectives could drive Private Howard to his base – and the military police even agreed to refill the Morris and the jerry cans with fuel.

Swift and Weighton were offered breakfast, and then allowed to bunk down in a couple of cells for a few hours to get some sleep.

For once, Swift slept soundly, uninterrupted by the usual dreams and nightmares from his time at the Somme. By the time they finally set off, it was approaching midday.

Despite his escape from the hangman's noose, as the journey progressed Swift detected an air of melancholy about Private Howard, rather than the elation he would have expected. Eventually, with some prodding, the soldier explained why.

'Thing is, Chief Inspector, I've lost two good friends. I'll never be seeing Archie again, and that makes me sad. And I thought my cellmate in Shepton Mallet was a no-good rapist – that was what he was convicted of being. But when he told me his story,

I realised he weren't a lot different to me. He weren't no rapist – he just made the mistake of loving up a married white woman. Thing is, Mr Swift, a black man's word is never believed. That's who your hangman was here for, and now he's gone. Name of Augustus Booker. Please think of him in your prayers, Mr Swift.'

The nearer they got to Cottingham, the more morose Theo seemed to get.

'They won't let me forget, Mr Swift. Those white officers. I'll be a marked man from now on, especially if the four you've caught hang for their crimes. Thing is, we thought we were escaping those Jim Crow laws coming over here to fight Hitler. But we didn't escape. No sir. That there Jim Crow just took flight and followed us here.'

By the time they reached the Cottingham base, Theo Howard had told Swift all about recognising Rushing and Dean from among the white supremacists back in Detroit. How they'd stood in front of his car, preventing Theo and Bessie, and the baby Bessie was carrying, from moving into their new home.

When they finally dropped him off outside Thwaite Hall, Swift asked the question that had been nagging at his mind.

'Do you know whether Bessie had a boy or a girl, Theo?'

There was a look of sadness on the soldier's face.

'I don't rightly know, sir. Bessie and me, we split soon before I came out here, before the baby was even born.'

'Well, you should write to her, Private Howard. Explain what has happened to you, what you've been through. Ask for a photograph of your child.'

'Well, that's something I'd love to have, Mr Swift. Do you think she'd ever take me back?'

'That I can't say. But a letter can be a powerful thing. If you get your words right, who knows?'

'Thing is, I'm not much good at reading and writing, Mr Swift. I certainly don't have a way with words. Would that be something you might be able to help me with?'

'Of course. With pleasure. I would consider it an honour.'

35

Before they got back to Alfred Gelder Street, they stopped at a newsagent's shop to buy a copy of the *Hull Daily Mail*.

'Blimey, that's quite a spread, sir,' said Weighton, as they unfolded the broadsheet paper to look at the front page. 'I can't remember the last time the war wasn't the lead story, and they've given Carver top billing. Holdridge won't be best pleased about that.'

Swift chuckled. The headline was POLICE HEROINE TRAPS US ARMY KILLER GANG. Swift wasn't entirely sure that didn't constitute a contempt of court, given the four white US officers had so far only been charged, rather than found guilty. But perhaps the newspaper editor had decided to go out on a limb. There was a photo of Holdridge, flanked by Carver, holding forth at the press conference on the steps of the Alfred Gelder Street headquarters, and also the same photograph of the Black Legion uniforms that had been used alongside the film review a few years earlier. Inside the paper, under Feather's byline, came column inch after column inch of in-depth reports. Pen portraits of each of the four victims, but also some of the background to the accused – or as much as the newspaper was legally allowed to print. The missing link that the detectives ought to have found out for themselves earlier in the inquiry was that Captain Rushing – the one who'd tried to escape when the police moved in – had originally started a medical degree, before getting thrown out for unspecified 'disreputable behaviour'. That, and his own tragic and violent family history.

'We missed all the fun, sir.'

'We were doing our duty, Weighton. And we succeeded.'

'You don't mind Holdridge milking the glory, then, sir?'

'Always the way. Always will be. They take the credit when others do the dirty work, and shift the blame when anything goes wrong. It's always deputy heads that roll, never the top man's.'

'I don't think that's an analogy I want to dwell on, sir. Not given how close Private Howard came to losing his life.'

'Sorry, Weighton. You're quite right, of course.'

'Do you think Holdridge will let Carver stay on the team with us now, sir?'

'I should jolly well hope so.' He poked his finger at her photo in the paper. 'She's a bloody good policewoman, and I don't want to lose her.'

When they got back to Alfred Gelder Street, Carver was waiting for them in the incident room.

'Any luck? With Theo Howard?' she asked eagerly.

Weighton gave the answer as Swift looked on like a benign uncle, although their wide smiles had already given the game away.

'We did indeed, although it was touch-and-go. Your boss has friends in high places, WAPC Carver. Show her the letter, sir.'

Swift got it from his pocket and handed it to Carver.

'Gosh, sir. Do you know Winnie personally, or something?'

'I don't, Carver, no. But I know a man who does, and thankfully that connection came up trumps.'

'I'm so delighted,' said Carver. 'It was the last piece of the puzzle – if you hadn't managed it, I'd have just felt so awful.'

'So would I, Carver,' said Swift. 'So would I.'

'Shall I put the kettle on, sir?' asked Weighton. 'We could celebrate with our usual cup of tea.'

'That's an excellent idea, Weighton. In a moment. Before that, could you give me and Carver a couple of ticks alone? There's something I need to discuss with her.'

Carver and Weighton both frowned.

'Of course, sir. I need to go the gents anyway after our trip.'

Once he was out of the room, Swift turned to Carver, who looked as though she was about to be bawled out over some error or other she didn't even realise she'd committed.

'It's nothing to worry about, Kathleen,' he said, using her Christian name deliberately to try to put her at her ease. 'I just wanted to start off by congratulating you. I was very impressed by your performance on your first case – and what a case it was.'

'That's kind of you, sir. But I thought we all worked well as a team.'

'We did indeed. Which is why I'd be honoured if you'd agree to join us full-time as our detective constable.'

He was delighted to see her face break into a broad grin, and at that moment Swift realised that if he'd ever been blessed with a daughter, a girl like Kathleen Carver would be exactly who he wanted. But before she had a chance to agree, he continued.

'Before you say yes, I have to warn you, it's not entirely in my hands. I'll have to clear it with DCS Holdridge first. But I need to know before I approach him that it's something you'd want.'

'Yes, yes, of course, sir. I'd be absolutely thrilled. And I wouldn't let you down.'

'All right, then. Tell Weighton to keep my tea hot for me. I'll go and see the DCS right now.'

Holdridge – for once – grudgingly gave Swift some praise.

'You did well, Chief Inspector. We all did.'

Swift had to clench his teeth to avoid guffawing. *We*? Holdridge himself had contributed next to nothing. In fact, if anything he'd been a hindrance, as usual. But now wasn't the time to point that out – not when Swift needed a favour.

'I was particularly impressed with Kathleen Carver, sir. She did a tremendous job, and I'd like to reward her with a full-time place on the team. As a detective constable.'

'A *woman*? As a detective? Have you gone out of your mind, Swift? It's far too dangerous work. I mean, perhaps I could see my way to letting her join your team full-time as an auxiliary, but certainly not as a detective constable.'

Swift had two pieces of information up his sleeve to use as bargaining chips.

'That's a shame, sir. Times are changing. The East Riding force already has a woman constable helping in CID.'

'*Really*? I hadn't heard that before. Nevertheless, it's not the way we do things in Hull.'

Swift had expected this to be the outcome.

'Well, have a think about it, sir. Don't reject it out of hand.'

'I already have thought, Swift. And the answer is no. The best I can offer is to keep her as an auxiliary, but attach her to your team.'

'As you wish, sir, of course. By the way, we did manage to save Theo Howard's neck.'

'You did? But I thought he was due to hang this morning.'

Swift got out the letter from Churchill, and put it on the desk under Holdridge's nose. His superior read it with a look of amazement on his face.

'Good grief, Swift. How the hell did you manage to get a personally signed letter from Churchill?'

'I have friends in high places, sir. A very close friend who is Churchill's doctor. You'd do well to remember that.'

Holdridge glowered at him. 'Is that a threat, Swift?'

'Not at all, sir,' Swift replied, making sure his face was a picture of innocence. 'Quite the opposite, in fact. I was just thinking it might be useful to a man in your senior position, what with honours lists and so forth. Have you been properly rewarded for all your good work yet? I mean, as well as leading the team which cracked this case, you also had a prominent role in the Great War, too, didn't you, sir?'

'Well, yes, Swift. I did, as a matter of fact. Not on the front line, of course. But a lot of important strategy work went on behind the lines.'

'Well, I could always put a word in if you like, sir.'

'That's jolly decent of you, Swift. Come to think of it, why don't we have a snifter to celebrate a successful end to this case. I've got a very good single malt in the drinks cabinet there.'

'I won't, sir, thank you. I have to drive back home to Beverley. As you can imagine, I'm already quite tired.'

'Of course, Swift. I understand. But you're a good officer, you know. Sometimes a bit of an awkward bugger, but if there's anything else I can do—'

'Well, there is actually, sir. As you mention it. If you could perhaps give the Kathleen Carver situation a little more thought. I really would like to appoint her as Hull's first female detective constable. You never know, you might get your photograph in the papers swearing her in, sir. That would be a feather in your cap, you know, if I did happen to mention your name to my friend who knows Winnie.'

The trap had snapped shut. Holdridge looked as though he knew it, too.

'There is that, I suppose, Swift. You make a good point. Let me have another think about it, and I'll let you know as soon as I can.'

'Thank you, sir.'

With that, Swift said his goodbyes and left.

He didn't have to wait for Holdridge's decision.

The man's vanity was such that there wasn't much of a decision to make.

Driving the Morris back to Beverley after the team's celebratory cup of tea, he felt elated, but utterly exhausted. For the last twenty-four hours, he'd been running on adrenaline alone. Somehow, he needed to relax and calm down – and he knew exactly the way of doing that.

Blanche seemed happy enough to see him, even though she'd been neglected these past few days, with Swift tied up with the murder inquiry, and then trying to save Theo Howard. She nuzzled his face and pricked her ears, whinnying at the same time. And she didn't seem in any way frightened by the strange-looking stick he was carrying.

They cantered out across the Westwood, enjoying the late-summer evening air. Behind the golf clubhouse – an adapted disused windmill – he could see the last of the day's golfers finishing their round before the light finally faded.

On the first fairway, Swift allowed the horse's canter to become a gallop, and then they turned down the second fairway before slowing to a trot near the tan gallop – and the site where the torso of Ulysses Grant had been discovered. The police tape had long gone, the bark of the track smoothed over. In years to come, no one would know about the gruesome discovery just beyond Black Mill.

Swift dismounted and tied Blanche's reins to a tree.

Then he walked onto the sixth tee of the now empty course.

This was the moment he'd been waiting for. One he feared would never happen. Perhaps, given his tiredness after his and Weighton's marathon journey, it wasn't the best time. But something inside his head was making him do it.

And he'd practised for long enough in the back garden of the Beverley house, even – sometimes – into the night, prompting the neighbours to shout at him to shut up on more than one occasion. But Swift was driven. He needed to perfect his technique.

Playing with the rubber practice balls was one thing. This would be the first time since before the Great War, when he was just a teenager, that he'd hit a ball in anger.

He'd studied other – two-armed – golfers playing this hole, about 180 yards, but steeply downhill, over the wooded old chalk quarry. Most of the good ones chose a 6- or 7-iron – according to the recently introduced numeric notation, though Swift still thought in terms of a mashie niblick – allowing the ball to run down onto the green after clearing the wood. The shot was totally blind – there was a viewing platform next to the tee to climb up on to check the green was clear. But Swift knew the course was empty.

He teed up his ball on the wooden peg, and took one practice swing with his left arm. It hurt, as he knew it would. And the club he'd selected was a spoon – he knew he didn't have the same power as able-bodied golfers.

In his pocket, he had one spare ball. He'd allow himself one reload if things went wrong.

He swung the club.

It seemed to make a good connection – and there was no sound of the ball crashing through the branches and undergrowth.

Re-energised, he leaped onto the viewing platform to try to see where it had ended up. But the light was too dim now. He could barely even see the flag on the green.

He untethered Blanche, and then carefully led her down along the path through the wood. Once he got beyond the trees, he swung himself into the saddle again, and they climbed the brow of the hill that led down to the wire-fenced green.

He scanned his eyes left and right, trying to see the ball.

It wasn't until they were about twenty yards from the green that he spotted it, nestling just ten feet beyond the flag.

He cursed himself for not bringing a putter. But then he'd never really expected to strike the ball properly, never mind get it on the green in birdie territory.

He tethered Blanche to the wire fence, then climbed it, intending to retrieve the ball. It seemed such a waste not being able to take the birdie putt.

When he got to the flag, on impulse he took it out, and laid it on the green out of the way.

He only had the spoon club in his hand, but that would have to do.

He held it like a putter, and took one practice swing.

Then he lined it up.

He struck the ball.

At first, he thought he'd narrowly missed and the ball was lipping out. But it seemed to do an entire tour of the cup, before dropping in.

He'd done it!

A birdie two, and a satisfying end to a satisfying day.

36

It wasn't, however, quite the end of the day for Swift.

By the time he'd got Blanche back to the stables, and he'd driven the Morris home, tiredness overwhelmed him. Each of his limbs felt as though it had hundreds of tiny lead weights attached. Everything ached – not just his shoulder where the harness for the prosthetic joined. Perhaps the golf hadn't been such a good idea when he was already exhausted. Adrenaline had kept him going, but only for so long. He was like a torch whose batteries were almost dead, only able to give out a feeble, flickering light.

He slumped in his armchair, and rewarded himself with a pipe of tobacco for a job well done.

As he tamped down the tobacco in the pipe bowl, he heard the noise of something falling over in the garden outside. Probably one of the neighbour's cats that insisted on wrecking his lawn, although his unwieldy practice golf chips had also gouged out plenty of divots.

He struck a match and began to light the pipe. At first, he couldn't get it to catch, then his second match was extinguished in a draught of cool night air from the direction of the kitchen.

Perhaps he'd somehow forgotten to close the back door. But the armchair was so comfortable, he couldn't rouse himself to check now – he'd look at it when he went to bed.

Third time lucky, and he managed to light the pipe and puffed away on it contentedly. It wasn't a great habit, he knew, but had been one of the few luxuries he'd been able to enjoy in the trenches. Margaret had hated the smell – many times she'd threatened he had a choice of his beloved pipe or her, but not both. In the end, though, she'd been lured away by the person he least suspected.

Another slight noise.

Had something got into the kitchen?

Then suddenly his neck was yanked back and upwards.

Something was tightening round his windpipe.

Some sort of wire noose.

He gasped for air.

He tried to clutch at whatever it was with his good hand, but his attacker only tightened his grip still further.

'Hello, Mr Swift,' a voice said from behind him. ''Appen yu'd fergotten about me.'

Swift recognised the voice at once.

Lewis. Ron fucking Lewis. Albeit this seemed to be Lewis with his Hull dialect now fully let loose.

The man now grabbed Swift's good left arm to stop him struggling, keeping the wire noose – or whatever it was – squeezed tight.

Then something was in front of Swift's eyes.

A flash of metal in the dim light of the table lamp.

Swift tried to focus, even though he felt as though he was about to black out from lack of oxygen in his lungs, as he still fought for what little air he could breathe.

He saw the golden lion first, then the ring filled with the colours of the Union flag, then the black swastika.

Finally, the sharp-pointed lapel pin. Lewis was holding the fascist membership badge like a dagger, with the point of the pin aimed at Swift's eyes, although Lewis himself was still out of sight behind the armchair, reaching round in front of Swift's face.

Close enough, though, to smell the man's foul, beery breath.

'You see a bit too much, Mr Swift. Caused me a lot of problems, you 'ave, yer fucker. Lost my nice little number at t' docks 'cause I 'as ter lie low 'cause of you lot. You won't bloody care about that, though, will yer. Err nerr. Sat here in yer fancy Beverley 'ouse, wi' all yer posh neighbours.'

The pin of the badge was even closer now, perhaps an eighth of an inch from Swift's right eye. He reflexively wanted to blink, as though that might protect him and his sight.

But he forced himself to keep both his eyelids open. He didn't want to show the fear he felt. He just hoped Lewis wasn't quite as in control as he seemed to be making out. Did his lapsing into Hull-speak suggest his attacker himself was on edge – was that something Swift could work on and turn in his favour?

Lewis's mouth was now right up against his ear, but the tightness of the noose prevented Swift moving his head to look at him.

'I've had enough of yer bloody nosiness, I 'ave. So I'm gunner teach yer a lesson. They might still employ you wi' a gammy arm, but you'll be fuckin' useless wi' no bloody eyes. They'll get rid o' you, just like the docks got rid o' me. Yer won't be able to see fuck all after I've finished wi—'

The sound of repeating, angry bells from the main road stopped Lewis's rant mid-sentence.

Ringing, ringing, ringing.

The bells of emergency vehicles.

As suddenly as the wire noose had tightened round his neck, it slackened, and Swift heard Lewis turn and run.

The detective took a series of deep breaths, and leaped to his feet as quickly as he could, rubbing the skin of his neck to make sure there was no serious damage.

He raced into the kitchen. The door's lock had been picked – the pick itself left in there as Lewis made his escape.

Swift saw the faint outline of a body jumping down from the left-hand side garden wall into a neighbouring garden. He knew that, with his disabled arm, he couldn't chase the man.

Meanwhile, a furious rapping had begun on the front door.

'Police! Open up!'

Swift ran through the hall and opened the door, to be confronted by Poskitt, Verrill and a handful of uniformed East Riding constables.

'Are you all right, Mr Swift?' asked Poskitt. 'Your neighbour reported hearing a noise that he thought might be an intruder.'

'I'm fine,' said Swift, still rubbing his neck. 'It was Ron Lewis. He broke in and attacked me. But he's escaped over the garden wall.'

He showed the constables through to the back door, and then the route Lewis had taken under the cover of the blackout darkness – out over the neighbouring gardens towards the Westwood and the racecourse. Two of them raced in hot pursuit, while Poskitt detailed Verrill and the others to go back out to the main road and head to the Westwood that way.

'What was he trying to do?' asked Poskitt. 'Was he threatening to hurt you?'

'I think he was trying to blind me,' said Swift. 'Using that.'

He pointed down to the lapel badge, lying on the floor – the twin of the one Swift had safely locked in a drawer upstairs. He prayed Poskitt wouldn't conduct too fine a search of his own house. Hopefully they would just dust the back door lock for fingerprints, and take Lewis's discarded fascist membership badge away as evidence.

Some thirty minutes or so later, once Poskitt's team had confirmed that Lewis had disappeared into the night, and after they'd completed their initial evidence-gathering, Swift was able to settle back in his armchair and finish his pipe. His heart rate had finally returned to normal.

No sooner than he'd sat down, there was another frantic knock on the front door. This time Swift was careful to keep the security chain on, and only open it as far as the chain allowed.

In the dim light of the torch the man carried, pointed down at the floor so as not to alert the ARP wardens, Swift could make out it was his neighbour, Maurice Blenkinsop, carrying something in a sack.

Swift took the chain off, but didn't invite him in, although the man looked as though he expected him to.

'Are you all right, Chief Inspector?' asked Blenkinsop. 'It was us who heard the noise in the back garden and called the police. I heard the bells.'

'I'm fine, Maurice. Thank you. It was something and nothing. The Beverley police have it all under control.'

'What, like an attempted break-in?'

'Something along those lines.'

Lewis had got away – but they might be able to pick him up later by checking in his usual haunts in East Hull.

Then Swift looked again at the sack Blenkinsop was carrying.

'What have you got there, Maurice? It looks heavy.'

'It is an' all. Thinking of you, I remembered.' He proffered the sack to Swift. 'It's your bloody car jack. I forgot to give it you back.'

Swift laughed.

The missing car jack that he'd thought at one stage had cost Theo Howard his life.

'Is there something funny, Chief Inspector?'

'No, no, Maurice. Thank you.' He placed the jack on the floor in the hall. 'Look, I'd normally invite you in for a nightcap to say thank you for alerting the police, but I've just this minute finished a difficult and exhausting case. I'm going to get an early night. We'll do it another evening.'

'Not to worry, Chief Inspector. That's what neighbours are for. I'll bid you goodnight then – you have a nice kip.'

The man tipped his hat, then turned and made his way back to the main road, torch still facing down towards his feet to avoid the beam alerting those who were patrolling the blackout – and to guide his way.

As he got to the pavement, a couple of young women passed by, and the ghostly reflected light highlighted the face of the nearest of them.

She had the same small, pretty facial features of Sarah Houghton – and for a brief moment Swift thought it was indeed Sarah, reincarnated.

Then he realised it was just a trick of the blackout.

She actually looked nothing like her.

But as he stood on the doorstep, watching the pair of young women walk towards the town centre, then disappear into the black night, the image of Sarah's face wouldn't go away.

He remembered what he'd whispered to her, to that unhearing body laid out in the tent outside the ruins of the Scarborough Street air-raid shelter.

I don't know what kind of madman or madmen have done this to you, Miss Houghton. But we're going to find them and make sure they pay for their crimes. You can be sure of that.

Nothing would bring Sarah, Jessica Pickering, or the two American soldiers back to life, but he'd kept his promise.

And for Swift, that was the next best thing.

Author's Note

This book is a work of fiction, but many of the background events to my fictional story actually happened – so it may be useful for readers to know what of that background was true, and what wasn't.

Firstly, and to me most shockingly (although to others it may be common knowledge), Shepton Mallet prison *was* used as an execution centre by the US Army under the 1942 United States of America (Visiting Forces) Act. Eighteen men were executed, the majority for murder, but six after being convicted of rape, which hadn't been a capital crime in the United Kingdom for more than a hundred years. The British government 'lent' the Americans the services of hangmen Thomas and Albert Pierrepoint. One of those executed for rape and murder was the black GI, Private Lee Davis, after a court martial lasting just one day, and despite serious inconsistencies in the evidence against him.

Intriguingly, in 2003 Channel 4 was accused of suppressing a documentary which exposed the fact that a disproportionate number of those executed were black soldiers. One of the programme's consultants said he was told it was because the film was too critical of the United States in the aftermath of the 9/11 attacks. Channel 4 denied the claims, and the documentary was later shown, although in what critics alleged was a 'graveyard slot'.

The novel's story about Churchill and Roosevelt intervening to stop an execution at Shepton Mallet never happened in real life, as far as I know. And the fact that I've allowed my fictional Churchill to do this should not be seen as in any way counter to the allegations of racism Britain's wartime leader has faced in recent years. Similarly, although Charles McMoran Wilson was a real person, he appears in this book in an entirely fictional way, and his allusion to what are now seen as some of Churchill's more controversial views is also an invention on my part.

Although my black GI characters are fictional, the disturbances at the Sojourner Truth Project are based on truth, and were the forerunner of the Detroit Race Riots, which were in turn a catalyst for the so-called Battle of Bamber Bridge, where tensions over the mistreatment of black GIs in the UK by white officers led to exchanges of gunfire between black and white US troops in the Lancashire village of the same name.

My plot line involving the KKK offshoot the Black Legion is entirely fictitious, and the group is indeed thought to have disbanded in the 1930s. However, Ku Klux Klan involvement in the US military is well documented: for example, Klan members paraded on a US base in Vietnam following the murder of Martin Luther King Junior, and the KKK actively recruited members of the military throughout much of the twentieth century. The film *Black Legion*, starring Humphrey Bogart and mentioned in the novel, was indeed released before the war, but the *Hull Daily Mail* review of it is fictional.

The port battalion of black GIs based in Cottingham featured in the book is a fictitious one. However, there was a real US Army port battalion based in the village, although on a different site. As recounted in the novel, the black soldiers were generally welcomed by locals, according to the *African Stories in Hull and East Yorkshire* project which is available online at www.africansinyorkshireproject.com. However, the site also documents the story of one Cottingham family who'd become friendly with, and received regular visits from, a black GI. That prompted the soldier's (white) colonel to visit the family home, asking them to 'refrain from entertaining black servicemen, as mixing was not permitted; we just don't do that sort of thing'.

The Imperial Fascist League was a real organisation, but their involvement here and at this stage of the war is fictional. The racial slurs against Dixie Dean actually happened, but the link to the Imperial Fascist League is entirely fictional.

Don't try to find the Devil's Chimney if you're in one of the real tidal caves under Flamborough Head: it's fictional, the name borrowed from the Isle of Wight.

Most of the bombings and air raids referred to in the novel were real events, overlaid with my fictitious murder story, with the exception of the ice factory bombing, which again is entirely fictional.

Acknowledgements

This book was written during various pandemic lockdowns, so I was unable to visit Hull as much as I would have liked, and it also hampered some of the in-person research I wanted to conduct. I've tried to faithfully represent the horrors the city faced during the war so stoically, but if there are nevertheless mistakes, I humbly apologise.

Once again, I'd like to pay thanks to my small group of beta readers, particularly Stephanie Smith. She was ably assisted for this novel by two fellow Hull City fans whose families lived in the Hull or East Riding areas during the Second World War – retired sports photographer Dave Richardson, and Not 606 message board stalwart, Spencer Buttle. They both pointed out some of my errors and made valuable suggestions, while otherwise no doubt busily watching (sadly only via iFollow) The Tigers secure their first championship trophy for more than fifty years.

Sensitivity consultant Helen Gould also gave some very useful insights, several of which I've taken on board.

Above all, my heartfelt thanks to the teams at my publishers, Zaffre Books, and literary agency, Peters Fraser and Dunlop – particularly my editor Ben Willis, and agent Adam Gauntlett – both of whom have always been hugely encouraging and a joy to work with.